the
wife

ML Roberts

A division of HarperCollins Publishers
www.harpercollins.co.uk

For my husband.
His constant support has been everything.

Harper*Impulse* an imprint of
HarperCollins*Publishers*
The News Building
1 London Bridge Street
London SE1 9GF

www.harpercollins.co.uk

This paperback edition 2018

First published in Great Britain in ebook format by
HarperCollins*Publishers* 2018

A catalogue record for this book
is available from the British Library

ISBN: 9780008119461

Set in Birka by Palimpsest Book Production Limited, Falkirk,
Stirlingshire

Printed and bound by CPI Group (UK) Ltd, Croydon, CR0 4YY

MIX
Paper from
responsible sources
FSC C007454
www.fsc.org

Prologue

Sometimes you look at people and you think their life is perfect. You envy them, what they have, what you *assume* they have. The perfect marriage, perfect careers, perfect home. They have it all, or that's how it seems to those on the outside. But sometimes, behind those closed doors of that seemingly perfect home, secrets live in the shadows, just waiting to reveal themselves. Secrets that make that perfect life more fragile and fractured than anyone could imagine. Secrets that cast a darkness over everything, even when the sun is shining.

I had secrets.

And my life wasn't perfect, even when I thought it was.

We all had secrets.

We all told lies.

We all had a darkness that blocked out the sun.

No ... my life wasn't perfect ...

Chapter 1

'Come on, Michael. Dance with me.'

'When was the last time you saw me dance, Ellie?'

I lean back against the wall, the edge of my mouth twisting up into a smirk. 'Our wedding.'

'Almost fourteen years ago.'

I put down my gin and tonic and reach out and grab him by his belt, pulling him towards me, smiling as my mouth almost touches his. 'But they're playing our song.'

'We have a song now?' He arches an eyebrow and gives me the kind of grin that made me fall for him in the first place, all those years ago.

'For a supposedly intelligent man you can be such a dick sometimes.'

He laughs, a low, husky laugh and I close my eyes as he kisses me, just a small kiss, his lips barely graze mine, but it's enough. 'We don't *have* a song, Ellie,' he whispers.

I let go of him and pick up my drink, taking another sip as my eyes scan the room. I'm not the biggest fan of Michael's work gatherings, but as one of the university's leading professors, a respected academic and head of the English Studies

Department, it's my duty, I suppose, to be by his side at these events. And I'm used to them now. In the beginning I'd always felt slightly out of place, as if I didn't belong in this world. I never went to university, I wasn't born into a family with those kind of aspirations. My family was nothing like Michael's. My family was a mess, but I was determined not to go down the route everyone expected me to take. I was determined to become successful against all the odds, and so far I've been very lucky. I've achieved that success.

Michael leans back against the wall next me and I turn to face him. 'We do, actually. We have a song. You just never remember what it is.'

He frowns and I look into his eyes and I can tell he genuinely wants to remember what that song is, but he can't. And it doesn't matter anyway, not really. I just like bringing it up, watching him squirm slightly as he tries his hardest to recall something that, in his world, isn't all that important.

'Liam'll dance with me.' I smile, and Michael returns it.

'Any of the men in this room would dance with you, Ellie. You're like a breath of fresh air around here.'

'You're hardly stuffy professor material yourself ... Oh, hang on, there he is ... Liam!' I wave frantically across the room at Liam – Dr Liam Kennedy BS, MSc, PhD, to give him his full title, although, there are probably half a dozen letters I've missed off there – one of our closest friends and a visiting lecturer here at the university.

He turns to acknowledge me, throwing me a wide smile before he takes a drink from the tray of a passing waiter and makes his way over to us. 'He still won't dance with you, huh?'

Michael rolls his eyes and holds up his hands in a gesture of defeat, shaking his head, but he's smiling too. 'I know when I'm beaten. You two go light up the dance floor. I need to have a word with Laurel about Monday's department meeting.'

'Still using your charm to kick-start that research project, huh?' Liam smirks.

'Works every time. Oh, and don't wear him out, Ellie. We're playing squash tomorrow, and I need him at his best if we're going to have any hope of beating Harry and Ed. I swear those two are taking something ...'

I watch him head off in the direction of Laurel Greene, another colleague; watch the way her eyes light up as he approaches, because that's the effect my husband has on people, especially women. He's handsome, charming and fun, even if he doesn't dance. Popular with both students and staff, he's a big part of this university, deeply committed to his work, sometimes a little too committed, but that's who he is. And I knew that the day I fell in love with him.

'You okay?'

Liam's voice drags me back from my thoughts and I look at him. 'Yeah, I'm fine. A little tired, but it's been a busy week.'

'Another drink?'

I nod and follow him to the bar, waiting until I have a fresh gin and tonic in my hand before we resume our conversation.

'So, how's the new spa coming along?' Liam asks as we commandeer a quiet table near the back of the room and sit down.

'Well, thankfully, the grand opening is going ahead next Friday, as planned. Bob, my builder ...'

Liam's face breaks into a grin. 'Bob the builder? Seriously?'

'I know, believe me, I've been listening to the same joke for two months now. I'm as sick of it as he is. Anyway, he's due to sign off on the work Monday morning, meaning we can now start moving things in and get everything organised ready for Friday.'

'Your fourth business, huh? You're killing it, Ellie Travers.'

'Well, I might not have any letters after my name, but I haven't let that hold me back.'

'Three salons and now a day spa, what's next for your empire?'

I take a sip of gin and quickly glance across the room. Michael's charming the Bridget Jones pants off Laurel Greene. I can see, even from over here, how much he's got her wrapped around his little finger.

'If there were degrees given out for flirting, huh?' Liam smirks.

'It's just who he is, you know that. Besides ...' I turn back to face Liam, leaning back in my seat and crossing my legs. 'I've never really been Little-Miss-Wallflower, have I?'

He laughs, a louder, slightly more raucous laugh than Michael's, but even though there are some distinct differences between the two men, they're more like brothers than best friends. They met, as students, at this very university – Michael studying English Literature, Liam Biochemistry. They both became lecturers here, until Liam left to focus more on his work as a research scientist, but he's retained visiting lecturer status here at the university. At a couple of universities across the UK, actually. He's a very well-respected figure in his field.

'No, Ellie, you could never be described as a wallflower.' He leans forward, clasps his hands together on the table. 'So, are we going to have that dance, or not?'

I cock my head, smiling slightly. '*You* know what my and Michael's song is, don't you?'

'Beyonce. *Crazy in Love*. Your first-dance wedding song.'

'I knew that.'

I feel hands on my shoulders and I tilt my head back to see Michael behind me. 'No you didn't. Are you done schmoozing Laurel now?'

'I wasn't schmoozing anyone.' He joins us at the table, stealing a sip of my gin. 'I thought you two were going all "Saturday Night Fever"?'

'Yes, well, the moment's passed.' I retrieve my drink and throw Michael a smile. 'Besides, I didn't want to tire him out.' I jerk my head in the direction of Liam. 'You're both on the wrong side of forty now, so ...'

'You let her get away with talking to you like that?' Liam winks as he gets up, leaning over to plant a quick kiss on my cheek, slapping Michael's shoulder as he slides past him. 'I'll leave you guys to it. I've got a meeting first thing in the morning, before that squash game, so I'm calling it a night. See you both tomorrow.'

I watch him stride through the crowd of people, stopping every now and again to say a few words to old colleagues and friends before he disappears from sight.

'Maybe we should call it a night, too,' Michael sighs, checking his watch. 'You must be shattered, the week you've had.'

'I'm okay.'

He looks at me. 'Are you?'

'Michael, I'm fine. Really.'

He stands up and holds out his hand and I take it as we head towards the exit, his fingers curling around mine, and I squeeze his hand a little tighter as we walk.

'I'm really proud of you, Ellie.' He stops and pulls me into his arms, kissing the tip of my nose. 'And I don't think I tell you that enough. You deserve the success you're finally getting. It's been a long time coming. After everything you've been through ...' His expression changes, for the briefest of seconds, a fleeting moment that only someone as close to him as me could possibly have noticed, before he pulls it back and his smile returns. 'Potential Local Businesswoman of the Year, huh?'

I smile back, tugging gently on his shirt collar. 'Hey, slow down, okay? There are only rumours of a nomination at the minute, let's not get too excited.'

'Ellie!'

A loud, deep voice aimed in our direction cuts through the noise and I look over Michael's shoulder to see Ernie Waterford approaching: Michael's predecessor as Head of Department and a lifelong mentor to my husband, not to mention a good friend.

'Looking stunning, as always.'

Michael moves aside, allowing Ernie to envelop me in a big bear hug, the scent of cigars and port filling my nostrils. 'Flattery will get you nowhere, Professor.'

His booming laugh almost drowns out the music and I

glance over at Michael, who throws me a knowing smile.

'Persistence is in my blood, Ellie. I'm still trying to work out how that man there snared a woman as beautiful as you, but if he ever leaves you ...' He winks at me and I laugh, too. Ernie's harmless flirting has been part of our lives for as long as I can remember now, 'he'd be an idiot,' he adds, throwing me another wink before he heads off in the direction of the bar.

Michael slips an arm around my shoulders, gently kissing the side of my temple. 'I don't think that's something we need to worry about, do you? Neither of us is going anywhere. Are we?'

I slide my fingers between his and I smile, turning my head so my mouth catches his, and

I taste gin on his lips as he kisses me quickly. 'I hope not.'

Chapter 2

I used to love early mornings. That time of day when it can feel as though you're the only person awake, when everything is calm and peaceful. I used to crave those snatched hours alone – it's the perfect time to think, when all those thoughts that may have felt jumbled before suddenly start to make sense. But now – now things are different. Things have changed. Nothing makes much sense any more, there's too much to think about, too many thoughts crowding my brain and it doesn't always make for those calm and peaceful hours alone I was once so fond of. I found myself waking early this morning; found myself down here, in the orangery that stretches the entire length of the back of our beautiful home on the outskirts of the County Durham countryside, drinking tea and thinking, about all those things I'd rather forget. Nights like last night; parties, dinners with friends, they help push the memories to one side, for a little while, but they'll never go away. They always come back.

Curling my legs up underneath myself I settle back into the comfortable couch that looks out over our sprawling garden. A neat, raised decking area leads out on to a perfectly manicured lawn, its flat, green surface interspersed with patches of shrubbery and strategically placed pot plants. There's a magnolia tree near the centre of the lawn, two apple trees to the side, and at the back of the garden there's a small vegetable patch, which is – was – very much Michael's baby. My fingers don't even come close to being green. Next to that is a sky-blue painted summer house, its front porch decorated with various terracotta pots, all housing an array of multi-coloured pansies. That summer house is my office. *Was* my office. I used to love working out of that summer house, it was my haven. Once. Now my office is in a side room next to the small indoor swimming pool we had built onto the back of the orangery a couple of years ago. A room that used to house towels and robes, but they're now kept in a large storage box at the back of the pool area. I needed that room. I wanted that room. A strange choice, maybe, given that we have three spare bedrooms upstairs, but I wanted that room.

I stare back outside, watching as the sun starts to break through the early morning cloud, casting shadows over the summer house. Casting shadows. Something I've become all too familiar with. Shadows. Darkness. Even my beautiful garden feels different, now.

Over the years we've turned that garden from nothing but grass and wasteland into a rustic, colourful space. We worked hard to make sure it was perfect, for us. For what we needed – wanted it to be, and I look over towards the back of the garden, to a corner adjacent to the summer house. It's empty now, that corner, we don't need what used to stand there, not any more. I wanted it gone.

I don't go out into the garden all that much any more. I don't have the time. I'm too busy. I'm about to open another new business, a day spa, and that's taking up a lot of my time. Too much of my time, some would say, but keeping busy is important. Over the past year and a half I've opened a third hair and beauty studio – I already have one in Newcastle and another in Durham – as well as taking on this day spa. I've never really been one to take it easy. I find that even harder to do now, despite people telling me to slow down. It isn't that simple, it never has been. It's even less so, now.

I close my eyes for a second, just for a second, and then it's almost as if the silence suddenly hits me, making me aware of its presence, and they spring open. I walk over to the French doors in front of me, and I know I won't be able to stop myself from doing what I seem to do on an almost daily basis now. But they say we all have a touch of OCD inside us, somewhere. I just need to make sure that door is locked. What's so strange about that? And as my fingers close around the metal handle I inwardly scold myself for being so paranoid. Of course it's locked. I check every night, before we go to bed. Every morning, when I come down here. Every time someone goes outside, I check the second they come back in.

Leaning forward, I rest my forehead against the cool glass door, my fingers tightening around the handle as I close my eyes.

The sound of birds chattering out in the garden brings a smile to my face. I find their noise quite calming. I love to hear them out there, starting their day. The peace and quiet these early mornings bring is something I never take for granted. But that peace is suddenly rudely interrupted by the doorbell ringing, and I glance up at the clock on the wall. It's just gone eight-thirty.

I wrap my robe tighter around myself and head out of the kitchen, into the hall. There's only one person comfortable enough to visit us at this time on a Saturday morning and, sure enough, when I open the door he's there on the step, a wide grin on his face as he holds out a box of something that smells very much like freshly baked pastries. I smile and lean back against the doorpost, folding my arms.

'Didn't you have a meeting this morning?'

'Cancelled. Rescheduled for Monday, so, as I was up and about and on the road I thought I'd stop by and bring breakfast.'

I take the box of pastries from him and stand aside to let him in, nudging the door shut behind me before heading back into the kitchen.

'Michael not up yet?'

'It's eight-thirty on a Saturday morning, Liam, so no. He's still in bed. Do you want some tea?'

He nods and leans back against the island in the centre of the room, glancing behind him into the orangery, where my pot of tea and crumb-scattered plate are sitting on the table next to the couch.

'You didn't much fancy a lie-in yourself, then?'

He looks at me, but I don't answer that. I know what he is getting at. 'Are you thinking of hanging around here until you and Michael leave for your squash game?'

'If that's okay?'

I smile slightly and flick the switch on the kettle. 'It's okay. You can make the tea. I'll go see if Michael's awake.'

I head back upstairs, back into our room, and Michael's very much awake. He's sitting up in bed with his laptop open, his reading glasses perched low on the end of his nose as he types away. And he doesn't hear me come in at first, he's that engrossed in whatever it is he's doing. It's not until I'm almost right there beside him that he looks up and smiles. But I also don't miss the speed at which he slams shut his laptop.

'Where'd you get to? I woke up and you weren't there.'

'You were in a hurry to come and find me, then?' I jerk my head in the direction of his laptop as I fling open the wardrobe and search for something to wear.

'Just thought I'd get a jump on Monday's meeting. Get some notes down.'

I loosen my robe and let it fall to the floor, and I flinch slightly as I feel Michael come up behind me, feel him slide his arms around my waist, his mouth brush my shoulder so lightly his lips barely connect with my skin.

'Come back to bed,' he murmurs.

'I can't.' I shrug him off and turn around, reaching for the dress I'd dropped to the floor when he'd touched me. 'Liam's downstairs. His meeting's been moved to next week, so he decided to swing by here early. He's brought breakfast.'

Michael sighs and drags a hand through his hair, and then he reaches out and wraps his fingers around my wrist, causing me to drop the dress again. I raise my gaze and look at him, and the expression on his face – it's one I've become all-too familiar with these past few months.

'Last night, Ellie – last night, at the party, you were fine. *We* were fine, we were good. We had a nice time, right?'

'Yes. We had a nice time. It was good to get out. And I'm still fine now, Michael, okay? I'm just tired. These last few weeks have been crazy, what with the new salon and the spa, so, you know? I'm just tired.'

'Look, I know we haven't ...'

He leaves that sentence hanging, loosens his grip on my wrist and drops his gaze, dragging a hand back through his hair again. And then his eyes meet mine and he smiles at me, just a small smile, but I needed that to happen.

He pulls me into his arms, kisses the top of my head, and for a few seconds he just holds me tight and I cling onto him, breathing him in.

I look up at him, and his mouth catches mine, just a quick kiss. But I take it.

'We're going to be all right, Ellie.'

He lets go of me and steps back, and I watch as he pulls on his jeans, looks in the mirror, running both hands through his hair to tidy it up.

I turn around and crouch down to pick up my dress, stepping into it, but as I reach behind me for the zipper I struggle to pull it up, and he's there; he takes my hand and he pulls it away, slowly sliding the zipper up, and as he does that he gently kisses the back of my neck, and I shiver. The first time he ever did that, kiss the back of my neck, I shivered.

'I'm sorry, Ellie.'

I know he is. I'm sorry too.

I turn around and pull him to me by his shirt collar, quickly kissing his slightly open mouth.

'Go see Liam. Go on. Go plan your squash strategy or whatever it is you do before one of your games. I'm going to finish getting ready. I need to stop by the spa later, make sure everything's going to plan.' I smile and I cup his cheek and kiss him again, stroking his skin with my fingertips. 'Go. I'll be down in a few minutes.'

I let go of him and I watch as he leaves the room, waiting until I hear both his and Liam's voices echo up from the kitchen downstairs before I head into the en suite.

I've got a busy day ahead. And maybe that's just as well.

Chapter 3

Long hours are something Michael and I are used to. Sometimes we can be nothing more than passing ships in the night. Days can blend into weeks before we realise we haven't spent any real time together. We both love our work. We both *need* our work, now more than ever. But over the past few months the hours we work are increasing, the days are becoming longer. Our life, it's changed. It had to. We changed. What happened, it was always going to change us. It would have changed anybody, but for us – Ellie and Michael Travers, the perfect couple, because that's how people saw us, how people still want to see us – for us, those changes are something I'm still trying to cope with.

I switch on the kettle and start laying out the breakfast things just as Michael comes into the kitchen, his head down as he sorts through the post.

'Anything for me?' I ask, leaning back against the counter, wrapping my arms tighter around myself.

He looks up, his eyes meeting mine for the briefest of seconds before his gaze drops back down to the letters in his hand. He shakes his head, keeping his eyes down, and I drop my own gaze, catching a glimpse of my bare feet, the shocking-pink nail polish I'm wearing – courtesy of some last-minute product testing yesterday at the spa – a sharp contrast against the dark tiled floor. And as I raise my head and check the time I realise I'm running late. I need to be at the spa in an hour and I'm not dressed yet.

I pour myself a mug of tea and make to leave, but I stop as I reach the door. I turn back around to face Michael but his head is still down. He's checking over some papers he's just taken from his briefcase. This is what it's like now. Sometimes. The silences, the heavy atmosphere. Painful memories engulf us, both of us, constantly, but we're finding different ways of dealing with them. I still need to talk about what happened, but Michael thinks we've talked enough. He's wrong.

'Will you be home for dinner tonight?'

He slowly raises his head, his eyes once more meeting mine, and he holds my gaze a little longer this time, but not long enough to make me feel as though anything's changing. We haven't really moved forward, we haven't yet got past what happened. We're not the same people we used to be, not behind closed doors anyway. We used to be happy, we used to be close, we had everything. Now I don't know what we have any more.

'I'm not sure. I have a department meeting at five, and then evening tutorials. I'll probably just grab something in the pub. I said I'd meet Liam for a quick drink after work, so ...'

He trails off and looks down again. That's it. He's severed

that communication, and I watch him slide those papers back into his briefcase, slip on his jacket, grab his keys from the dresser. As he heads towards the doorway I'm still standing in. I feel my stomach jolt as he comes closer, and he stops, turning his head to look at me.

'I'll try not to be too late.'

I nod, and I take the small smile he gives me, close my eyes as he leans in to kiss my cheek. And I watch as he strides down the hall, without looking back.

It wasn't always this way. Not so long ago we could barely make it out of the house on time because morning sex and breakfast together was an all-important part of our day. We had it all, we *were* that couple. Ellie and Michael Travers. Happy. Successful. So fucking perfect that our friends used to tease us incessantly, claim that nobody could ever live up to what we were. Or so we thought.

I glance at the clock again. I'm pushing it, timewise. I really need to get ready, so I head upstairs, but I'm only halfway up when I stop, turn around and come back down. I need to check that Michael locked the door behind him. Our home, it's quite isolated. A converted barn set in its own grounds, our nearest neighbours are within sight but not walking distance. It's all very private.

So, I just need to check that Michael locked that door. But of course he's locked it. He's as paranoid as I am. Now.

Chapter 4

If somebody had told my thirteen-year-old self that one day I'd be a successful businesswoman running three beauty salons and a day spa; that I'd be married to a gorgeous, brilliant professor, I'd have laughed in their faces. My thirteen-year-old self had no ambition. No prospects.

I was brought up by my grandparents in a small mining village in County Durham. The kind of place where everyone knows everybody and nobody's business is private. Mine certainly wasn't.

I'd just turned thirteen when I went to live with them, an angry, disillusioned teenager who fought against everything. I had my reasons.

People didn't think I'd amount to much, not even my own family. They assumed I was too damaged, and maybe I was. I certainly spent the first few months I was with them proving everyone right. I didn't try hard at school. I didn't think there was any point. My grandparents had done okay, they didn't have much but they had enough. They'd spent their life 'getting by'. Managing. And for them that was fine. For a while I thought that was fine, too, and nobody encouraged me to try otherwise.

By the time I'd turned fifteen I'd realised I wanted more than that. 'Getting by' wasn't enough. I wanted to buck the family trend and *be* someone. Do something with my life. I wanted to show the small, insular community I was growing up in that the damaged kid I once was could be something more than just another casualty of a fucked-up family.

I stared working harder, grew a thicker, tougher skin, learnt how to look after myself. I channeled all my anger and frustration into proving everyone wrong. Nobody thought I could do it. But I did, do it. I became someone. I *did* something. And I did it all on my own. When nobody else believed in me, I had to. Michael believed in me. Michael was the icing on the cake, so to speak. To have a man like him – a handsome, clever, successful man, from a background the complete polar opposite of mine; to have a man like him fall in love with me, that's when my world became complete. But now – now my world is becoming increasingly less certain. My world is changing. My world *has* changed ...

'It looks like you're all set for the opening on Friday, then.'

I swing around at the sound of his voice, my heart beating hard against my ribs. I'd been so deep in thought there, he gave me a shock. 'Jesus, Liam, don't creep up on me like that! What are you doing here anyway?'

'I'm on my way to a meeting in Newcastle, so, I thought I'd pop in, see how it was all going.'

I walk back behind the front reception desk and switch on the computer. I need to check all our booking systems are up and running before we open the spa in just a couple of days' time.

'It's all going fine.' I raise my gaze and smile slightly, but I'm too busy for his company this morning. I can do without any more distractions. I already have enough.

'Good.' He rests his forearms on the counter and leans forward, clasping his hands together. 'So, are you going to show me around?'

'I'm really busy, Liam. There's so much to do before Friday, and I'm swamped here, so ...'

He steps back and holds up his hands, an apologetic smile on his face. 'It's okay, I get it. Michael said you were snowed under.'

'You've seen Michael?'

He slides his hands into his pockets and I grab a pile of folders from the desk and walk back out front, quickly glancing down at my scribbled, handwritten schedule for the day. I haven't had time to print out a neater, more detailed, version.

'Just for a few minutes. I needed to stop by the university to sort out a few things. I'm giving a lecture there tomorrow afternoon.'

'Is he okay?'

'He's fine. Any reason why he shouldn't be?'

I look at him, and I frown, because he's been through enough himself to know that seeming okay and actually being it are two completely different things.

'Are *you* okay, Ellie?'

'I'm fine ... *shit*!' A handful of papers slip from the folders I'd bundled into my arms, landing on the floor in a scattered heap and I crouch down to retrieve them.

'Here. Let me get those for you.'

Liam crouches down too, but I hurriedly grab the papers myself, shoving them back inside the folders. 'It's okay, I can manage. Thank you.'

His hand briefly but gently brushes against mine, and he pulls it away, sliding it back into his pocket as he stands up.

'You should take things a little easier, Ellie. You're working yourself into the ground.'

'I don't want to take things easy, Liam. This is what I do. I work hard.'

'At the expense of everything else?'

I narrow my eyes as I look at him, leaving a couple of beats before I respond to his comment. 'Not everything.'

He drops his head and laughs quietly, smiling slightly. 'No ...' He raises his gaze, his expression slowly changing, and then I suddenly realise something, and a wave of guilt washes over me.

'Oh, Jesus, Liam, I'm sorry. The divorce ...'

'Finalised this morning. It's all official now.'

I go over to him, and I reach out to touch his arm, squeezing it gently. 'So it should be me asking you if *you're* okay.'

'It's not like we didn't know it was coming, Ellie. Keeley left me a long time ago. This is just the paperwork. Our marriage, that was dead before she even walked out.'

'Yes, I know, but ...'

'It's a divorce, that's all.'

He fixes me with a look, he's shutting me down, ending that conversation, and I understand. He doesn't like to talk about it, says it doesn't matter any more. But everything matters, in some small way, even if you try to convince yourself that it doesn't. It all matters.

'I'm still sorry.'

'Don't be.' He smiles, and I pull my hand away and clutch those files closer to my chest, returning his smile. 'Well, I'll leave you to it. Like I said, I just wanted to see how things were going here.'

'Are you sure ...?'

He holds up a hand and I stop talking. 'Ellie, I'm fine. I'm fine.'

'Okay.'

'And you need to remember what I said, all right? Take things a bit easier. Make some time for yourself.'

I throw him a small smile. 'Is that an order?'

'Maybe ...' He smiles too and turns to leave, walks away, but I wait a few seconds; wait until I hear his car drive off before I go outside. I need some air. I've been cooped up inside ever since I got here a few hours ago, and the smell of fresh paint and cleaning fluid is giving me a bit of a headache now.

'Is there anything you need me to do, Ellie?'

I turn my head to see Carmen, the spa's manager, join me outside. 'Actually, yes. Could you give the linen suppliers a call? We need to make sure those towels Libby put through on a last-minute order yesterday are going to arrive before Friday.'

People told me I should never have taken on this spa, that I should have stuck with the salons, concentrated on those. The timing wasn't right to start something like this. They were so wrong. The timing was perfect. This hasn't just been a new business venture for me, it's been the distraction I needed to get me through the past few months. Distractions. They've become such a big part of our life, and they never used to be. We didn't do distractions, before. We hadn't needed them. Michael and I, our work has always been important to us, we've always been busy people, but now – now I think he's using work as an excuse to prevent himself from being alone with me for too long, that's *his* distraction. One of them, anyway, because I fear he has others. It's a creeping fear that's been bubbling beneath the surface for a while now, but I don't think it's unfounded. And he has no idea how much that hurts me.

'I'll get straight on to that.'

Carmen's voice drags me back from my thoughts and I smile at her. The last thing I want is for anyone to think that Michael and I aren't okay. We're fine. It's just that we used to be so much more than fine.

'Thanks, Carmen. That'll be a big help. Anyway, if you could also keep an eye on what's happening out here for a little while I'd be really grateful. I've got a few things I need to be getting on with, so I'll be in my office if anyone needs me.'

I head back inside, back to my office just behind the reception area.

Closing the door behind me I open a window, just wide enough to let in some air, and I sit down at my desk, leaning forward to pick up the photograph I've got standing on it. It's a photograph of Michael and I, taken about three years ago on holiday in southern Spain. We love Spain. It's been our go-to destination for years now, ever since our honeymoon in Valencia. We've travelled throughout most of the country, stayed in some of the most beautiful and unusual hotels, met the most incredible people; made plans to buy a holiday home out there, one day. Maybe. But that was before. We haven't spoken about those plans or even mentioned the prospect of another holiday over there, not for a long time.

I reach out and run my fingers lightly over the photograph as I remember how happy we'd been, back then. I know he feels guilty for what happened. I know that's partly the reason why he distances himself from me in the way that he does now. It's because he still feels that guilt. But he shouldn't. I don't want him to.

I put the photograph down and spin my chair around so I can look out of the window. It's a beautiful spring day, warm for the time of year, the kind of day when everything should feel pretty much perfect. I used to think *we* were pretty much perfect, it certainly felt that way, at times. And then I drop my gaze, my eyes focused on my hands clasped together over my stomach and I know that we were never perfect. Even before everything changed, before the guilt and the doubt, before all that happened, we still weren't perfect.

There's a niggle in my mind. My gut is trying to tell me something.

Swinging my chair back around I pick up the phone and punch in the number for Sue, Michael's secretary. She answers after a couple of rings and I lean back and swing my chair around to face the window again as I wait for her to speak, and when she finally does her tone is crisp and businesslike.

'Good afternoon, Professor Travers' office.'

'Sue, hi. It's Ellie.'

The second she hears my voice her tone switches to informal and friendly, and I smile to myself. I like Sue. She's worked with Michael for years. I'm not sure how he'd cope without her now. And when it comes to his timetable and schedule she's got a photographic memory.

'Ellie! It's lovely to hear from you, how's everything going over at the spa?'

'It's all going to plan, fingers crossed. Opening on Friday.'

'That's wonderful news. I'm so pleased for you. Michael said you'd been working incredibly hard to get the place up and running as soon as possible ... Anyway, I'm sure you're still extremely busy, so, what can I do for you? Do you need to speak to Michael? Only, he's not in his office right now, but I can take a message.'

'No, it's fine. I don't need to speak to him. Listen, Sue, I was just wondering, does he have any tutorials this evening?'

'I don't think so ... If you can bear with me for one second, though, I'll just double check his schedule.'

'Thank you.' I hear her start typing, and while I wait I reach behind me for that photograph, and I look at it again, narrowing my eyes slightly, tilting my head to one side as I stare down at the smiling image of my husband.

'No, Ellie, he doesn't appear to have any tutorials in his diary for tonight.'

Sue's voice cuts through my thoughts, although it takes a

second for her words to register with me. 'Okay.' I distinctly remember him telling me that he had evening tutorials this morning. 'He *does* have a department meeting, though, doesn't he? I'm sure he said he did. Five o'clock, is that right?'

'Yes, that's right.'

'I'm just trying to plan dinner, that's all. We haven't spent an evening together, at home, for a while now, what with me getting the spa ready to open and his busy schedule, so – I just hoped we might be able to manage that tonight. Some time together.'

I wonder, did it seem as though I was over-compensating just a bit too much there? To the outside world we're over what happened, we've moved on. And Michael has moved on. I'm still trying to.

'You work too hard, both of you.' Sue's tone is mock-scolding, but she just cares about us. We tried to keep what happened as private as we could, but it was inevitable that people would find out. And some of those people, they still treat me as though I'm made of glass. I'm not. I'm tougher than some give me credit for.

'At least we're lucky enough to enjoy what we do.'

'That's very true. You take care now, you hear? And good luck for Friday.'

'Thanks, Sue.'

I hang up and spin my chair back around, placing the photograph back down on the desk. Was Michael lying to me? Does he put all his tutorials in his diary? I don't know. But I know that he never used to make excuses to avoid spending time with me. There once was a time we'd do anything we could to grab just a few precious hours together, yet now, it's almost like we're living separate lives.

Breathing in deeply, I exhale slowly, as though I'm ridding myself of those negative thoughts.

What was my husband hiding?

Chapter 5

'How did your tutorials go this evening?'

Michael looks up from his books, takes off his glasses and slides them into the top pocket of his shirt. And his expression – I can tell he's slightly confused. I don't usually ask about tutorials, they're not something we ever really talk about. He likes to keep some kind of student-professor confidentiality thing going, but in this case, there weren't any tutorials, were they?

'Tutorials?'

I watch his expression change, almost a little too quickly there. I think he's just realised what he told me this morning.

'They went fine.'

He slips his glasses back down and drops his gaze, and that's how it is. How it's been for months now. And it isn't fair, it isn't how it should be, but it's his way of dealing with everything – it isn't mine.

'Did you see Liam? In the pub, I mean.'

He lets a couple of beats go by before he slowly looks back up at me, and his expression is verging on exasperated now; he doesn't even attempt to hide that frustrated sigh.

'I'm extremely busy, Ellie. As you can see.'

He indicates the pile of books in front of him, and I get the message. Sometimes it's just easier to give in rather than fight.

I walk over to the fridge, take out the bottle of wine I opened last night and I pour myself a glass. I don't ask Michael if he wants one. When we're alone, like this, even those simple, ordinary exchanges are rare. I keep my back to him, taking a long sip of wine, closing my eyes as the cool liquid slips down my throat, settles in my belly – that familiar alcohol-hit my welcome friend once more, though Michael thinks we're becoming increasingly closer these days.

'Ellie ... I'm sorry.'

He comes over to me, pulls me into his arms, and before I can take another breath he's kissing me. A beautiful, slow, deep kiss, and I wind my arms around his neck as I push myself against him, his erection digging into my thigh and I gasp quietly as he slides a hand up under my skirt, pushing my underwear aside as he lifts me up onto the countertop. I can't remember the last time we had sex outside the bedroom; spontaneous, unexpected sex. I can't actually remember the last time we had sex, the last time we both wanted it. So this is a surprise, and even though I think this might be his way of stopping dead a conversation he doesn't want to get into, I think we need this. I know I *want* it, now that it's happening. I want *him*.

Placing my hands palm-down behind me I lean back as he pushes inside me, closing my eyes as I feel him move, feel his hands on my knees keeping my legs apart, and I bite down on my lip as his thrusts start to pick up pace, quicken slightly, almost as though he's taking an element of frustration out on me, or maybe that's just me over-thinking this; the reasons why he's acting this way, now. But the sex is slightly rough, and that was never Michael's style. And then, as if he's just realised what he's doing, he slows down, his thrusts suddenly become more gentle, measured.

I keep my eyes closed, keep my head thrown back, but then I feel his hand slide around onto the back of my neck, forcing my head up, making me look at him as he comes with a force so brutal it almost tears the breath from my body, his eyes burning into mine, and it's only when he's done that he breaks that stare, drops his head, but he keeps his hand on my neck. And nobody says anything. I can't. I don't think I could get the words out. My throat feels tight, and my heart is beating so fast and so hard it's difficult to catch my breath.

He slowly raises his gaze, but we remain silent. I think we're taking a moment, to remember who we used to be, what we once were. Who we've become. Sex, when it happens, has been almost paint-by-numbers for us since – well, for a while now. He hasn't done *this*, hasn't touched me in this way for so long, and as I stare deep into his eyes I feel as if I'm breaking into a million tiny pieces. I feel as though I'm shattering from the inside out, I'm confused. This – us, this isn't what we do; isn't what we've done for so long, and there are reasons for that. Have we suddenly got past those reasons? No. So this – this only makes everything all the more confusing.

He suddenly lets go of me, and without saying a word he

heads off into the hall, to the downstairs bathroom. I stay where I am, leaning back against the counter, turning my head slightly to stare outside. It's dark now, but our decked terrace and part of the garden are illuminated by various solar-powered lights, and for a few seconds that's what I focus on – the lights. It's only when I hear Michael come back into the kitchen that I pull myself together, take a deep breath, and I smile at him. Just a small smile, and I have no idea if it got as far as my eyes but it was a smile.

'I'd better go and get cleaned up, too.'

But as I edge past him he gently takes hold of my arm and stops me, swinging me back around to face him.

'I really am sorry, Ellie.'

He keeps saying that, all the time, he keeps saying he's sorry, keeps apologising.

I turn around to face him. 'What for?' Given our circumstances, that's a loaded question, and he knows that.

He bows his head, runs a hand along the back of his neck, and he's about to say something when his phone rings, and I'm not sure whether I'm irritated by the interruption or relieved that it may have stopped us from embarking on another of those conversations we just can't seem to handle.

He picks his phone up from the table and looks at the screen. 'I need to get this.'

I nod, and the second he gets up and turns his back to me I practically run upstairs, not stopping to take a breath until I'm safely behind the privacy of our bedroom door. That's when I take a second to breathe, to compose myself. He's lying to me. I'm almost sure of that now. He's lying to me. And there has to be a reason for that. He wouldn't lie to me unless he had something to hide. Or maybe he's just trying to protect me. Maybe that's all he's doing, but I don't need protecting. All I want is for what happened ... I don't want him to lie to me.

I head into the en suite. I need a shower. And when I'm done I pull on sweatpants and a t-shirt and I look at my reflection in the full-length mirror by the window. Turning sideways I lay a hand on my stomach, and I close my eyes, keeping them squeezed tight shut as my breath catches in my throat; as I feel my heart start to race, my skin become clammy, I can't breathe, for a second or two. I can't breathe. I get them every so often, these brief panic attacks that come from out of nowhere, sweeping over me with a brutal force. But I'm learning to handle them, or I'm trying to. And once again I flick that switch that pushes everything to one side, drop my hand, and step back from the mirror, swallowing down breath as it finally dislodges itself from my throat. I need another drink.

Back downstairs Michael's nowhere to be seen, he's not in the kitchen. I go into the orangery, but he isn't in here either. And then I look towards the double glass doors at the far end of the orangery, the ones that lead through to the extension that houses the swimming pool. He's there, poolside, pacing up and down, still talking into his phone, his hand running continuously along the back of his neck, and for a second or two I don't move, I just stand there. Watching him. And then he stops pacing, faces the floor-to-ceiling windows that look out onto the garden. He leans forward, presses his

34

forearm up against the glass, drops his forehead so it rests against it.

I move a little closer, my eyes fixed firmly on him. He's still talking to whoever it is who's decided that calling him this late is a good thing. Maybe it's just Liam, but their phone calls to each other usually last about three seconds, just long enough to make sure they both know where they're meeting, what time their squash game or football match is. They're not exactly your heart-to-heart kind of friends. Are any men?

I go back into the kitchen and pour myself another glass of wine before I head into the living room, switch on the TV, trying to keep things as normal as possible. Until Michael walks into the room.

He places a fresh bottle of wine on the table beside the couch and throws himself down onto the chair by the fireplace.

'Is everything okay?' I ask, not missing the slightly weary expression on his face.

'Everything's fine. It was just one of my students. She needed some help with a project I've set for a group of them, that's all.'

I feel my shoulders tense up. *She* needed some help? What kind of help?

He sits back in his chair and he smiles at me. 'Come here. Come on.' I get up, let him pull me down so I straddle him, and I close my eyes as he kisses me; as his fingers lightly stroke the base of my spine, causing my skin to break out in goose bumps. 'I've told them they shouldn't call this late, but, you know, they keep telling me I'm their favourite professor, who am I to let them down when they need me?'

I can't help smiling too. This is what he does, how he reeled me in all those years ago with that disarming smile and those bright blue eyes. But I still want to ask him questions, ask exactly who he was talking to, why they were calling so late, was this really just about help with a project?

'Michael ...'

He gently pushes my hair back off my face, lightly kisses my slightly open mouth.

'This is what I do, Ellie. It's what I've always done. And I know what you're going to say but I'm not going to compromise my students in any way. If they need my help, at any time, I'll give it to them. I thought you understood that.'

'I do, it's just ...'

'It's my job. To look after my students. It's my job. Okay?'

He looks at me, his blue eyes burning deep into mine. He's ending this conversation. He's told me as much as he's willing to tell.

I climb off him, go back over to the couch, and I anticipate the coming silence. He won't want to do this, he won't want to go where I'm heading.

Silence. Loaded with secrets. Hurt. Guilt.

'It's been over a year, Michael. And nothing's changed.'

He drops his head, a sign that he doesn't want this. And I can see what he's been trying to do, all night. He's been using his charm, using that smile, using sex to try and distract me. To try and stop me from doing this. But that only works for a short time. And this, what I'm seeing now, his body language, I've seen it all too often over the past few months, and a knot of frustration pulls tighter inside my gut. We're done here.

And he doesn't make any attempt to stop me as I get up and leave the room, and that breaks my heart. It kills me.

I feel tears start to stream down my cheeks as I run upstairs, and I hate that I'm still crying. Is he really just accepting this as us now?

I get ready for bed on auto-pilot, going through the motions until I can finally crawl under the covers and wait for sleep to take over. But it's not coming easily tonight, and I lie there, staring at the wall, until I feel Michael slip into bed beside me; feel his arms wrap around me from behind, pulling me back against him and I close my eyes as his fingers slide between mine. We'll go to sleep, wake up in the morning, and everything will be back to that new normal that fills our days now. A kind of normal I'm having to get used to, even though it's not one I want. But this is the way it's been for over a year now. The way I fear it's always going to be. And while Michael may be willing to accept that, I'm not sure I can ...

Chapter 6

'Hey! What are *you* doing here?'

I'm surprised to see Michael at the spa. He hasn't set foot in the place since he came with me to view the building a few months ago.

'You left your phone on the kitchen table. I thought you might need it.'

'Oh, right ... thank you.'

I look at the screen, see that there are about a dozen missed calls I'm going to have to return.

'Sorry ... I was in such a rush this morning, I forgot to make sure I had everything. I hope this hasn't made you late.'

He smiles at me, jerks his head back towards himself and I step out from behind reception, let him pull me into his arms, quickly kiss the tip of my nose, and I scrunch it up, laughing quietly.

'I haven't got a lecture until ten-thirty. You haven't made me late.'

'Can you stay for a coffee? I could show you around ...'

I feel his body stiffen, almost as if a switch has been flicked and he lets go of me, pulls his phone from his pocket and looks at it. 'I'd better get going. I still have to prepare some notes.'

Disappointment floods me, but I'm not going to push it. There's no point. 'Okay. Well, thanks for this.' I hold up my phone and he throws me another smile before he turns away and heads out, stopping to talk to a couple of staff members who are hovering around in reception before he leaves. I watch closely as he exchanges pleasantries with Gillian, one of my masseurs, laying a hand gently on the small of her back as he leans in to her, both of them laughing at something he says. He's a born flirt, my husband. He's always been that way, he can't help himself, charm oozes from every pore, and I think a lot of women find the fact that he's an English literature professor but looks more like a movie star quite appealing. It was probably half the reason I was attracted to him, if I'm being honest. But the way he's talking to them, when he finds it so hard to say anything to me, it's like a knife in the back.

I turn away and busy myself sorting paperwork behind reception, and when I glance back up Michael's gone, but as I look outside, I see he hasn't left yet. He's leaning back against his car, his phone to his ear. I come out from behind reception and go over to the huge bay window that overlooks the front grounds and car park. He's still talking into his phone and he's smiling. It looks as if whoever he's talking to – it's a friendly conversation, I'm guessing.

I fold my arms and take a deep breath, briefly closing my eyes. I'm letting way too much get to me lately. Maybe everyone's right, maybe I *am* working too hard, but what choice do I have? I'm not the kind of person to sit back and let someone else take the reins. Besides, having something to focus on, it's necessary.

Dropping my head, I take another deep breath, and when I look back up Michael's getting into his car. I watch as he pulls away, drives out of the grounds. But I don't move, I stay where I am, even though he's out of my sight now. He's out of my sight …

*

'I seem to be getting a lot of male visitors this morning.' I glance up as Liam sits down opposite me at a table out on the terrace. I'm taking a break, but I'm still surrounded by paperwork. I just thought a few minutes out in the sunshine might be nice. I thought it might help to clear my head. It hasn't.

'Well, I knew you'd be busy, so I thought I'd bring you some lunch.' He slides a tub of salad towards me, the corner of his mouth twisting up into a smirk.

'There better be a sandwich to go with that.'

He reaches into his jacket pocket and pulls out two triangle-wrapped sandwiches. 'There you go. Ham and cheese okay?'

'Perfect. Thank you.'

'Are you lecturing this afternoon?' I ask between mouthfuls of salad and sandwich.

He shakes his head, taking a sip of coffee as he looks around at the newly landscaped grounds that surround the terrace that leads out from the spa's garden room.

'No. I'm heading back to the lab. Got a couple of meetings this afternoon plus a mountain of paperwork to catch up on.'

'But you still found time to go and buy me lunch, huh?'

I smile and he returns it. 'Don't want you going hungry. You can't run an empire on an empty stomach.'

I sit back and briefly drop my gaze. 'Did you and Michael ...?' I look up, my eyes meeting his. I need to know if *he's* lying to me, too. 'You met for a drink, right? Last night?'

Liam frowns slightly. 'Yes, we did.'

'Okay.'

'Something wrong, Ellie?'

'He's lying to me, Liam. He said he had tutorials last night, but he didn't. There was nothing in his diary, I checked with Sue. So, where was he? Between leaving the university and meeting you, where was he?'

Liam's head drops, his hands clasped tightly together, and for a few, long beats he says nothing. But he knows, he understands what Michael and I went through; the reasons why we are the way we are now. That's why I can talk to him.

'I don't know, Ellie,' he sighs, raising his gaze and dragging a hand back through his hair. 'I don't know where he was.'

'Did he say anything to you?'

'Jesus, Ellie, come on. We don't sit there and share emotional shit. We don't do that.'

I look at him and I suddenly realise how tightly my fingers are gripping the arm of my chair and I quickly loosen that grip, feeling my shoulders sag as I do so.

'Look, I know that what happened ...' He drops his head again, and I don't miss the way he wrings his hands together.

He's frustrated, I can tell. 'Nobody expected you to get over it in a fortnight, it was never going to be that simple, but, maybe now's the time to start dealing with it. Properly.'

'I'm dealing with it, Liam. You, of all people, know I'm dealing with it.'

His eyes are back on mine and he's still frustrated, he isn't hiding that fact.

'Yeah. I guess you are.'

He stands up. He's calling an end to this conversation, one I'm not even sure got started. There was more I wanted to say. Even though he doesn't know everything, nobody does, he understands enough. And I need him, to talk to.

'I should be going. I don't want to be late for those meetings.'

'He won't talk about it, Liam. He won't go there. I mean, sometimes it's like he refuses to acknowledge it even happened. Is *that* the best way to deal with it?'

He shrugs and that irritates me, it really does. 'Maybe, in this case, it is. I mean, how are *you* dealing with it, Ellie? Hmm? How are you *really* dealing with it, because, there are times when *you* don't want to talk about it either.'

I look at him and I want to say something but I don't know how to respond, because he's right.

'Sometimes talking isn't always the answer, Ellie. You know that better than anyone.'

I stand up, gather my things together and start to make my way back inside. It looks as if we're finished here.

'Ellie, come on. I'm sorry, okay?'

I turn around and he comes over to me; he takes my hand

and he gives it a gentle squeeze, his thumb running lightly over my knuckles. He doesn't want me to go back inside angry or upset. I get that. He's a good man, Liam Kennedy. A good friend, to both of us ... though a better friend to one of us.

'Okay. You're sorry.'

He smiles, I smile too, and the mood is lightened. Sometimes he's the only one who can make me smile.

'Are you coming to the party on Saturday?'

It's Michael's birthday at the weekend. We always have a small house party when it's someone's birthday, even though Michael told me he didn't want anything this year. He was happy to just let this birthday slide by. But I think we need to at least try and keep up some level of normality. It's what he keeps telling me to do, after all. Carry on as normal. Forget what happened. Move on. So we're having this party. If we start pulling back from our friends they're only going to continue with the pitying looks and the questions I can't answer. I don't want people to know the truth; know that I'm terrified of losing my husband, scared of the secrets he's keeping. Scared that history could repeat itself.

'Are you sure you should be having this party, Ellie? I mean, the spa opens on Friday ...'

'It's keeping me busy, Liam. I need the distraction.'

'Haven't you got enough of those?' He raises his eyebrows.

I start to walk back inside and he follows me, falling into step beside me, and I don't answer his question. I don't think he was expecting me to.

'Nobody says you shouldn't keep busy, Ellie, it's just that, all these distractions ...'

'They're necessary. All of them.'

We stop walking and I turn to face him.

'Thanks for lunch. That was really kind of you. But you should probably leave now, if you want to miss the worst of the early afternoon traffic.'

'Dismissing me, huh?'

I smile slightly. I don't want him to think I'm being a complete bitch. I'm not. I just think we're wasting time now. 'Are you coming? To the party?'

'I'll be there, you know I will.'

'Good.' I reach out and gently touch his arm, giving it a small squeeze as I lean in to quickly kiss his cheek. 'And I really am grateful for lunch. Sometimes I forget to eat, you know?'

'Yeah. I know.'

I step back and turn to go.

'Ellie?'

I spin around, frowning slightly. 'Yes?'

'Do you need any help? With the party?'

I shake my head. I can manage. 'No. Thank you. Michael doesn't want a huge fuss, so I'll be fine.'

'Okay, well, good luck for Friday. And I'll see you both soon, all right?'

'Yeah. See you soon.'

I watch him leave, watch as he lifts a hand and drags it back through his hair as he walks away. Is he frustrated with me? I feel as if everyone around me is frustrated. Everyone has something they're not saying. Something to hide ...

Chapter 7

I lean back against the counter and sip my wine, watching as our friends and neighbours chat and laugh. The party's in full swing now. And as I look around me, it really is as if nothing has changed.

I turn away to refill my glass and I realise how nice it is to have the house full again. It feels good to hear laughter and music, any noise that helps drown out the lingering feeling of guilt.

I take another sip of wine. I need the Dutch courage and just as I'm about to turn back around, plaster on my perfect hostess face and join the party, I feel someone sidle up beside me, feel his hand brush mine as he takes the bottle from me and refills his own glass. I turn my head slightly and I smile at Michael, and his mouth catches mine in an unexpected kiss, which causes a small shiver to course right through me. But I know he's just playing to the crowd. These brief, snatched moments when we're in public; when we're surrounded by people, that's when I can pretend everything's how it used to be, how *we* used to be. Before I questioned everything, before *he* became swathed in guilt and remorse for something he had no idea could have turned out the way it had.

He pulls back and his eyes meet mine, and I feel a wave of love so strong for this man it almost knocks the breath right out of me. And I wish with all of my heart that I knew how to fix what was broken, I really do. Brushing it under the carpet, ignoring it, that's become the chosen option. Maybe it's the only one we have left now, I don't know.

He smiles at me, cups my cheek in the palm of his hand, his thumb lightly stroking my skin as he leans in to me, his mouth brushing against my ear. 'You look beautiful tonight,' he murmurs, his breath warm on my neck, and I bite down on my lip as he steps back from me, throws me one last smile, picks up his wine and walks back out into the party. That's it. The moment's gone. He's played his part, done his bit. But I need him to *show* me that he loves me. I need him to make me feel as if he means it; make me feel the way he used to make me feel, when we're alone, not just when we're surrounded by others. I want him to listen to me and not walk out of a room or make excuses not to talk. I need him. And I love him. Of course I do.

A hand suddenly touching my arm makes me jump back, my heart beating ten to the dozen as I fall back against the counter, struggling to catch my breath.

'Jesus, Ellie, I'm sorry ... I'm sorry.'

'Oh God. You scared the hell out of me!' I laugh a bit too loudly to cover up the panic that shot through my body.

I look up at Liam and his expression is genuinely apologetic. He didn't mean to scare me. 'It's fine, really. I'm just exhausted, what with the spa opening yesterday, and organising this party.'

'The one that Michael didn't want.' He leans back against the counter beside me and folds his arms, staring out ahead of him.

'The one we needed to throw.'

'Why?' He turns his head to look at me. 'Because you want everyone to think everything is normal?'

'Nothing's normal any more, Liam. I'm just trying to keep up a pretence, that's all. It's what Michael wants. And you didn't *have* to come tonight. Not if you didn't want to.'

'Michael's my best friend. *You* know how important you are to me. Of course I had to come.'

He reaches behind him for the bottle of Scotch on the counter, grabs a tumbler from the tray and pours himself a drink.

'You should come and join the party. People are starting to ask why you're hanging around in here.'

I watch him head back out into the crowd, and he's right. I should go and join the party.

Glancing around me I try to find Michael, but I can't see him. Maybe he's outside. It's a beautiful evening and the orangery doors are wide open, so I look out there. And, yes, there he is, standing at the edge of the decking, a little way away from everyone else who's ventured outside on this beautiful spring evening. He has his phone to his ear, surprise surprise, his head down. It'll just be work. Something's come up, that's all it'll be. Nothing is happening here. I know that. Don't I? He's just talking to one of his students, a work colleague, nothing is happening.

I can't stop myself from turning back around to watch my

husband. He's still talking into his phone, his body language only slightly animated, and when he smiles and laughs I feel my stomach dip. Well, as long as *he's* fine. He's not letting what happened affect him. I feel angry, envious that he can just push it aside as if it never happened. I can't do that. I can't. I can't pretend, like he can.

Without thinking I put down my drink and slip away into the hall. I go upstairs. I need a few minutes alone. Going into our room I head over to Michael's side of the bed, crouching down in front of the small chest of drawers, and for a second I just stay there, I don't move. Am I really doing this? Is this what it's come to? Is this the woman I'm turning into?

I reach out and slowly slide open the top drawer, leaning forward to peer inside, but a sudden noise coming from the landing outside makes me jump. I almost fall backwards as I let go of the drawer handle and I have to grab hold of the duvet to steady myself. There are voices outside in the hallway and I realise now that it's just friends from the party looking for the bathroom. My heart is still hammering away against my ribs.

Deep breath. Calm down, Ellie. I peer back inside the drawer. The contents are lined up neat and tidy – a couple of pens, a notebook, some papers he's using to help his research. Michael's writing another book and he likes to make notes before he goes to sleep.

I reach inside and lift up the notebook, but there's nothing underneath it. Did I think there *would* be? I open it, still not entirely sure what I'm looking for, but I quickly flick through it anyway. And there's nothing but page after page of Michael's ridiculously neat handwriting. What was I expecting to find, exactly? I don't know, because I'm not thinking straight. I just know that he's hiding something from me. Again. Something's going on. Michael's behaviour – it's familiar. He's been like this once before. *It's happening again.*

I sit down on the edge of the bed, crossing my legs. up underneath myself, the noise and the chatter from the party drifting upstairs. I look at the picture of me and Michael hanging on the wall opposite our bed. One of our wedding photos, blown up and framed in all its perfect glory. Two smiling, incredibly happy people, madly in love. We had everything. We had it all, that perfect life, that exciting future ahead of us. Until it was all snatched away, just like that. We lost it all.

There was a time when I thought nobody knew me better than my husband. When I fell in love with Michael, I fell hard. I fell so hard, because I never thought a man like him could love someone like me. He was the charismatic one, the centre of attention. I was the adoring wife. But he's underestimated me. You see, I'm not ready to lose my husband. So whatever's going on, whatever he thinks he can hide from me, I'm going to find out what it is. Whatever it takes.

Chapter 8

'Do you want some breakfast?'

Michael throws a pile of files down onto the countertop and reaches for the coffee. 'No, I don't have time. I'm already late for a meeting with my research students. I'll grab something at work.' He takes a sip of coffee, slides a hand onto the small of my back. 'And where are *you* going to be spending your day today?'

I turn to face him, his hand moving around to rest on my hip. 'The spa.'

He smiles, and for a moment everything feels like it used to. He cups my cheek, leans in to kiss me slowly, and I close my eyes and take this moment because it'll soon be over.

'I'd better go.' He steps back from me, throws me one last smile and grabs those files he'd discarded not thirty seconds ago. 'I'll see you tonight.'

'Hang on ... Michael!'

He stops before he reaches the door, and I can tell from the way his shoulders sag that he's frustrated. He just wants to get out of here.

'How about I cook tonight? I'll get a bottle of that wine you like, make you your favourite ...'

'What's going on, Ellie?'

I'm actually quite stung by his question, by his tone of voice. It's verging on suspicious, as though he thinks I'm doing this because I have some kind of ulterior motive. And maybe I do, but only because I'm trying to save something here. I'm trying to save *us*.

'I want to cook my husband dinner. There's nothing strange in that.'

'You've just opened a new business, and when you open a new business you're usually there more than you're here. You don't have time to cook dinner.'

'I'm *making* time. Maybe I need to do more of that.'

He throws back his head and sighs quietly, backing off towards the door. 'No, Ellie, you really need to stop this.'

'Stop what, Michael?'

'You're fishing. I know you want to talk, but it's over. Done. Finished. I don't know how many times I can say that. And dragging it back up, it isn't going to do anyone any good. So you need to stop pretending to be housewife of the year and let's get back to normal. Okay? Let's do that.'

I lean back against the counter. My fingers grip the edge. Tight. It makes me angry that he issues instructions and expects me to obey them. He thinks he can control how I'm feeling, but that isn't his right. He doesn't get to tell me what to do.

'Ellie? Look at me.'

I do as he says. I raise my gaze and I look at him, right

into his eyes. He has the most beautiful eyes. Piercing. Bright. Almost cobalt blue in colour. Eyes that looked into mine that first night we met, and I knew then that I wanted to be with him.

And his voice, it's a little less harsh now.

'We need to move on, Ellie. What happened ...'

For a second there's a connection. Something we very rarely have any more, but right now, I feel its brief but powerful presence.

'It's going to be okay. And I need you to believe that, Ellie. I can't keep telling you, every day. So, I just need you to believe it. Believe *me*. Please.'

I want to believe him.

I watch as he drops his head, runs his hand along the back of his neck, and then he raises his gaze and his eyes lock on mine. 'I understand that what happened – what I did ... nobody expected you to get over it in a heartbeat, but you said you would. You wanted to. It's been a while now. Hasn't it? It's been a while. Long enough.'

There's that silence again.

'You can't let it take over, Ellie. You can't, so please, let's just try and move on. All right?'

He briefly drops his gaze again, and I hear him breathe in deeply, see his shoulders stiffen.

'I need to go. I'm late.'

I smile and I nod, I let him think he's won, but I know what he's doing. I'm the one in control here, not him.

I encourage the kiss he plants on my cheek. I let him go. Watch him leave the kitchen, hear him out in the hall collecting his things together, and I wait until I hear his car drive away before I move. I need to be at the spa in a little over an hour but there's something I have to do first.

I head upstairs, along the first-floor landing to the set of stairs that lead up to a small roof-space conversion that houses Michael's office. I know what I need to do. As I approach his office there's a louder voice inside my head telling me I have no choice.

My husband is distracted. More distracted than usual. He may try to cover it up with charm and smiles and kisses but he needs to be focused on me. His wife.

I push his office door open and walk inside. The room is a cluttered mess of books and files, a wall of shelves filled with more books and papers that have spilled over onto his desk, the floor, but he knows where everything is, or so he tells me. It's an organised mess, but not the kind I could work in.

I head over to the window, peering outside, just to make sure that he's gone. It's all quiet out there, nothing but the sound of birds chattering and the distant noise of traffic. It's an ordinary, everyday morning.

I sit myself down at his desk, looking at the photographs he's got scattered about the surface, in amongst the piles of papers and books – us on our wedding day; on holiday, in Andalucía; one of us with Liam taken at a university Christmas party a few years ago. So happy. The three of us. There've been no photographs taken in the past year. Nothing on display, nothing anywhere to act as a reminder.

I switch on Michael's desktop computer. He has his laptop

with him, but I'm assuming everything he has stored on that will be on here, too. I feel no guilt, no nerves. This is my right. I scan the icons on his screen, looking for the one I need. One I'm sure he hasn't password-protected, and then I see it. His tutorial timetable pops open, filling the screen, and my eyes flick over the coloured blocks he uses to distinguish his students. They each have their own personal colour. That's just the method Michael likes to use and my eyes continue to scan the document. A name in a light-green block, and even though the colour isn't in any way significant, the name might be. Ava. The only female student he has a tutorial with today. Do I know who she is? No, I don't. But I know what she might be. There's a twisted sense of relief as I stare at the screen. I have something to work towards now. I have something to focus on.

Her tutorial is at twelve-thirty this afternoon. Scribbling the time down on a piece of paper I shove it into my pocket as I close the timetable down. I go to switch off the computer when my eyes fall on the email icon staring back at me from the screen, my hand hovering just slightly above the mouse. Do I dare? Is this who I've become? Yes. I think, maybe, it is.

My hand falls back onto the mouse and I move it slowly towards that email icon, stopping only briefly as a flicker of rationality creeps in, but it's soon pushed aside and I click down on the mouse. But whatever it was I was about to do, it's halted. He's password-protected his email account. So he does have something to hide.

Shutting the computer down, I get up and go over to the window once more, resting my forehead against the glass as

I stare outside at the view, at the surrounding houses in neighbouring fields, all of them set in miles of countryside, green fields dotted with more houses here and there. I can see for miles from up here in the roof space. It's peaceful and beautiful and this house – I loved this house. When we first moved in here we had so many plans, it was our little corner of the world, our hideaway, a place where no one could get to us. After that night – what happened – my initial reaction was to run, to leave it all behind, everything we'd created here, all those plans. Michael thought that staying here – he thought it was for the best. He thought that facing up to it all might help fix what was broken, but maybe it can't be fixed?

Finding the slip of paper I'd pushed into my pocket just a few seconds ago, I start to play with it, twisting it between my fingers. I can almost feel the lies, they're so real to me now. I know they're there, I know he's telling them. I'm …

Something crashes downstairs.

Jesus!

It's just the post – that noise that nearly stopped my heart beating, it was just the post being pushed through the door. I know that. The postman is walking down our driveway. I got such a shock I've hit my head slightly on the glass. A dull ache spreads across my forehead. I need to stop this. I need to pull myself together.

I get up and walk out onto the small landing here on the top floor. There are only three rooms at the top of the house – Michael's office, a tiny bathroom and a box room that Michael uses to store his overflow of books, files and papers. I very rarely come up here. It's Michael's floor, really. His space.

Back down on the first floor I slip into our bedroom, tidy myself up. I tie my hair back, apply a little more make-up. I'm painting on that mask again, putting up that shield. I stare at my reflection in the mirror. Ellie Travers stares back. Confident businesswoman. Loving wife. Loving wife who's snooping around her husband's things. What are you not telling me, Michael?

As I turn to head back downstairs, something catches my attention. I can hear something, a noise; it's vague, a low, heavy rumbling ... where's it coming from? It's getting louder and there are raised voices now, they're outside. Shouting. I quickly move into the empty bedroom to my right to get a better look out the window, my heart beating so fast I think it might explode. There's someone outside. Is it her?

Get a hold of yourself, Ellie. It can't be.

As the refuse lorry rumbles down the lane my eyes close with relief. All I heard was the bins being emptied. That's all. My paranoia, that unwelcome rush of anxiety, it's ramping up when it should be waning now. I should be able to deal with it all, after fourteen months. But I can't. Or I won't. I don't know.

It's then I realise which room I'm standing in. It's empty. There isn't even a bed in here. The walls are painted a bight lemon yellow and the carpet's a soft, plush cream pile, but that's all there is – painted walls and cream carpet. Maybe we'll get around to making this more of a room and less of an empty space one day, but not yet. There's no hurry. It's not as if we need another guest room right now.

The view is pretty from this room. It gets a lot of sun in

the afternoon, on the days when the sun dares to make an appearance. That's why I painted the walls yellow, to make the most of the sunshine. I wanted this to be a bright and happy room.

The sound of my phone ringing out from the kitchen startles me. It's becoming exhausting now, this almost constant fear that something is going to happen. I need to get my shit together.

Closing the door, I run downstairs towards the ringing phone. It's Carmen, at the spa. It's time to focus. But as I listen to Carmen's update, my fingers curl around the scrap of paper in my pocket. This is far from over.

I love my husband.

My husband loves me.

Nothing, and nobody, is getting in the way of that.

*

'Ellie! How lovely to see you!'

Sue's smile beams out as I walk into the outer space that houses Michael's office, and the offices of two of his fellow English professors. It's a bustling, busy area comprising three desks for the secretaries, countless filing cabinets, a large table with two desktop computers on it at the back of the room, next to a huge wall of windows that look out over university grounds, an old battered leather sofa positioned beside a large, ornate fireplace, which Sue always makes sure is decorated beautifully at Christmas, and a small kitchen area with a kettle, microwave and a Belfast sink. It's actually all rather homely, given that it's a workspace.

'Are you here to see Michael?'

'I was just on my way to the spa, and seeing as I was passing I thought I might pop in, say hello. Bring him some lunch. Is he in his office?'

'I think he's just finishing a lecture, but he's due back any minute now. He's got tutorials this lunchtime. Can I get you a coffee? A cup of tea?'

'No, thank you. I'm fine. I'll just wait, if that's okay.'

'Of course it is ... Oh, speak of the devil. Here he is.'

I turn to see Michael stride through the door, his expression a mixture of surprise tinged with something else – is that anger? But then his expression quickly changes and he smiles at me, that easy-going smile I'm all-too familiar with. He wasn't quick enough. I can tell he's using that smile to mask something; whatever it is he's hiding from me.

I know what you're doing, Michael. I'm your wife. Remember?

'Darling? What are you doing here?' He takes a step towards me, leans in and gently plants a kiss on my cheek, that smile still there on his handsome face.

'I was on my way to the spa and I just thought I'd pop in and bring you some lunch, seeing as you missed breakfast this morning.'

His eyes meet mine. It feels as if he's searching my soul. 'Sue, can you stick the kettle on, please?'

'Of course. Are you sure you don't want anything, Ellie?'

'I'm fine, thank you.'

Michael nudges his office door open with his shoulder.

'I've got tutorials in a few minutes. Did you want to see me about anything in particular?'

'I was just passing. I thought it might be nice to drop by and say hello, that's all. Does there have to be a reason for your wife to pop in and see you?'

He glances over at Sue, but she's in the kitchen area chatting to April, one of the other secretaries. They can't hear us.

'It's just not something you make a habit of. It never has been.'

'Do you want me to leave?'

I can't stop the slightly irritated edge to my tone and he narrows his eyes as he looks at me.

'No, Ellie, I don't want you to leave. But I don't have a lot of time. Like I said, I have tutorials.'

Sue comes back over and hands Michael his coffee, his face breaking into a smile as he takes the mug from her.

'Thank you, Sue.'

He turns his attention back to me.

'Come inside. I've got a few minutes to spare before my first student gets here.'

I follow him into his office and close the door behind me. He puts down the pile of folders and books he was carrying and leans back against his desk, folding his arms, his eyes boring into mine.

I don't think he wants me here, and I know why. But I'm not going anywhere, yet.

I go over to him, take hold of his shirt collar, my lips brushing the side of his neck as I lean in to him. 'You said you had a few minutes,' I murmur, sliding a hand around the back of his neck, my fingers playing with his hair, stroking his skin.

He lets out a low groan as I press myself against him, drops his hand to my bottom as I kiss him. *It doesn't take much, Michael, does it?*

'Do you remember those days when you'd come visit me at work, at the salon?' I whisper, as his fingers dig into my thigh, push me harder against him. 'You'd meet me for lunch but we'd always end up never leaving my office. Remember?' I push his head back slightly so I can look at him, look right into those beautiful blue eyes. 'Those days when we couldn't keep our hands off each other. I miss those days. Don't you?'

His hand slides up under my dress and I gasp quietly as he touches me, as his lips brush the base of my throat, his thumb stroking my inner thigh.

He takes hold of my hips and swings me around, pushes me back against his desk. I wind my fingers in his hair and pull him down. I kiss him. I breathe him in because I love him. My husband. *My* husband.

I wrap my legs around him, feel his hand on my lower back push me against him, and then, almost as if a switch has been flicked, he steps back from me, drops his gaze for a second or two. And when he raises it I can see how on edge he is now.

'What's all this about, Ellie?'

'What's all this *about*?' I frown, but his expression doesn't waver. 'When did stopping by your office become something you're suspicious of?'

'It isn't, I just ...' He sighs quietly and pushes a hand back through his hair. 'It just isn't what you do. Bringing me lunch, dropping by to say hello. That isn't what you do. You've never done that, so why now?'

'Now I have a business not fifteen minutes away from your office, Michael.'

I watch as his expression turns from one of suspicion to one of guilt, almost. But he still wants me to leave. He isn't making a secret of that. It's written all over his face. He wants me to go. But that only makes me more determined to go through with this, because I need to know now. I need to fucking know.

'Look, Ellie, I know things have been a bit strained lately ...'

He leaves that sentence hanging and I almost laugh at his simplified summing up of the past few months. He thinks things have been strained *lately*? Things have been strained for a long time now; he just chooses to ignore that fact. But I don't want him to be suspicious of anything, not now. I can't risk that. If he thinks I'm being irrational or that my behaviour is changing – if he *is* hiding something, that would only alert him to that fact, give him a chance to cover his tracks. And I need to know if something's going on. I need to know if there's something – some*one* – standing in the way of me getting through to my husband. Something that threatens *us*. I need to know that. I need to make sure history doesn't repeat itself, because he sure as hell isn't doing that. I have a mission now, something to focus on, something that's giving me back a little bit of that control I felt I was losing.

'Anyway, I really need to prepare for this tutorial ...' He slides his hands into his pockets and walks behind his desk, firing up his laptop, 'and I'm sure there are things you need to be getting on with.'

I watch him for a few seconds, his gaze dropping to the laptop screen, and then he checks his watch and I'm sensing a slight hint of irritation coming from him now. He really does want me to go, right now. Is there a reason for that? Is it guilt? More guilt? He doesn't want me to come face to face with this student who's about to turn up here, at his office, for their lunchtime tutorial, is that it? Is that why he wants me gone? Because his body language, Jesus, it's screaming at me to leave.

'Yes. You're right, there are lots of things I need to be getting on with.'

I look back over my shoulder, outside into the outer office, but there's no one out there except Sue and April. It's quiet, even though it's lunchtime.

'I should be home for dinner.'

His voice causes my head to shoot back around.

'Providing nothing comes up, of course. You know how it is sometimes.'

Yes. I know how it is. I know how it's become. I know 'sometimes' is turning into 'most of the time', and I feel my stomach twist itself up into a tight knot as I catch him checking his watch again.

'Okay, well, I'll see you tonight.' I reach into my bag and take out a small plastic box, placing it down on Michael's desk. 'Your lunch.'

He looks down at the box, but he just leaves it there. He doesn't touch it.

'Are *you* going to be working late?' he asks, raising his gaze, and I look at him. His expression is verging on hopeful. Is that what it's really come to now? How desperate he's become to make sure we spend as little time alone together as possible?

'No. I don't intend to be. I'm learning to delegate more, Michael. I'm trying not to drown in my work quite so much, not when there are other things I need to concentrate on.'

I don't know whether he can read between the lines of that sentence, whether he realises that that was a dig, a hint. I don't know if he'd even acknowledge it if he had. But even though I leave his office, leave the outer office, I don't leave the building. I didn't come here to waste this chance, to not see what I need to see, I came here for a reason, and it wasn't just to bring Michael lunch. That was nothing more than my excuse.

I remain outside in the corridor, stepping back against the wall alongside a large display cabinet and I pull out my phone. I check the time. If she's the punctual type she should be here any second. I'm feeling strangely invigorated. The rush of adrenaline is both breathtaking and frightening and I don't know who I've become, how I got to this point. I just know I can't leave it alone now.

The sound of chatter coming from the entrance invites my attention and I turn my head slightly, putting my phone to my ear as I embark on a fake conversation. A group of three young women stop outside the open door to the outer office I've just left. They chat for a few seconds before saying their goodbyes and I watch as two of them head off in separate directions, leaving one still there outside the office. I'm guessing that's Ava. She's dressed in an unflattering long sweater and boyfriend jeans, her dark hair pulled back into a loose ponytail, but she seems pretty enough. And as she glances back over her shoulder, casting a wave in the direction of someone I can't see from where I'm standing, she smiles and her whole face lights up. She's really pretty, actually. The knot in my stomach returns, pulling tighter as I see Michael come to the door, watch as she turns around to face him, and her expression changes again, her smile growing wider. As does Michael's. They start talking, but I obviously can't hear what they're saying and I shrink back into the shadows, just in case Michael's gaze wanders, but he seems too focused on her.

I keep the phone to my ear, although I've stopped pretending to talk into it, I'm too busy watching my husband. I watch Michael lay a hand gently on the small of her back, guiding her inside. I'm almost sick in my mouth.

I slide my phone into my pocket as I calmly walk outside, but the second air hits me I have to stop and lean back against the wall. My heart's still beating wildly and that knot in my stomach is so tight now it hurts, but I know what I saw – the way he smiled at her, touched her; the look on her face the second *she* saw *him*. I know that look only too well.

Chapter 9

I'm in the kitchen, cooking a dinner I'm not sure we'll finish eating when Michael finally gets home. We may not even start, I don't know. I'm just trying to keep up some kind of routine.

I glance up at the clock as I hear him out in the hall, and I feel that familiar ache in the pit of my stomach, that nervous anticipation, that worry – is tonight the night something changes?

A loud crash from the garden startles me.

'Ellie?'

Michael runs into the kitchen, crouches down to pick the wooden spoon I've dropped in shock up off the floor.

'Are you okay?'

'I ... I heard something, out there. Out in the garden. And the security light ... the light's been triggered.'

He goes over to the back door and I close my eyes as I wait for him. I'm so on edge these days. Lack of sleep and working too hard, I guess it's all building up. It's coming to a head. I love my husband but we never were tied to each other. But now – now I dread being alone. I'd rather have Michael here, rather endure the silences and that painful gap that's growing wider between us as each day goes by; I'd rather have that than be alone. Here. In this house.

'It was just a fox.'

I look up as Michael comes back inside; watch him as he locks the door, I watch him closely. Has he flicked both locks?

'They knocked a couple of pots over, that's all.'

'Okay.'

He comes a little closer and I crave his warmth, his attention.

'Everything's fine, Ellie. All right? It was just a fox.'

He steps back and the gulf between us widens again.

'I'm going to grab a quick shower before dinner.'

I nod and return to the stove.

The doorbell ringing makes me jump again and I take a second to pull myself together before I go out into the hall, checking the small black and white security monitor by the door first to see who's outside. It's only Liam.

'Hey ...' He frowns. 'Are you okay?'

I fold my arms and throw him a small smile. 'I'm fine. Just tired, that's all. When did you get back from Berlin?'

'Landed about an hour ago. I'm on my way home from the airport, but I found this in my car, Michael must've left it there. And as I have to pass your place on the way to mine, I thought I might as well drop it off.'

I take the jacket Liam holds out, his fingers accidently brushing mine as I gather it up, laying it over the crook of my arm.

'Thanks. Do you want to stay for dinner? I've got a casserole on the stove. There's plenty.'

He shakes his head and steps back from the door. 'I'd love to, but I've got a meeting first thing, not to mention copious notes to write up for a conference I'm attending next week, so ...' He shrugs and gives me an apologetic smile, 'I'll pick up a take-away on the way home. Are you sure you're okay?'

I nod and try to muster up a more convincing smile. 'Yes. Michael's just grabbing a shower, then we're going to have dinner, maybe grab an early night.'

Liam drops his gaze, scuffing the toe of his boot against the step, his hands in his pockets. He doesn't say anything and even when he raises his gaze he just smiles at me again as he starts to walk backwards towards his car. 'I'll see you later, huh?'

'Yeah. Later.'

I close the door before his car's left our driveway, flicking the locks and double-checking them before I hang up Michael's jacket. And I'm about to go back into the kitchen. I should check on that casserole, but I don't. I stop and I glance quickly up the stairs. I can hear Michael moving around up there. I can hear his voice. He's talking to someone.

Taking a deep breath, I turn back to look at the jacket Liam's just returned. It really has come to this.

I slide a hand into one of the pockets and feel around inside but there's nothing in there. So I try another pocket. Still nothing. But I'm sure this jacket has an inside pocket and I reach around to find it. And the second I put my hand in there I feel it. A slip of paper. A receipt, maybe? I pull it out and look at it. It *is* a receipt, for lunch at a Spanish restaurant in the city. The same restaurant we used to love going to, but we haven't been there for a long time now. *We* haven't been there, but he obviously has, and I check the date – it was a few days ago, his lunchtime visit. Just a few days ago. I scan the receipt more closely. Definitely a meal for two. He wasn't alone.

Shoving the receipt back into his pocket I glance up the stairs again. His voice is a little more muffled now. It's barely audible. He must've gone into his office. It isn't Liam he's talking to ... so who is it?

Climbing the stairs, carefully, quietly, I try to avoid those steps that I know have creaking floorboards. He's still just that little bit too far away for me to make out what he's saying.

I make my way along the first-floor landing, again moving slowly so as not to make a sound, but I stop when I reach the bottom of the stairs that lead up to the top floor. His voice is a little louder now, but he's definitely inside his office and the door is closed, so whatever he's saying – whoever he's talking to, I still can't make anything out. And then it goes quiet, and I hear him moving about again, so I turn to go, but he's already coming down the stairs. I dart into our bedroom, pretend to look for something I don't need.

'Ellie?'

I turn around and he's standing there, in the doorway.

'I needed a change of shirt. I splashed something on this one.'

He comes over to me, takes the shirt I don't need from my hand and tosses it onto the bed. 'What's going on?'

'I need to change my ...'

'Why were you really at the university today?'

68

I laugh quietly, fold my arms across my chest and step back from him, shaking my head. 'You think I had some ulterior motive for dropping by to leave you lunch?'

'I don't know what to think, Ellie. I don't. I mean, there are times when you're fine, you're good; times when everything is normal ...'

'You think everything is *normal*, Michael?'

He takes a step towards me, reaches out to take my hand and I let him, his fingers curling around mine. It's a feeling I'm so unfamiliar with now, him touching me, so when it happens, even under these kind of circumstances, I take it. Because I just want to feel him touch me again.

I drop my gaze and look at his hand holding mine.

'Please, Ellie, don't do this.'

'Who were you talking to? Just now?'

He lets go of me and narrows his eyes, pushing a hand back through his hair. 'Jesus, what the hell is wrong with you? You turn up at the university, out of the blue, you demand to know who I'm talking to ... whatever the hell you think is going on it's all in your head, okay?' He jabs the side of his temple hard as he says that, his eyes darkening as he stares at me. Yeah, he's angry. So am I. I've been angry for a long time. I have every right to be. 'And that call was to Neil Haywood, a colleague of mine from Edinburgh. He's visiting the university next week for a guest lecture. I just wanted to make sure he has all the details he needs before he gets here.' He pulls his phone from his back pocket and holds it out to me. 'Go on. Check my call history if you don't believe me.'

I lean back against the wall and fold my arms tighter against myself. I don't know what to feel now. I don't. 'I'm not going to do that.'

'Look at me.'

I slowly raise my gaze, my eyes meeting his. The darkness has lifted slightly. He's trying to understand what's going on in my head.

'Nothing is going on. Okay? Nothing's happening, everything is fine. And you can't – you can't keep doing this, it's not healthy.'

I pick up the shirt he threw down on the bed and slide it back onto the hanger.

'Ellie? Are you listening to me?'

'I'm not one of your students, Michael. Don't talk to me like I am.' I swing back around to face him. 'Or maybe you'd prefer it if I was one of your students.'

'What the fuck is *that* supposed to mean?'

'Nothing ...' I start to walk away, out of the room. I'm done here.

'No, you don't get to walk away like that. Jesus ... *Ellie*!'

I stop in the doorway, but I don't turn around.

'Ellie?'

I stay still, I don't move. I just lean against the doorpost and sigh.

'I'm sorry,' he says quietly, and I ache for him to touch me, to make all this shit go away. I want it all to go away. I want my husband back. 'It's been a long day. I'm just tired.'

Excuses. That's all they are. He makes them regularly. He's too tired to talk, too exhausted to go over it all again. Didn't the counsellor help us? She helped *him*. Nothing helped me.

But even *she* never got the full story, did she? And he's still okay with that. I'm not.

'How about we eat dinner, then have an early night, hmm?'

I slowly turn around. I look at him, but his eyes – he doesn't look at me the way he used to look at me. There's always a hint of something else there now. Is it pity? I want my fucking husband back.

'When I tell you I love you, Ellie, I mean it.'

'I know.' *Liar.*

'That's what we need to concentrate on, okay? Us. Everything else – all of that, it's in the past. It's over. It's over. I promise.'

Michael – he needs a distraction, something to stop him from going over and over it all in his head; something to take away his guilt. I think he needs that. And I think he's found her, his distraction. My husband's lying to me and that's not right. None of this is right.

'It's over,' I whisper. I'm just telling him what he wants to hear, and whether he believes that or not – no. He'll believe it. He'll tell himself that he's managed to pacify me. That's exactly what he'll do. Because he's done it before, so many times.

He smiles and he takes a step forward. Yet, when he touches me, as his thumb gently strokes my jawline, his mouth lowering down onto mine, I actually let myself believe that everything's fine. It's all going to be all right. But that only lasts a second because, okay, he's kissing me, and the kiss is soft and warm but there's no passion there. That rarely makes an appearance now. We barely touch each other in that way any more, and when we do have sex it's as though we just go through with it every so often to tell ourselves something, and I don't even know what that something is. It feels as if we're clinging onto what remnants of a relationship we have left, and that breaks my heart a million times over. I want it to be so different. I want him to want me the way he used to want me, fuck me the way he used to fuck me.

'Michael ...'

He slides his thumb over my mouth, silencing me, shaking his head as his eyes stare deep into mine. 'No, Ellie.' He steps back from me, slips his hands into his pockets. 'I'm going to have a quick shower, then we'll eat. Okay?'

Nothing is okay.

I know he's lying.

I know he's hiding something.

I know that he wants me to move on and forget, but I can't do that.

I won't, do that ...

Chapter 10

I throw my bag down on the floor and lock the front door behind me, grabbing the handle and pulling it towards me, just to make sure it's secure.

I know Michael's home, his car's in the driveway, he's early. It's just gone four-thirty and I've only popped back myself to pick up some papers I need from my office for a meeting at the spa in an hour.

I glance through into the living room as I walk past, but it's all quiet in there. He isn't in the kitchen either, so he must be upstairs.

I go to my office, find the papers I need and head back out into the hall, sliding the files into my bag before I make my way upstairs. And I'm about to call out Michael's name, but I stop myself. I can smell paint. Fresh paint. We aren't decorating, we haven't talked about making any changes, haven't talked about repainting anything.

I climb the stairs slowly, and when I reach the landing, when I see where Michael is, what room he's in, it feels as though someone's reached into my chest and yanked out my heart.

'What are you doing?'

He spins around, almost dropping the paintbrush in his hand. 'Ellie! I didn't expect you home just yet. I wanted to surprise you.'

I look around me. Three of the walls are still sunflower yellow, but the wall he's standing in front of is now half-painted a deep purple colour.

'Don't,' I whisper.

He frowns. He doesn't understand, but he should.

'Put the brush down.'

'Ellie ...'

'Put the fucking brush down, Michael.'

He narrows his eyes, watches me as I move towards him. And then it hits me, like a volcano erupting inside of me. The anger. The pain. It spills out of me, so fast I can't control it.

I run towards him, snatch the brush from his hand and I slap him. Once. Twice. Again, harder. I want to lash out, hurt him, the way he's hurt me, by doing this. But he grabs my wrist, he grips it tight, because I'm fighting this. I'm fighting *him*.

'You had no right to do this.' I hiss, my eyes burning into his. 'You don't touch this room, you don't *do* that.'

'Ellie, we talked about this ...'

I wrench my wrist free of his grip. 'No, Michael, *you* talked about this. And I told you I didn't want it. Not yet. It's too soon.'

'You weren't thinking straight back then.'

I look at him. I shake my head. What happened to us? 'Fuck you.'

'Jesus Christ, Ellie, come on!'

'Put it back how it was and don't touch it again.'

'This isn't rational behaviour.'

'And you're not being fair.'

'Ellie ...'

'Leave this room alone. Do you hear me? Leave this room alone.'

*

'I don't think he meant to hurt you, Ellie.'

Liam hands me a bottle of beer and sits down opposite me at a table out in the pub's riverside beer garden. I needed to talk to someone. I needed a friend.

'Did you know what he was going to do?'

'No, I didn't, but, you know, maybe he's right. Maybe it *is* time to do something about ...'

The look I shoot him shuts him up, but his frustrated sigh tells me he's on Michael's side over this one.

'I'm sorry, I just think ...'

'I don't care what you think.'

His eyes meet mine. 'You should care what I think. You should try listening to people every now and again because, contrary to what you might think, they're only trying to help you.'

I hold his gaze. 'And is that what *you're* doing? Are *you* only trying to help me?'

He doesn't answer that. He just continues to stare right

into me, until I finally break the stare, looking down at my beer.

'I'm sorry, you didn't deserve that.'

'You don't need to fight all the time. You don't always need to be so defensive. People care about you. Let them do that. People worry about you. *I* worry about you.'

'He shouldn't have done it. Not without talking to me first. He was wrong to do what he did. He was wrong.'

I glance out over the river. It's a beautiful evening, warm and sunny, and the banks of the river are busy with people out for a walk, enjoying a drink, making the most of the good weather we've been having lately. I've always liked it here.

'Hey.'

Liam's voice pulls me back from my thoughts and I turn to face him. He smiles at me and that, somehow, makes me feel a little better. That smile.

'I'd like to think that's what I'm trying to do, Ellie. I'd like to think I'm trying to help you.'

I leave a beat or two before I say anything and I smile back. 'You are.'

He is.

Helping me ...

Chapter 11

It's Saturday and I'm busy going over the books from the Durham salon. I'm popping in there later, after I've dropped by the spa. My new business is really taking off and I'm so lucky to have an amazing team of people looking after the place because I can't be there all the time. I have four businesses to oversee, so I need a good strong team of people behind me, to help me. I have that.

I look up as Michael walks into the kitchen, throwing his kit-bag onto the floor before he goes to get himself a cup of coffee. I'm still angry at him for what he did yesterday, but I'm not letting him see just how much it affected me. He didn't do it out of malice, I get that now, but he still should have understood why I reacted the way I did. But, like everything else, we haven't spoken about it any more. It's become something else we've just swept under the carpet.

'You're going out?'

He looks at me, leaning back against the counter as he takes a sip of his coffee. 'It's Saturday. I always go to the squash club on a Saturday.'

Not always. He never used to go *every* Saturday, but lately – yeah, lately it's been that way.

'What's the problem? You're going to work, so ...'

'There's no problem.'

He takes another sip of coffee, puts down his mug before he heads back towards the door, and as he passes me he gently squeezes my shoulder, drops a quick kiss on my forehead. 'Have a good day, darling. I'll see you later.'

He goes back over to his bag, picking it up and throwing it over his shoulder. I drop my gaze, go back to checking over those books. 'What time are you going to be home?'

'I'll probably grab some lunch with the guys, and then I need to stop by the university later to pick up some papers, so, I'm not sure when I'll be back.'

I look up to see his retreating figure head out into the hall, watch as he stops by the line of coats hanging up by the door, his eyes falling on that jacket Liam returned.

'Liam dropped it off a couple of nights ago. Said you must've left it in his car.'

I continue to watch as he rummages around in the pockets. *Oh Michael, I know what you're looking for.* I can't quite see from where I'm sitting, but the fact that he puts his hand straight into his jeans pocket makes me think he's slipped that receipt in there.

He says nothing more to me as he lets himself out and closes the door behind him.

I get up and go out into the hall. Glancing down at the security monitor I watch as Michael's car pulls out of the driveway and I turn around and take his jacket off the hook by the door, immediately feeling around for the inside pocket. It's empty. He *did* take that receipt out of there, but I check the other pockets anyway. I might have missed something. No. They're all empty.

I hang the jacket back up and sit down on the stairs, dragging my hands back through my hair. Our Saturdays, they used to be good. They used to be something we enjoyed. If I had to work then, yes, he'd play squash, maybe organise something with Liam. But if I wasn't working we'd always do something, even if it was just going into Durham to look around the shops, take a walk along the river, have lunch outside if the weather was good. We'd always do something, together. Now it seems he can't wait to be apart from me.

I stay there, at the bottom of the stairs, for a good few minutes, just staring at that small black and white security monitor, even though nothing is happening. It's all quiet outside, but I keep staring at our empty driveway, at the shrubs and pots of flowers that dot the gravel and block-paved space. It's all quiet.

Suddenly I don't want to be here, in this house, alone. I get up, grab my coat, and I let myself out. I'm not going in to work, not yet. There's nothing urgent waiting for me. I don't know where I'm going. I just know that I need to get away from here, for a while. I need to be somewhere else. So I get in my car and I drive. I turn up the radio and I try to drown out that silence I'm so tired of now. I just drive, until I find myself passing a supermarket. I pull into the car park, stop the car and turn the music up a little louder, and for a few minutes I sit there, listening to a song I don't know as I look out around me, at people going about their lives with no idea how much mine has changed. So much, I don't recognise it any more. And then that numbness hits me again, washing over me with a breathtaking speed, and I breathe in deeply, try to compose myself because I can't sit here all day. I have to do something.

Reaching over onto the passenger seat I grab my bag. I can't remember if I put my purse in there before I left the house. Yes, it's there, and I breathe a sigh of relief. I'll go and do the food shop. I'll do something mundane and ordinary and try to forget all the crap that's complicating my once beautiful, perfect life. But as I walk across the car park it's as if all eyes are on me, as though every person here can see my pain so clearly, a loneliness that's so glaringly obvious to everyone I can almost feel their pitying looks boring into my back as I pass them. So I keep my head down, grab a shopping trolley from outside the store and go inside. But I still feel exposed, and yet, at the same time, it's as if I'm the only one here. I'm in a busy supermarket, surrounded by noise and chatter, and yet, I feel alone.

I raise my head slightly, just to see where I am, which aisle I've just walked into and I stop by the milk, my eyes scanning the shelves, but I'm looking at everything and seeing nothing. So I just reach out and grab something, anything. I don't care. Just putting something into the trolley fills me with a sense of relief, as if I'm less exposed now I've actually started to do what I came in here to do. What *did* I come in here to do? I did a big food shop two days ago, there's nothing else we really need.

I continue my slow walk up the aisle, glancing at the shelves as I pass, watching as everyone around me picks up items, talks to the person they're with. Almost everyone is with someone. But even those who are alone don't seem to have that weight on their shoulders that I feel I carry constantly now. They're walking around with a sense of purpose, while I don't even know what I'm doing in here. I have one carton of milk in the trolley and no idea what else I'm looking for. So I just start to grab things, anything – a can of soup, a packet of pasta, bread, cereal, teabags, even though I know we don't need any of it. I·want to get out of here now. It's time to go to work. I need to take my mind off all of this. I need to grab onto reality.

'Ellie?'

A voice behind me makes me jump, causing me to drop the jar of marmalade I was holding, and I watch as it clatters against the metal of the shopping trolley, landing on its side next to a loaf of bread.

'You not at work this morning?'

I look up. It's Liam. And my eyes lock on his for less than a heartbeat before I drop my gaze, glancing down at the basket in his hand. It's filled with things he probably does need, as opposed to my randomly filled trolley. 'I'm on my way to the Durham salon. I just needed to pick up a few things first.'

And then I realise something and I frown, and he doesn't miss that change in my expression. 'Is there something wrong, Ellie?'

'I thought you'd be at the squash club this morning.'

'I was. I've just come from there, but there's nothing

happening. Most of the guys are away on business this weekend, so there's not really a lot going on.'

'Was Michael there?'

It's his turn to frown, and that causes my stomach to twist up into that all-too-familiar knot of fear, anxiety once more taking over. 'No, he wasn't.'

'It's just that – he said he was going there. This morning, when he left the house. He said he was going to the club.'

'Well, I didn't see him ...'

More lies. My husband. The liar.

I start to push the trolley towards the check-outs, but Liam puts a hand on my arm to stop me, and I stare down at his fingers grasping my wrist.

'Is something wrong, Ellie?'

He repeats that question and I just look at him. I don't want this conversation here. In fact, I'm not sure if I want this conversation at all.

'Okay. Let's go for a coffee.'

'I need to get to the salon.'

I try to push the trolley away again but his fingers tighten around my wrist. 'We're going to grab some lunch, all right?' He loosens his grip on me and I drop my gaze again, eyeing those random items of food in my trolley. 'All right?'

'Yes. Okay.' I look up at him and I don't know if I feel angry or sad or frustrated. I don't know. I just know that my husband is lying to me. 'Let's go.'

Liam smiles, but I don't smile back. I'm not really in the mood for smiling. I'm not really in the mood for lunch, either, but I don't think I have much choice as far as that's concerned.

And I know that Liam – he's going to try and take my mind off something that can't be ignored, but ultimately, he's going to fail. Because I can't ignore it. I can't ignore any of it. Not any more ...

*

'You're selling the house?'

I've become so selfish lately, so consumed with my own problems that I forget to take notice of what's going on in our friends' lives. But Liam's our closest friend, and I had no idea the repercussions of his divorce had come to this.

'Well, Keeley wants her half of the equity.' He shrugs. 'It's time to move on, I guess.'

'I'm assuming you'll be looking to buy a new place of your own?'

'I've been checking out a few properties, yes.'

'Anywhere in particular?'

'Somewhere between Durham and Newcastle, I thought. That would make my commute to the lab a little easier, seeing as I'm there most of the time at the minute. But I'm definitely looking for a smaller place. If it's just going to be me.'

His eyes meet mine and I look down, reaching for the salt at the exact same time that he does, our hands clashing together, and I quickly pull mine back, laughing as he does the same.

'Ladies first.' He smiles and I return it. I'm glad I bumped into him now. I'm glad of the company. I don't think I'd really wanted to be alone today. It's just that house, the irrational feelings it can kick up inside me sometimes.

'Ellie?'

I hadn't realised I'd drifted off. 'I used to have friends, Liam.'

'You still have friends.'

I raise my gaze and my eyes once more meet his. 'They're all too scared to be alone with me these days. It's fine, in a crowd, at parties, weddings ... They don't know what to say to me. I mean, they think me and Michael are fine, but they still don't know what to say ...'

I leave that sentence hanging and drop my head again, watching as I absentmindedly fiddle with the salt shaker.

'They're still there. All of them. They're still there.'

I slowly look back up and I smile slightly. I have to stop this self-pity because he's right. My friends *are* still there, they haven't distanced themselves from me, it's the other way around. I'm the one who can't face the girls' nights out or the weekends away. I'm still being invited, I'm just making excuses not to go.

'You need your friends. You need *me*.'

'Yes. I do.'

He breaks the stare and looks down, picking up his fork, although all he does is move his food around the plate a bit.

'That jacket you dropped back for Michael a couple of nights ago ...'

He raises his head, his eyes back on mine. 'What about it?'

'I found something. In the pocket.'

He frowns, putting down his fork. 'Found what?'

'A receipt. For that Spanish restaurant – the one me and Michael used to go to regularly.'

He's slightly confused now, I can tell.

'It was for lunch there. A few days ago.'

'So?'

'So, we haven't been there for a long time. Not since … It was *our* place. Why would he go there without me? And who was he with, huh? Who did he take?'

Liam sighs and it's one filled with frustration as he picks up his fork and resumes eating. He isn't even entertaining this conversation. And I want to tell him I dropped by the university, I want to tell him that, too; tell him what I saw, but I stop myself, I pull back because I'm not sure he wants to hear that, either.

'I think I'm losing him, Liam.'

He keeps his head down and I watch him, the way he stabs his pasta with a fork, the sound of metal hitting china loud enough for me to hear above the noise of the busy bistro.

'When he touches me, which isn't all that often, it doesn't feel like it used to. *He* doesn't feel like he used to.'

'Have you talked to him?' Liam asks, but he keeps his head down. And there's a slight edge to his voice, a hint of frustration, and I don't want to push him away too, I really don't.

'I've tried. But you know how it is, he doesn't want to listen.'

Liam looks up and sits back in his seat, his eyes finally meeting mine.

'I love him, Liam. And yes, I've told him that. He knows I love him. And I know – I *think* he loves me …'

'You *think* he loves you?'

I break the stare this time, glancing around the bistro at couples and families and groups of friends all enjoying lunch. The place is full of laughter and excited gossip, conversations that aren't darkened with unfounded suspicion and doubt, like mine are.

'How long is it going to take? How much more do we have to go through before it pulls us so far apart we can't ever come back together?'

'I can't answer that, Ellie, you know I can't.' He sighs again, running a hand back through his dark-blonde hair, and I turn my head back around to look at him, but he's turned his attention to the people around us now. And I just watch him for a few seconds. I try to read his expression and I start to feel that guilt hit me again. I keep dragging him into this, into my and Michael's problems, but he was involved too, to some extent. He went through it with us; he knows how hard it's all been. He understands. He's been there for me. More than Michael has. But I still feel that guilt, sometimes.

'Surely we didn't go through all that shit just to lose everything?' I say quietly, and I wait for him to respond, but he doesn't, not really. Instead he checks his watch and continues to eat as though I hadn't uttered a word, hadn't asked that question.

'What if he keeps putting those barriers up?'

Again, no response.

'I *know* Michael's hiding something.'

He finally looks up, laying down his fork, his attention is on me now. 'Hiding what?'

'I don't know ... I don't know anything for sure, I just ...'

I sit back. I can feel that weariness start to flood my body again. That doubt, that uncertainty, it's rushing forward, threatening to overwhelm me, but then I remember what I saw, at Michael's office. I remember the way *she* looked at him, the way he looked at her. I remember that. I remember what's gone before too. I remember the past. And now that doubt and uncertainty is being chased away by a fire in my belly. I have a mission, right? I have a job to do. 'He's looking for a distraction.'

'And you're not?'

Liam looks at me, right into my eyes, and I drop my gaze, because he's right. We're both looking for distractions. We both need them, and that's part of the problem. 'I saw her.'

'Saw who?'

'Ava.'

I wasn't going to say anything about this, but I really can't stop myself. I can't.

'Who the hell is Ava?'

'One of Michael's students ...'

'Jesus Christ ...' He throws back his head. He's not even attempting to hide his exasperation now. And I can see it on his face. It's not there as much as it is on Michael's – that expression I'm all too familiar with – but it's there all the same. The disappointment, the frustration, the wishing I'd just drop all this shit and get on with my life. It's there, now, I can see it clear as day.

'And you think, what? That he's sleeping with her?'

His bluntness shocks me a little, but maybe he's just doing that to try and make me see things more clearly, but I know what I saw. And I don't want to argue with him. I don't need that. 'The way he looked at her ... the way *she* looked at *him*, there was something else there ...'

I leave that sentence hanging, because I'm not entirely sure how to finish it, and Liam, he stays silent for a few seconds, his eyes down, and now I'm wondering if I should've confided in him at all. Maybe I should've kept this to myself, until I had something more concrete. Until I knew, for sure.

'My husband refuses to talk to me. He refuses to talk about something that we still need to talk about, *I* still need to talk about. It doesn't matter whether *he's* moved on or not, I haven't. *I* haven't. And if he's looking for some kind of distraction ... Is it my fault? Have I pushed him into this?'

'Pushed him into what?' He looks up, and his eyes – that frustration is still there, but there's something else. He understands, all too well. 'What exactly do you think is going on, Ellie?'

I let a couple of beats go by before I answer him. 'What if it's happening again?'

My voice is barely a whisper. I'm not crazy. I'm not imagining anything.

'What am I supposed to do? Just fall into line, suck it up and wait for him to get whatever he's doing out of his system? Is that how it works now?'

'Maybe he's just found his own way of dealing with things.' He finally faces me again, and looks at me hard. 'And you have yours.'

He holds my gaze for the briefest of seconds, and then he's signalling for the bill. He's calling an end to this now. And I feel that rush of guilt return.

'I'm sorry. I shouldn't keep using you as a sounding board, it isn't fair.'

And it isn't, but right now *life* isn't fucking fair, and I'm tired of everyone just expecting me to be over this. To forget. To accept that things have changed. To move on. I'll move on when I'm ready, and I'm not ready yet.

'I'm always here, Ellie, if you need me. You know that.' His tone has lost that slight edge now, and I smile, reaching for his hand, but he pulls it away as the waitress places our bill on the table. I just wanted to thank him, for being here. For listening to me, again.

'Liam, I ... thank you.'

'Are you going to be okay?'

I nod. I'm going to be fine.

'Come on, let's get out of here ... Look, I've got nothing on this afternoon, do you want me to come over? Keep you company?'

I look at him, and his expression's one of concern now. Jesus, I don't need *his* pity, too. 'I don't need babysitting.'

'That's not what I meant.'

'No. I know it isn't, I'm sorry.'

'I haven't got anything planned, and if Michael's not home ...'

'I said no, Liam.' I hold his gaze, because I mean it. I don't want him to come home with me. I don't need him to do that. I don't need looking after. 'Besides, I'm not going home. I'm going to work.'

'Okay.' He holds up his hands in a gesture of surrender. 'I get the message.'

I gather up my things and fish my car keys out of my bag, and then I hesitate for a second. I give his offer of company a second thought. If Michael still isn't back. Then I push that thought to the back of my mind. I need to be on my own now, to think.

'I really am grateful, Liam. For everything.'

We fall into step alongside each other as we walk to our cars, the silence between us so different to the one that constantly haunts Michael and me. This one is a friendly, comfortable silence, whereas the ones that have gradually developed between me and my husband – they're laced with unspoken words, locked-away feelings, they're tinged with guilt.

'Hey. Come here.'

We stop by my car and I turn to face Liam; let him pull me in for a hug.

'Remember what I said, all right? I'm always here, if you need me.'

I step back from him, and I smile. 'I know.'

I watch as he heads down to the street, to his own car, wait until he's driven away before I get into mine, and once again I just sit there. I don't make any attempt to drive away, not yet. I turn on the radio and I sit back and look outside at the busy street. I need another minute, that's all. And as I sit there my mind goes back to that phone call I heard Michael make just a couple of nights ago. Was it really just a work colleague he was talking to? He offered me his phone, told me I could check for myself, but that could've been nothing more than him calling my bluff. He knows I would never do that. I couldn't *be* that woman, except, I am. I *am* that woman.

I close my eyes and sigh quietly. Has it helped? Offloading all my crap onto Liam's shoulders? I don't know. I don't know if anything *can* help. I just know that I've started something I have every intention of finishing now. And if I have to do that alone, then that's fine, I'm okay with that. It might even be better that way. But I need to know what my husband's hiding. I need to know who my husband's seeing; why he's lying to me. I need to know what he's doing when he isn't with me. I need to know. And I'm going to find out.

Chapter 12

'Liam told me you bumped into each other today.'

'We did.' I hand Michael a glass of wine and sit down on the couch by the fireplace, curling my legs up underneath myself. 'We went for lunch, at that new bistro not far from the Durham salon.'

I haven't asked him where *he* went today, why he wasn't where he said he would be. I haven't asked him anything. I'm biding my time. Waiting until he trips himself up, gives something away, because he will. He thinks he can hide behind his charm, use that smile to disguise his deceit. *I'm watching you, Michael. I'm watching you.*

'So, what did you talk about?'

I take a sip of wine. 'Nothing in particular.'

'Did you talk about us? About me and you?'

I frown slightly, because that's a strange question. Would he be angry if he thought I was talking about us?

'We talked about a lot of things. But, yeah, I mentioned us.'

It's hard not to, when it's all I can think about most days. Us. What we had. What I want back, at any cost.

'Do you remember who we used to be, Michael?'

'We're still those people, Ellie.'

'Are we?' I don't want him to answer that. He doesn't need to. 'Do you remember who we were?'

He looks at me, and there it is, that change of expression, the fear that I'm about to launch into that conversation he continually avoids, and I wait for the inevitable shut-down.

'We loved each other.'

That throws me slightly. I wasn't expecting an answer, I was expecting the usual barriers to come up. He used the past tense; we *loved* each other, that's what he said. Loved. I still *love* him.

'We were those people who loved life and lived it, every day, like it was the last one we were ever going to experience.'

My wonderful, idealistic husband. It can never be that way again, and I think, deep down, even he knows that.

'What happened changed that. What happened changed everything.'

'For a while, yes. It did ...'

'For a *while*?' I put my drink down and sit up, my eyes fixed on his. He is going to listen to me now and he is going to understand the pain and the fear I still feel, every day. 'I lost our baby, Michael. I miscarried our child, I ... you think that changed everything for a *while*?'

He gets up and comes over to me, sits down beside me. He takes my hand and he brings it to his mouth, kissing it gently, and I'm so angry at myself for crying now. So fucking angry.

'We can't go on like this, Ellie. We can't. It isn't good for us. It isn't good for *you*. I hate seeing you like this.'

'Then let me talk, Michael. Please. Let me talk about it.'

He drops his gaze, but he keeps hold of my hand, his fingers tightening around mine. 'Ellie, sweetheart, I just think – I think that dwelling on it, on what happened, it's unhealthy. We can't change anything, we can't turn back the clock ...'

'I know. I know that, but – do you know how difficult it is for me? To keep all this shit bottled up inside because *you* don't want to talk about it?'

'We've talked about it so many times, Ellie. We've been over and over it, so many fucking times, and it needs to stop now. It needs to stop.'

'And what? That's it? Where does that leave *me*, Michael? Hmm? Where does that leave *me*? Should I be – I don't know – grateful that *you're* over it?'

'That isn't what I meant ...'

'I still need to talk, Michael. *I* still need to talk; do you understand that? Because I don't think you do. Oh, you'll give your students all the time they need, *they* can talk to you, but your own wife?'

'Ellie, come on ...'

'*They* can talk to you, Michael.'

He slowly raises his gaze, his fingers gripping my hand tighter still.

'What's going on here, Ellie?'

I pull my hand away from his. I sit back, pull my knees to my chest, hugging them to me as I stare out ahead of me. I take a deep breath. I don't want to go there again, I don't want to keep remembering, but the memories are racing forward now. They're too powerful to ignore.

'When I woke up, in hospital – when I woke up, and you told me ...' I drop my head, bite down on my lip, I don't want to cry any more. 'When you told me we'd lost the baby, I felt so empty, Michael. So fucking empty. It felt like – like I'd died, too.' I look up, turn to face him. 'Like *we'd* died.'

'Ellie ...'

He reaches for my hand again and I let him take it. 'We didn't just lose a baby, did we? We lost *us*?'

He rests his palm against my cheek, his eyes looking deep into mine, and I feel a wave of love so strong for this man flood me. It knocks the breath right out of me.

'No, my darling, we didn't. We didn't.'

I think we did.

'It's like you've forgotten our baby ever existed,' I whispered, covering his hand with mine, our fingers sliding together. 'And I can't do that.'

He sighs quietly, squeezes my hand gently. 'You were hurting so much, Ellie. I just didn't want to hurt you any more.'

'I felt so alone, Michael. A huge part of me had been ripped away, taken from me in a way that ...' I don't finish that sentence. I can't. Losing the baby was painful enough, but remembering the way it happened ...

'We had it all planned, remember? Names. The books we'd read to him or her. The school we wanted our child to go to. Where we were going to take our son or daughter on his or her first holiday ...'

'Don't do this to yourself, Ellie, please.'

I look away, look down at my arms hugging my knees. 'I wanted that baby, so much.'

'*We* wanted that baby. It hurt me too, losing our child like that.'

My head snaps up, my eyes meeting his. 'Did it?'

'You really have to ask that?'

'You were ready to get rid of the nursery. Ready to paint over the past like our baby had never existed ...'

'That's not what it was like, and you know that. Losing the baby hurt me too, Ellie.'

'It's just that, you were so busy telling me we had to put it all behind us, had to forget ...'

'I didn't tell you to forget about the baby. I never once told you to do that.'

'Losing our child makes up so much of what happened that night, Michael. So forgetting isn't something I can do. Even if *you* can.'

I want to ask him who Ava is. I want to ask him, but if I mention her name, if I go into specifics he'll think I've been spying on him. And he'd be right, that's exactly what I'm doing, but I don't want him to know that. So I can't mention her. Not yet.

'I worry, Michael. That it's going to happen again, that history is going to repeat itself and I can't go through it a second time, I can't ... I can't do it.'

He looks at me, right into my eyes. He's throwing me a silent instruction. He's telling me to end this, to stop this, to shut up.

'It won't happen again. You think I'd *let* that happen again? I didn't let it happen the first time, I had no fucking idea ...'

He rakes a hand back through his hair, briefly turning away

from me. I'm making him relive everything he's succeeded in pushing to the back of his mind, but it happened, and I can't forget it. He wants to. And when I don't allow that, this happens. 'Don't ask me to change who I am, Ellie, because I can't do that.' He turns back to face me; his blue eyes have darkened now. He wants me to get this, to listen to him. To obey. 'What happened was a mistake. A tragic mistake ...'

I can't stop the laugh escaping. He's almost trivialising what happened. And then I look at him, right at him. His eyes bore deep into mine and I can see the faint trace of his own pain still there. He just refuses to share it with me and that's what upsets me. That's what's helping to tear us apart while I'm struggling to keep us together.

'Please, Ellie, I'm begging you now. Stop this. Please.'

He reaches out and wipes a tear from my cheek with his thumb.

'I know that – what you went through, it affected you so much more than me ...'

'You weren't there,' I whisper, closing my eyes as I try not to remember that night, but it's impossible. I can't forget it. I'm not sure I ever will, it's still there, every terrifying, devastating second, embedded in my brain like a permanent memory that can never be erased. People keep telling me it can be erased, but it can't. People tell me I'm refusing to let it go, but how can I? So much was taken from me that night. So much was stolen from me, and I can't get it back. We changed, that night. We changed, forever.

'You think I don't know that? I *know* I wasn't there, Ellie. I *know* I couldn't get to you in time ...'

'You're not here now. Are you?'

He frowns. 'What's that supposed to mean?'

I turn away from him. I don't want to start that conversation. It's not the right time. 'Nothing. It doesn't mean anything. I'm just tired.' I take another deep breath, turn back to look at him, smiling slightly. I don't want to push this. I need to step back. Keep watching him. I'll find out what I need to know. I just need to be patient.

I let go of his hand and stand up, walking over to the window. It's dark and it's raining, a hard, heavy kind of rain that hits the ground outside with a force that sends splashes of water high into the air, and I wonder where this storm came from all of a sudden. It's been such a beautiful day. I never saw this coming. But sometimes we don't see things coming. Even when the signs have been there, signs we should've picked up on, dealt with, stopped in their tracks before they grew into something terrifying. Dangerous. Tragic.

Sometimes we don't see things coming ...

Fourteen Months Earlier ...

'Is everything okay?' I ask Michael as he sits down and begins searching through a pile of papers that has been there on the kitchen table since he came home from work a couple of hours ago. I know better than to move anything of his that might be work-related. 'Is it something important?'

'Hmm? Sorry?' He looks up, his eyes meeting mine.

'Whatever you're looking for. Is it important?'

'No ... No, it's just something I might need for this meeting tonight.' He smiles at me, and I join him at the table, pouring myself a glass of water. I'm craving wine, beer, a strawberry Mojito. I'd kill for a hit of alcohol, but at just over thirteen weeks' pregnant Michael won't even let me sniff the cork from the bottle of red he and Liam shared the other night. But we've been trying for so long to have this baby, so I'm quite happy to sacrifice anything for our child.

'You seem a little on edge.' And he does, just a little. I can see it on his face. 'Are you sure everything's okay?'

'Everything's fine, Ellie. There's just a lot going on right now, that's all. We're trying to set up a new research project, hire another member of staff, and on top of that we've still got tutorials, student mentoring. You know I don't like to neglect my students. It's a busy time.'

'You can deal with that kind of stuff with your eyes closed.' I rest my elbow on the table, cup my chin in my hand and I smile at him. 'You got a new fan club yet? Any fights over the front row in the lecture theatre?'

My husband. The handsome professor. He's been the focus of a fair few crushes in his time, but I think he secretly likes the attention.

'I can't help being the Indiana Jones of the English Literature world, can I?' He grins, and I throw him a look.

'I think you're over-selling yourself a bit there.' I get up and go to check on the chicken roasting in the oven. 'Do you *have* to go out tonight?'

'I promised Laurel and Frank I'd meet them for dinner. We really need to push forward with the decision on this new staff member, but if we can't agree on who's best for the post ...'

'As Head of Department shouldn't you have the final say?'

I feel him come up behind me, his arms pulling me back against him, his hands resting lightly on my stomach. 'I don't run a dictatorship. I'd like us all to agree on this one.' He kisses the side of my neck and I feel a hot shiver race up my spine. I've loved this man for so long now, and there are days when I still wake up and wonder how I got so lucky; why this clever, handsome, funny man fell for me.

'I really wish you could stay at home,' I murmur, laying my head against his shoulder, his breath warm on my neck.

'I wish I could stay at home, too.'

'I was going to take a long, hot bath. Who's going to wash my back now?'

His hand moves up to touch my breast, his thumb flicking over my nipple, and I close my eyes and bite down on my lip as his mouth brushes over my shoulder. 'These get bigger during pregnancy, right?'

I gently elbow him in the stomach, and he cries out in mock pain.

'That kind of remark is beneath you, professor.'

'Oh, I can be as shallow as the next person, believe me.'

I turn around and laugh as he pulls me back into his arms. 'I love you so much, Michael.'

'I love you more.'

My eyes flicker shut as he kisses me. I slide my fingers into his hair, his hand on the small of my back keeping me pressed against him.

'I've just got to make a quick call, okay? I need to speak to Liam before I go, make sure he's all right. All this business with Keeley is really getting to him, even though he won't admit it.' He grins at me and kisses the tip of my nose. 'I'll be right back.'

I lean back against the counter, still smiling as I watch him almost run out of the kitchen, hear him bound up the stairs, and I let a hand fall onto my stomach. There's no bump there yet, nothing to let anyone know that we're finally pregnant, but *we* know, that our baby is finally on his or her way, and it makes me smile, every day. That little person inside me, they are going to be so loved because we have waited so long for this child.

I shift my gaze from the doorway to the table, my eyes falling on the pile of papers Michael's left there. There's something just poking out from the middle of the pile. It looks like an envelope. And I don't know why, but I go over and I slowly slide the envelope out. I pick it up, turning it over in my hands.

'Put that down, Ellie.'

My head shoots up the second I hear his voice. I don't even get a chance to glance down at the envelope, but my fingers refuse to let go of it.

He comes over to me, takes the envelope from me and slides it into his back pocket. 'It's work, Ellie. Nothing for you to be concerned about.'

'I'm sorry, I don't know why I did that ... it must be my hormones. This pregnancy's already turning my brain to mush.'

He smiles and takes my hands in his, pulling me against him as he kisses me quickly. 'You just concentrate on taking care of yourself, and our little one. Okay? You don't need to worry about anything.'

I look up into his eyes and I nod, and the more I look at him the more convinced I am that he has something on his mind. But it's a busy time of year, and now he's Head of Department his workload's increased, so maybe he really has just got a lot on.

'You *can* talk to me, Michael, if you need to – if you just want to offload. I know how important it is to do that sometimes ...'

'Ellie, I'm fine. I'll just be a lot better once we finally decide on this new member of staff. We need that lecturer in place as soon as possible, *then* I'll relax a little more. I promise.'

'Okay.'

I throw him a small smile and step out of his arms. I need to retrieve that chicken from the oven now. I don't even know why I've cooked it, considering I'm home alone tonight, but I've developed one hell of an appetite since I got pregnant. And I don't mind cooking for one.

'Are you going to be all right on your own tonight?'

I switch off the oven and turn around to face him. 'Why wouldn't I be?'

'I can get Liam to come over. He's not doing anything, and he's all on his own too, so, if you want some company ...'

'I'll be fine, Michael. What's wrong with you? It's not like this is the first time I've been home alone, is it?'

'It's the first time since we found out you were pregnant. I just want to look after you. Is that such a bad thing?'

'Well, that's very sweet of you, but you've never felt the need to go all protector on me before.'

'Because I know what's good for me.'

I laugh quietly, because he's right. I'm no princess. I've never really wanted to be looked after. I was brought up to be tough, to look after myself. I didn't really have a choice. And Michael got that. From the second we met, he got that.

'I'm going to make myself some dinner, watch some TV – all the stuff you hate – then I'm going to have a bath and an early night. That's my evening sorted. So, try not to wake me up when you come home, okay?'

He smiles slightly, raising an eyebrow as he slips on his jacket. 'It's dinner with Laurel and Frank, Ellie. It's hardly a night out clubbing. I'll probably be home before you're in bed.'

I go over to him, pulling him to me by his jacket collar. 'That would be nice, if you could do that. We could have that early night together.'

I kiss him, and he laughs low and deep, his mouth still resting against mine and I feel that shiver surge up my spine again.

'Maybe I'll skip dessert then, huh?'

'You do that.' I give him one more kiss before pushing him away. 'Now get out of here. I need to eat.'

He picks up his wallet from the dresser and stops in the doorway, his expression a little more serious now. 'Are you sure you're going to be okay?'

'Go, Michael.'

He smiles, and I return it and I watch him leave again, wait until I hear his car drive away before I turn to check on the chicken. And I realise I'm not really all that hungry any more, but despite that I still pick at the crispy chicken skin, pulling a tiny bit off and eating it. Usually I'd rip the lot off and devour it in a heartbeat. I love everything that's bad for me – chicken skin, chocolate, copious amounts of coffee, but right now ... right now I don't want any of it. And I don't know why, I'm just putting all these weird, unexplained feelings down to being pregnant.

I grab some foil and cover the chicken. I might feel like something later, after I've had that bath. Michael's right. I need to relax; I need to take it easy, for the baby's sake.

I head upstairs to our bedroom, pull my hair from its ponytail and go into the en suite to remove my make-up. I've had three meetings and a visit to the doctor's today, and when I look at my reflection in the mirror above the sink I can see the toll a busy day has taken on me. I look exhausted. I look even more tired once that mask of make-up's been removed, but I feel a little better after a quick shower. I scrapped the bath idea; a quick shower is a much better option. A long bath would only have seen me lie there, going over and over all of today's meetings, and that isn't relaxing. I need to switch off for a little while, although that's never been something I've found easy to do.

Pulling on a pair of comfortable lounge pants and a t-shirt I blow-dry my hair and pile it up on top of my head, and I smile as I look at my reflection now. By day I'm all business suits and heels, but once I'm home I like nothing better than my sweatpants and oversized shirts.

Going out onto the landing I make my way to the top of the stairs, but I don't go down. Instead I turn around and go into the room next door to ours – the room that's slowly being turned into a nursery. I just want another quick look in there, to remind myself that we've finally done it. We're having our baby. And even though we're six months away from meeting our son or daughter, I'm slightly impatient. I wanted to get things moving immediately, even though we've only known about the baby for a few weeks. And we haven't told anyone our news; we haven't made it public yet. Well, we've told Liam, but he's almost like family. And he's the only other person who knows, but we trust him not to breathe a word to anyone, not until we've had the scan next week. Then we'll tell the world, I'll shout it from the rooftops, and I smile to myself as I look around the freshly painted room. Liam and Michael finished it over the weekend, although I could have done it myself a lot quicker. For a couple of academics they're way too easily distracted, and I smile again as I remember the way I'd had to nag them into making sure it was finished by Sunday afternoon, the promise of a full-on roast dinner going a long way to helping them achieve that deadline.

We've gone for yellow on the walls. It's going to be a little while before we find out the baby's sex, but I'm not really someone who goes in for that pink for a girl, blue for a boy thing. I'm sticking with neutral and I like yellow. It's a happy colour.

My phone suddenly rings out from the bedroom, causing me to jump, and I silently scold myself for being so on edge. I'd just been a little too lost in my thoughts there.

I almost run back into the bedroom, grabbing my phone from the dressing table, and I'm slightly out of breath by the time I answer it.

'Ellie? Are you okay?'

'Michael ... Yes, I'm fine. I just left my phone in the bedroom – had to run back in here to answer it.'

'Will you just take it easy? Please? Look, I've spoken to Liam again, and he isn't busy, so, if you want to him to come over just give him a call. All right?'

'Jesus, Michael, I told you, I don't need babysitting.'

'Can you just humour me, Ellie? Please?'

I lean back against the dressing table and smile. 'I'll think about it. But I'm fine on my own. I'm looking forward to a bit of me-time.'

'Well, just call him anyway. Let him know you're okay.'

I throw my head back and sigh, but it's not an irritated sigh. It's nice that he's worried, that they're *both* worried. I just don't need keeping an eye on.

'Are you going to be like this throughout the entire pregnancy?'

'Pretty much.'

I laugh quietly, a wave of love for this man washing over me, so strong it feels like a punch to my stomach.

'I love you, Ellie.'

Another wave. Another punch to the stomach.

'Yeah. I love you, too.'

He ends the call and I slide my phone into my pocket as I head back out onto the landing, closing the door behind me. But as I reach the top of the stairs I hesitate again, this time my gaze turning towards the small staircase that leads up to Michael's office on the top floor. It's not a room I go into all that often. It's his space. But for some reason I'm heading in that direction now, and I have no idea why. Maybe it's because he isn't here. Maybe it's because I actually want to take a look at just what it is he keeps in there, or maybe I'm just bored. Curious. Whatever the reason, I'm in here now.

I leave the door open so I can hear the phone or anyone coming to the front door, and I stop and glance around at the clutter that fills the room. It looks a mess to me but Michael swears he knows where everything is. My own office, in the summer house out in the garden, is very different. My shelves are filled with box files and small, neat piles of magazines and journals, whereas Michael's shelves are stacked high with books and papers and I smile at his ordered chaos.

I go over to his desk, walking behind it, smiling again as I look at the one, single photograph he has standing on it. Us. Together. Not long after we'd met. But we were already in love. He'd reeled me in with that almost disarming charm of his, made me crazy about him with that smile. And then I look up, and my eyes go straight to the battered old sofa in the corner of the room. The one he refuses to get rid of it because he insists it's too comfortable to throw out. And as I look a little more closely I notice a box that seems to have been shoved underneath it. Curiosity gets the better of me and I come out from behind his desk and go over to the sofa, crouching down as I try to pull the box out, but it's wedged firmly underneath. I fall back on my haunches, landing cross-legged on the floor as I try to catch my breath. And I'm just about to have another go at retrieving that box when a noise – it sounds as if it came from outside – causes me to pause for a second. What was that? That noise? Are those pregnancy hormones making me paranoid now? I don't move. I stay where I am as I strain to listen again, but I don't hear anything. It's probably just this house. It has a lot of creaks and quirks; it's what makes it so perfect. To us.

Hauling myself up off the floor I forget about the box and head out of the office, pulling the door closed behind me. I make my way downstairs, and as I reach the hall I can hear the sound of the TV coming from the lounge, and I pause for a second, my brow furrowing in a confused frown. I don't remember switching it on, but it could have been Michael. Maybe he wanted to catch the news before he went out.

I think nothing more of it and make my way into the kitchen. The chicken's still there on the countertop, covered in foil. I'm still not all that hungry, so I leave it where it is and start to make myself a cup of tea. But as I switch on the kettle I hear another noise: not the TV, it's definitely not the TV. It sounds as if it's coming from outside, so I head into the orangery, take a quick look out into the garden, my eyes darting this way and that but I can't see anything. What am I looking for, anyway? I glance outside again, at the garden swathed in darkness bar a few solar lights that edge the terrace, but there doesn't appear to be anything untoward out there. Although, as I narrow my eyes slightly, take a longer look, I notice a terracotta pot lying on its side, rolling back and forth, as though it's just been knocked over. That could just be a fox, or a cat from the farm in the next field. They're always finding a way into our garden, knocking over pots, invading Michael's vegetable patch. I'm just being unnecessarily paranoid tonight, and I'm blaming my over-protective husband for that. His need to protect me has made me almost believe that that's what I need. To be protected. I don't. This house – the barn it once was, it's old. It has creaks and noises that Michael jokes are the ghosts of the cows who used to live in here trying to freak me out, which he thinks is incredibly amusing, but it does make me a little nervous, sometimes. Irrationally so, I know. Liam's a scientist, he keeps telling me ghosts don't exist but there are times when I beg to differ, and those are usually the times when I'm alone in the house. Is that what's happening here? Are the ghost-cows coming out to play? I shake my head, getting rid of my own stupidity. It was a fox, that's all, upending my plant pot.

I go back into the kitchen, silently scolding myself for being so jumpy, and I make that cup of tea, take it into the living room. But I've started to convince myself that something isn't right now. I need to go back outside and check that everything's okay, so I put my tea down on a side table and head back into the kitchen, folding my arms against myself as I walk. I'll go into the garden, take a quick look outside. Even though I know nothing's wrong, I just need to put my own mind at rest now. I'm being silly and irrational, but once I've done this unnecessary recce I'll go back inside and call Liam. Just for a chat.

I reach for the door handle, and as I pull it down the smell of that freshly roasted chicken fills my nostrils. I think my appetite's coming back now. Once I've done this; once I've called Liam, let him know I'm okay, I'll make a nice green salad, cut up some bread I baked yesterday. I'm actually starting to worry that the prospect of becoming a mother is making me seriously domesticated now.

I start to pull the door towards me, a slight breeze blowing in from outside as it slowly opens, and then I hear it – that sound, a scream that barely has time to resonate before it's quickly stopped, and it takes a second before I realise it was me. I was the one screaming; the one who was silenced by a hand being clamped heavily over my mouth.

It was me, who was screaming ...

Chapter 13

It was me who was screaming ...
Michael blamed himself for not protecting me. He blamed himself for everything, but it wasn't his fault.

It wasn't.

Not really.

I pull my knees to my chest and hug them tightly as I sit in the corner of the room that should have been our baby's nursery. The light, bright yellow walls are almost taunting me, smiling down at me, reminding me of what this room should have been.

The people Michael and I should have been.

Parents.

Fourteen Months Earlier ...

I can't feel anything but fear. It's all-consuming. As I'm slammed back against the glass door I want to cry out in pain, but I can't; that hand is still clamped firmly over my mouth.

I close my eyes, squeeze them shut, try to pretend this is a dream. I'm going to wake up any second now because *this isn't happening*. And then the hand is roughly removed, and I let out a gasp, double over, clasp my stomach. I need to protect my baby.

A smell of a strong floral perfume fills my nostrils and I look up, my head seemingly taking an eternity to raise itself – it feels like everything is happening in slow motion right now.

'You're prettier than I thought you'd be.'

Her words both confuse and terrify me, and I back up against the door, my hand still splayed out over my stomach. I don't know what to do.

'How did you get in here?'

Her eyes glance over my shoulder at the door behind me. 'You made it too easy.'

I frown, look behind me. I remember Michael took the rubbish out a couple of hours ago ... We always check every door is locked before we go to bed, before we go out. Always, without fail. At least I thought we did.

'I was just going to rock up on your doorstep, invite myself in, but, you know, it was nice of you to give me an easier entrance. Glad I checked first. All I had to do was scale that fence and there I was, out there, in your garden. Michael talked a lot about his garden. He's got a vegetable patch, right? Over by the summer house?'

Who the hell *is* she? How does she know about Michael's vegetable patch, my summer house? How does she know where we live?

She raises her eyes to the high ceiling, her mouth falling slightly open, and I watch her – this woman who's invaded our home. I watch as she looks around her, turning a full three hundred and sixty degrees, spinning around until she's back facing me. 'You have a lovely home.' She drops her head forward, her eyes staring straight at me. 'And you ... Ellie, isn't it?' Her head falls to one side again as she looks me up and down. 'I don't know ... I guess I expected someone ...' She lets that sentence tail off, but her eyes continue to stare right through me, and I feel that fear rising, I'm terrified. 'It doesn't matter ...'

She shakes her head as she turns away, walks back out into the kitchen; and that's when I reach behind me. I try to fumble for the door handle, shifting my body slightly, I don't want to turn my back on her for too long, I just need to see what I'm doing. But that was a mistake, turning away from her, even for a second; she's behind me before I can grab hold of the handle. The kick she gives to the back of my legs knocks the breath right out of me, and I fall to the ground, hitting my head on the tiled floor as I land. Her fingers grasp my wrist, drag me up off the floor, a wave of pain shooting up my arm. I must have landed on it. But I don't have time to dwell on that. I don't even have time to take another breath before she's thrown me back against the floor-to-ceiling window, her fingers winding in my hair, yanking my head back. Her sweet, cloying perfume is unbearably strong, and I feel a sickening jolt of fear at what this woman might do to my baby.

'He loves *me*. Did you know that? Me and Michael, we were meant to be together. We're *going* to be together.'

I don't know what she's talking about, I don't understand …

'You have no idea, do you?' she sneers, tugging at my hair, and I cry out as another wave of pain hits me, one that feels like my hair is being ripped from the roots. 'No idea that your husband is in love with another woman. With *me*. Your husband loves *me*.'

I shake my head. This is not true. It can't be.

'I knew it the second I saw him. I knew he was the one. Michael knows it too, he just won't admit it, not yet. But he will, eventually. All that time he spent with me, all that attention he showered on me, he wouldn't have done that, would he? If he didn't love me. So, you – I need to deal with you. You're just getting in the way now. You're getting in the way of me and him being together.'

She lets go of me, pushes me back against the glass with a force so hard I'm surprised it didn't shatter, and I stay completely still for a second or two as the breath is forced out of me, painful and ragged as it escapes the confines of my throat.

My hands don't leave my stomach. I'm desperate to protect my baby. I have no idea what this woman wants, because, what she's telling me it makes no sense.

I slowly raise my head, but her eyes are down, they're looking at my hands resting on my stomach, and her expression changes so quickly it's utterly terrifying, because she's guessed now.

'You're pregnant.'

It wasn't a question, but I nod anyway. I can't breathe, can't speak; I just want her out of my house.

'You're having Michael's baby?'

She doesn't wait for my answer, and the terror that swamps me as she rushes towards me is suffocating, the kick to my stomach devastatingly brutal, and I cry out as my legs give way beneath me. I hit the floor again, and she continues to kick me. She's screaming words I can't make out. She's hysterical. I squeeze my eyes shut as kick after kick rain down on my body. The only thing I can do is curl my knees up to my chest, keep them there, try to maintain some kind of makeshift shield for my baby. I can't even cry. I'm too terrified, too scared of what's happening here.

And then it stops, just like that. But I stay curled up; the foetal position seems the safest place to be right now. I keep my eyes closed, and I try to breathe through the pain, aware that, suddenly, all has gone quiet. I can only hear my panicked breathing, my heart hammering hard and fast against the threatening silence. She hasn't gone. I know she hasn't. I can still feel her here, in this room, I just don't know what she's doing. And I want to look, I want to see what's happening, but I can't open my eyes. My brain isn't letting me. It's almost like it's shutting down all my senses, one by one.

'You can't have his baby. You ... *you* can't ... have his baby ... he doesn't want you any more ...'

Her tone is calmer, she's lost that hysterical edge, but that just makes it even more terrifying. Each word she speaks is filled with an unspoken, sinister threat, and I feel hot, angry, scared tears finally start to roll down my cheeks. I'm helpless, but I need to do *something*. I need to get out of here. Is this woman high? Or is she just fucking crazy? I don't know ...

My eyes spring open as she grabs hold of my arm, yanks me up from the floor, presses her hand against my stomach. She's staring at me as though I'm nothing. Nobody. 'You can't have his baby,' she repeats, her voice barely audible, and as she puts her other hand over my mouth the smell of her perfume hits me again, causing me to gag. I can barely breathe. 'Do you hear me?' And then she laughs, just a small, quiet laugh; and she steps back, removing her hand from my mouth. 'You know what? It doesn't matter.' She shakes her head, continuously, over and over again. It's terrifying to watch. Her eyes stay locked on mine, but she isn't speaking now, and I don't know whether this silence is better or worse.

She breaks the stare, her eyes darting this way and that, as though she's looking for something. I don't know what, and I don't care; I just want her out of here.

'What's in there?'

She jerks her head in the direction of the indoor swimming pool at the far end of the orangery, the dim lights that surround the small oval pool making the water seem almost blue, what little of it you can glimpse from back here.

'You can see what it is,' I reply, my flippancy instantly rewarded with a slap across the face, so hard it snaps my head around.

I reach up, touch my cheek, the skin burning from where her palm caught me, my heart racing so fast now it's painful. Hard to breathe. I feel a terrifying inevitability, and I wonder if it's best to just let this happen. Let her do whatever it is she's come here to do. I don't think I have the energy to fight her. I feel an overwhelming exhaustion flooding over me, taking charge of every sense, every emotion.

Her hand clamps around my wrist, pulling me back from those dark thoughts, and I suddenly find myself being dragged along behind her, towards the pool, my legs crashing into tables and chairs. She doesn't care that she's hurting me

And then everything starts to fade.

Everything goes black ...

Chapter 14

Yellow is such a happy colour, but this isn't a happy room any more. The day I returned home from hospital, the day after I miscarried our baby, I stripped this room of all the furniture, got rid of all those things we'd already bought even though we'd only known our child for a short time. I got rid of it all. And even though none of it was Michael's fault, for a while I couldn't help but throw some element of blame in his direction. I was angry. I was upset and confused and angry. How could he not have noticed her behaviour? How could he not have seen this coming? He was her lecturer, for Christ's sake! He'd tutored her one-on-one; hadn't he noticed *anything*? Hadn't he seen some sort of sign? I didn't understand how a man as intelligent as him could have missed something like that. So I blamed him, and that was unfair, but I'd needed to blame someone at the time. We were both to blame, really. Both of us. All of us.

I get up off the floor and leave the room. It still hurts to be in here sometimes. But even though people tell me I should change the colour scheme, turn it back into the guest room it originally was, I can't do it. I can't ... I can't forget.

I go back into our bedroom, walk over to the window and look outside at the garden – at the higher fences Michael had erected after that night. Security cameras were installed all around the house, locks put on all the outside gates. I couldn't feel safe until something had been done. It's just that: I don't feel safe. I'm not sure if I'll ever feel safe again.

My eyes shift to the corner of the garden, to that space next to the summer house; that empty spot where a swing used to stand. Michael had bought it just two days before that night. I remember the huge grin he'd had on his face as he'd lifted it from the back of the car and hauled it into the garden. I remember him and Liam trying to build it, testing it to make sure it was safe, and I can't help but smile slightly at the memory of them pushing each other like a couple of kids – the way I'd laughed so hard at their messing about – and I'd known, right then, that Michael was going to be an amazing dad. And then *she* came along, that night happened, and our entire future, everything we'd planned, was all ripped away from us, just like that. So yes. I blamed him. For a while.

'Ellie?'

I don't turn around. I don't reply. I continue to stare out across the garden. I feel him come up behind me, and I flinch slightly as he touches my hip, causing him to pull his hand away. I want him to touch me, yet there are times when I hate it. His touching me. No wonder he's looking for a distraction. And maybe that's also why his touching me makes me flinch – because I know he's touching someone else?

'We really should think about redecorating that room ...'

'Because a lick of paint will help erase the memory? You tried that once before, remember? And I told you not to touch that room again.'

'Ellie, will you look at me, please?'

No. I won't look at him. Why should I? Why should *he* get to say how this all works?

'This isn't helping. This behaviour ...'

I swing around and stare at him, this man I fell hopelessly in love with all those years ago. And I know he's changed. Forgetting and moving on, that's how he's dealt with it; but I'm not him. The repercussions of those events spread wider than just that one night, and Michael blames himself. But he shouldn't. He shouldn't blame himself. Like I said, we're both to blame. We both made mistakes.

'What we did ...'

He shakes his head as he backs out of the room, and I start to feel that barrier slowly rise up between us again. 'No, we're not doing this, okay?'

'Because *you* don't want to?'

'Because you're going to make yourself ill if you don't stop this. Every time I think you might be ...'

'What, Michael? Every time you think I might be *what*? Getting over it? Forgetting it?'

He turns his back to me and walks out onto the landing.

I let him leave. I have to think of another way to win this. I have to find out what's really going on with my husband. Only then can I start to fix what's broken ... if I want it to be fixed at all.

Chapter 15

My father wasn't a good man. I'm not saying he wasn't a good father; he was, in the beginning. Before I knew the kind of man he really was; before I realised why my mum was always so sad, so reclusive. Their marriage was a lie, from start to finish. A web of deceit that ended tragically when my mum took an overdose of whisky and pills that saw her go to sleep and never wake up. Because she didn't want to wake up. Because of what my father did. Because of his cheating. Because of his lies.

And I couldn't stop it from happening. She hid how she was feeling just a little too well, even though we all knew something wasn't quite right. Everyone knew she was unhappy; that much was obvious, even to me, and I was barely a teenager when I lost her.

Nobody had known just how deep her sadness had run, even after she'd found the courage to leave my dad. She kept it hidden from me, as much as she could – tried to make life after my father as happy as possible – but it became too hard for her. My mum was a good woman. She was one of the best. Kind. Caring. There wasn't anything she wouldn't do for anyone, including my bastard of a father. She didn't deserve what he did to her. His selfish weakness destroyed her, and I never forgave him. I never will. He killed my mum; that's how I see it. Cheating, lying, deceiving – those actions destroy people. So to think that my own husband could be part of something like that ... I won't let it happen. I'm not my mother. She didn't fight. I will.

Digging my hands into my pockets, I continue my walk through the centre of Durham. It's one of my favourite places. Wandering around the compact streets of this small city is something I love to do. It's calming – a chance to gather my thoughts, think about everything more clearly – and when the sun's out and the weather's a little warmer, as it is today, it fills me with peace. Out here, amongst all these people, I'm exposed, yet I don't feel scared. Not today. Today I'm focused. I'm not feeling fragile or frightened; I'm fine.

Passing the small university bookshop on the corner, I start walking along a familiar street. One Michael and I know very well. We've been here so many times. I'm heading towards the Spanish restaurant we used to visit frequently, before that night. The same restaurant I know he's been to recently, without me. I found the receipt, I saw the evidence, and that bill was for two meals. So, he didn't come here alone. Maybe he was just having lunch with another staff member; it's a possibility, but I doubt that was the case. He wouldn't come here. Not here. He wouldn't use this place for anything work-related; it was always our special place. And the thought of him sharing that with someone else ...

I reach the restaurant and push open the door, the smell

of paella, garlic and freshly baked bread hitting me head on, causing my stomach to rumble. I didn't even realise how hungry I was until I came in here.

I look around until I catch the eye of a young waiter, someone I don't recognise. I haven't been here for so long that most of the staff seem different. New. This is a city with a big student population, and a lot of them find work in the many restaurants and bars, so it stands to reason there'll be high turnovers of staff in places like this. Is that why Michael felt it safe to come here without me? Because no one would recognise him, no one would care; no one knows us well enough to tell me he's bringing someone else to *our* restaurant?

The waiter throws me a friendly smile as he comes over, and I ask if I can have a table away from the window, a quiet table, at the side of the restaurant. I'm looking for somewhere with a good view of the room, a place where I can easily see the entrance but also remain slightly secluded, and the table he seats me at is perfect. I thank him and take the menu he offers me, ordering a glass of Rioja Blanca and some bread and olives before I'm left alone to check out the rest of the menu, although I already know what I'm going to order. My favourite Tapas dishes – Gambas Pil Pil, Albondigas and Escalivada. I feel like something familiar, and I haven't been here for so long, just the thought of those spicy prawns, the beautifully cooked pork meatballs in that wonderful tomato sauce and those Catalan style roasted, chargrilled vegetables … it's making my mouth water. I'm almost forgetting why I've come here. It isn't for the food at all; I'm here on the off chance that I might see something, anything, that can help me work out what's going on in Michael's world, because for too long now it's felt like we've been living in two completely different ones. And I know that that receipt I found means something – I know it was only one, just one receipt. There's no evidence he came here any other time. I have no reason to think he's going to turn up here today; no reason to think he's made this a regular haunt with someone new. But I have no reason to think he hasn't. So I'm here, and maybe I'll continue to come here for lunch more often. Maybe I need to put more time in at the Durham salon. Spend more time at the spa, so I can be closer to here.

I take a sip of wine and glance around the restaurant at the random mix of people all enjoying their lunch. I'm the only one dining alone, but that doesn't bother me.

A fresh group of people are entering the restaurant now, and I can hear the waiter asking them to follow him to their table. I turn my head to see if any of those people are my husband and for a brief second that small, rational part of my brain makes me wonder what the hell I'm doing here. Do I really expect Michael to walk in, with another woman, on the day I decide to come here?

Sitting back in my chair, I continue to watch everyone around me, and I wonder if any of their lives are as messed up as mine. I'm not sure anyone's could be. But I know that what people choose to show to the outside world isn't necessarily the reality. And I allow my mind to wander back to memories of my parents' marriage; the way they'd acted happy, put on a united front whenever they were out in public, at family parties, gatherings, trips to the supermarket; anything that involved them being seen together. As I grew older, I could hear the arguments that quickly blew up once they were back behind closed doors; I was old enough to hear those rows, but not the accusations. I had no idea what they were arguing about, not at first. But once I realised what was really going on, that's when I knew how quickly things – *lives* – could start to fall apart.

Because of them, I avoided relationships; anything that had even the vaguest hope of turning serious, I shut it down. Walked away. I never let myself get involved, fall too deep. I always took a step back from anything that I thought could hurt me. Until I met Michael. Michael was different. The second we saw each other – the first time he smiled at me, the way his hand touched mine as we reached for the same bottle of wine – I knew then that he was different. *He* was the man who made me realise all men *weren't* like my father. Not all men cheated. Not all men lied. Not all men made you feel worthless and alone. Michael *was* different ... or so I thought.

I look up as my food is placed in front of me, and the incredible smells that fill my nostrils help drag me back. I need to stay focused.

I thank the waiter, ask for a bottle of still water and look down at my food, picking up my fork and gently stabbing a large prawn, the garlic-laden juice dripping from it as I lift it up and pop it into my mouth. It tastes wonderful, and as I chew slowly a hundred and one memories of mine and Michael's trips to Spain flood my brain; memories of a life I loved, and I'm not willing to let that life drift away from me. Not without a fight.

I'll find out what's going on.

I'll find out if he's lying; if he's cheating.

I'll find out if he really is just like my father. I'll find out the truth.

And I'll deal with it.

Chapter 16

'Am I driving tonight?' Michael throws his bag down onto the kitchen table. He doesn't even bother with pleasantries any more. It's like we've forgotten how to communicate sometimes, and the fact that he seems okay with that – I struggle to get my head around it.

'No. I'll drive.'

We're going to a dinner party to celebrate the anniversary of a couple we've known for almost ten years now. We are both aware that we will need to pretend tonight. Pretend we are still *that* couple. The ones who managed to pull through together, despite it all; still perfect. The pressure of this pretence makes me want to scream.

'I'm going upstairs to take a shower. Is my grey shirt clean?'

I nod and take a sip of the tea I've just poured as I watch him leave the kitchen, hear him head upstairs. He's left his bag on the table, his jacket slung over the back of a chair, his phone hanging precariously from the top pocket.

I wait until I hear the shower switch on, I put down my tea and I quickly rescue his phone before it drops to the floor; but instead of putting it somewhere safe, I keep hold of it. I turn it over in my hand and look at the screen, but I stop myself from doing what I really want to do – check his messages. Read his texts. Look at his call history. Am I really that person? That kind of wife?

The landline suddenly rings out, its sharp, shrill tone jarring against the silence, causing me to almost drop Michael's phone. The slightest sound still has the ability to make me jump, and I reach behind me for the TV remote, switching it on for that background noise that helps drown out the perpetual, threatening silence. The ringing stops, abruptly, so Michael must have answered it. Sure enough, he calls down from the top of the stairs.

'That was Laurel on the phone.' I hear him run downstairs, and I quickly slide his phone into the back pocket of my jeans. 'She needs me to pop back to the university, sign a couple of things concerning grants for a new research project. I should have done it before I left … I forgot. You know how it is.'

I don't, actually, but I leave it at that. I don't think he's lying to me this time. If that had been her, this woman, this *girl*, she wouldn't call him on the landline. She wouldn't be that stupid. That indiscreet. I think he's telling the truth for now. He has to pop back to work. Fine.

'Call Rachel and let her know we might be a few minutes late, okay?'

He issues that instruction without even looking at me, out the door before I have a chance to acknowledge him. And it's only when I hear his car leave the driveway that I realise I still have his phone. He threw his jacket back on without even checking it was still there in his pocket.

I reach around and pull it out of my jeans, laying it down on the countertop. I look at it. I don't do anything else, just look at it, because he could still come back for it if he realises soon enough. But if he doesn't ...

I glance over at the TV screen and focus on the local news programme that's just started, and then I remember I need to call Rachel. Let her know we may be running late. So I quickly call her, and once I've done that I check the time. I don't think he's coming back for his phone. And it's there now, calling to me.

I pick it back up and head towards my office at the far end of the orangery. But the second I open the doors of the pool house, I stop walking. I stand perfectly still, and, as I always do when I come in here, I remember. A lot of people still find it strange, that I have my office here, in this place, considering what went on just a few feet away from where I'm standing. And I can't always explain the reasons why I've forced myself to come in here on an almost daily basis. Facing up to what happened is just something I need to do.

I look down at the water. I've always liked being surrounded by water. I grew up by the coast, spent a lot of summers at the beach. My grandma and grandad used to take me there a lot after my mother died. I think they sensed it was like an escape for me. Somewhere that allowed me to forget. Somewhere that made me feel happy. All they'd wanted was for me to forget the bad times and get on with my life. And that's all Michael wants me to do too, isn't it? Forget, and move on with my life.

Crouching down I drop my hand into the water, let my

fingers trail through it, backwards and forwards. It's almost hypnotic ... What am I doing? I've been gifted this window of opportunity, and I can't afford to waste it.

I snap myself out of that near-trance-like state I was close to falling into and head over to the small room in the corner that now serves as my office. There's not a lot of space in there, but it's big enough to house a decent-sized desk, a couple of filing cabinets, and some shelves. And there's a huge window that means the room always gets a lot of light, as well as a decent view out over the garden. A view of the summer house that was once my haven. The space beside it that was supposed to be our child's play area. I lean back against the wall and close my eyes, my fingers tightening around Michael's phone as my breathing quickens, the pain of losing that life I wanted, that life I was living; it still hurts in a way nobody will ever understand.

Inhaling deeply, exhaling slowly, I pull myself together. Sitting down behind my desk, I switch on my laptop and lay my own phone down beside Michael's, my heart beating like a jackhammer as a mixture of nerves and—am I finding this exciting? So many emotions are fighting inside me these days, it's hard to tell which ones win out. And maybe exciting is the wrong word, but I'm feeling something. The anticipation of relief, perhaps. That I will soon know so much more about my husband than I clearly do at the moment. First I need to check his messages, even though I don't expect to find anything. Michael is clever; if something were going on, if he was doing anything he shouldn't, I doubt he'd leave any evidence on his phone. My scan over his texts proves me right

– there's nothing even slightly incriminating there. I still know *something* about my husband, then.

I start tapping away at the keyboard, watching as a list of instructions pops up on my screen, and my stomach dips as the realisation of what I'm about to do hits me again. But this is necessary. I can't have him accepting that this life of distractions, silences and resentment is our life now. I can't. I won't.

Picking up my phone, I follow the steps listed in the instructions, and I watch as my plan kicks into action. The knot in my stomach tightens because of what I'm doing here – I'm tracking my husband. I'm installing an app on his phone that allows me to see where he is, where he goes, who he calls and texts. I'm still amazed at how readily available this kind of thing is. And yes, there is part of me that knows that this is wrong, but I also know that this is the only way that I can begin to rebuild my sense of trust in Michael.

Sitting back in my chair, I close my eyes. I don't feel guilty for doing this. I have nothing to feel guilty about. I'm trying to save our marriage, trying to put our life back together, because *he's* given up. He's too scared to face up to a guilt he doesn't need to feel, and if he'd only let me tell him that, let me talk, I wouldn't have had to do this. He gave me no choice. This is *his* fault. *His* doing.

I open my eyes and lean forward, checking both phones before I log out and shut down my laptop, but not before I've quickly cleared my search history. I have no reason to think Michael would ever check that, but I'm playing this safe. I'm done now. I'm going to fix this.

Sliding both phones into the back pockets of my jeans, I make my way back through the pool house, the orangery, out into the kitchen. But only to put Michael's phone on the countertop. I need to get ready for this dinner party now.

I wander upstairs to shower and change, and I'm busy pinning up my hair when Michael returns.

'Ellie?' He walks into the room looking slightly flustered.

'Yes?'

'Did I leave my phone here?'

I turn back to face the mirror, sliding the last pin into my hair. 'It's downstairs, on the kitchen counter.'

'Oh. Right ... Any calls?'

I turn back around to face him. 'Were you expecting any?'

'No ...'

'There were no calls. And you need to get changed.'

I sit down on the edge of the bed and slip on my heels – bright green strappy sandals to match the dress I'm wearing. Bright clothes, bright shoes. Both match my slightly brighter mood.

'Ellie?'

I stand up, my eyes looking straight into his. After what I've done tonight, I should probably feel guilty. I don't.

'You look beautiful.'

He used to tell me that all the time. Not so much these days. And I think it's *his* guilt that's making him tell me that now. I didn't miss the slightly panicked look in his eyes when he asked me if he'd left his phone, whether there'd been any calls. I saw it.

I respond to his comment with a small smile, because I think he does mean what he says when he tells me I look beautiful. But I don't feel it. I haven't felt it for a long time. The bruises and the cuts she inflicted on me, they healed, in time. They faded. But everything else ... the loss of my child, I'll never get over that. That pain will never fade, because she not only took my baby, she took away any chance I had of conceiving again. Those kicks to my stomach, they damaged me too much. Physically, as well as mentally. She changed me, hurt me, in every way possible, and that can never heal. The fear she instilled in me – for months afterwards I was afraid of my own shadow. I still am at times, so that – that will never leave me. I'm not who I want to be any more, and I certainly don't feel beautiful. I feel empty and sad, and I'm angry. I'm tired. But I'm determined to change that, to get *me* back; get my husband back; get *us* back.

I'm not losing this fight.

*

I don't want to be here, making small talk, even with people I love. My brighter mood was only temporary, retreating back into the shadows the second we stepped inside Rachel and Harry's newly decorated home. I thought it might be easier, this evening, putting on that show. It isn't. I watch Michael. He seems much more at ease with this act tonight. He isn't struggling at all; he's all smiles as he laughs and jokes with Liam and Harry and Ed while Rachel and Claire busy themselves clearing plates and glasses from the dinner table. I'm watching this perfect picture of suburban domesticity play out from outside on the patio. I feigned a slight headache, said I needed some air.

'Are you all right?'

I turn my head to look at Liam as he joins me outside.

'Claire said you had a bit of a headache.'

He pulls a packet of cigarettes from his pocket, and I frown slightly. I thought he was trying to give up.

'Do you mind if I smoke?'

I shake my head. He slides a cigarette out and lights up, taking a deep draw on it as he looks back at me.

'So? *Are* you all right?'

'I'm fine.'

'What are you doing out here, then?'

'I'm tired, Liam. Of all this.'

He leans back against the fence and takes another drag on his cigarette. 'Michael seems okay with it.'

'I'm not talking about Michael. I can see he's fine about it.'

'Has something happened?'

'Like what?'

He shrugs and stubs his cigarette out on the fence behind him before he tosses it into the ashtray Harry's left on the wooden picnic table. 'I don't know. You just seem more on edge than usual.'

I take a sip of my drink and look at him, trying to force a smile because I'm not really in the mood for a conversation. 'Nothing's happened. It's just that, this all becomes too much sometimes. All this pretending, the way he treats me in public ...' I drop my gaze, staring down at my bright green sandals, my shocking pink nail varnish. Outwardly I'm bright and colourful, yet inside I feel nothing.

'When we get home, it's like he flicks a switch and all of a sudden I'm nothing to him. I'm just this obstacle, this thing that's getting in the way of his world carrying on the way *he* wants it to. But what about *me*, huh? What about *my* world?' I raise my head and my eyes meet Liam's, but he doesn't respond. I don't really expect him to. 'It hurts, that's all.'

He comes over to me, places a hand on my hip and he leans into me, his breath warm against my neck as he speaks. 'He's an idiot.'

His words shock me. I've never heard him talk about Michael that way. They're friends. Best friends. Almost like brothers. So to hear Liam speak that way was unexpected. And I watch as he walks back inside, goes straight to the fridge and takes out a beer, downing a large draft. For a second I can't move; I just stand there, watching from outside as everyone carries on as though everything's normal. I'm almost jealous that they're able to do that.

I go back into the kitchen, and I start to pour myself a glass of wine.

'You're driving. You've had enough.'

Michael takes the bottle from me before I can fill my glass, and I close my eyes, just for a second. I need to breathe. He's right. I can't drink any more; I *have* had enough. Unfortunately.

'I'm sorry.'

'Here.'

He hands me a glass of lime and soda and I take it from him. 'Thanks.' We can't have anyone thinking our marriage is in trouble. We can't have people knowing how broken we are. We've never rowed in front of our friends; in front of anyone. We've never even shared so much as a niggle, a random barbed comment. It isn't what we do. Not in our friends' eyes. We're Ellie and Michael. The perfect couple. That couple who faced tragedy and still remain closer than ever. Yes. That's who we need to be again.

'You need to make more of an effort, Ellie, or people will start to think something's wrong.'

I look at him, my expression one of disbelief. I'm not even trying to hide it. 'Because everything is just perfect, right?'

He bows his head, quickly runs his hand along the back of his neck, and then he reaches out, takes my hand in his and pulls me towards him, kissing me gently, an action so unexpected I didn't even have time to take another breath before his mouth was on mine. Is this real? Or just a façade?

'We don't have to stay much longer, all right?' he whispers, cupping my cheek, his thumb lightly stroking my skin, and I feel a million confused, messed up emotions flood my brain.

I nod, and he smiles – just a small, brief smile – before he pulls away and re-joins Harry, Ed and Liam. And as I look over towards our group of friends, Liam's eyes meet mine and he throws me a friendly smile – one I return.

'I really admire you, Ellie.'

Claire joins me at the back of the kitchen, helping herself to the wine I so badly need and can't have. Not until I get home, and then I can drink until I forget everything.

'Admire me? Why?'

She takes a sip of her wine and looks at me, narrowing her eyes slightly, her expression telling me I should know exactly why she admires me. I don't.

'The way you and Michael have stayed so strong, after everything that happened. It would've tested most couples to their limit.'

'It wasn't easy, Claire.'

'Oh, no, Ellie, I know that. I'm not saying it was easy, God … I didn't mean it that way, I just …'

'No, Claire, I'm the one who should be sorry. I'm just a little tired. It's been a busy week at the spa, problems at the Newcastle salon … It all just piles up sometimes, you know?'

Claire smiles, and I breathe an inner sigh of relief. These people are the last people I should be taking anything out on.

'I just think the way you and Michael came back from what happened – that would've pulled most couples apart. I'm not sure Ed and I would've coped as well as you two did.'

We really seem to have done a good job of lying to our friends. And part of me feels guilty for that, for letting them think that we dealt with everything so much better than we really did. Why couldn't we have told them the truth? What would've been so bad about letting them know that we aren't so fucking perfect after all?

The sound of Rachel and Harry's eight week old daughter crying from the nursery upstairs bellows from the baby monitor on the countertop, and I watch as Rachel says something to Harry before running out of the room. It's Liam who glances over at me again, not Michael. Not my husband. He can't even look at me, and that rips me apart inside. The fact it's Liam who senses that only makes it worse. But it's Claire's hand on my arm that pulls me back from a dark place I don't want to go to right now. I've been there enough times over the past few months.

'It must still be hard, Ellie. For you and Michael.'

I turn my head to look at her, plastering a smile on my face because that's what I need to do. I need to smile and pretend I'm fine, I'm okay, I'm over it, all of it. 'It was, in the beginning, but things are much better now. And I have Michael. We have each other.'

Do we?

She squeezes my hand, her smile reassuring, not full of pity like it used to be. 'I envy what you guys have. You're so strong.'

She envies us. She thinks we're strong. How would they feel if they knew the truth? If they knew how weak Michael and I really were?

'Life goes on. Besides, my work keeps me busy. And speaking of which, aren't you booked in for a pamper day at the spa next Friday?'

'I am, and I can't wait! Thank you so much for the vouchers; I'm going to use them all.'

I smile at her, thankful that we've finally changed the subject. But I'm still counting down the minutes until it's an appropriate time for Michael and me to make our excuses and leave. These evenings are tough, which is why we don't do them so often any more, but every now and again we feel obliged to come out, show our faces. We have to keep up those appearances.

Claire turns to top up her wine and I stare out ahead of me, watching closely as Rachel reappears, whispers something to Harry. It's his turn to go and see to their daughter while she re-joins the conversation, and I watch as Michael leans in to her, says something to her that makes her throw her head back and laugh. I watch as he rests a hand on her hip, and I narrow my eyes slightly even though I know he and Rachel would never do anything like that; not to me, not to Harry. This distraction Michael's found – she isn't a friend of ours, she's a stranger, at least to me. A student to him. Michael would never stray so close to home, he's just a very tactile, very charming, flirtatious man. He always has been; it's what makes him so attractive.

I keep watching him, the way he can still charm women he's known for almost a decade, and I can completely understand why his female students fawn over him so much. But reciprocating those feelings – after what happened, after what *she* did, for him to take that risk – is he really that insensitive? That naïve?

Despite their own husbands watching on, Claire and Rachel continue to play up to my husband's harmless flirting, but they've known Michael a long time. They know this is just the way he is, and then I wonder if these people – people I still call my friends – I wonder if any of them would lie for him. Cover for him. Keep his secrets, and me out of the loop. It's something that makes the knot in my stomach tighten a little more, pulling so hard I find it difficult to breathe for a second or two. Could I be the only one who knows nothing?

The last to find out about my husband's infidelity? Alleged infidelity; I still have no proof. Not yet.

'Come on, Ellie. Come and join us.'

Claire's voice breaks through my thoughts and I shake that new paranoia away, although I think it's already found a home amongst the rest of my jumbled theories. It won't go away now, I'll be watching them, all of them, a lot more closely.

'Ellie?'

'Oh, sorry, yes. Yes, of course. I'm coming.'

I head over to them, and as I approach the group Michael holds out his hand, and I hesitate, just for a beat or two, before I take it. Before I let his fingers curl around mine, squeeze my hand tight in his; before I allow this charade to carry on a little while longer. But I refuse to accept that it will be this way forever. I will change it. I've already started.

Chapter 17

It's raining; the kind of rain you usually only see in movies or on TV. The kind that can't possibly be real because it's coming down so heavy. Too heavy. But it's raining like that now, here, as I sit in my car, watching a cascade of huge raindrops pelt down onto my windscreen, the noise they're making so loud it's quite unnerving.

I'm parked up in the back yard behind the Durham hair studio waiting for this shower to pass. Even the short dash from my car to the back entrance of the salon will see me soaked through if I attempt to leave just yet, so I sit tight, watch the rain continue to fall, straining my neck to look up at the sky to see if there's a break in those dark, threatening clouds overhead. There's a small sliver of light in the distance. I just have to wait. It'll be over soon.

It's been a day or two now since I installed the spyware app on Michael's phone, and so far he has no idea it's there. I need it to stay that way. Over the past few days there's been nothing strange that's caused me any concern, given me any reason to think something's going on, not yet; but that doesn't mean he's innocent. That doesn't mean he isn't seeing someone, isn't mentoring this student just a little too closely. So it's staying there. Because I'm not letting this go. Not until I know what's going on.

There've been phone calls to fellow staff members, texts to a couple of his other students to arrange tutorials, but nothing suspicious, and no contact with this girl called Ava. No texts, no calls. Nothing. He hasn't visited anywhere that's made me think anything untoward is happening – he's been to a different university building, which isn't unusual; he went to football last night and the pub afterwards, and then he came home. Went straight to bed, left me downstairs watching some box set or other. We barely spoke this morning. I was up before him, ate breakfast alone, watched a bit of TV, caught up on the news, and by the time he came downstairs I was ready to leave for work. Now I'm checking that's where he went, too. Did *he* go straight to work?

I stare down at my phone at the very second an alert flashes up on the screen. He's making a call. I feel my heart start to beat out another hard, heavy rhythm, because this app ... it records any calls Michael makes from his phone. I can play them back, listen to them, all of them. But so far he hasn't called *her*. Is he calling her now? Is he arranging another lunch? An innocent tutorial? An afternoon in a cheap hotel? I hate myself for the way my brain works now, for the shit it kicks up and makes me believe, but I do believe it. I believe he's doing something, my husband. I believe he's living another life outside of ours because ours is falling apart, and he can't deal with that. Instead he's just chosen to ignore it; to avoid the issue.

It's quickly become an obsession now, this desperate need I have to know my husband's whereabouts. To see whom he talks to, whom he contacts. Every time my phone flags up an alert, every time I know he's calling someone, I find myself burning up, my stomach contracting with nerves and apprehension. I feel sick. Anxious. Desperate to know his secret. This is what it's come to, what *I've* become – the kind of woman who spies on her husband. But I think I have good reason. Just the thought that he could be speaking to her, right now, it turns my stomach. It makes me feel – angry? I don't know if it's anger I'm feeling. I think it's more sadness. I'm sad that this is what our lives have become.

Sitting back, I close my eyes and take a few long deep breaths as that knot in my stomach tightens once more, my fingers grasping my phone. I'm on edge, because I need to hear that conversation he's just had. The tracker has him at work, but that means nothing. That doesn't mean he's making a work-related call.

I look down at my phone, log onto the app, hold the phone to my ear as the recorded call plays out. He was calling Laurel. Something about a conference in London.

I stop listening. Log out of the app. My shoulders sag, my breathing slows down, I have a few more minutes of respite, some short-lived relief before the paranoia and the anxiety kicks in again. Because it will kick in. It never goes away now, not really; it just lies dormant, waiting to unleash itself at any given moment.

I glance out of the car window. The rain's eased off, I can make a break for it; so I tuck my phone back into my bag, grab my laptop from the passenger seat and make a run for the salon's back door.

Once inside, I have a brief meeting with Tanya, the salon's manager, before I make some coffee and head into my office. I spend a lot more time holed up in my offices at the salons now, way more than I used to. I used to be out on the salon floor at any opportunity. I had my own client list, people who would come only to me because they trusted me, not just with their hair but with their secrets, too. They could talk to me, about anything – family members they despised, friends they didn't really care about and ones they cared too much for. I used to hear some eye-watering stuff; it's surprising what people will tell their hair stylist, the trust they put in someone they only see once every few weeks. And I loved it, being out there amongst everyone, joining in with the gossip and the chatter. But now – now I prefer the solitude of my office. I like – I *need* – the privacy. I still go out there sometimes, as I have one or two regulars who refuse to let anyone else touch their hair, and I'd like to keep them. They've been good to me over the years, and their loyalty hasn't gone unnoticed. When I couldn't face coming into work after the miscarriage, they stuck by me. They waited. So I owe it to them to make the effort when they need me. But anything else, I leave that to my amazing team of stylists.

I've just logged onto my spyware account on the laptop when a knock at the door interrupts me, and I quickly shut the lid as Tanya pokes her head inside.

'Liam's here, Ellie. You busy? I can tell him to come back later.'

I shake my head, keeping the laptop lid closed. 'No, it's okay. Tell him he can come in.'

I get up and come round to the front of my desk, leaning against it as Tanya goes back outside to fetch Liam.

'What are you doing here?' I ask, folding my arms as he closes the door behind him, a mug of coffee in one hand. 'And will you stop getting my staff to make you coffee?'

'I can't help it if I'm irresistible.' He smirks, but I'm not really in the mood for his humour today.

'What are you doing here?' I repeat, hoping to get an answer this time.

'I'm lecturing at the university. I told you, remember? At Rachel and Harry's dinner party. I've got a series of guest lectures this week.'

'I've had other things on my mind. It might surprise you to find out you're not always at the forefront.'

He takes a sip of coffee, ignoring my probably slightly unnecessary barbed comment, and I know his eyes are on me as I go over to the filing cabinet in the corner of the office. I can feel them boring into the back of my neck. 'Anyway, I haven't seen you since the dinner party.'

'I know. I've been busy. You've seen Michael.'

'Yes. I have.'

I turn around, clutching the file I was looking for to my chest. 'I assume you've just stopped by here to kill some time?'

He puts down his mug and smiles slightly. 'Guilty. Although, since I'm here, you couldn't fit me in for a trim, could you?'

I place the file down on my desk and walk over to him, running my fingers through his hair. 'Hmm ... this *could* do with some tidying up ...' I tug lightly at the hair at the back of his neck. 'It's grown a little out of shape. I'll get Ola to sort you out. She hasn't got anyone in until eleven thirty.'

'Can't *you* do it?'

'I'm busy.' I step away from him and sit back down.

'Doing what?' He folds his arms and leans back against the desk.

'I'm just busy, Liam, okay?'

He says nothing for a couple of beats, and then he leans right back, reaches out and flips open the laptop lid. And I'm not quick enough to close it before he sees what pops up on the screen, although I don't think he quite realises what it is, not at first. But it's piqued his interest enough for him to come back behind my desk for a closer look, which I try to discourage by attempting to minimize the image. But his hand covers mine before I get that chance, stopping me from doing anything.

'What *is* that, Ellie?'

I fling his hand off mine and try to shut the lid again, but again he stops me, grabbing my wrist this time, his fingers gripping me tight as he leans forward and looks at the screen.

'Jesus Christ ... you're *spying* on him?'

I manage to wrench my arm free of his grip, stand up and go over to the small window at the back of the office, folding my arms against myself as I look outside. The weather's still dull and miserable, and those huge raindrops are back now, falling heavily from a leaden sky, hitting the roof of my car with such force I'm afraid they might dent the bodywork.

'He's having an affair, Liam. I know he is.'

Liam doesn't say anything, he doesn't respond, and when I turn back around he's still staring at the laptop screen.

'You're recording his phone calls?'

I nod, even though Liam isn't looking at me. He's still staring at the screen.

'You're tracking him?'

'You're stating the obvious now. You can see what I'm doing.'

He turns around to face me. 'You really think he's having an affair?'

'Yes. The signs are there, I just need some proof.'

'And then what?'

I drop my gaze, and close my eyes again. 'I just need some proof, Liam.'

'You know that shit's illegal, don't you? What you're doing, the *way* you're doing it ... you're not concerned about that?'

'Are *you*?'

He frowns, leans back against the desk, sliding his hands into his pockets. 'This isn't *about* me, Ellie.'

I look up, I'm slightly angry now. He's seriously going to stand there and lecture me? 'I just need some proof.'

'Why don't you just follow him like normal suspicious wives do?'

He doesn't even hide the sarcasm, and I feel my hackles rise slightly as I push him away and slam down the laptop lid.

'Come on. Let's get you outside, let Ola sort your hair out.'

'And what are *you* going to do, huh? Come back in here and listen to your husband's phone calls?'

I stare at him, right at him, I look deep into those steel-grey eyes of his. He has no right to question my actions. He probably knows exactly what my husband is up to. He could be hiding shit from me too. I can't trust anyone now. But even if he *did* know anything, I don't think he'd ever confront Michael about it. He has no reason to.

'Look, forget sorting my hair out. Why don't we go grab a coffee? I don't have to be at the university for another hour ...'

'Like I said, Liam. I'm busy.'

I'm dismissing him now, avoiding his gaze as I sit back down behind my desk and open the laptop lid. And he leaves me to it. He knows when to let things go, and I'm grateful for that. I'm really not in the mood for this conversation. Am I scared he'll tell Michael what I'm doing? After all, he's going to be seeing my husband later; he could quite easily let him know that I'm spying on him. But I know Liam. And I know he won't say anything.

Chapter 18

The lunchtime rush at the restaurant is dying down a little now as people drift back to work or college or wherever it is they're supposed to be this afternoon. I'm supposed to be at the spa, but I'm thinking of calling Carmen, telling her something's come up; that I can't make it for our planned meeting. It's only to discuss the prospect of putting the spa out there as a possible wedding venue, nothing urgent. One of our clients, a County Durham-based wedding planner, mentioned the idea last week when she came in for a massage therapy session. She persuaded us to think about it, claiming to already have couples who would love to get married in the grounds of my newly opened business after a handful of brides-to-be had contacted her following recent visits to the spa. And I can understand why. The old building I've had renovated and transformed is set in acres of beautiful landscaped gardens, both front and back. I can completely see why people would want to get married there. And if the weather's bad we also have a large, currently empty room at the back of the spa that has no real purpose yet, and rather than me using it as an extension of the café next door, maybe it would make more business sense to turn it into a fully fledged wedding venue. Fran, the wedding planner, was quite confident it would be a viable route to take, and I *have* been thinking about it. It just hasn't been at the forefront of my mind, that's all. It isn't something we need to do right now. It can wait. There's a lot more to think about anyway, before I even begin to put that plan into action; a lot more people to talk to, figures to look at. We're really just at the putting-out-feelers stage at the moment, but as I stir my coffee I wonder if I should put Carmen in charge of getting the ball rolling. At the very least she can make a few calls. I don't want Fran to think I'm not taking her idea seriously. I am. I'm not that blinkered by Michael and the prospect of our life falling apart that I'm willing to see my business fail, too.

I glance around the almost empty restaurant. There are still one or two tables occupied, but we'll all have to leave soon. They'll need to close up, get ready for the early evening rush. So I finish my coffee, slide my bag up onto my shoulder and get up, pulling my phone from my pocket, dialling Carmen's number as I walk out into the afternoon sunshine. I leave a lot of the responsibility for the spa's day-to-day running on her shoulders, and I feel guilty about that, I really do. But she's one of my best managers, one of my best friends, an absolute gem of a person. I trust her implicitly. She's been with me since I opened my first salon in Newcastle all those years ago, and I can't think of her not being a part of my team. That's why I have to be careful not to take her for granted. But she understands that things have been difficult since –

well, since everything. And she understands now when I tell her I have to miss our meeting.

I start to walk up the steep bank that leads to the cathedral, feeling the early summer sun warm on the back of my exposed neck. I took a chance on the weather, leaving my jacket in the car, which in this part of the country can be a bit of a risk. We've been known to have four seasons in one day in this neck of the woods, but today we've struck lucky. The weather seems to be pretty much settled. The sky's almost devoid of clouds; only a few tiny scattered ones have dared to break up the almost cobalt blue colour above me, and I slip my sunglasses down over my eyes as I turn a corner and start heading towards the cathedral. A beautifully imposing building set on a rocky headland, it looks down over the medieval city of Durham and the River Wear below. It's another of my favourite places. I come here a lot, sometimes just to sit outside on the vast expanse of bright green lawn and people-watch. Sometimes I go inside, lose myself in the stunning surroundings, something that never fails to overwhelm me. I never cease to be in awe of this place, no matter how many times I visit. There's a sense of calm that can take over the second you step inside, a peace – pure peace. I let nothing else invade my thoughts when I'm in there. The last time I went inside was just after I'd miscarried, when Michael started to drift away from me; and yet, at that time, I had no idea he'd continue to drift so far, seek solace with another woman. That I would become too much for him. That my questions, my need to talk, my constant reluctance to let the past go and move forward would become a barrier he refuses to break down.

Today, I'm not going inside. I sit down on the lawn and hug my knees to my chest, watching as others file into the cathedral or wander around outside. It's quite busy due to the sunshine. I'm not the only one sitting out here making the most of the weather; there's everyone – pensioners enjoying a day out, coach trips full of tourists here to spend a bit of time in this beautiful city, students snatching some sun in between lectures. Students. Is *she* here? Ava? Even in my head I spit out her name, this woman who's threatening everything I have.

So far there've still been no calls between them, my husband and his distraction. No texts, no communication that I can see, and for a fleeting second I begin to wonder if my frequent visits to the restaurant are nothing more than a habit I now can't find it in me to break. And I can't break it; I can't stop myself from going there, because the second I do they'll turn up, I know it. The second I decide to stop going, stop enjoying my lonely lunches, they'll arrive for one of their illicit ones. And I'll miss it. I'll miss my chance to gain that proof. Just because they haven't spoken on the phone, just because the contact on that score has been zero, doesn't mean contact isn't happening. Maybe Michael has a burner phone, a second phone he uses only for her. A phone he uses to set up his sordid meetings; a phone I'm unaware of. I find my skin prickling at the possibility; at my own naïveté.

I bow my head briefly, closing my eyes, taking a long, deep breath. And when I open them I stare up at the cathedral and let a rare moment of calm flood through me. I breathe in slowly, and exhale even slower. I let my mind almost shut down, free itself of all the doubt and the pain.

I remember the night I met Michael like it was yesterday. He'd just left university; I wasn't long out of college. We'd both been at a housewarming party held by a mutual friend, a pretty civilised affair compared to some of the house parties I'd been to. It was all expensive wines, cocktails and Waitrose canapes, and I can't help but smile slightly at the memory of my friend Isla and me commenting on how our own house parties had never consisted of anything more than sausage rolls, sparkling wine and lager – whatever we could cobble together on the tight budget we'd had to live on at the time.

I remember Isla wandering off into the garden to talk to someone she'd had her eye on for a while, and that's when I'd gone into the kitchen to top up my wine; when my hand had brushed against his as he'd reached for the same bottle. When I'd looked up and fell into those ice blue eyes, I was lost from that very second. This young, idealistic English lecturer had me in a heartbeat, but I was still wary. The constant memory of my father made me take a step back from any kind of relationship that veered too far from friendship; and besides, I had no idea if a man like him would want someone like me. Could he see the damage? Could he sense how wary I was?

But he took no steps back. He talked to me. He asked questions, seemed genuinely interested in who I was, what I was in the process of doing – opening my first hair salon. It was about to happen. Everything was about to happen, my life was about to start, the night I met Michael.

We sat on the stairs for most of the night, drinking wine and talking. We never really saw much of the party. He made me laugh. He made me feel calm and happy. He was different. He was the one who changed every misconception I had about men. About relationships. He changed it all.

Two days later we met up again, this time at a pub in the centre of Durham. Our first date. A beautiful evening, one that was warm enough for us to sit out in the riverside court-yard, drinking beer and sharing stories. He'd wanted to know about my family. I hadn't wanted to tell him. I'd thought it was too soon; thought the truth would scare him off. He was so handsome, looking at him took my breath away. He could have anyone; why would he want me? But he did. And that's when I knew – that's when I was certain he was the one, the man I was going to marry. That's when I fell in love, so hard I still feel my stomach flip, even now, when I remember that night by the river.

We'd taken a walk through the city after dinner at the small Spanish restaurant, the one I now spend my lunchtimes in, waiting for him to turn up with his distraction. We'd walked, his hand holding tightly onto mine, and for the first time in my life I'd felt happy. I'd felt free of all the crap my father had caused me to feel. Michael had taken that and tossed it away; he'd fixed me. Until now.

Hauling myself to my feet, I check my watch, slide my bag up onto my shoulder and walk away from the cathedral, back down the bank towards the streets of Durham city. I spend another half an hour or so staring blankly at shop windows, feeling the calmness that had filled me such a short time ago slowly begin to drain out of me. I start to panic. My heart starts to race. I suddenly feel exposed, as if everyone can see so clearly the fear that lives within me now.

I head into the marketplace, cutting through the crowds of people milling about by the statue in the centre of the square, sitting on benches, taking in the afternoon sun. And as I walk, that's when I notice something; it's just a fleeting glimpse out of the corner of my eye, but it's enough to make me stop. To take a longer, second look.

I sidle up beside the statue, peek around the side of it, glance over towards the pub across the square. It's him. It's Michael, standing outside, talking into his phone. I keep my eyes on him, but his conversation is short. He slides his phone back into his pocket and checks his watch. Is he alone? I don't shift my gaze. I keep watching as he glances back inside the pub, leans against the wall outside and folds his arms. Is he waiting for someone? My heart is racing even faster now, hammering violently against my ribs, and I try really hard not to let my breathing get out of control. But as I continue to watch my husband, outside a pub in Durham City Centre, in the middle of a weekday afternoon, that suffocating panic only becomes more stifling. And yet, I don't want the safety of my car now. I want to see who my husband's waiting for, what he's doing here. Why didn't I check my phone earlier? I would've seen where he was; I could've come here sooner. That was a lapse on my part. My mistake. I'm not usually so careless.

I blink quickly in case I miss something, and then he glances behind him again, and I feel my heart beat even harder, even louder, as someone comes out of the pub. Someone. *Her*. Ava. His pretty little student. His distraction. She comes outside, and he smiles at her, rests his hand on the small of her back, and my stomach knots up so tight I feel sick.

They start walking towards the bookshop side by side; he's pulled his hand from her back now. They aren't touching each other, but that means nothing. It doesn't mean he isn't taking her to a cheap hotel later for an afternoon fuck – he's fucking someone, because he sure as hell isn't touching me any more.

I watch them until they disappear from my view, and while part of me wants to follow them, confront them, confront *him*, I don't. I can't. Not yet. I don't have the proof, nothing concrete, not even this afternoon's meeting is enough, despite the fact I'm more than sure that I'm right now. He's sleeping with her, he's using her to distance himself from me. His wife. The woman who lost our child because another of his deranged, deluded, obsessed students thought she loved him. He was only mentoring her, that's what he told me. Like he's mentoring this one? My husband is a very caring man; he looks after all his students. He *cares* about his students. Their futures. But I worry about his methods now. I didn't think twice about it before. I had no reason to. He *gave* me no reason to. Until that night. Michael always has been the kind of lecturer who goes above and beyond the call of duty for those he feels warrant that level of attention. Is that what caused that crazy bitch to lash out the way she did? Was she just reading the signals wrong, or *had* there been something going on? What did he do to make her think he was hers to take? Is that what *this* one thinks, too? Does *she* think she can have him? Take him from me? Has he told her what a burden I am to him now? How I aggravate him, irritate him; how every time I open my mouth to speak he winces, because he assumes I'm going to start asking questions I still need answers to? He thinks I don't see that expression on his face, don't notice it, but I do. I see it all too often, and I know that's why he's been driven to this. By me? Have I driven him to fuck other women?

I sink to my haunches, lean back against the statue and close my eyes, breathing deeply in and out, until I remember where I am. I'm not alone out here, so I drag myself to my feet and start walking again, in the opposite direction to where Michael and his distraction went. His distraction ... I think I need to stop calling her that. *Has* she distracted him? Has *she* turned my husband's head? Is this one different, or is it just as I imagine it was with the other one? Is my husband getting too close? Are his mentoring methods giving these girls signals they can't help but act upon? Either way, this one has become an unwelcome part of my life now, and I don't want her there, but I can't help but acknowledge her presence. Ava.

I don't share, Ava, and you need to know that.

Every fibre of my being still wants to turn around and follow them. Confront them. But I know I can't do that, not yet. I'll have to make do with tracking his movements. Listening to his calls. Reading his texts. Which is why I pick up pace as I make my way to the multi-storey car park, hurrying up the concrete steps to the floor where I left my car a couple of hours ago.

I climb into the driver's seat, pull the door closed and lean back, closing my eyes again, I feel safe now. I'm alone in my car, cocooned in my own private fear, my paranoia. My guilt? No. I still feel no guilt. I've got nothing to feel guilty about. I think *he* has.

Reaching into my bag, I pull out my phone and log onto my spyware account. I need to see where he is. Where he's gone. If only it could tell me whether she was still with him.

I feel hot, angry tears start to burn behind my eyes, and I quickly wipe them away. It's been a hard day, one full of memories of a life I'd loved living. One full of fear for the life I'm losing. For the man I can feel pulling further and further away from me.

Michael was different.

Michael loved me.

He really was different.

But now I don't know.

Chapter 19

I stand by the window, looking outside at the garden. That corner by the summer house still lies empty, still waiting for me to plant that tree, another thing I'll probably never get around to doing.

I look down into the empty wine glass, my fingers gripping the stem so tight they're almost turning my knuckles white. I don't even remember drinking the wine, but I must have. At some point. There are a lot of things I don't remember these days. And a lot I'd rather forget. Why do the bad memories so entirely smother the good ones?

I hear him – Michael – come into the kitchen, but I don't turn around. Instead I watch his reflection in the window, watch him open the fridge and take out a beer. Watch him pull off the top and drink down a mouthful before he places the bottle down on the counter and leans back against it, his eyes glancing over towards me.

'I've been thinking, Ellie.'

So have I. Too much. I don't enjoy it, thinking. It hurts; it's confusing. Painful. 'About what?'

Do I say something? What I saw this afternoon, the image

of him looking at her, walking alongside her; it's imprinted in my brain, embedded there on a loop. So, do I say something? Or do I stay quiet? Keep bottling this all up, until what? Until he leaves me? Until I lose him forever?

'Why don't we get a dog?'

I swing around so fast I almost lose my balance and fix him with a look of disbelief, but his expression is just confused.

'You always wanted a dog, remember?'

I wanted a dog as part of that little family we were about to create. I wanted a dog for our child, so they could grow up with a pet, a little companion to play with, I wanted that fairy-tale perfect world.

'I don't want a dog, Michael.'

He frowns. 'You used to.'

'I used to be pregnant.'

His expression changes, the confusion evaporates, and I can see fear in his eyes now. Fear that I'm about to broach *that* subject.

What are you scared of, Michael?

'Maybe a dog would help, you know?'

'Help?' I splutter the word out; it almost escapes as a laugh. I really can't believe I'm listening to this; that he's saying *this*.

'Help you get over …' He stops. He shuts up, kills that sentence dead, because he knows that completing it is wrong. It's so fucking wrong. But I can't pretend he didn't start to say it. And neither should he.

'Get over what, Michael?'

He looks at me, his blue eyes sad, but there's no guilt there. He looks at me, and I feel my heart break a million times over as I remember what we used to have, who we once were. 'Don't go there, Ellie. Please. Let's not do this. I just thought ...'

'I lost a baby, and at the same time I had any chance of conceiving again taken away from me, and you think a dog is going to help me get over that?'

'You need something else to focus on.'

'I have my work.'

'You're hardly ever there these days.'

'I don't want a dog, Michael. Okay? A dog isn't going to help anything. What would help is *you* talking to me ...'

He shakes his head, raises his hands in the air to silence me as he starts to back away, towards the door. He's retreating, taking himself out of this situation before it turns into everything he spends his time avoiding. I want to ask him why he's doing this to me, why he's making me feel so angry and frustrated. Why he's making me feel so lonely. I want to ask why he's fucking another woman to avoid facing up to *this*.

He grabs his jacket from the coat rack, hanging it over his arm as he leaves the house, slamming the front door behind him. I can't explain how much his behaviour hurts me.

I sink to the floor, the sound of glass shattering on the solid black tiles echoing around the empty kitchen. I must've let go of the wine glass. I place my hand down to steady myself, forgetting all about the broken glass beside me. I don't even feel pain as tiny, sharp shards stab into my palm. I feel nothing. I don't see the blood. I don't register that I'm hurt. I feel nothing. Just numbness. A cold, sweeping numbness.

I close my eyes, sit back against the window and breathe.

I breathe, because sometimes I forget to do that. And still I feel nothing ...

*

My eyes flicker open, slowly, and I blink a few times as I try to focus, try to read the time on the clock on the wall, but I don't know how long I've been out of it. Did I faint? Fall asleep? Pass out? I can't remember what time it was when I closed my eyes.

I glance over at the TV still playing away in the corner of the living area of our open plan kitchen. A familiar soap opera is on, so it isn't that late. And then I feel it. The pain. My throbbing palm feels like it's on fire, and I raise it up slowly, wincing as I see the cuts, the blood, the shards of glass embedded into my skin. I tilt my head to one side, slowly and carefully pulling the shards of glass from my palm, which makes me wince again. It hurts, a burning pain that spreads far beyond my injured hand.

Tossing the pieces of broken glass to the floor, I raise my hand up again, strangely fascinated by the patterns the rivulets of blood are making as they snake their way across my palm, dripping slowly and steadily onto my jeans. But it takes a second or two before I realise I have to do something. Do I need stitches? I don't want to go to hospital. I don't want to leave the house. The house I'm alone in, again, because my husband still can't face talking to me.

I want to cry. I feel stupidly weak all of a sudden. Or am

I constantly weak, and I just insist on ignoring that fact, blocking it out?

I place my other, cut-free hand onto the floor next to me and push myself to my feet, keeping my injured hand aloft as I head into the kitchen. I grab a towel from the drawer, wrap it around my hand, watching as the blood soaks through the linen and I lean back against the counter and bow my head. I should get it looked at. I don't think a plaster is going to stop the bleeding.

Reaching for my phone, I'm about to call Liam when I notice an alert on my screen. Michael's made a call. Or someone's called Michael. I check the tracker, try to see where he's gone; he might have gone to Liam's. He hasn't. He's at the pub, the one close to his university building, and for a second I forget the pain that's starting to travel up my forearm. I'm too consumed by thoughts of who my husband is with, what he's talking about. Is he talking to her? To Ava? Does he listen to Ava? Does he let *Ava* speak, or is it all just sex? What kind of distraction is she? What kind of sex do they have?

The pain I momentarily forgot comes back with a vengeance, hitting me head on, and I squeeze my eyes tight shut, biting down on my lip even though I know that won't help. I'll call Liam, then I'll take some painkillers. That might ease it slightly.

I can tell Liam wants to know what's gone on, but I don't go into any detail. I tell him I've cut my hand, tell him I'm not exactly bleeding out but I'm not sure whether I need to go to Accident and Emergency, and if I do I can't drive myself. I tell him enough not to worry him, but I need him to come over.

He's on his way, so I take the painkillers, wrap a fresh towel around my hand and go upstairs.

I run my injured hand under the tap in the bathroom, watching as the blood disappears from my palm and swirls around the white basin, down into the plughole. It's hypnotic. I stay in the bathroom, mesmerised by my injury, until I hear the front doorbell ring. And the sudden noise cutting through the silence makes me jump, makes me knock my hand on the tap and I cry out as my already tender hand receives a fresh assault. My nerves are still shattered, more so when I'm left alone in this house. And Michael knows that. And still he chooses to leave me here. Alone.

Wrapping the blood-stained towel back around my hand I run downstairs, check the security monitor on the hall table just to make sure it's Liam. It is. I open the door to let him in and he kicks it shut behind him, his expression one of exasperation mixed with concern. Is he getting tired of me, too? He's the only one I can talk to, seeing as Michael wants us to hide the real truth from the rest of our friends. He doesn't want their pity. Neither do I. I just want us to be honest with each other, how we used to be.

'Give me your hand, come on. Let me look at it.'

I hold out my hand and Liam removes the towel, tossing it to the floor, and I watch as he runs his thumb lightly over the scattered, criss-cross cuts on my palm. His thumb is covered in my blood now, and I look at him briefly before dropping my gaze back down to my hand.

'Where's your first aid kit?' he asks, his fingers now grasping my wrist as he raises my arm up.

'In the kitchen. The cupboard next to the cooker.'

He keeps hold of my wrist as we head into the kitchen, blood trickling slowly over my arm as we walk, and I look down. Specks of it decorate the tiled floor, but that doesn't bother me. It'll wash off. My husband sleeping with one of his students – that bothers me. Blood on the tiles, I can fix that.

Liam holds my hand under the tap in the kitchen sink and once more I watch as my blood washes away down the plughole.

'Keep it there.'

He crouches down, retrieves the small first aid kit from the cupboard next to the cooker, and then he's back up beside me. He switches off the tap, takes hold of my wrist again and checks my palm for any smaller shards of glass that might still be in there. When he's satisfied they're all gone, he gently washes my cuts with antiseptic lotion, which stings a bit, but I try to ignore the discomfort and bite down on my lip again, even though that doesn't help ease anything.

We stay silent as he washes my cuts and dabs cream onto them, which makes me wince again. But the bleeding seems to be subsiding now.

'You don't need to go to A&E.' He reaches into the first aid kit for a bandage. 'But you will need to be careful with this hand for the next few days.'

His tone is authoritative, almost like he's speaking to a child. He's very business-like, which surprises me. *Have* I done something wrong? Something to upset him? Or am I just so paranoid these days that I think I'm pissing everyone off? Jesus, this self-pity has got to stop.

I watch as he wraps the bandage around my palm, fastening it tight, just the tiniest amount of blood showing itself now. And the pain is lessening slightly, but that could just be the ibuprofen kicking in.

'There.' He steps back from me, starts putting the first aid kit back together, tucking it away in the cupboard. 'Are you going to tell me how it happened now?' He faces me, his tone still a little cold, his expression only slightly warmer.

'Have I done something to upset you?' I ask, walking over to the fridge. There's another bottle of wine in there, and I need a drink.

'I take it you and Michael have had another row.'

It isn't a question, it's more of a statement. And I can't stop the snort of disdain from escaping as I twist the cap off the wine bottle with my uninjured hand. 'I wish we could *get* to the stage of rowing.' I pour us both full glasses of wine, sliding one towards him. 'We rowed in the beginning, but now – it's pretty difficult to row when you barely speak to each other any more.'

He looks at me, ignoring the wine. And then I realise he's also ignored my earlier question. *Have* I done something to upset him?

'I didn't tell him. What you're doing. I didn't tell him anything.' Liam's eyes fix on mine, holding my gaze. He wants me to believe that what he's telling me is true. I believe him. He hasn't told Michael anything; if he had, I'd know.

'I didn't think you would.'

'That sure, huh?'

My eyes remain locked on his. 'That sure. Yes.'

The corner of his mouth twists up ever so slightly, it's barely a smile. It's not even a smirk, but it's something. 'You need to do what you need to do, Ellie.'

I lean back against the counter, sipping my wine.

'And you shouldn't be drinking, if you've taken painkillers.'

'You're not a doctor.'

'I am, actually. Just not *that* kind of doctor.'

I smile at him, grateful that he's here, that I don't have to be alone in this house tonight. 'What did you mean, before? I need to do what I need to do?'

'If you think he's having an affair ...'

'I do.'

His eyes meet mine again, but again he stays silent for a good few beats. 'Okay.'

That's all he says, he leaves it at that, and I frown. I'm a little confused now. But I don't push it. 'I saw him. Michael. I saw him today. This afternoon, in Durham.' I down another mouthful of wine. It's helping to dull the ache in my hand; helping to dull the pain, bring that numbness back. 'He was with *her*.'

'Her?'

'Ava.'

Once more I spit out her name, and Liam almost flinches, my tone is that harsh.

'He was coming out of a pub, the one just off the market square. She was with him. I saw them walking away together.'

Liam doesn't respond, doesn't ask what my reaction was to seeing my husband with another woman. A much younger woman. He remains silent, and I look down into my glass and realise I've downed that wine in a stupidly quick amount of time. It's gone straight to my head. I feel a little woozy now. A little dizzy.

'Put the glass down, Ellie.'

I can just make out Liam's words, although he sounds as though he's speaking from far away now, like he isn't in the room with me, he's somewhere else.

I reach behind me and place the glass down on the countertop, the sound of it toppling over onto its side, crashing onto the work surface, it makes me flinch, but the glass doesn't break. It just rolls from side to side, until Liam comes over and uprights it. Uprights me, because I feel like I'm falling, my knees are so weak now.

I feel his hand on my lower back, guiding me away from the counter, tiredness sweeping over me like a blanket of darkness until I have no choice but to close my eyes. My head feels heavy, my entire body sagging against his, but his arms catch me. I hold onto him, my fingers gripping his shirt as he sits me down on the armchair by the pantry door.

'You need to be careful, Ellie. Are you listening to me? You need to be careful.'

I blink rapidly, try to re-focus. Everything feels blurred. Surreal. I try to wake myself up, but I'm still so tired. It must be the wine and the painkillers and the fact Michael chose to walk out on me. Again. As always, we try to start a conversation, it comes back to the one thing he can't cope with, and he walks out. It's an exhausting cycle that neither of us can seem to break free from, but at least I feel like I'm trying. I'm not sure *he* even wants to.

'Ellie? Look at me, Ellie. Did you hear me?'

Liam's face slowly comes into focus, his eyes fixing on mine. He's so serious sometimes, Dr Liam Kennedy. 'You – you said I had to be – had to be careful.'

He crouches down in front of me, takes my uninjured hand in his, squeezing it gently. 'I care about you, Ellie. I care about Michael. But you – you're the one I'm worried about. What you're doing ... You just need to be careful, okay?'

I nod, pull my hand away from his. I'm still a little confused. But the wine and the painkillers have exacerbated my light-headedness. I might not even be hearing him right.

'Okay.'

He stands up, strides back into the kitchen, opening cupboards and taking out coffee, mugs, milk. 'I'll stay with you until Michael comes home.'

If he comes home. He's never stayed out all night before, but that doesn't mean he won't. We just haven't reached that stage, not yet. But we probably will at some point. I seem to be pushing him more than usual, making him less inclined to stick around when we're alone. When we're with others, he lights up, becomes the Michael I fell in love with. I quite obviously can't become the Ellie I once was, the Ellie he loved. I've changed too much. And that scares me. So much scares me these days; the things I'm willing to do now; the things I've already done ...

'I need to sleep,' I say quietly, staring down at my bandaged hand. The blood seems to have stopped seeping through, just the odd tiny speckle of red showing up on the cream coloured bandage. And the pain seems to have dissipated for now. But it'll be back. It always returns. It never leaves.

I look up as Liam crouches back down in front of me, his expression warmer. Kinder. No, I don't think I'm pushing him away. He'll always be here, he promised me that. He promised he'd always be the friend I needed. Always. The only friend I can talk to.

'Okay, let's get you to bed.'

He holds out his hand and I take it, letting him pull me up from the chair, and I keep hold of his hand as we make our way upstairs. I just want to sleep now. I want to close my eyes and forget this day happened. Forget every day since that night happened. I want to close my eyes and wake up in a world where I can turn back time, live that life I was living before, with my handsome husband and our beautiful baby and that little dog I'd always wanted. Our perfect family. Our perfect life.

But we were never perfect.

Nobody is.

We really weren't ...

Chapter 20

'You should have called me. Last night.'

I don't even turn my head to look at him as he joins me in the living room. I'm sitting on the couch, legs curled up underneath me, a mug of tea cradled in my hands. The hot liquid irritates my injured hand slightly, but I get a strange kind of comfort cradling a hot drink like this.

'Would you have come home?'

I don't move my eyes away from the TV. I'm watching breakfast television, but I have no idea what the presenters are talking about. I think they're interviewing someone about their latest TV show. I'm not really listening. Everything is just white noise. And I'm aware of Michael still in the room, of him sitting down on the arm of the chair to my left, but I don't look at him; I keep my eyes on the TV screen.

'You were hurt, Ellie. Of course I would have come home. Why didn't you call me? Why call Liam?'

'Liam wasn't busy.'

'Neither was I.'

I finally turn my head to face him. My husband. Handsome and rugged with his grey-flecked hair and sexy stubble, those ice blue eyes of his so beautiful and bright. Does Ava look into those eyes and love him like I do? The thought of her looking at him in any way makes me feel sick, and I turn my head away again, stare back at the TV. They're doing the weather now. It looks like it's going to be another sunny day here in Durham.

'I wasn't busy, Ellie. I just needed some air, a breather. I needed some time out.'

'Time away from me?'

He doesn't even attempt to hide his sigh. It echoes around the room, heavy and laden with frustration. And I feel my insides twist up, pull tight until I'm breathless. Until the pain becomes real, until I feel tears start to prick at my eyes; but I refuse to let them fall. I can't cry. I don't *want* to cry. I don't want to let him know how much this is tearing me apart.

'I want you to talk to me. That's all. Is that really too much to ask? Because – because I can't understand why you find that so hard to do.' I turn to face him again, but he's looking down at his hands clasped between his knees. *We* let this happen. Us. *We* were to blame. *We* let that night pull us apart, let its consequences crush us, destroy us. *We* let that happen. It's no one else's fault. 'I just – I just want you to understand how empty I am, inside.'

He doesn't say anything, he just keeps looking down at his hands.

'Why can't you talk to me, Michael? Why can't you bring yourself to listen to me? Don't you care what I'm feeling ...?'

'You should be over this by now, Ellie.'

His words slice through me, unexpected and brutal, his

tone harsh. And I want to retaliate, I want to fight back, but the words won't come out; they're stuck in my throat, choking me.

'I've done everything I can, to make this go away ...'

'Make this go *away*?'

'I've done everything I can, Ellie, to try and make this better. *I've* done everything I can. What happened – I didn't encourage her, do you understand that? I was her lecturer, that's all I was, whatever else she read into that, that wasn't my fault. She gave me no signs, no signals, nothing to make me think she would do what she did, and I'm so sorry that she put you through all of that. It kills me every day to think what you went through. What she did to you. But it has to be over. It needs to stay in the past. Things need to change. *You* need to change. It's time you started making an effort now, for everyone's sake.' He stands up, heads towards the door. But he stops when he reaches it, turns back around, and he looks at me. 'I love you, Ellie. *That* will never change ...'

He leaves that sentence hanging, almost as if he's about to say *not yet*. But he doesn't. He just turns and leaves the room.

I put my mug down on the table beside me and pull my knees to my chest, hugging them tight, once more staring back at the TV. He still loves me. There's still hope. Does he love her, too? Does he love Ava? No. She's just his distraction, remember? That's all she is. All she'll ever be. I'll make sure of that.

*

I head across the gravel car park, which isn't easy in heels, and make my way up the stone front steps of the spa, throwing Carmen a brief smile before I retreat into my office. I don't even stop for coffee. I need to log on and find out where my husband is. Where he's been. He left for work early, much earlier than usual, and I need to find out if he went straight to the university, or if he went somewhere else first.

During the short drive here, my stomach was clenched so tight with nerves it hurt. And yes, I could have checked his whereabouts before I left for work; but if I'd done that, if I'd found something I didn't want to see, I don't think I would have made it out of the house today. Sometimes the need to watch him, track him, listen in to his phone calls, read his texts – sometimes the need to do all of that, it's becoming obsessive. So, I need to be out of the house. I need to grasp onto some level of normality, no matter how fragile that grasp may be. Besides, once I get the proof I need I'll stop this. I'll stop tracking him, stop having lunch in our restaurant, day after day. I'll stop it all. I promise. And I think I'm getting close to finding that proof. To finding out what my husband is really up to. I just need to see him touch her in a certain way, see him kiss her, anything that tells me there is something more between them. Or something that tells me there isn't, because so far I have nothing concrete. But I know. I know something isn't right. Trust your gut – isn't that what they say? Well, my gut is telling me he's lying.

I fire up the computer, wait for the screen to light up, to kick into action, and as soon as it does I log onto my account, scanning the screen for the information I'm looking for.

I frantically check where he went after he left the house this morning, because I'm sure he didn't go straight to the university, and I'm right. He drove into Durham, yes, but he wasn't anywhere near his building, not first thing. And from his movements it looks like he parked his car on the bank that leads up towards Gilesgate and then walked into the city. That's what I'm assuming. I look closer at the screen, at the route he took, where he ended up; and when I check the location I see it's a small café near Elvet Bridge. He used to have breakfast at home. We used to have breakfast together. We used to love those mornings when we'd drink tea, watch the news, talk about work and the things we had planned. Holidays. Days out. Children. A future.

I rest my elbows on the desk and clasp my hands together, dropping my head, closing my eyes. My heart's beating so hard, banging against my ribs with a breathtaking force, and I squeeze my eyes tight shut, breathe in deeply, try to ease my hammering heart. And then my eyes spring open. I slam the laptop lid shut, stand up, kick my chair back under the desk. I walk over to the window, dragging a hand back through my hair. I'm trying to slow my breathing down as I stare outside. It's another beautiful day, but I don't see that beauty so much now. I should be at home, with my baby, enjoying the sunshine out in our garden with the puppy running around my feet. I should be a mother now. And I'm not. I never will be. My life has changed beyond anything I'd ever imagined, and I'm scared and sad; but I won't let Michael do this anymore. I won't let him ignore me.

I flip open the laptop again, log out and switch it off before I leave the office. There's somewhere I need to be; something I need to do ...

Chapter 21

Slipping my sunglasses up onto my head, I push the café door open, the smell of freshly brewed coffee and just-baked pastries hitting me immediately. I haven't had any coffee this morning, so I order an Americano and wait while the young woman behind the counter makes my drink.

The café is busy, full of students and shoppers, possibly tourists too. This is a city that attracts a lot of tourists, especially when the weather's good like it is today. And this café, I haven't been in here before; it isn't one of my regular haunts. Is that why Michael chose it? Is that why he came here? Because it's somewhere new and different, somewhere he can take Ava without the threat of me walking in?

I look down at the counter and realise I've been drumming my fingertips on the glass. Another nervous tic. I pull my hand away, reaching into my bag for my purse, and when I open it I see the picture of Michael and me I carry around with me constantly. My handsome husband, so happy, so alive. When he looks at me now, he's so dead behind the eyes it breaks my heart.

'Can I get you anything else?'

The woman's voice yanks me back from those thoughts and I look up, blinking a couple of times as I try to regain my focus. 'No, I ... No. Thank you.' I take my coffee, scanning the room for a free table, but then I stop. I turn around, go back over to the counter, reaching into my purse for that photograph.

'Excuse me ...'

The young woman comes over to me, and she smiles. A genuinely friendly smile. 'Something I can help you with?'

'Yes, actually ...' I twist the photograph between my fingers, a sudden moment of clarity hitting me as I realise what it is I'm about to do here. But the image of him touching *her* – Ava – yesterday, in broad daylight ... he shouldn't be touching her. He shouldn't be doing that.

I turn the photograph around, showing it to the woman behind the counter. 'This man, was he ... was he in here, earlier today?'

Her expression changes slightly, her eyebrows furrowing together in concentration as she looks at the photograph. And then she looks up at me, and I can tell she's wondering why I want to know, why I'm asking. But she knows that's not really her business.

'I think I saw him this morning, around eight thirty.'

'Was he alone?'

Her expression becomes a little more wary now, like she's nervous of answering any more questions for fear of where this is going. But I need to know. She's going to tell me.

She shrugs, and that irritates me, I feel my skin prickle. She must've noticed if he was alone. Or if he had company.

She must have. Is she lying, to save herself from becoming involved in something she doesn't understand? I don't blame her. Sometimes I wonder if I come across as slightly unhinged. I don't think I do. I'm only asking a simple question.

'Just tell me, yes or no. Please. Was he alone?'

I'm almost begging now, so desperate am I to gather more information on my lying, cheating husband. Desperate. It's a word I'm becoming all too familiar with.

'No.' She whispers the word, her gaze dropping, but I didn't miss the pitiful expression on her face.

She turns away to serve another customer, and I can practically feel the relief flooding out of her. She didn't want that conversation to go any further. Neither did I. And then I silently berate myself for not asking who he was with – was it another man? An older woman? *Her*? I should've asked, because he could've been with anyone. Laurel. Frank. Maybe even Liam. No. He wasn't with any of them, I'm sure of that. But then, how can I be sure of anything any more?

Sitting down at a just-vacated table near the window, I keep hold of my coffee until the waiter's wiped the tabletop clean, and then I place the mug down and sit back in my seat. I stare outside at the already busy street, despite it still being relatively early, the photograph of Michael and me still in my other hand. I look at it, my thumb flicking the bottom corner back and forth in a slightly manic fashion. I can't help it. Can't stop it. That small, frantic action is calming me. But then I stop, toss the picture onto the table next to my mug of coffee and stare down at it. When was that photograph taken? I briefly close my eyes, trying to grasp the image, and it takes a second, but then I remember all too clearly. It was taken at a barbecue at Ed and Claire's, just a couple of months before that night. Before everything changed. And I feel my heart ache, a pain that takes my breath away. I have to close my eyes again, just for a second, until the pain eases.

I take a sip of coffee, pick up the photograph and slide it back into my purse before I stand up, grab my bag and leave the café.

He wasn't here alone.

*

'Ellie?'

I swing around, the sound of my heels click-clacking on the floor suddenly silenced as I stand still. Liam looks at me, frowning slightly. It doesn't suit him. Frowning. It clouds his features, makes him look angry.

'What are you doing here?'

'I came to see Michael.'

His frown deepens, and he slides his hands into his pockets as he walks towards me.

'Do you know where he is? Is he in his office?'

'What do you need to see him for?'

I narrow my eyes as he comes closer. 'That's not really your business. Do you know where he is?'

'Don't *you*? I mean ...' He shrugs and takes another step towards me, 'you're the one tracking him. Aren't you?'

I lean back against the wall. He joins me, keeping his hands in his pockets as he stares straight ahead.

'I know he's here. In the university, in this building. I don't know which room he's in.'

He takes a hand out of his pocket and rakes it back through his dark blonde hair. Liam doesn't seem to be greying as quickly as Michael, but maybe that's just because of his hair colour. Michael's darker, the grey shows up more.

'You need to be careful.'

'You've already told me that.'

He turns his head to look at me. 'And you're, what? Ignoring my advice?'

'I'm not *taking* your advice, Liam.'

'I don't know where he is. Try his office.'

'Okay.'

I pull myself away from the wall and start to walk down the corridor towards Michael's office.

'Ellie, hang on. Wait a second.'

I turn back around. 'What?'

'You're not being careful, are you?'

'Was he with you?' I ask, ignoring his comment. No, I'm probably not being as careful as I should be, but I'm losing patience now. I don't have time to be careful.

Liam frowns. 'When?'

'This morning. Was he with you? Did you meet him for breakfast, in a café on the corner of Elvet Bridge?'

'No, I wasn't with him. I haven't even seen him today.'

I drop my gaze, fold my arms. 'Then I'm guessing he was with her.'

'Maybe he was.'

My head shoots up, my eyes meeting his. 'Do you *know* something?'

'I don't know anything. And neither do you.'

'I saw him with her. I told you that. I saw him, they were together.'

He holds my gaze for a second or two before jerking his head in the direction of a room to his left. I follow him into the empty room, closing the door behind me.

'If you really think he's sleeping with someone else, Ellie, why don't you do this properly? Hire a private detective, if you have to. A professional. Someone who can find out whatever it is you need to know without *you* having to do what you're doing right now.'

'I wouldn't be able to settle.'

I lean back against the door, absentmindedly fiddling with the bandage still wrapped around my injured hand. I can't stop. It's oddly comforting.

'This is a situation you can't control. You might think you can, but you can't.'

I look at him, tilting my head to one side. 'I think you're wrong.'

He comes over to me and takes hold of my right hand, which stops me from fiddling with the bandage. 'Why don't you let *me* keep an eye on him?'

I frown, pulling my hand away from his as I slowly shake my head. 'No. Why the hell would I let you do that?'

'Because you're making yourself ill, Ellie.'

'I'm fine.'

'I don't think you are.'

'I don't need your help, Liam. I'm perfectly capable of keeping an eye on my own husband.'

'And if he finds out what you're doing? That you're tracking him?'

'There's nothing wrong in wanting to know what my husband is doing behind my back.'

'Let me do *something*, Ellie. Please.'

He's almost pleading with me now, but there's something there behind his eyes that worries me slightly. I just don't know what. I don't know why.

'If you want to keep an eye on him, keep an eye on him. I can't really stop you, can I?'

'So, does that mean you'll stop tracking him the way you're doing? You'll stop listening to his phone calls? Will you stop, and let *me* see if I can find anything out?'

'And how are you going to do that? Are *you* going to start following him?'

'I don't need to. We're like brothers, remember? We're close. He talks to me.'

'You think he's just going to *tell* you what's going on?'

'Just trust me. Please. If Michael's doing anything he shouldn't, I'll find out, I promise.'

'How do I know you'll tell me the truth? How do I know you're not already covering for him? Michael trusts you, Liam. If he told you anything ...' I look up at him, my eyes locking on his. 'How good a friend *are* you to him, huh?'

'I'm not covering for him, Jesus, Ellie, come on! If he's having an affair I will tell you. I will get you some proof, and I will tell you. Okay?'

I drop my gaze, but I keep my hand in my pocket despite the overwhelming urge to start pulling at that bandage again. It's like I need to be doing something constantly, otherwise it feels like my brain will explode.

'I can't trust anyone. Not even you. This is something I need to do for myself. I need to see it for myself.'

He reaches out, tucks a finger under my chin and tilts up my head, a small half-smile on his face. He's a handsome man. Tall – slightly taller than Michael – with deep, steel-grey eyes, dark blonde hair that he keeps constantly pushed back off his face, and a neat beard, which isn't something he's always had. He used to be clean-shaven, never even letting a few days' worth of stubble grow, but the beard suits him. I think he should keep it.

'Let me help you, Ellie.'

I look at him, up into his eyes, and I think he really would tell me if Michael was having an affair. I really think he would. I think …

'Why didn't you tell him? When you found out what I was doing, why didn't you tell him? He's your best friend, and like you said just now, you're as close as brothers. So, why didn't you tell him?'

He doesn't answer that. He pulls his hand away from my face and takes another step back, sliding his hands back into his pockets, but his eyes stay fixed on mine.

'Did you *want* to? Tell him?'

He briefly drops his gaze, lifting it after a couple of beats. 'I don't know. I guess there was a part of me that felt like I needed to.'

'Why?'

'So we could finally put an end to this.'

I look at him, and I don't need to ask what he means by that because I know what he means. I know.

'But you didn't.'

'No. I didn't.'

'I need to go ...'

I take hold of the door handle, but before I can turn it his hand covers mine, stopping me from doing anything. 'When I said be careful, I meant it. What you're doing is dangerous. You really should let me help you. If Michael *is* having an affair, he's a very clever man. He isn't stupid.'

'What's that supposed to mean?'

'He'll know how to cover his tracks.'

'So, I'll uncover them.'

'Let me help, Ellie. Please.'

He isn't pleading now, he's almost demanding. Issuing an order. 'Okay. Help, if that's what you want.'

I just want an easier life – I want my old life back, I don't want *this* any more.

He pulls his hand away from mine, lets me open the door. 'Does that mean you'll take a step back?'

I look at him again, and I nod. But I have no intention of taking any steps back, I'm just telling him what he wants to hear. It's easier that way.

'All right.' He can't hide the relief in his voice, and that's fine. He can think I'm stepping back, think I'm leaving this alone, but I'm not. I'm not leaving anything alone.

Chapter 22

I didn't go and find Michael in the end. I didn't confront him. I left after that conversation with Liam. I went back to work, had lunch at the Spanish restaurant as usual and took a walk around Durham. I kept to my now obsessive routine. It's what keeps me going. It's why I wake up in the morning; my reason for carrying on.

I curl my legs further up underneath me as Michael comes into the orangery, a newspaper tucked under his arm, his reading glasses pushed up onto his head.

'What are you doing in here?' he asks as he sits down on the chair opposite mine and opens his newspaper. He's asking me a question, but I don't think he's interested in my reply.

'It's not unusual for me to sit in here.' I keep my gaze focused on the garden, on a flock of birds – I don't know what kind, but they're small, I'm guessing sparrows – huddled together on the bird table, picking away at the food I left out for them.

I can hear Michael flicking the pages of his paper. This silence between us is something I still can't get used to. I don't want to get used to it. I hate it. It's sad and frustrating, and it shouldn't be this way.

I stand up and walk over to the window, staring outside again, at the birds still huddled around the feeder. I keep my back to Michael, sliding my hands into my pockets. The only sound breaking the silence are the birds outside and the rustling of his newspaper as he turns the pages.

'You left without breakfast again this morning.'

I turn around, lean back against the glass and wait for him to respond. But he doesn't; not at first.

'I grabbed something at work.'

'You didn't even stop for a coffee somewhere first? You left quite early today. You had time to stop for a coffee.'

He gets up out of his chair, moves a little closer to me, and I hold his gaze. I need to see his eyes when he tells me whatever it is he's going to tell me next.

'I went straight to work, Ellie.'

Our eyes stay locked, and the silence surrounding us now is stifling, the air thick with his lies. I know he's lying. *He* knows he's lying. The first time he's lied to me outright. And maybe that's what I needed, to hear him lie to me like this.

After a couple of loaded beats, he backs away, sits back down, opens up his newspaper like that exchange never happened. I stay backed up against the window. I keep watching him, my lying husband. My cheating, lying husband. And then I turn away again, look back out of the window, the heavy beating of my heart filling my ears, a new sound to help break the silence.

'Do you want a cup of tea?'

His voice startles me slightly, and I flinch, taking a deep

breath before I turn around to face him, shaking my head. 'No. I'm fine.'

He closes his paper, flinging it down on the table beside him. 'Is this the way it's going to be forever now, Ellie? The silences, the questions ...'

'This is *my* fault?'

'Well, it isn't *mine*.'

I laugh. I can't help it. I'm so fucking tired now. 'What do you want me to do, Michael?'

He sits forward, clasps his hands together. The look he's giving me is verging on pitying. I don't want his fucking pity, I want his love. His support. I want my husband back.

'It hurt me, too, Ellie. Losing the baby, coming to terms with what happened to you ...' He drops his head, and I see his shoulders visibly hunch up then relax as he takes a deep breath. I still don't understand why he finds it so difficult to talk about this. It's confusing. When I was in hospital – when they told me we'd lost the baby, told me I may never be able to conceive again – he was there for me. He cried with me, held me; for those first few days, he was the husband I needed. And then it all changed. One day *he* changed. He started shutting me down, refusing to talk about it any more. Does he really still think that a couple of days was all I needed to get over everything?

'What happened? To make you this distant; to *keep* you this distant? I thought we were supposed to be getting through this together. That's what you told me, that we'd get through this together.'

'Nothing happened.' He raises his gaze, his eyes meeting

mine, and the look he gives me now breaks my heart. We're getting nowhere. We're not moving forward, we're stagnating. No, we're not even doing that; we're drifting further apart. 'I just think – a lot of time has passed now ...'

'And time heals everything, right? She kicked our baby to death, Michael. I was supposed to be keeping our unborn child safe, and I couldn't do that. She killed our baby. She took our baby from us, took our chance to be parents away. And I have been dealing with that, dealing with everything, all on my own, because *you* refuse to talk to me. You refuse to let me talk to my friends ...'

You lie to me.

He slams his fist down on the table beside him, causing the vase that was standing on it to vibrate, and I jump, falling back against the window. His eyes are dark now, his expression cold. He finds it so hard to be patient with me these days.

'I love you, Ellie, I really do, but you are making it so difficult for me right now to be close to you.'

He stands up, and I watch as he rakes a hand through his hair, throws his head back and lets out another heavy, frustrated sigh.

'I did everything I could to make this better. I tried, I really did ...'

'You *tried*?'

Past tense. He tried. And all I feel now is that numbness creeping back, sweeping over me, engulfing me.

'When did you *try*, Michael?'

All of a sudden the numbness recedes, the darkness pushes

189

back and I move towards him. There's a strength inside me now that I wasn't aware of before.

'What *did* you do, huh? To make this better? What did you *do?*'

'I talked to the counsellor. I went because you wanted me to, because I thought it would help, and I sat there and I held your hand and we tried to talk this out. I talked to someone, *we* talked to someone ...'

'But we didn't talk about everything, did we? We couldn't ...'

'We talked as much as we could, Ellie. You were there; we talked enough to be able to move on, to some extent. It's *you* who's so bloody insistent that we continue to drag it all up. That isn't helping anyone. All it's going to do is hurt more people in the long run. Hurt *us*. We can't grieve for the past forever. We can't change what happened. It's time to leave it alone now. It's time to start living again.'

He turns to go.

'I'm not having this conversation ...'

'That's right, walk away like you always do. Where are you going this time, Michael? What distraction are you looking for now?'

He strides towards me, his face a mask of anger and frustration; the pity's gone now. But he doesn't scare me. He'd never hurt me, not physically. No matter how hard I push him, he'd never hurt me that way.

'Do you know how crazy you sound, Ellie?'

He almost hisses the words out, his fingers jabbing at the sides of his temple as his eyes bore into mine. I don't think I sound crazy at all. I think I'm justified in wanting to know why, fourteen months on, my husband still can't talk to me about what happened. I think it's quite fair of me to want to know if he's seeking solace in the arms of another woman, leaving me to deal with the pain and the memories all on my own. When *he* should be helping me. And he isn't. He hasn't.

'Tomorrow I'm going to buy paint for that room ...'

'*That* room ... you can't even say it, can you? You can't even call it the nursery ...'

'Because it isn't a fucking nursery, Ellie. It never was.'

The flat of my palm connects with his cheek before I even realise what I'm doing, the slap so hard it sends tingles vibrating all the way up my arm; but I'm not sorry. He deserved that.

His eyes continue to stare right into me as he raises a hand to his cheek; but he doesn't react, doesn't respond. Instead he just turns and walks away. It doesn't matter what I do, how far I push him. He always, eventually, walks away.

I sit back down on the couch, clasping my hands together, wincing slightly because my injured hand is still sore.

The front door slamming shut makes me jump, even though I know it's just Michael. Leaving. And I look up, out into the quiet, empty kitchen. I'm alone, again. Just me and my paranoia. My fear.

I get up. I need to check he's locked the door behind him. And as I walk through the kitchen I flick on the TV, something to drown out the silence. I need some background noise. I need my own distraction. Is that what he's doing? Is that where he's gone? Has he gone to *her*? To Ava?

Pulling at the door, I check that it's locked. I slip on the chain and slide the bolts across, top and bottom. He'll have to ring the doorbell if he wants to get back in. If he comes home. I need to feel safe while I'm here on my own.

Feeling around in my back pocket for my phone, I pull it out, sitting down on the bottom of the stairs as I log onto the spyware app. I sit back against the wall, draw my knees to my chest and watch as the tiny green dot moves slowly across the screen, tilting my head to one side as I squint slightly, trying to make out exactly where it's heading. And it feels like an eternity passes before it stops, but as I look up at the clock in the hall I see it's only been a little over ten minutes. He can't have gone that far.

Sitting forward, I bring the phone closer to me, staring down at the screen. Where is my husband tonight? Where has he run to this time? It takes just a second or two for the address to pop up in front of me, a street name I don't recognise. Which means he hasn't gone to any of our friends. He hasn't gone to any of his work colleagues – unless one of them has moved house, but he hasn't mentioned anything. Why would he? We don't indulge in small talk any more; I have to keep reminding myself of that. We don't talk about work, our colleagues ... we don't share so much these days.

The address is in Durham – Chester-le-Street – so it isn't that far from here. No one we know lives in Chester-le-Street. No one *I* know lives in Chester-le-Street.

A sudden knock at the door makes me jump, my phone slipping from my grasp, and I quickly glance over at the security monitor by the door. It's Liam. I'm not in the mood for him tonight. I need to be alone.

I get up, retrieve my phone from the floor and move slowly across the hallway. I remove the chain and pull back the bolts; I open the door, but I don't stand aside to let him in. I stay firmly rooted in the doorway. I don't want to let him in. I want him to go away. I want to find out what Michael's doing at this unfamiliar address, although I'm already certain I know who he's with. It has to be Ava; it has to be her.

'Is Michael in?' Liam asks, taking a step forward; he thinks he's coming inside. He isn't.

I narrow my eyes, the look I give him full of suspicion. 'Why didn't you call him first? You never just turn up like this.'

'I do, actually. I quite often *just* turn up like this. And I was on my way back from a late meeting at the university, so that's why I've just dropped by, on the off chance. So quit with the paranoia Ellie, okay? There's nothing weird going on. I just wondered if he wanted a quick drink, that's all. And I could do with having a word with him about Saturday's squash game. You going to let me in?'

I fold my arms, still clutching my phone in my hand, although I'm trying to discreetly slide it up the sleeve of my jumper. I don't want him to see it. I don't want him to think I'm doing anything I shouldn't.

'Michael isn't here; he's gone out. And I'm really tired, so ...'

'You had another fight?'

'You say that like it's all we do.'

'Isn't it?'

'Like I said, Liam, I'm really tired. And Michael isn't here.'

'Do you know where he's gone?'

He's trying to catch me out, I know he is, but I won't give him the satisfaction of winning this one. 'I'll call you tomorrow, okay?'

'Ellie ...?'

I shut the door in his face. I don't want his company tonight. I don't want anyone's company. I want to know where my husband is.

Sitting back down on the stairs, I watch the monitor, waiting until Liam finally gives up and drives away. But I stay where I am. I do nothing for a few minutes. I just sit there, staring at the screen.

I check my phone again. Michael's still at that unfamiliar address.

I get up and grab my jacket, slide my phone back into my pocket as I quickly set the alarm, pull the front door shut behind me and lock it, checking it twice, three times before I head over to my car. My husband is with *her*, I know he is.

Tonight's the night I get the proof I need.

Tonight, I'm putting a stop to this shit. I'm ending it.

I'm ending it all.

Chapter 23

The roads are quiet as I follow the instructions barked at me by my sat nav, the cold, disembodied voice intermittently interrupting the music I've got playing quietly in the background.

It's been almost forty minutes since Michael arrived at that address. And he's still there. Forty minutes, and he hasn't moved, hasn't left, and I feel my stomach twist up, pushing the breath out of me. I don't know whether I'm angry or scared. I just feel sick.

I turn a corner into a brand new housing estate as my sat nav informs me I've reached my destination. I crane my neck as I slow my speed down. I need to find Michael's car. And then I spot it, parked outside a neat little detached house with hanging baskets and a perfectly manicured front lawn. It can't be hers, surely; she's too young to own her own home, isn't she? And I still don't know if this is her house yet. I'm just assuming. But who else does Michael know around here? Is he shagging every woman on this street? I close my eyes and grip the steering wheel tight. My thoughts are becoming dangerously irrational now.

So you see, Michael, I'm not crazy! How can I be crazy if I know I'm thinking irrationally?

Taking a succession of deep breaths, I open my eyes and throw back my head, trying to compose myself. Because if he *is* with her, I'm going to confront them. I'm going to put an end to it. That's what I said I was going to do, and I'm doing it. I just need to see them, together, in that house ...

Getting out of the car I'm thankful it's quiet. It's late, almost dark; curtains are being drawn; everyone's behind closed doors, getting on with their lives. I'm out here, because my life is on hold. I'm just waiting to see if my husband really is cheating on me.

I lean back against the car, which is parked across the street from Michael's, and I look over at the house, the one I'm assuming he's inside. The only one on this street with the curtains still left open. I can see a TV on in the corner of the dimly lit living room, but I can't see anyone inside, despite the fact it's quite obviously occupied. Someone's definitely home.

I keep my eyes focused on that house, glancing around me every now and again to make sure I'm not being watched. Maybe I'd look less suspicious if I took a walk up the street. I can do that. As long as I don't take my eyes off that house.

And I'm just about to pull myself away from the car when I notice something, some*one,* coming into the living room, and I narrow my eyes, my heart beating so hard I can barely hear anything else. The sound fills my ears, echoing around my head. It's her. I can see her clearly now as she draws the curtains. It's Ava. I know it is, despite the fact I've only ever seen her a couple of times before, both times from a distance. But I know it's her.

Her dark hair hangs loose around her shoulders; she's wearing an oversized t-shirt and shorts. Are they that comfortable with each other now? Have they reached that stage already?

She starts laughing and turns her head slightly, looking behind her, and my fingers grasp the car door handle as I try to make out who she's talking to. Is it Michael? Is it my husband? It's *his* car outside; is she talking to *him*? Is *he* the one making her laugh? He used to make *me* laugh like that ...

She draws the other curtain, shutting off my view, and I feel ready to explode. It's like I have a volcano of emotions bubbling away inside of me, just waiting to erupt. I can't hold them down any longer. I need to end this.

I step out into the road. This is it; I'm going to get my proof. I didn't see Michael, but his car is there. What the hell am I waiting for? Of course he's inside. He's in there. He's been in there for almost an hour, with *her*. Alone. Together. Has he fucked her yet? Is that what they've been doing while I've been alone? Laughing. Fucking. Talking. Everything *we* don't do any more.

I'm almost on the other side of the street, almost there, outside that house, and I'm filled with a strange mix of emotions now. My heart's thud-thud-thudding wildly, pumping the blood through my veins at a breakneck speed that sees me stop, just for a second, to catch my breath. I need to breathe, need to compose myself before I confront my lying, cheating husband. Before I confront her. Ava. His whore.

Pushing both hands through my hair, I throw back my head and take a long, deep breath, exhaling slowly. I'm ready for this. I'm ready for it, all of it. But then a hand suddenly grabs my arm and I swing around, ready to scream, but he shakes his head, putting a finger to his mouth to silence me as he drags me back across the road.

He slams me back against the car. Am I scared? No. I'm fucking angry.

'Did you *follow* me?' I ask, trying desperately to get my breath back. My throat's so tight now I can barely breathe.

'What did I tell you, Ellie? I told you to leave this to *me*.'

I laugh. He's kidding me, right? 'You didn't answer my question, Liam. Did you *follow* me?'

'Of course I fucking followed you. You were about to do some crazy shit. I could tell, because you're *so* transparent ...'

'And you can read me so well, huh?'

'Like a fucking book. I've known you too long, Ellie. I know the way you work, way better than Michael ever could. And I'm not going to let you go in there, all guns blazing, when you don't know what the situation is. You don't even know if he's in there.'

'That's his car, Liam. Look. Over there, parked right outside her house. I saw her inside ...'

'Did you see *him*?'

'That's his car.'

He looks at me, just looks at me, he doesn't say anything. And I feel that anger steadily rise. He had no right to do this, to stop me. He had no right.

'I could've put an end to this, Liam. I could've stopped this, right now, tonight.'

'By what? Confronting them? You don't even know what the fuck's going on!'

'He's having an affair.'

His eyes burn into mine, even here, in the darkness, I can see the fire behind them. 'He's having an affair ...' He trails off, turns his head away from mine, and he laughs. A small, sharp laugh, and then he looks back at me.

'Liam, I'm ...'

He shakes his head. Opens the car door. 'Get inside. I'm not doing this out here. We're going home.'

*

He kicks the front door shut and strides across the hallway into the kitchen, making straight for the bottle of Scotch Michael keeps on the counter. I don't follow him, not straightaway; I need to make sure the door is secure first. I slide the chain on, pull the lock across; it's a habit now. As with checking my phone, it's become an addiction. Even now, as I finally head into the kitchen, I'm pulling it out of my pocket, checking where Michael is. He's left her house now. He's on the move. Is he coming back home? Back to me? Or is he still with her? Has she gone with him? Are they heading somewhere together? My head's so full of questions that it's spinning, making me dizzy.

'Put it down, Ellie.'

I raise my gaze, but I don't do anything. He doesn't get to

order me around; that isn't his place. 'He's on his way home.'
I don't know that for sure. I don't know where he's going, but
I'll find out. I'll keep track of him, all night if I have to.

'Just put the phone down. Please.'

'You should go. It's late.'

'I'm not going anywhere. Not when you're like this.'

'I'm fine.'

'You're fine, huh? You think what you were about to do
tonight – you think those are the actions of someone who's
fine?'

I finally put my phone down and drop my gaze, staring
down at my still-bandaged hand. But I don't say anything.
I'm too tired to argue, and I think he is too.

I hear Liam place his glass down on the counter; feel him
come closer, his voice softening. He has way more patience
with me than Michael does.

'Do you want me to stay, Ellie?'

'It's late. You need to get some sleep. You have work in the
morning.'

'Do you want me to stay?' he repeats, and I look up. I feel
calmer now. Liam does that to me; he calms me. He gives me
a kind of peace I don't get from Michael. That's why I need
him.

'Yes. I want you to stay.'

He smiles, and I feel that calm start to flood through me
now, easing the tension, sweeping the anxiety away, and I
welcome that. Even though I know it's only a temporary
feeling. I just need these snatched moments of calm. A time
to forget. Pretend. Be somebody else, someone whose life isn't

falling apart. Liam allows me to be that person. He allows me to live those moments.

'I'm going to grab a quick shower.'

I start to walk away, but he grabs hold of my hand, stopping me from moving any further away from him, and I swing around to look at him, his eyes burning into mine. It's time to pretend now. Time to forget. Time to be somebody else for a little while. There's no Michael. There's no Ellie. There's no Ellie and Michael.

'Do you want me to join you?' he murmurs, his lips brushing the side of my neck as he leans in to me, a tiny shiver shooting down my spine, and I smile. I let him pull me a little closer. I let his fingertips stroke my cheek, let his hand rest gently on the small of my back. I let him kiss me ...

Chapter 24

Ten Months Ago …

I don't know why we're here. I don't want to be here. I didn't want this party, neither did Michael, not really. He's just trying to get things back to normal. Trying to get *us* back to normal. I think he's wasting his time.

Four months ago, something devastating happened.

I lost our baby.

Four months ago, I was also told I would never have another one.

Four months ago, our lives, our whole fucking world, it changed. Forever. And I can't deal with it.

'Don't you think you've had enough, Ellie?'

I look at my husband. Renowned English Literature lecturer. Handsome. Popular. Everyone loves Professor Michael Travers, including those who have no right to.

I drain my glass of whisky, my eyes never leaving his. 'I'm not even close.'

'Jesus Christ …'

'Denial is your way of dealing with things, Michael. Drink is mine.'

'I'm not talking to you in this state.'

'You don't talk to me in *any* state, do you? You don't even touch me ... when was the last time we had sex? Hmm? When was the last time you made me feel *anything?*'

He moves a little closer, his eyes blazing, his voice so low it's almost a hiss. I'm pushing him. Fine. That's good. He needs pushing. 'I'm not doing this here, Ellie. Pull yourself together, for goodness' sake.' He leans in even closer, his mouth almost touching my ear as he speaks. 'Let's just move on, okay?'

He backs off, turns around and walks away, back to the party. Our anniversary party. Fourteen years we've been married. Fourteen wonderful, happy years. Ellie and Michael – the perfect couple. Even tragedy couldn't tear us apart, at least, that's what everyone thinks, thanks to Michael's desperate need to paper over the cracks of a marriage that's breaking. Cracks that are growing bigger by the day.

I pour myself another drink, swallow the whisky down in one; I can feel it burn my throat, settle in my belly. But it's going down like water as I'm feeling no effects, I'm not even remotely drunk. I wanted the edge taken off. This hasn't even clipped it.

'Hey.'

Liam's hand lightly brushes the small of my back as he joins me at the counter in the kitchen. I look up at him. 'Hey.'

He grabs a beer from the fridge and leans back against it,

looking out ahead of him. 'It was nice of Ed and Claire, to organize this party.'

'Yes. It was.'

I drop my gaze, stare down into my empty glass.

'Not in the party mood though, huh?'

I throw him a small smile. 'People just want me and Michael to get back to the way we were.' I shrug. 'They want us to be happy.'

'*Are* you? Happy?'

I hold his gaze, he knows the answer to that. He doesn't have to ask that question. 'Are *you?*'

He comes over to me. He returns his hand to the small of my back, and leans in so close to me I feel his breath on my neck. 'I could be happier.'

I watch him walk away. Dr Liam Kennedy. Tall, handsome, my husband's best friend. *My* best friend.

Grabbing what's left of the bottle of whisky, I slip outside into Ed and Claire's garden. It's quieter out here, bar one or two smokers over on the terrace. I just need some air, to escape the pretence for a few minutes.

Sitting down on the edge of the decking, I wrap my fingers tight around the neck of the bottle, but I resist taking another drink. Now the fresh air's hit me my head's spinning slightly. Maybe Michael's right. Maybe I have had enough. For now.

I throw back my head and breathe in deeply – once, twice, each time exhaling slowly. I try to do this sometimes, these breathing exercises, to try and control the panic that often builds up inside of me. Because of what happened that night. But those exercises don't always work. That night affected me too much, damaged me too much. The bruises may have healed, but the emotional pain is still raw. Every time I close my eyes I can still feel the punches and the kicks, I can still see her face ...

I pull myself to my feet and head back inside. Michael's talking to a group of his friends from the squash club, but he glances over – a glance so brief I almost miss it. He's making sure I'm okay, that's all. He needs me to be okay.

'Ellie, come and tell us all about the new spa you're planning to open.'

Claire's voice cuts through my thoughts and I look at her, forcing a smile onto my face. Talking about work is always a welcome distraction, so I start to tell my friends about my new business venture, losing myself in talk of facials and massages as I try to pretend everything is normal. It's only when I glance up and see Liam watching me from across the room, when he smiles at me and I feel something burn up inside of me, that I know nothing's normal. I don't think it ever will be again.

I leave my friends chatting happily about the prospect of a free spa day that I have just mentioned, and I go back into the kitchen. A small glass of wine isn't going to hurt. My head feels clearer now I've come back indoors.

Sipping my wine, I stand against the archway that separates the kitchen from the family area of Claire and Ed's spacious open-plan living space. Perfect for parties. Even those I don't want to be a part of. I used to love parties. I loved being around people, but now I find their pity and their questions too much. And yet, being alone scares me. I don't like my own company for too long. I've never felt vulnerable before, but I do now. And I hate that feeling.

I look around; I'm searching for Michael but I can't see him anywhere. Maybe he's gone outside, I don't know. I'm not even sure I care. I'm so tense tonight, I'm finding it harder than usual to keep this charade going. So, when Liam's eyes meet mine once more from across the room, I allow myself a smile – a smile he returns. I know Liam well. I've known him longer than I've known Michael, but Michael doesn't know that. We never told him that we knew each other before. That we'd slept together before, a long time ago. Liam didn't think it was important that Michael knew, he didn't think it mattered. But now that Liam is suddenly such a big part of my life, in a way I never expected he would be – *does* it matter?

I look away and take another sip of wine. For some reason there's a knot of excitement unravelling in my stomach now. One that seems to unravel much faster as I catch sight of Liam laughing at something Ed's said. And then he turns his head and his eyes meet mine again. Another smile. But his eyes are saying something else now. And I get the message.

I drag a hand through my hair, make my way back into the room. I start a conversation with Katie, Ed and Claire's neighbour. Something about a holiday she's just returned from, but I don't know where. I'm only half listening.

He's moved closer now. I can smell his cologne, I know it's him. Glancing outside, I catch sight of Michael on the terrace, deep in conversation with some of his university colleagues.

For a few more minutes I give Katie my full attention. It was Thailand, the holiday she's just returned from. And I listen as she tells me of the food she tried, the full moon party she attended, the stunning hotel she and her partner stayed in. I listen, but all the time I'm aware of Liam almost touching me. His hip gently nudges mine, his hand accidently brushes my bottom as he slides past me and I feel my heart start to race as I look back outside, at Michael. A man who doesn't touch me that way anymore. A man who doesn't want me, like that, anymore.

We've been joined by another of Claire's neighbours now, so I excuse myself from the conversation, back away a little, deliberately knocking into Liam, hard enough for him to get what's happening here. He drops his hand and it catches mine, just briefly, but long enough for him to gently squeeze my fingers before he quickly pulls his hand away. He knows what's happening. Liam knew what I needed before. He knows again now. We both do.

He resumes his conversation with Ed, but I know he's watching me as I leave the room and make my way upstairs. It's much quieter here. There are three bathrooms in Ed and Claire's house so it's not like there's hordes of people hanging around up on the landing.

Leaning back against the wall beside the main bathroom door I take a second to think about what I'm doing here. What *am* I doing here? Is this nothing more than a knee-jerk reaction to the way Michael's making me feel tonight? Am I drunk? Not thinking straight? It might be all three, but right now I don't care, I'm just tired of feeling empty and alone. I need something that actually makes me feel like I exist.

I hear him bounding up the stairs. I know it's him, and I

smile. He's keeping a safe distance between us, just in case anyone else is around ... He pushes open the bedroom doors, looking inside each one of them to check that no one is there. I think we're alone, but glance through the corridors once again to make sure. Just one more room to check. The bathroom.

He edges past me, drops his hand and slips it into mine as he nudges open the bathroom door, checks to make sure it's empty. And without looking at me he pulls me inside, kicks the door shut behind him, slamming me back against the tiled wall before I have a chance to take another breath. And it hurts. The pain is real, but it's what I need, I need to *feel* something. Because for months I've felt numb, a continuous dull ache. But right now, I feel *everything*.

My heart feels like it's beating out of my chest, banging against my ribs as I look at him – right into his steel-grey eyes. I want him. I want *this*. And he knows that.

The corner of his mouth edges up into a smirk and I gasp quietly as he slides both hands up under my dress, his fingers trailing so lightly over my skin they're barely touching it. I can't breathe, but I like the feeling, and as he grabs hold of my underwear, ripping it off in one rough yank, the sound of the flimsy material tearing echoes around the empty bathroom. I feel dizzy, excited, sick with nerves. This is wrong, I know it's wrong. My husband is downstairs, right now; he's just a flight of stairs away but it's because of him I'm doing this. He won't touch me. Won't talk to me. It's *his* fault, *he* drove me here. Doesn't he understand? I need *this*.

Liam presses a hand against the side of my neck, gently pushing my head back, just a touch. I groan quietly as his lips graze the base of my throat; as his fingers stroke my skin, dig into my thigh. My skin feels like it's on fire, I'm burning up. I want all of this and so much more, I don't want him to stop.

He cups my bottom, lifts me up and I wrap my legs around him. I want to see him as he pushes inside me but, as his mouth touches mine, my eyes start to close. He's kissing me, gently at first. A once-familiar kiss. Back then it was okay, for him to do this, to kiss me. To fuck me. Now it's dangerous. Now it's wrong, but he's making me *feel* again, with every fibre of my being. I need Liam to be the one I take my frustration out on, to be the person I use to vent my pain and anger, I need him. And I want him. God help me ...

His fingers intertwine with mine up against the wall as the kiss becomes harder, deeper, more urgent. It's overwhelming, the intensity. It's wrapping itself around us, engulfing us, and I open my eyes again. I want to look at him, as he fucks me.

I grip his hands tighter. I can feel him inside me, his eyes burning into mine as his thrusts become harder. They're verging on violent, but I crave this beautiful pain that is telling me I'm alive. Telling me I don't always have to live in that new, sad, dark world, not all the time. I can escape, when I need to. So, when he suddenly stops, when he pulls out of me, an overwhelming feeling of emptiness washes over me. It's unexpectedly brutal, and for a second I forget to breathe.

But before I can get that breath out he's swung me around so I'm facing the wall. He grabs hold of me, pulls me back against him and I cry out as he slams back into me, his fingers digging into my flesh as he pushes deep, angles my body in a way that enables me to feel every inch of him. But I need to look at him, I want to see him in a way that I can no longer see my husband. I need to see him do *this*. I need to realize what's happening, and I buck back against him, pushing him out of me so I can turn around. He gets it now, he knows. We're not done yet.

His mouth twists up into a slight smile, and I close my eyes as he kisses me again; a slow, deep kiss that grows in intensity as he lifts me up into his arms. He's back inside me in a heartbeat, my fingers winding in his hair, his breath hot against my neck, and the one thing I'm not feeling is guilty. I'm filled with so much anger and fear, there's no room for guilt. Here, in this room, with this man, I'm the woman I want to be again. And that's all I care about.

I drop my head, and bury my face in his shoulder. I grip his hands so tight I must be hurting him, and I can already feel that inevitable climax coming, spreading through my body like a beautiful wildfire. My skin's still burning, and I want to scream so loud, let all that frustration out, but I can't, not here – so I bite down on my lip as my body jolts and shakes in his arms. I can barely breathe, my heart's beating so fast and so loud it's all I can hear. I don't even know if he's come too, all I'm aware of is what's happening inside of me, when *he's* inside of me. Dr Liam Kennedy was my drug of choice once before. He's become that again.

Unwrapping my legs from his hips, I let my feet hit the floor before I push him away. It's just a gentle nudge, but I want to look at him now we're done. I want to see his face, to know he understands what this is. And then I reach out and clutch him by his shirt to pull him back towards me, his hands slamming up against the wall by my head as our mouths crash together in a deep, almost animalistic kiss. I scrunch his shirt up tighter in my fist, and I bite his lip. I want to drown in whatever this is. I've tasted escape now. I want more.

'Are we really doing this?' I whisper.

He doesn't answer my question. He just kisses me again, a kiss so hard it pushes my head right back. And then he pulls away, throws me another slight smile, and he walks out of the room. I hear him head back down to the party. Back to my husband, his best friend. A man we've both been lying to, for a very long time ...

Chapter 25

So many lies. I can't seem to escape them. Can't seem to stop living them. There is so much I can't let go of.

Liam.

I can't let go of *him*. I need him. We've been sleeping together for ten months now, mine and Michael's anniversary party was just the start of it. For ten months he's been giving me everything my husband can't or won't give me. Liam keeps me from falling over the precipice I threaten to tumble over so frequently these days.

I'm spying on my husband because I think he's sleeping with another woman, and yet, I'm sleeping with his best friend. I'm almost certain my husband is having an affair, yet I'm having one of my own. But he drove me to it. He practically pushed me into Liam's bed with his lack of concern, his unwillingness to be the support I needed at a time when my world was falling apart. It still is falling apart. He's no different to my father, with his lies. His deceit. But I'm not my mother. I won't lie down and take his shit, I'm fighting. Liam's nothing

212

more than the support I need as I try to put my life back together. That's all I can allow him to be. My support.

The first time I met Liam Kennedy, a year or so before I met Michael, I wasn't in a good place. My father had tainted the way I saw men, making me wary of contemplating anything other than friendship. That was probably why I was drawn to Liam. He wasn't looking for anything serious either, he just wanted someone to hang out with. Someone to sleep with, without the complications of a full-on relationship. That suited me just fine. Sex without the mess, without the threat of any heartache.

We'd met at the local pub, at a party to celebrate the pub football team's win in some tournament or other, I don't remember what, exactly. I don't even remember how I'd ended up at that party, but I remember the first time I saw Liam. He'd been standing by the side of the bar, close to the doors that led from the pub to the beer garden out back. He'd had a pint in one hand, the other gesticulating wildly around his head as he regaled some story to his group of friends. And it must've been a funny story because I also remember the laughter, so loud it had almost drowned out the music.

I remember the night I met Liam. My first night with Liam.

The night it all started.

The night that meant he was now linked to us, our lives; everything that would happen, he was going to be a part of it, because of that night.

I quickly pull myself back from that memory; back to the here and now. It's the present I need to concentrate on, not the past.

'I should be going.' I sit up, hugging my knees to my chest as he comes out of the bathroom. 'Michael's probably home by now.'

But he won't wonder where I've been. He won't ask what I've been doing. That would mean starting a conversation, something my husband is apparently terrified to do these days.

'Will he care? If you're not there?'

Liam sits down, runs his fingertips lightly up and down my calf, sending shivers racing up my spine. Liam gives me everything Michael won't. Everything my husband refuses to share with me, it feels like Liam allows me to have it all. I can close my eyes and lose myself in him, let the sex engulf me. I need the release, because the darkness always returns.

I take his hand, watch as his fingers curl around mine. He wants me to stay. 'I'm not sure *what* Michael cares about anymore.'

'So, stay a little longer.'

I let go of his hand, climb off the bed and reach for my clothes. I get dressed, keeping my back to him, and it's only when I look outside, when I realize that dark and unwelcome world I now inhabit is drawing me back towards it, that I know I'm not ready to face it just yet.

I turn around, lean back against the window sill, and look down at my hand. The cuts from the broken wine glass are still clearly visible, but they're healing now.

'I wish things had been different, Ellie.'

I look up, frowning slightly. I'm not sure what he means by that. 'Different ...?'

'Back then.'

'Back then it was nothing more than meaningless sex, Liam.'

'And now? What is it now?'

I don't know. Yes. I do. I know. 'It's still meaningless sex.'

He gets up, walks over to me. Tall, toned and muscular in ways Michael isn't, Liam has stronger arms, a harder body. He does things to me Michael would never do, and I'd never given that a second thought before. But now I crave the sometimes twisted sex we have. That passion. That red-hot need to feel another body invade mine. I don't want to be loved, I just want to be touched. Taken. Made to feel like a woman again instead of an empty shell.

He stops in front of me, naked and beautiful and I don't know why he's still alone. He's handsome, intelligent, funny and kind. Why did Keeley leave him? What made them drift so far apart? There seemed to be no reason for their marriage to end in the way that it did. Maybe they just fell out of love, it happens.

He slides a hand onto my neck, pushes my head backwards, his lips brushing the base of my throat and I groan quietly. He's making me want to stay, and I need to go. I can't stay here, in this bubble, forever.

'When can I see you again?' he murmurs, his mouth touching mine. I close my eyes, let his words vibrate against my lips, feel his breath fall into me.

'I don't know,' I whisper. But I need it to be soon. I can't wait too long, I don't like giving the darkness time to take over completely. As long as I can take a step back every now and again, I can cope. Maybe I'm becoming too dependent on this man, I don't know. I don't care. All I know is that when he's inside me I forget all the pain. I feel part of something again, part of some*one*.

I place a hand on his chest, my fingers splaying out over his skin. I feel his heart beating against my palm and I look up at him. I touch his jaw line, his neat, dark-blonde beard, his mouth. I run my thumb over his lower lip, tilt my head to one side as he grabs my wrist. He pulls my hand away from his face, and I fall backwards against the window sill as he kisses me, sliding his hand between my legs. He's keeping me from going anywhere.

I pretend to resist, but he knows that's a game. I don't want him to stop, I want him to continue to take away the pain until I don't need him anymore. But we can't keep doing this forever, he knows that; I made it clear from the start. And we both know the rules.

'I have to go.'

I pull his hand from between my legs and head for the door. I do have to go. I need to check where Michael's been today. What he's been doing. Who he's been talking to. I've spent enough time here, I've had my fix, I'm okay now.

'Ellie?'

I stop in the doorway, turn back around to look at him. His eyes lock on mine, but neither of us says anything. We don't need to.

If I want my husband back, we can't do this, forever …

Chapter 26

I sit back and listen as Michael's voice floats out from the tiny speaker I've attached to my laptop. It increases the sound quality of his recorded phone calls only slightly, but it's enough. None of his calls have been to her, which makes me even more sure that he has a separate phone he uses to talk to her. But that doesn't stop me from listening to all of his calls. Even if they're not to her, I have to listen to them, I might miss something if I don't. One small, miniscule detail could pass me by if I skip over stuff, so I listen to everything. No matter who he's talking to.

He ends this particular call to Laurel. A conversation about a staff meeting and a lecture he's giving at a university in Cardiff next week. See? I didn't know he was going to Cardiff. Maybe he did tell me, I can't remember, but I'm almost sure he didn't. And I'd have missed that, if I'd skipped over that call. Is he taking *her* to Cardiff? Ava? Is that why he didn't tell me about the trip? An overnight stay. Time away from me.

The front door opening downstairs signals Michael's arrival back home, and I quickly log out and close the laptop down.

He's late, as usual, although there's no such thing as a regular time for him to come home nowadays. But it's later than it ever used to be, when everything was normal and happy. When we had a future.

He's in the kitchen when I get downstairs, fixing himself a drink. He accuses me of drinking too much, but he's no saint.

'Good day?' I ask, in a vain attempt to elicit a response.

'It was okay. Same old, same old.'

I think you're lying, Michael. I think you do so many things you never used to do before, so I'm not buying the 'same old' line.

I wait for him to ask me how my day went, but he doesn't. Instead he turns away and goes into the orangery. He sits down and takes out his reading glasses. Then he opens his newspaper and hides behind it, because that's what he does now. He hides behind anything he can to avoid talking to me.

I start making dinner. A stir-fry. Something quick. Easy. Something we'll push around our plates while we pretend that everything's okay. That this is normal. But I'm not willing to accept this existence. I'll expose my husband's affair and I'll end it. I'll make sure his distraction is gone for good because I can't go through this all again. History is not going to repeat itself. But at least this one – Ava – is going to be easier to deal with.

As I prepare dinner, the only noise in the room is the sound of the TV playing away quietly in the background. I can't live with the silences, they're becoming more and more painful to deal with. So I fill them with music or the news, or I switch over to some banal reality TV show in the hope that he'll react, because he hates them. As do I.

I serve dinner, and he joins me at the table. He folds his newspaper, lays it down beside his plate, picks up his glass and takes a sip of wine. I gulp mine. I need the alcohol hit, more and more as each day passes. Liam and alcohol, my two necessary crutches.

'How's the mentoring going?' I ask, knowing that that will, at least, cause him to raise his head. Which it does.

'Why do you ask?'

'I'm interested in your work, Michael. I always have been.' I pick up my napkin, scrunching it up in my fist. 'Look, I know you have this student/professor confidentiality thing, but don't you think that's a bit, you know? A bit of an over-reaction? I mean, it's not like you're discussing their medical records or bank details. Why the need for such secrecy?'

I don't care now. I don't. I need to ask questions, it's the only way I can get to the truth. I need to push him, until he tells me what I need to hear. I can track his whereabouts, listen in to his calls, read his texts, but I want to hear him *tell* me. Something. And he will. I'll make him, if I have to.

'There *is* no secrecy, Ellie. It's just not something I think *we* need to talk about.'

'Why not?'

He looks at me through narrowed eyes. He doesn't like it when I talk like this. I'm being confrontational, I know, but I'm starting to lose patience. How many times has he lied to me? How many times has he done that?

'I have work to do in the office.'

He throws his napkin down, pushes back his chair and leaves the table. But as he passes me he stops, rests a hand lightly on my shoulder and gently kisses the top of my head.

'Get some rest, Ellie. You work too hard.'

I let him go. I listen as he climbs the stairs. One flight. Two. He's gone straight up to his office.

I look down at the napkin bunched up in my fist and I squeeze it tighter, so tight my knuckles turn white. When I loosen my grip, it falls onto my plate, into my half-eaten food. I watch as it slowly becomes soaked in soy sauce, and as I watch I'm aware of a sharp pain coming from my hand. I look down. I've been picking at the scabs on my palm, scratching away until I drew fresh blood. I hadn't even been aware I'd been doing it, but now the soy sauce-soaked napkin is peppered with droplets of blood, the red and the brown slowly merging together in a dark, mud-coloured mess.

I inhale deeply before I finally get up from the table. I fetch the small first-aid kit from the cupboard and I wash the reopened cuts, carefully placing plasters over them; there's not enough blood to warrant a bandage. And then, like a robot programmed to carry out these everyday tasks, I clear the table. Stack the dishwasher. Fill up the coffee machine and switch it on. I pour myself a glass of whisky and down it quickly, closing my eyes as the warm liquid settles in my stomach. That one was for medicinal purposes. But then, aren't they all?

Raising my eyes to the ceiling I wonder if Michael really has got work to do. I doubt he does. It's his go-to excuse when he doesn't want to talk – he has work to do.

Sighing quietly, I head out into the hallway, stopping at the foot of the stairs. I turn around, look at his jacket hanging on the hook by the door, and without hesitation, without any hint of guilt, I rifle through the pockets, finding nothing more than a receipt for his newspaper and his glasses case. But that means nothing. It's easy to cover your tracks when you're doing something you don't want anyone to find out about. I should know. Which is why I don't trust him. I know the signs, I've been playing this game for a while now, and I'm good at it. Is he?

I go into our room, check my reflection in the mirror. I look okay. Not too tired. You could even describe my complexion as slightly glowing, and that's all down to Liam. Sex and time away from this charade fills me with a renewed energy, something that keeps me going until I need to keep running on empty. And I briefly wonder if this was how I looked before everything happened. Did my complexion ever glow back then?

A sudden noise from outside on the landing jolts me from that thought; makes me spin around. Even when I'm not alone in this house my nerves are on edge. It'll be nothing more than a beam creaking, but for the briefest of moments I'm wracked with memories I won't ever forget. The fear. The noise. The blood ...

My phone vibrating in my pocket drags me back from those memories and I quickly take it out. There's an alert flashing up on the screen; Michael's making a call, to a number I recognize as Bill Franklin's, a member of his faculty. Another work call, but I'll still listen to it, later. When he's asleep.

Sliding my phone back into my pocket I look up at the wall facing our bed, at the picture hanging on it. Me and Michael on our wedding day. Sunshine, happiness, laughter, that's what I remember about that day. A darkness hides the sun now. I can't remember the last time I felt true happiness. I'm happy, for a few brief minutes, when I'm alone with Liam. It's a kind-of happy, anyway. Something that masks the sadness, for a while.

'Ellie?'

I turn to face him. He looks tired as he stands in the doorway, his reading glasses in one hand, his other pressing down on the bridge of his nose with his thumb and forefinger, his head down, eyes closed. 'I thought you were working.'

'I am. I just need something from the car. I left some papers in there.'

I turn back to look at the picture on the wall; let a couple of beats pass before I turn to face Michael again. 'How *is* work?'

He slowly raises his head, and I fix my eyes on his. I look right at him, wait for him to tell me about Cardiff, because he just forgot, right? He forgot to tell me he was going away.

'Work's fine. I just have a lot to catch up on, that's all.'

'Your students keeping you busy, are they?'

He narrows his eyes, that familiar, weary expression taking over his face. 'Where is this going, Ellie?'

I leave another beat or two before I answer him. He's defensive. That means I've touched a nerve. 'It's just a question, Michael.'

You won't be able to keep her a secret for much longer, Michael.

The Wife

Your car was outside her house, you were in there, with her, I know you were. It's only a matter of time now, before I find that cast-iron proof I need. It's only a matter of time …

'I need to go fetch those papers from the car.'

He's shutting me down, as he does so often these days. He's ending it, before I start asking more questions. Before I start pushing him, he's putting a stop to it. And I'm too tired to fight it tonight. But I will fight it.

I want my life back.

I want Michael back.

I don't want *this* …

Chapter 27

It's a busy day at the spa. We have a, thankfully very well-behaved, hen party spending the day with us today; there are also a couple of clients with birthdays and an anniversary treat, amongst many others. My new business has really taken off. The spa has appeared in lots of features in the local press and a regional news programme filmed a lovely piece on us for TV that went out a few nights ago, which has brought a lot of new business in. I'm happy, at work. It's a necessary distraction.

I've been busy today making sure we have everything set up for a meeting tomorrow about expanding into the wedding venue side of things, but my staff seem to be doing an amazing job of keeping this place running. And I need that, because there are times when I can't focus. When I'm somewhere else, not concentrating on work. When I'm wondering where my husband is.

I still have lunch most days in the Spanish restaurant, even though I've all but convinced myself Michael probably hasn't been in there again. The tracker has never put him there, but I still go. Just to be sure. Just in case.

The Wife

My phone signals an alert and I pull it from my pocket, look down at the screen. It's a text, from Liam. He's coming to the university this afternoon to set up another run of guest lectures, and he wants to see me. Do I want to see *him*? Today?

I stop outside the pool room – a huge glass-walled extension we had built onto the back of the building that looks out over the grounds and gardens. It houses the swimming pool, two hot-tubs and a sauna. Most of the loungers that surround the large oval pool are occupied by guests this morning, decked out in white robes drinking mocktails and prosecco while they relax after treatments, looking forward to lunch. It's a sight that makes me happy, seeing another venture slowly become a success; a reminder that, in spite of everything that's happened, I haven't let any of it affect my work.

I turn around and lean back against the glass as I call Liam back.

'Hey.'

'Can you get away?' he asks, and for a second I just let the sound of his voice fill my head.

'I don't know. I'm busy today. Come and see me here, at the spa.'

'You sound like you're summoning me.'

Maybe I am. He's going to come anyway. 'I can't leave here, Liam. If you want to see me …'

'I'm on my way.'

I end the call, slide my phone back into my pocket, and I can't keep the smile off my face. I like having sex with him, here, in my office. I think it's the danger, I get off on it. I like that feeling of possibly being caught, even though I know we won't be. But Liam isn't putting us in danger. My distraction is harmless. Michael's isn't.

Michael. I haven't checked his whereabouts for a while now, so I pull out my phone to see where he is. I check the tracker. He's at work. Or he's in his building, anyway. He's at the university. But that means nothing. *She* could be with him, in his office. He's also made a few calls this morning, all work-related by the looks of it. And there's been one call to him. A number I don't recognize this time. And that makes my stomach turn, I've never seen that number before. Is that *her* number? Ava's? Has she made this easy for me now?

I take a deep breath, put my phone away and head back to my office. I might just have time to check that call before Liam gets here.

'I'm taking a break for lunch now, Carmen. Can you take charge for an hour or so? There are a few things I need to catch up on in the office. Oh, and Liam's on his way. Tell him to come straight through when he gets here. Thanks.'

Am I playing with fire? Sailing a little too close to the wind? Are Liam's visits becoming so frequent that others may start to suspect something's going on? I don't think so. I think we're okay. My husband, on the other hand, his time may well be up. Soon.

Closing the door behind me I head straight for my laptop, slip the earphones into my ears and log into Michael's call history. I find that call that was made to him – the one from a number I don't recognize – and I play it back, my heart hammering so hard I have to turn up the volume. And it's

226

Michael's voice I hear first. A simple '*hello*'. He sounds distracted. A female voice answers him, tells him she needs to see him. Needs to talk to him. His voice becomes slightly more agitated as he tells her she shouldn't call him on this phone. I feel sick. Is it her? Is that what *she* sounds like? He tells her to stop by his office as soon as she can, before that afternoon's lecture. And then he ends the call.

It's her. I know it's her. Ava. I'm certain of that now.

I sit back in my chair, stare blankly at the laptop screen. I don't know what to do. That conversation didn't exactly incriminate anyone, it didn't give me anything that told me they're definitely having an affair, but his voice – he sounded irritated. Slightly angry. She shouldn't be calling him on that phone ...

The door opening pulls me back from my paranoia and I look up. I see Liam closing the door behind him, and just the sight of him makes a little of that paranoia disappear. For now.

'Was it my idea?'

Liam frowns; he doesn't know what I'm talking about.

'To keep our past a secret from Michael? Was it my idea? I can't remember ...'

I trail off, stand up and go over to the window to pull down the blind, plunging my office into semi-darkness. There wasn't all that much of a past to keep secret, in reality. What Liam and I had before, it was nothing more than sex. Pretty much exactly what we have now, except I wasn't married then. But I don't feel married now. I feel like I lost my husband a long time ago, but I'll get him back. This, what I'm doing, sleeping with Liam – I see it as a kind of therapy. It's keeping me on the right side of sane; without this release I'd be on the brink of a breakdown. This helps keep that at bay.

'I really don't think it matters anymore, Ellie.'

I turn around, tilting my head to one side as I look at him. 'Maybe not.'

He throws his jacket down on the couch in the corner and comes over to me. He cups my cheek, leans in to kiss me and the second his lips touch mine I feel that release start to build. I feel the paranoia recede a little further, allowing the escape to begin. I feel the darkness lift; my temporary respite is here.

I loosen his shirt, slip it back off his shoulders. Sometimes I just need to feel his skin against mine, warm and hard, his strong arms holding me close, keeping me safe.

For a second or two we just look at each other, and I'm aware of my heart pounding, pushing the breath out of me in short, sharp pants as his mouth lowers down onto mine. I crave the way he kisses me. I crave the taste of him, the smell of him, he's my medicine.

He reaches down, lays a hand on my leg and he keeps it there, he doesn't move it. I feel his fingers dig into my flesh as his eyes bore into mine. He's teasing me, taunting me, he doesn't make it easy but that's why I need him. He forces me to play these games until I have no other option but to give myself to him, and I want him to take me, to bring a small shard of sunlight into my darkened world. I want him to touch me, I want him to push the pain away. I want him inside me.

I keep my eyes locked on his as he slides my dress up over

my thighs, tugs at my knickers, nudging them down, and I help him. I wriggle out of them, kick them away, let him push my legs apart with his knee, and my heart is pounding so hard it's threatening to break through my ribs. Outside I can hear the sound of the spa going about its daily business, while I'm in here, doing this, but it's that danger of being caught that drives me. The excitement is addictive.

I place my hands on Liam's naked chest, look back up into his deep, grey eyes. His skin is warm and smooth, taut beneath my palms. I kiss his slightly open mouth. I breathe him in. Escaping. I'm not here anymore, in this cruel world I've been forced to live in. I'm not there. I'm somewhere else, that place I want to be, where Michael and I have a future. Where our child is alive and we've never known the kind of heartache we live with every day now. I'm somewhere happy and bright, as light as the yellow on the walls of our dead child's nursery. I'm there. Liam takes me there, he always does. He touches me, and I come here.

I bite down on my lip, throw back my head and close my eyes as he pushes his fingers inside me, his mouth covering my neck in tiny, featherlight kisses. My heart's beating impossibly fast, my body wracked with the most beautiful shivers. He's doing what he knows he can do so well, bringing me to a crashing climax, one silenced by his mouth covering mine. He swallows down my moans, takes my pleasure as his own, and when I'm done he instructs me to open my eyes and look at him, right at him. He knows what he does; he gives me the strength to carry on, the energy I need as I try and put my shattered life back together. That's why I can't let him go, I can't stop this. I won't.

'She called him,' I whisper as I run my fingers ever-so-lightly over his rough jaw line. 'I listened to it. The call. I heard them, talking.'

He takes hold of my hand, strokes my knuckles with his thumb, but I keep my eyes on his.

'Michael was your best friend back then, when we were together. Why did you never introduce me to him?'

I'd never really thought about it at the time. I'd never questioned the fact that Liam had never once introduced me to *any* of his friends, not just Michael. I'd never met any of them and I hadn't questioned it because what we'd had, it was nothing. Just sex. And I'm not even sure why I'm questioning it now, I just want to know.

I feel his hand squeeze mine a little tighter, but he doesn't break the stare. His eyes continue to burn into mine. 'Michael was – he would've drawn you in, Ellie.'

I frown. 'Drawn me in?'

'All he needed to do was smile and women came running. *You* came running. Eventually. At the time, I didn't want to lose you, so, I kept him in the background.'

'And now we're doing the same to him.'

'No. This isn't the same.'

I slide a hand onto his back, stroke his skin with my fingertips. I don't know if I'm done with him yet. 'You said you didn't want to lose me.'

'I didn't.' He shrugs. 'But you went anyway.'

'I thought you didn't want anything serious?'

'I didn't.' He steps back from me, grabs his shirt from the floor and puts it back on. I stay where I am, watching him. 'But you stopped returning my calls, so ...'

He leaves that sentence unfinished, and I frown again. But I don't dwell on it. I have enough to think about. What happened in the past, between me and Liam, well, that's *in* the past. I need to focus on the future.

I go over to him, press my body against his. I kiss him, feel his fingers wind into my hair, pulling my head back. I let him push me against the wall, let his fingers scratch lightly over my skin, his beard rough against my neck as he kisses it. His mouth touches mine one more time before he takes his jacket and leaves. We're done, for now. And that's fine. I'm okay with that, I have work to do. He gave me what I needed, it's time to get on with my day.

I quickly pull myself together, open the blinds, call Carmen to let her know I'll be out for the rest of the day.

I'm going to see my husband.

Chapter 28

Iknow he has a lecture this afternoon. I know, because he mentioned it in that phone call. He told her – Ava – to come and see him, in his office, before that afternoon's lecture. So, I went home after Liam's visit and accessed Michael's timetable from his desktop computer. I found out the time of that lecture. A lecture I'm assuming *she's* going to be attending. That's what I got from that call. Because I'm still certain it was her. He never called her by her name, but I know it was her, calling my husband. Asking to see him. To talk to him.

What about, Michael? What does she want to talk to you about? Your trip to Cardiff? A couple of sordid hours in a cheap hotel? What does she need to see you about, Professor Travers?

I'm at the university now. I'm going to that lecture, because I need to see them together. I need to see, for myself, those tell-tale signs. I need to do *something*. And I don't want him to know I'm here, that would be pointless, so, I need to stay back, just until the lecture starts. Then I'm going to quietly sneak into the back of the theatre, and watch him at work. Watch *her*, at work. Stealing my husband. Fluttering her

232

teenage eyelashes at a man old enough to be her father. A man she can't have. None of them can have him, and Michael, he needs to realize that he has to stop this, he has to put an end to these infatuated girls, he has to stop playing up to them. It's dangerous. Look what happened before. The repercussions are slowly destroying us, and we can't deal with it a second time. We can't.

I stand back as the last of the students file into the lecture theatre. Michael's already inside, I can hear him, chatting away as he sets up, his deep voice easily heard even though he's right down there on the floor. It's not the first time I've sneaked into one of his lectures, it's just that, all the other times I've done it, he knew about it. He knew I was there, and it was fun, watching him. This isn't fun. This is necessary.

I slip inside behind the last of the students, find a seat at the very back of the hall, and already my eyes are scanning the room. Is Ava here yet? Please don't make this a wasted journey ... no, she's here. She's down at the front, where else would she be? I can just about make her out, and I squint slightly, to make sure, but then she stands up and I can see her face a little more clearly. It's definitely her. She's wearing that same unflattering jumper she was wearing the first time I saw her, skinny jeans and black ankle boots, her dark hair pulled back off her face in a loose ponytail. Even from way up here I can't fail to notice how pretty she is. How young she is. Just like the last one. The one who invaded our home, kicked our baby to death. So, my husband – he needs to put a stop to this. To *her*. He needs to rid himself of his distraction. Am I going to have to do it for him?

I watch her as she laughs with her friends, and then I glance over at Michael, but he isn't looking in her direction. He's talking to another student, a young man wearing a Foo Fighters t-shirt, ripped jeans and Converse trainers. But *she's* looking at *him*. At Michael. She's watching him, talking to this student, even though she's still chatting to her friends. And I wait for him to turn and see her watching him, but it doesn't happen.

He calls an end to the chatter, asks everyone to sit down. Be quiet. And within seconds he has them all in the palm of his hand. My husband. The popular professor.

I spend the next hour watching both of them, trying to catch a glimpse of them glancing at the other, but I've either blinked and missed it or it just hasn't happened. Should that surprise me? After all, if something's going on between the two of them, the last thing Michael will do is anything that could give them away. So I wait, I stay put until the lecture ends. Until he dismisses them, starts packing away his things. I stand up and back off into the doorway, I can't stay seated now. Everyone's leaving, he'll notice me if I stay. So I hide in the doorway, keep my eyes on him because she's still there. She's still there, even though her friends are leaving, filing out up the stairs towards the entrance I'm standing just outside of, far away enough to remain unnoticed but close enough to see what's happening.

I wait, craning my neck above the crowd of students still streaming out of the lecture theatre, because I need to see what's going on now. Has she left? Is she still down there? I can't see ... no. She's still there. She picks up her files, hugs them close to her chest, and I feel my breath catch in my throat as she walks over to Michael.

I edge closer to the doorway, giving myself a slightly clearer view, and I watch as she approaches him. I watch as he turns around and throws her a smile, but it's a very brief one. It's almost as if he's remembered where he is, and that smile is wiped off his face in a heartbeat.

He leans in closer to her, rests a hand on her arm. They exchange a few words, she doesn't take her eyes off him. Are they arranging the trip to Cardiff? The hotel they'll sleep in? The room they'll fuck in? Is that what's happening here?

I feel my stomach turn over and over as I continue to watch their exchange. She takes her phone out of her pocket, finally pulling her eyes away from Michael as she scrolls down, looking for something. She shows him the screen, and he scribbles something down on a piece of paper, tucks it into his pocket. Will that piece of paper still be there when he gets home? Will I be able to find it? See what he's just written down?

Nausea floods me, rising up from my belly into my throat, but I swallow it down. I need to stay here, I need to watch this, until it ends. Until she leaves. Only then am *I* leaving.

She puts her phone away, starts talking to Michael again, and he stands there, listening to her. Her listens, to *her*. He doesn't listen to me. And that fills me with an unbearable sadness, a dark anger; it's becoming harder to control so many conflicting emotions.

He reaches out, places a hand on her shoulder, and he smiles at her. She smiles back. He squeezes her shoulder and turns away from her. It's over. Whatever that was, it's over. She's heading out now. It's my time to leave. He can't know I was here.

I make my way to his office, to see Sue. I really can't remember whether he told me about Cardiff or not, but I'm still convinced he didn't. Because he wants to take *her*. He doesn't want me to know, he's going to spin me some lie, I'm sure of it now. But Sue won't be aware of that. She'll just assume I know about his trip, that he's told me, because that's what husbands do, right? They talk to their wives. They tell them when they're going away. They talk to them. But *my* husband – I think he's going to lie to me. Again.

'Ellie! What a nice surprise. Michael isn't here, though, he's just finishing a lecture.'

'Oh, that's a shame. I was hoping to catch him. I was on my way into town to pick up a few things for the spa, and I just wondered if he needed anything. Never mind. It's not important.'

'I can pass on a message, if you like? Get him to call you.'

'No, it's fine. I'll call him myself … Actually, before I go, Sue, you couldn't check his calendar for me, could you? Some friends of ours are organizing a dinner party next week and I need to check when Michael's free. You know, when he hasn't got an evening of tutorials or meetings.'

'Just let me look for you … well, as you know he's in Cardiff next Monday and Tuesday, but apart from that …'

'Cardiff?'

Sue frowns. 'He's giving a guest lecture there next week. Didn't he tell you?'

236

I wave a dismissive hand in the air, I laugh it off. 'You know, he might've done, but I've had so much on my mind lately what with all the publicity for the spa and now the wedding venue side of things taking off, I totally forgot about Cardiff!' I check my watch. I need to leave now, before Michael gets back. 'Anyway, I'd better go. I need to be back at work in half an hour.'

Sue smiles at me. She's bought my act, she's given me what I need. I can mention Cardiff now, and Michael will *have* to tell me. Whatever lie he was planning to spin me, he can't do that now.

He's going to tell me everything.

Eventually.

Chapter 29

'What were you doing at the university this afternoon, Ellie?'

I leave a brief silence before I answer him. 'I came to see you, but you were busy. Is that a problem?'

He sits down and drops his head, clasps his hands together between his knees. I see his shoulders sag, hear him sigh. *I'm* the problem. And I don't want to be that anymore, but he's forcing my hand, he's making me do these things, to save *us*.

'I'm sorry I didn't tell you about Cardiff.' He looks up at me. His expression's changed now. It's softer. Kinder.

Is that because I almost caught you out, Michael?

'You might've mentioned it.' I shrug. 'We've both been really busy. Things get left out. Forgotten.'

You're forgetting me, Michael.

He nods, and I can see him wringing his hands, does he know he's doing that?

'You have to stop dropping by like that, Ellie. Unannounced. I'm really busy right now, and I don't need ...'

He leaves it there, doesn't finish that sentence, and I feel another piece of me die.

He's slipping away from me, faster than I thought. I need to move quicker, fix this quicker.

'You don't need *what*, Michael? Me? You don't need *me?*'

'Not like this, Ellie.' The agitation has returned to his voice, his tone's harsher. Irritated. And that's all he says. He gets up, he leaves the living room, leaves me alone. Again. I hear him go into the kitchen, then head upstairs a couple of minutes later. I feel tears prick the back of my eyes and I blink hard, squeezing my eyes tight shut, I don't want to cry. Crying won't help anything.

I get up and walk through the kitchen to the orangery, down to the pool room at the far end of the house. I go into my office, fire up my laptop and I check to see if he came straight home, after work. He didn't. He went to see *her*. Or was she with him, in the car? Did he drive her home? Stop off for a quick one before he came back to me?

I sit back, look out at the pool, at the last of the slowly setting sun as it hits the water's surface, shooting patterns of light up at the ceiling. The swirling patterns of bouncing light are quite mesmerizing, and for a few seconds I just sit there, watching those patterns. And remembering, as I always do, when I'm in here.

The sound of something clattering outside in the garden jolts me from my trance-like state and I cry out in shock, a short but loud gasp. Any sudden noise still puts me on edge, especially when I'm in here. When I'm alone, in here ...

I get up, look outside, and I see a cat scampering across our garden. He's knocked over one of the terracotta pots on the summer house porch, that's all. It happens a lot; that cat seems to like our garden, so I should be used to this by now. Those sudden noises, these random sounds. I wonder if I'll ever get used to it.

I take a minute until my breathing has slowed down before I head back into the house. I might have a bath, try to relax a little. Try to forget, for a while, that my once happy life is now a sad and lonely one. And it shouldn't be that way, I won't let it stay that way. I won't.

As I walk through the kitchen, I hear voices out in the hall. Michael's, and Liam's. I take another deep breath before I go any further, folding my arms tight against myself as I leave the kitchen and head into the hall.

Liam sees me first, his glance over Michael's shoulder brief but I catch the slightest of smiles on his face. I smile back. Michael turns his head, but I receive no smile from him.

When did you become so cold, Michael? What guilt are you carrying that's made you treat me this way? Is this all because I refuse to forget? Refuse to play along, pretend that things didn't happen when we both know that they did? They happened, Michael … and I'm sorry …

He turns back to face Liam, and they finish their discussion. They're talking about some football game, it's just a flying visit, they're saying goodbye now. But before he goes Liam glances over at me again. He smiles at me, again, before he leaves. A smile Michael doesn't notice, why would he? He's already closed the door, he's about to head back up to his office but he stops at the foot of the stairs. He looks at me, at the palm of my hand decorated with plasters. It's been a few days since I accidently picked at the scabs there, but they're still healing.

'What've you done to your hand?' he asks. It's the first time he's shown any interest in my well-being in a while, and I feel oddly happy about that. I'm snatching for scraps, anything that makes me think he's still in there. My husband.

I turn my hand palm upwards, look down at the plasters. They need renewing again. They're starting to curl upwards at the edges, the packet might say they're waterproof, but they're not.

'I knocked it, at work. It reopened one of the cuts, that's all.'

The lies trip off my tongue now. Do they trip off his, too?

He takes my hand and runs his thumb lightly over my palm. He stares into my eyes, and for the briefest of moments I feel a flicker of hope. I see my husband.

'You need to be more careful,' he whispers, and he sounds almost caring. He then starts to make his way back upstairs, taking them two at a time. Is he that desperate to escape me?

'Michael?'

He stops just before he reaches the landing.

'Nothing. It doesn't matter.'

I don't know what I was going to say. Maybe I'd just hoped something would come, something that would make him want to stay down here, with me.

He sighs, turns back around and disappears from view. I hear him walking up the stairs to the top floor, hear him close his office door. He's gone. That's where he'll stay until it's time for bed.

I sit down on the bottom stair and glance at the security monitor by the door. It's quiet outside, but there's a slight breeze blowing, nudging the leaves and flowers of the potted plants and shrubs lining the driveway. And it's dark now. I should be cooking dinner but I'm not hungry. I don't think Michael is, either. I don't want to eat, I don't want to be in this house, tonight. I don't want to spend another lonely evening downstairs, alone, while Michael hides away in his office.

I pull myself to my feet and go to get my coat, my hand brushing Michael's jacket as I reach for it. The same jacket he was wearing at his lecture this afternoon. He put that scrap of paper he wrote on – something *she* showed him on her phone, he wrote it down and he slid it into this jacket pocket. I'm looking for it, but it's not there. His pockets are empty.

Slipping on my coat I glance upstairs. Should I tell him I'm going out? And then I remember, there's no need to tell him. He won't even notice I've gone.

Chapter 30

'Does Michael know you're here?' Liam closes the door behind me and I follow him into the living room.

'No, he doesn't. He won't even know I've gone out.'

Liam slides his hands into his pockets and looks at me. 'Are you okay?'

'He makes me feel like I don't exist.'

'Is that why you come to me? Do *I* make you feel like you exist?'

'You know that's why I come to you.'

'And what happens if Michael stops being this cold towards you? Is that it, for you and me?'

'Yes. Liam, come on, you know what this is for me. You know *all* it is for me.'

'And what if it's something else, for *me*?'

I frown, I wasn't expecting this. I'm not in the mood for analyzing relationships. 'We don't have feelings, Liam.'

'No, Ellie, *you* don't have feelings.'

Maybe I shouldn't have come here. I don't want this, it's confusing. 'I should go.'

I start to walk out the door but he runs over to me, grabs my arm. He stops me, from leaving.

'No, Ellie, please. Stay.' He swings me around, slides an arm around my waist. He pulls me against him and he kisses me slowly, his hand cradling my cheek and I melt into him. 'Stay the night,' he whispers. 'Leave Michael on his own, teach him a lesson. Let him worry about you. I want you to stay, Ellie. With me.'

I look up at him. He's serious, he wants this, but I'm not sure. What he said just then, I don't know where that's coming from. He's saying things now that are playing on my already messed-up mind. He's complicating a situation that can do without any more crap being heaped on it.

'I don't know …'

He drops a hand to my hip, slides it around so it cups my bottom and I try not to gasp, but I can't stop it from happening.

'Stay,' he murmurs, his mouth resting on mine, so close his breath is my breath.

I nod. I don't want to go back home. I don't want to go back to the man I love, because it's too painful. Too hard.

'I'll get us some drinks.' He lets me go and I watch him leave the living room, his long-legged swagger so different to Michael's.

I walk over to the window, look outside at the quiet suburban cul-de-sac. This house is on the market now. Liam's marital home. He's been looking at apartments and houses closer to Newcastle, where his offices and laboratory are. He wants rid of this place, it holds too many memories. And we all have memories we want rid of, don't we?

I close the blinds, I shut out the world. It's the way I like it, the way it's going to be, until the world I want has been put back together.

'Beer?'

I swing around at the sound of his voice, smile at him as I take the beer he holds out to me. 'Thanks.'

I sit down on the couch, cross my legs up underneath myself, taking a swig of beer as I watch him look for some music to play. The haunting intro to Pink Floyd's *Shine On You Crazy Diamond* floods the room, and I smile at him again as he sits down on the chair opposite me.

'You saw them live too, didn't you? Earl's Court, '94?'

I take another swig of beer. Give him another smile. 'This was the set opener. The first song they played.'

His eyes lock on mine, and already I'm beginning to feel better. My head's clearer, I don't feel so sad anymore. I don't feel alone.

'I love you, Ellie. You know that, don't you?'

His words slam into me, knocking the wind right out of me, but I don't break the stare.

'I've always loved you.'

He knows the score. He knows I can't love him back, how can I? I love Michael. I love my husband.

'You shouldn't.'

'Marrying Keeley, that was a mistake. I just – seeing you with him. With Michael. It fucking hurt, Ellie, that you chose him over me.'

'I didn't choose him over you, Liam. It wasn't like that. I had no idea you and Michael even knew each other, not until I saw you at our engagement party.'

He drops his gaze, but I keep mine steady, keep it focused on him.

'I should never have let you go.'

'You didn't *let* me go, I left you. I stopped returning your calls, I ignored your texts, I just walked away. What we had was nothing, it *meant* nothing.'

'It means something now.'

'To *you*. I'm not leaving Michael, do you understand that?'

'What if he leaves *you*?' He looks back at me, his eyes dark, verging on angry. 'What if he's already gone?'

'He won't leave me. He loves me.'

'So much that you think he's fucking one of his students?'

I slam my beer down on the table beside me, get up and head for the door, but before I reach it he's seized hold of my hand and swung me into his arms. His mouth crashes down onto mine before I have a chance to protest, his fingers clawing at my clothes and he's got me, I'm all in. I'm tearing at his shirt, pulling off his belt, I'm desperate to feel him now, even though I should walk away after what he said, but how can I? I walk away and I have nothing, no escape. I'm alone, if I walk away. I don't want to be alone. I like the way he makes me feel, I *need* him.

It's rough, hard, fast sex. The release we both need, we obviously have our own frustrations we need to vent. I scratch at his skin, bite down on his lip. My hips crash against his as he thrusts into me, there'll be bruises I won't even have to hide – Michael and me, we have sex so rarely these days. But that'll change. One day. Soon. And by that time the bruises will have disappeared. The scratches will have healed.

Hot, hard, frantic sex, it's what keeps me functioning. Keeps me focused. But I don't love Liam. I love my husband.

He pulls out of me, steps back from me, and I close my eyes, I wait for my breathing to slow down. I wait, before I look at him.

'You don't love me, Liam. Things have just been crazy these past few months, everything's confusing and ...'

'You don't *know* how I feel, Ellie.'

I hold his gaze, my eyes burning into his. 'I don't know how *I* feel.'

He sits down on the couch and drops his head into his hands, dragging them both back through his hair.

'I only married her – I only married Keeley because I thought it would help me get over *you*.' He slowly raises his gaze. 'It was a knee-jerk reaction.'

'She didn't deserve that.'

'No. She didn't.'

'Did she know? Keeley? Did she know, that you only married her as a distraction?'

'Of course she didn't know. And in the end she left me, so I got what I deserved, right?'

I go over to him, crouch down in front of him, take his hands in mine, running my thumbs lightly over his knuckles. 'I love Michael, Liam.'

He lets go of my hands, stands up, starts pacing the floor, raking a hand back and forth through his dark-blonde hair. 'Then why are you here, Ellie?' He stops pacing and turns to face me. 'Why are you here, fucking me, if you love your husband?'

'You know why, Liam.'

He holds my gaze, his eyes boring into mine. 'You really think he's having an affair? Or, is this all just something you're seeing in your own mind because you don't want to believe that what happened to you both was something that can't be fixed?'

I shake my head, fold my arms against myself. 'That's not fair. We're broken, but I *can* fix us.'

'You really think that?' He comes over to me, rests his palm against my cheek. 'Maybe you just need to face up to the fact you and Michael are over.'

I push his hand away, sit down on the arm of the chair. Is he right? Am I really seeing something that isn't there?

'Ellie, I'm sorry, okay? I just – I think you need to take a step back, look at the facts ...'

'You have access to drugs, don't you? At your lab?'

He frowns. My sudden change of subject has thrown him slightly. 'Yes, but ...'

'Truth serums. They exist, right?'

He sits down on the couch, clasps his hands together. 'Yes, in theory ...'

'Can you get hold of any?'

He laughs. I don't think he believes what he's hearing. Does he think I'm crazy? Does he think I'm losing it? Maybe I am. But I'm desperate now, to know the truth. Because I don't think I *am* seeing something that isn't there. I think it's all very clear, I just need some proof, that's all.

'Ellie, come on, are you serious?'

Deadly.

'I can't just walk into the lab and walk out with an armful

of drugs, it doesn't work like that. I mean, what the hell do you think you're going to do, huh? Even if I *could* get hold of anything remotely like that, what would you do with it? Slip it into his food, spike his drink? The effects of drugs like that – they're not even proven to work, not to mention the legal and ethical issues they throw up. What the fuck is going on in your head right now?'

I get up and walk out of the room, into the kitchen, and he follows me, of course he does. He grabs my arm and spins me around. His expression is a mixture of pity, frustration, anger. 'You're scaring me now, Ellie, do you hear me? You're really scaring me.'

'You won't help me?'

'To break the law? No. I won't. Do you have any idea of the kind of shit I could get myself into by helping you like that? It's ridiculous.'

'So, maybe I should just ask him outright? If he's cheating on me, if he's fucking one of his students. I should just ask him outright. Is that a better idea?'

'Better than drugging him, yes.'

I wrench my arm free of his grip and walk over to the counter. I pour myself a large shot of vodka and swallow it down in one mouthful, the clear liquid burning my throat. It's a feeling I'm used to, one I need.

'Or you could just try and accept what's happening.'

I look at him, I tilt my head to one side, and I frown. 'And what *is* happening, Liam?'

'You and Michael are drifting apart, it happens. What you guys went through, it would put a strain on any couple ...'

'Me and Michael aren't just *any* couple.'

'Aren't you?'

'You're supposed to be his best friend.'

'Best friends don't sleep with their mates' wives.'

I turn away from him, pour myself another vodka. The alcohol's going straight to my head because I've had nothing to eat for hours, and it's the first time I've really felt the effects in a while. I like it.

'He just needed a distraction, Liam, that's all. He needed something to help him deal with what happened.'

'What *did* happen, Ellie?'

I turn around, look right into his eyes. 'You know what happened.'

'I wasn't there.'

'You know what happened.' I resist pouring another drink, I think it would push me over the edge. 'And I don't want it to happen again.'

'He didn't know he had some crazy stalker student, Ellie.'

'But he knows about this one.'

He narrows his eyes, and scoffs quietly. He really does think this is all in my head.

'I need to find out, if he's sleeping with her. I just need to know.'

'And then what?'

'I'll deal with it.'

'How?'

Whatever it takes. That's how. But I don't tell *him* that. I don't tell him anything.

He reaches out and pulls me into his arms, and I willingly

fall against him. I'm too tired to talk any more, too exhausted to think straight.

He kisses the top of my head, his fingers sliding into my hair and I hold onto him. My safety net, my rock. Without him I'd have fallen a long time ago. He saved me. He's *saving* me. Isn't he ...?

Chapter 31

As soon as I wake up, in a bed that isn't mine, I panic. I regret staying out all night, what am I going to tell Michael? And then I remember. He's going to Cardiff next week. Without me. With Ava?

I look at Liam, still asleep beside me, and I slip carefully out of bed, go into the bathroom. I don't want to wake him yet. I need some time alone to think. Did I really ask him to get hold of a truth drug for me? Have I been watching too many movies? Looked at too many websites that are filling my head with outlandish ideas?

Looking in the mirror I see a woman I barely recognize staring back at me. I'm struggling to know who I am anymore, and there are times when I'm truly scared of what I'm capable of. And times when I know it's those moments that give me the strength I need to get through this. To fight for my husband. I *know* what I'm capable of. I know what I've done, and I survived, didn't I? Even if my baby didn't.

I quickly brush my teeth before going back into the bedroom. I don't even know what time it is, but it's daylight outside so it can't be that early, and then I glance at the clock and I see it's just gone six. It's very early. But I wake early a lot these days, that's what happens when you have a lot on your mind.

Sitting down on the edge of the bed I reach for my phone. I need to check where Michael is. He's at home. Of course he's at home, it's six in the morning. And he's made a call, to that number, to Ava. Late last night, he spoke to Ava. Because he realized I'd gone? Why didn't he call *me*? Didn't he care where I was? Didn't he fucking *miss* me? And then I double check his tracker history. He went out last night, too. Just after he made that call, he went out, to that address in Chester-le-Street. He went to *her*. He came home an hour later. And he still didn't care that I wasn't there?

Everything from anger to a crushing sadness fills my gut, tears streaming down my face, I want this to end, so badly it hurts. It kills me.

'Put it down, Ellie.'

I quickly wipe my eyes with the back of my hand, put the phone down on the bedside table. 'He went out. Last night. He called her, and then he went out.' I turn around, I look at Liam, another wave of sadness washing over me so fast I almost can't breathe. 'Why didn't he call *me*? I'm his wife ...' I drop my head, let those tears fall again, I can't stop them.

'Hey, come on.'

Liam tucks a finger under my chin, tilts my head up so I look at him. His eyes are kind, it's almost like he's forgotten how much of a crazy person I was last night. How desperate I've become. That's why I need him, to pull me back. To keep me this side of sane.

253

'Listen, Ellie, if Michael *is* having some kind of affair with this student, are you really going to forgive him?'

'Would he forgive *you*, Liam, if he knew you were sleeping with *me?*'

It's a mess. It's a god awful, complicated mess. Secrets and lies, betrayal and paranoia, they're all part of our everyday lives, now. There's no trust anymore. We've dug ourselves so deep into this pit of deceit we can't see a way out. There's so much we can't come back from.

I need to go home. I need to see Michael. I need to talk to him, and this time I'll make him listen. We can't go on like this, we can't, it's destroying everything around us. But Liam's pulling me back, towards that beautiful bubble we've created. Is there time? I need to see Michael ...

He pushes me down onto my back, gently nudges my legs apart, his hand trailing up the side of my body as he pushes inside me, and I don't fight it. I don't *want* to fight it. It's like a shot of calm, an injection of peace. When he's inside me I can think straight. I become the woman I want to be instead of the woman I've become, so I'm never going to fight this. Instead I close my eyes, arch my back, let him take my hand and push my arm above my head, my fingers gripping his as we make love slowly. He's flooding me with that calmness, it's like everything's running in slow motion, he's giving me time to catch my breath. And I don't even realize that I'm crying until I feel him kiss the tears away, feel his lips damp against my skin. He's telling me it's okay, everything's going to be okay, but it isn't. It can't be, not when we're surrounded by so many lies. So many secrets. So much betrayal. Nothing's okay. Maybe it never was. The lies started so long ago. That perfect life I thought I'd lived with Michael, it wasn't perfect at all. Not really. Even then I was lying to him.

The sex is over now, but Liam's hand still holds onto mine, and as I turn onto my side, as I face him, I remember those peaceful Saturday mornings when Michael and I would lie in bed like this in a post-sex bubble of happiness. I remember when he used to make me feel like the most beautiful woman in the world; his special girl, that's what he used to call me. Now I feel nothing but an emptiness that only Liam can fill. He makes me feel everything Michael doesn't. And that breaks my heart, but if I give this man up I risk losing myself completely. I can't afford to do that.

'I should go, soon,' I whisper, running my fingertips lightly over his jaw line, the roughness of his beard sending tiny shivers shooting up my spine.

He takes my hand and brings it to his mouth, kissing it gently, his eyes locking on mine. 'I used to pray that you and Michael wouldn't last.'

His words don't shock me as much as they should. Not after what he told me last night. Things he obviously meant. While I was asking him to smuggle me truth serums from his laboratory, he was telling me he loved me. That he'd always loved me. That he'd only married Keeley to distract himself from *me*.

I'm not that special, Liam. I'm really not that special.

'I'm not proud of it, but that's how I felt. I wanted something to come between you, to split you up, tear you apart, but believe me, Ellie, what happened – I wouldn't have wished *that*. Not that.'

I smile weakly and lean in to kiss him, let him pull me back into his arms, I feel safe there. But I can't stay here. I need to go.

I pull away from him and slide out of bed. I start to get dressed and he doesn't stop me. He knows the score. He can tell me he loves me a hundred times, it won't change anything. I love Michael, Liam's just my escape. My respite. My support. That's all he *can* be. And he knows that.

'Are you going to be all right?' he asks as I reach for my phone and slip it into my pocket.

'I'll be fine.' I try to give him a more convincing smile, let him know I'm really not that crazy. 'Liam, really, I'll be fine. I'll call you.'

'Ellie?'

I turn around, wait for him to come to me. He looks concerned. Worried. He needn't be, I'm okay now.

'You're not going to do anything stupid, are you?'

I frown. 'Like what?'

'I don't know. It's just, last night you were talking truth drugs and ...'

'And you were telling me you loved me. You changed the game, Liam.'

'This isn't a game, Ellie.'

I look at him, up into his grey eyes. 'I know.'

*

He's in the kitchen, when I get home, drinking tea and reading his newspaper like it's just another ordinary day.

The Wife

He looks up from his paper, his expression almost impassive, although there's a hint of a slightly puzzled frown there too.

'You've been out early.'

'I've been out all night, Michael.'

He puts down his paper and takes off his reading glasses. 'What do you mean, you've been out all night?'

'You really didn't know?'

'Where the fuck have you been, Ellie?'

No. No, he doesn't get to sit there and lecture *me*. That isn't happening. But at the same time, he can't find out that I know he went out too. He'd ask questions, and I can't have that; I'm not handing him an excuse to become suspicious of me. He can't ever find out I'm tracking him, I need to know where he is at all times. I don't have my proof yet.

'Where were *you*, Michael? If you slept in our bed, how could you not know ...?'

'I slept in the spare room.'

That throws me slightly, but it also explains how he could easily have missed the fact I wasn't home last night. The way we are, the lengths he goes to in order to avoid being with me, he wouldn't have bothered checking to see if I was in bed. He would've just assumed that I was.

'Why?' I whisper, because I'm scared now, that it's come to this, that point where he doesn't even want to share a bed with me. After coming home from seeing *her*? It's like another piece of that already fragile world I'm trying desperately to hold onto is crumbling around me.

'I went out, Ellie. Last night. I just – I needed some air,

that's all. I went out for a drink, a walk, to clear my head. And when I came back I assumed you'd already gone to bed and I didn't want to disturb you, so, I slept in the spare room.'

I stare down at my feet. He's lying to me. I know where he went, and he's lying. Again.

I try not to let the mess of emotions swirling around inside of me take hold, but it's hard. Almost too hard. And then I raise my head, I need to look at him now. 'It's happening again, isn't it?'

He frowns, but then his expression changes, becomes colder. 'No. Don't do this, Ellie. Don't go there.'

'Where, Michael? Don't go *where*? I mean, if *you* can't see the signs ...'

He gets up, sending his chair toppling backwards. 'What fucking signs, Ellie? Jesus, are we really going over this again?'

'Where did you go, when you went out last night? Where did you *go*? Did you go to *her*?'

He's confused now, but there's something there in his eyes, something he can't hide.

'To who? What the hell are you talking about?'

'Did you go to *her*? To Ava ...?'

Lie to me now, Michael, come on. I'm waiting ...

'Ava? What's going on here, Ellie? Because, right now, you're making no fucking sense.'

He's pushing me. I didn't want to mention her name, I didn't want to do that, but he's pushing me.

'Did you learn nothing? After everything that happened? You let them get too close, Michael. You let them get too close, give them too many signals ...'

'Ava is a student, Ellie.'

'I know.'

'How do you know *anything* about her?'

'I *don't* know anything about her. Apart from the fact you're letting her get too close. And when they get too close ...'

He shakes his head. He thinks I'm being irrational, I can see it in his eyes. He's going to make it sound like I'm imagining all kinds of shit that doesn't exist, like my crazy, mixed-up, over-emotional mind is making me see things that aren't there.

'I don't know how you even know about Ava – I don't know how you know about any of my students, but whatever you think is going on, you're imagining it. We've been here before, Ellie, it's all in your fucking head. I didn't encourage anyone, I didn't lead anyone on. And *nothing* is happening again. Okay?'

See? I knew he was going to do that. To think that. Because he assumes I'm nothing more than a messed-up wreck now. Too damaged. Too broken.

'Ava is one of the students I'm mentoring. That's all.'

'That's all *she* was too, Michael. The woman who kicked our baby out of me, the woman who killed our child. You were mentoring *her*, too.'

His eyes are fixed on mine, and even though I'm sure I see a brief flicker of sadness in them, his expression is mostly one of pity. He's constantly frustrated with me these days, but he just needs to know that I'm doing this to save *us*, he needs to realize that.

'Do you understand how dangerous your behaviour is becoming, Ellie?'

No, Michael, what you're *doing is dangerous, I'm just trying to keep us safe.*

'If you don't let this go ...' He turns away from me, rakes a hand through his hair before he turns back to face me. 'You need to let it go. Now. For all our sakes.'

There's something else in his expression now – fear? Panic?

Are you nervous, Michael? Of what I might know? What I've already found out?

'What exactly do you think is going on, Ellie?'

'I don't know, Michael.'

He holds my stare for a second or two before he laughs quietly, he's dismissing me as crazy again. 'No, you *don't* know.'

'Then tell me.'

'It's none of your business.' His eyes harden, he's looking right into me, and I feel my stomach contract with a new type of fear. Something darker. Something I can't explain. '*None* of your business.'

He's my husband. Everything he does is my business, but before I can tell him that he's left the room. Left me alone.

He goes upstairs, I hear him, just one flight this time. He hasn't gone up to his office, yet.

I stay rooted to the spot, I can't move. The room feels like it's spinning and I reach out to grasp the counter behind me, to steady myself. I can't remember if I've eaten today. I can't remember the last time I ate at all, I don't have much of an appetite anymore. Eating isn't high on my list of priorities, there are more important things to think about. But I need a drink, and I turn around and reach for the whisky on the counter. I fetch a glass from the cupboard, pour out a large measure and drink it down in one mouthful. The feeling of calm that spreads through me is instant, flooding my body and I close my eyes and breathe in deeply. Exhale slowly. I'm calm. I'm okay.

'Ellie?'

I open my eyes. Michael's standing in the doorway. He seems calmer now too. His eyes don't seem as cold.

'I'm going to spend the weekend at a hotel.'

I frown. I don't understand ... 'A hotel?'

'I fly to Cardiff on Sunday evening, so ... I've booked myself into one of the hotels at the airport. I think we could both do with some space, don't you?'

How much more space does he need? He couldn't be any further away and now he's walking away, again. Like he always does. He walks away, he leaves me alone, and he still doesn't get how much that hurts me.

'We both need some time, Ellie. To think.'

About what, Michael? About her? Ava? About how you're going to leave me?

'And when I get back ...'

He trails off, and slides his hands into his pockets. I feel sick, I feel like everything's falling apart, like I'm losing him too quickly, and the room, it's spinning again.

He eyes meet mine, and I reach behind me for the counter, gripping it tight. If I let go I'll fall, I know I will.

'When I get back, if things haven't changed – if *you* haven't changed, Ellie, then I think it's best if I move out. For a while.'

I feel my knees give way beneath me, feel them weaken and I grip the counter tighter. I will the room to stop spinning.

'I've done everything I can, to help you. I've tried, to help you ...'

Have you, Michael? Really?

'I did my best to make this all go away, but you refuse to leave it alone. And this is the last time I'm going to tell you this, because I'm tired. I'm tired of fighting this, of fighting *you* ...'

'I'm not fighting, Michael.'

'You are. You're fighting against everything I told you ... Everything I tell you.' He looks away again, and I see his shoulders tense up, hear him sigh heavily. 'Let it go, Ellie. Please. Because if you don't ... if you don't ...'

He doesn't need to finish that sentence, and I feel my stomach clench up, feel my heart start to beat so fast it hurts. He's slipping away from me and I'm scared. I'm so fucking scared.

I watch as he turns and walks away, and again I can't move. It's like I'm frozen; paralyzed. Have I just lost my husband? Have I given him, to *her*? Has he been using my behaviour as an excuse, to give himself a reason to leave me? A reason for him to feel better about leaving me for his teenage distraction?

A wave of nausea rises up from my clenched stomach, so fast I only just manage to turn around in time to vomit into the sink.

I hear his car start up, but I keep my head down. I hear him drive away and I feel a mixture of pain, anger and sadness sweep over me, so intense it's suffocating. He's left me alone, again. He left me alone that night, and he promised he would never do that again. He promised he would never leave me alone again.

Sinking to the floor I sit back against the kitchen cabinets and look around the room. The silence is terrifying. This house, I'm growing to hate it, it's just a reminder of everything we almost had.

Everything we lost.

I've lost enough ...

Chapter 32

I sit at the kitchen table watching Liam as he makes breakfast. I had to call him. I didn't want to be alone last night, the fear is becoming too much to bear. I can't cope sometimes, when I'm alone here. Every creak, every random, harmless noise, they all remind me of that night. They all bring back memories, cause those images I've tried to push aside to surge forward again. They make me realize that what happened, it's never going to go away. If I'm alone I can't cope with that realization. If Liam's with me, I'm okay. I can manage.

'Here. You need to eat something.'

He places a plate of scrambled eggs down in front of me. 'I'm not hungry.'

'I don't care. You're losing weight, so you're obviously not eating. And I'm not going to stand around and watch you make yourself ill.'

Michael hasn't noticed I've lost weight. Because Michael doesn't notice anything anymore. He chooses to ignore instead. To bury his head in the sand. He chooses distractions.

'I'll eat when I'm hungry.'

'Stop acting like a petulant child, Ellie, and just eat something. If not for yourself then do it for me.'

I scoop up a forkful of egg and swallow them down, but I'm resisting the food so much it almost sticks in my throat. It takes a mouthful of tea to dislodge it.

'I thought it might be nice to have a walk along the river this morning.'

I look at him as he joins me at the table; as he sits back and drinks his tea. He's made himself at home, but then, this place was always his second home anyway. He's always been too close. 'Okay.'

He looks at the plate of eggs in front of me. 'Eat some more, Ellie.'

He's talking to me like I'm a child, and I don't want that from him. He's supposed to make me feel like the woman I need to be, not some weak, pathetic person who needs to be looked after.

I eat a little more of the scrambled egg before pushing the plate away. That was enough, I don't need too much food. It upsets my stomach.

'While we're down by the river we could have some lunch. The weather's looking okay, we could sit outside.'

I pick up my plate and take it over to the sink.

'Ellie? Did you hear what I said?'

I turn around and stand with my back against the counter as he gets up and comes over to me. 'Our first date was a walk, down by the river.' I look up into his eyes. Am I pushing *him* away, too? 'Mine and Michael's. That was the night I knew I was in love with him.'

Liam drops his head and backs away from me. But he doesn't say anything. He remains impassive. Stays silent. And then he looks up at me and I realize how much I need this man. If I push him away I'm left with nothing. I really am alone.

'I'm sorry, Liam.'

He comes back over to me. He tucks a finger under my chin and tilts my head up, kissing me firmly on the mouth, forcing my lips apart with his. I reach out and grasp his t-shirt, pulling him against me, the kiss deepening, his mouth pressing harder against mine as he pushes me up onto the counter. He knows what I need, he knows how to fix me. At least, for now. He knows.

He's inside me. I feel him, invading me. But I want him there. I wrap my legs around him and lose myself in sex that means nothing and everything. I hold onto him, rest my chin on his shoulder as he thrusts into me, my eyes fixed on a photograph of me and Michael on the dresser. Me and Michael. Happy. In love. My husband's bright, beautiful smile lighting up his handsome face as he looks at me. He loved me then. He'll love me again.

I close my eyes, dig my fingernails into Liam's back as he comes, and I try to drag myself back to where I need to be – in the moment. I need to feel that release, that's why Liam's here.

I take his hand, I put it between my legs and I look at him as he touches me. I stare into his eyes as he brings me to a slow, calm climax, and all the time I don't take my eyes off him. It's intense, yet, at the same time, I'm not really sure what I'm feeling. There are so many parts of me that are still numb. Maybe he can't fix all of me.

He pulls his hand away and steps back from me, turns around and walks away. He senses I'm not in the mood for anything more than what he's given me. He knows me, better than Michael does. He knows me, and he knows he's done what he needs to do.

He leaves the kitchen and heads upstairs. I slide down from the counter, go over to the dresser, picking up that photograph of Michael and me. I struggle to remember those happy times, even though they far outnumber the dark ones we're so used to now.

Putting the photograph down I open the top drawer and reach inside, to the very back of it, feeling around until I find what I'm looking for. Another crutch. Another thing I need to help me get through each day.

I take the bottle over to the sink and pour myself a glass of water, swallowing down two of the pills, closing my eyes as they slide effortlessly down my throat.

'What've you just taken?'

I spin around, I hadn't heard him come back downstairs. 'Ellie?'

'They're for anxiety. They're herbal, nothing dangerous.'

He strides over to me, takes the bottle from my hand and looks at the label. 'Were these prescribed by your doctor?'

I walk over to the window, wrapping my arms around myself as I look outside. The sun's already high in the sky, casting shadows over the garden, making everything look picturesque and pretty. The garden I should have been sitting in, reading a book while my baby lay beside me, shielded from the spring sunshine. Sleeping.

'Ellie? Where did you get these?'

'I bought them online.' I turn around to face him. 'They're just herbal, Liam.'

'Jesus Christ ...'

'It's nothing sinister. They help me cope with being here alone, that's all. You know how hard it is for me to be in this house on my own.'

'You're not *on* your own, are you? *I'm* here.' He shoves the pills into his pocket. 'You think I don't know what these are, Ellie? I work in pharmaceuticals, for Christ's sake, I know this shit. You're done with these.'

I'm not going to argue with him. I should've been more careful, knowing he was here.

He comes over to me, and reaches out to touch my cheek. He smiles, and I smile too. I feel better when he's here, but when he isn't, I need something else to get me through each day, because I feel like they're all gradually becoming darker; like the world is slowly closing in around me, and I can't face that alone. I need something to keep me strong, to help me do what I need to do to get me and Michael back to where we need to be. Because what I might have to do in order to achieve that ... I need that strength.

'Go get dressed and we'll go for that walk. Okay?'

*

It's a beautiful day in Durham City. We've taken a walk through the busy centre of town, looked in the shops, visited the cathedral. Liam knows it's a place that gives me peace.

Just standing outside, looking up at it, I instantly feel a rush of calm, even though I know it's only temporary. Like sex with Liam. Temporary rushes of calm. I'm taking them all.

He held my hand, as we stood outside the cathedral. We shouldn't show any signs of affection when we're out in public, especially when we're here in Durham, there are too many people who know us. Our secret could become exposed, but his touch was discreet. He slid his hand into mine and he squeezed it tight, for the briefest of seconds, just long enough for him to let me know he was there. He was with me.

Now we're down by the river, sitting on a row of stone steps that lead down to the water, watching the rowers glide elegantly across it, their coordinated strokes mesmerizing as they push their boats along in a seemingly effortless motion. The cruiser is out today too, chugging up and down the River Wear, its outdoor deck full of people taking in the views of the cathedral and castle. It's a peaceful, beautiful day. But there's nothing peaceful or beautiful about my world now. My husband is in a hotel, because he can't live with me. My marriage is broken, because he can't leave his distraction alone. I'm lonely, but determined not to stay this way. Each day I try to summon up a new charge of energy, a new reason to climb out of bed and keep going, because there have been times when carrying on wasn't something I wanted to do. But then I think of Michael. And Ava. Of what I need to get back, no matter what. I *have* a reason to climb out of bed each morning. I have every fucking reason.

'What if he doesn't come home?' I'm not sure I meant to say those words out loud, I was thinking them. But they're out there now.

Liam picks up a stone and tosses it into the water, and I watch as it skims off the surface, bumping over the water in short, sharp hops before disappearing from view.

'Do you want him to?'

He looks at me, and I frown. 'Do I want him to come home? Of course I do.'

Liam turns his head away from me, picks up another stone, tossing that one into the water too. 'Did he give you an ultimatum?'

'What do you mean?'

He looks at me again. 'You know what I mean, Ellie.'

I start twisting my wedding band around my finger. 'He wants me to move on.' I shrug. 'It's all he's ever wanted me to do.'

'So why don't you just do that? If you love him that much, why *don't* you just let it go?'

'Because it's not that simple.'

'Isn't it? You went through a lot, Ellie, there's no question of that, but sometimes moving on is the best way to deal with it.'

'It isn't that simple,' I repeat.

He frowns, he doesn't understand. Nobody understands. 'Why not? I mean, if you're still finding it that hard to deal with, why not go back to counselling?'

'More counselling isn't going to do any good, Liam. Believe me.'

His eyes lock on mine, and I feel a cold shiver tear up my spine, despite the warm sunshine on my back.

'We could leave here, Ellie. Me and you, we could just walk away. Leave all this shit behind. We could start again.'

I look down at my fingers still fiddling with my wedding band. 'You knew the score, Liam.'

'I love you, Ellie ...'

I raise my gaze, hold his stare. 'You knew the score, when we started sleeping together. Don't make this into something else.'

He looks out ahead of him, clasping his hands together between his knees. 'Michael was my best friend. From the day we met, back in our university days, I knew he was going to be in my life for a long time. He was like a brother to me, yet the second I saw him with you ...' He turns his head to face me, his eyes boring into mine, 'I hated him.'

I swallow hard. He doesn't mean that. He doesn't. 'You don't hate him, Liam.'

He stares down at his clasped hands. 'Maybe hate's the wrong word. I resented him. I resented *you*, for choosing him.'

'I didn't *choose* him ...'

'What made you want him, and not want me? What made *him* so different?'

I don't want to talk about this. I don't *need* this. 'It was just timing, Liam.'

He stares out ahead of him again, and I'm not sure what's happening here. I'm confused. Those pills I took this morning, they're not working, they aren't easing my anxiety, they're not helping me cope.

'All those years, I resented him. For having you.'

It never felt that way. I never knew *he* felt that way.

'We can all put on an act, Ellie.' He turns to look at me. 'Can't we?'

Chapter 33

I pull the car into the parking space and turn off the engine. Yesterday's sunshine has given way to a cloudier Sunday, the grey sky scattered with heavy dark cloud. Rain's threatening. Heavy showers are forecast. A storm could even be on the way.

I sit back in my seat and take out my phone. I'm checking Michael's here, in the hotel. It wasn't hard to find out where he was staying, given that I'm tracking his every move. And now I need to know if she's here, too. If he's taking *her* to Cardiff. I need to know.

I'm giving him the space he so badly seems to want, but I'm not leaving him alone. He thinks it isn't my business, that Ava isn't my business, he thinks I don't need to know what's going on. He's wrong.

I slip my phone into my pocket and get out of the car, locking it before I make my way inside. I won't let him see me, of course, but I need to see *him*. I need to know if he's alone, or if she's here with him. Is that why he really wanted to spend the weekend at a hotel? Maybe he isn't taking her with him, maybe he just wanted some time alone with her before he had to go. My stomach tightens as a barrage of yet more irrational thoughts and theories flood my brain, they're relentless. Always nagging away at the back of my mind, giving me reason to think the worst. Because the worst could be happening.

It's busy inside the hotel's reception area, and that gives me a chance to slip by unnoticed and find a seat that gives me a good enough view of the lifts and the entrance. I can also see the corridor that leads down to the bar and restaurants. If he's still in the hotel, which the tracker tells me he is, then I'll see him, if he comes by here. And I could be here for hours, I don't care. I've brought work, magazines, I'll be fine. I can wait.

I settle back in my chair and look outside, up at the rapidly darkening sky. I'm sure I can hear a rumble of thunder some-where in the distance; it looks like that storm might be coming. But it doesn't seem to be bothering everyone outside, not those heading the short distance to the airport anyway, drag-ging their luggage, and in some cases their kids, behind them. A lot of them will be heading off to sunnier places, holidays. I idly wonder if any of them are travelling to Spain. A country Michael and I loved. Is he planning to take *her* there one day?

I snap out of those thoughts, bring my attention back to the hotel foyer. I can't afford to lose concentration, I don't want to miss him. I pull out a file from my bag, start skim-ming over the notes from a meeting Carmen and I had last week regarding the spa becoming a wedding venue, but it's nothing more than a cover, something to make it look like I'm just another businessperson. This hotel will be full of them. It's easy to blend in here.

My phone vibrating in my pocket distracts me, and I hurriedly pull it out, it might be an alert. Is Michael making a call? No. It's nothing. Just a message from my network provider, telling me about some deal or other. I'm not interested. I log onto the tracker app instead, check to see if I've missed anything. Liam distracted me a little too much yesterday. I'm still confused by his talk of walking away – of leaving Michael, for him. Why would I do that?

My heart leaps into my mouth as I look closely at Michael's call log. I did miss something. A call was made to him, from *her*. From Ava. Just an hour ago; it must've happened while I was driving here. She called him.

I reach into my bag for the headphones I carry around with me, slipping them on to play back that call, my skin prickling as her voice fills my head. A soft voice. A local accent. She wants to see him, sorry, *needs* to see him. I need him too, but he has no time for me. He has time for *her*.

He tells her to come here, to the hotel. She asks him why he's in a hotel, but he doesn't tell her the real reason. He makes something up about it being more convenient for his flight later today. He's lying. She tells him, again, that she needs to see him. He instructs her to meet him outside the bar across the way from reception, and I glance outside to the bar opposite. That storm I thought was coming seems to have given way to a brighter spell, the sun's out now. People are starting to drift out from the bar to the tables outside, and I crane my neck to see if Michael's one of them. If *she's* one of them. Is she here yet?

It's a quick conversation. They arrange to meet and end the call. I feel like I've been kicked in the gut. I keep the phone in my hand, I don't want to miss anything else, and it's just seconds before it starts vibrating again. I've turned it to silent, I don't want to draw any unnecessary attention to myself.

Looking down at the screen I see Liam's number flash up, and I don't want to answer it, but I do. He'll only keep calling if I ignore him.

'Where *are* you, Ellie?'

'Out. I'm busy going over some notes from a meeting me and Carmen had last week.'

'You couldn't do that at home?'

'I needed to get out of the house.'

He stayed over again, last night, because I wanted him to. But today I needed some space, so when he arranged to meet friends for lunch at the pub, I was relieved. I was hoping he'd stay out longer, not notice I was gone until later.

'Are you going to tell me where you are?'

I look back out of the window, I don't want to miss Michael. I don't want to miss Ava. 'Are you keeping tabs on me?'

'It's *you* who's the expert at that, remember?'

I say nothing, I don't offer a response. And then I hear him sigh down the line. He's realized he shouldn't have said that, even if it's true.

'I'm sorry, okay? I just don't want you doing anything stupid.'

'I'm not doing anything stupid.' I quickly glance around me, making sure I'm not missing anything. There are so many people milling about, I don't want Michael to slip by unnoticed. 'I'll be home soon. I promise.'

I end the call, put the phone down on the table in front

of me and I look outside again. There's a small round court-yard separating the reception area where I'm sitting from the bar opposite, but it's still close enough for me to make people out. To see faces.

My phone vibrates again. It's Liam, again, but this time I ignore it, because I can see her now, walking across the circular courtyard, her head down, arms wrapped around herself as she makes her way to the bar. My heart's hammering so hard as I look for Michael. He told her he'd meet her outside, and then I see him too, coming out of the bar. I see him smile at her, even from this far away I can see his smile. See her return it. He reaches out and touches her arm, guiding her to a table outside and I watch as she sits down; watch as he asks her something. I'm guessing it's what she'd like to drink because seconds later he goes back inside. It's all I can do not to go out there, to confront her. I was all ready to do that not so long ago, and I didn't have half as much evidence as I do now. Now I'm almost one hundred per cent certain this is an affair. This is his secret. His distraction. And yes, I have my own secret, my own distraction, but that means nothing. My secret isn't dangerous. My distraction is harmless.

I watch as Michael comes back outside, places the drinks on the table and sits down beside her. She starts talking before he's even taken his seat, and he places a hand on her arm and says something to her that silences her. She bows her head, looks down at the table. Michael's still talking. He still has his hand on her arm.

My stomach twists up into a tight knot. It hurts, but I can't tear my eyes away from my husband. From her. From the two of them together.

Ava looks at him again, and I move my head a little, to see if I can get a better view. She's smiling now. So is he. The liar. The cheat. His betrayal stings, it rips through me like a knife tearing at my skin.

And then I sense someone approaching my table, and my head snaps around as they sit down opposite me. It's Liam.

'How did you know where I was?'

'It doesn't take a genius to work it out, Ellie. You told me Michael was staying at an airport hotel and this is one we've both used before, so call it a lucky guess. The way you've been acting lately, the way you've been talking – I knew this was where you'd be. And your car's in the car park. But you need to come home now, okay?'

I turn my head to look back outside. He's still there, with Ava. My husband, and his distraction.

'He's over there.'

I'm guessing Liam follows my gaze, but he doesn't say anything, not at first.

'He's with *her*.'

'Come home, Ellie.'

I shake my head. 'I'm not going anywhere, not until I find out whether he's taking her with him to Cardiff or not.'

'And if he is? What are you going to do, huh? Are you going to – what? Physically drag her away from him?'

'He's *my* husband, Liam.'

'For how much longer, Ellie?'

I turn to face him. Why would he say that? 'You think I'm

just going to stand here and watch while *she* takes my husband from me?'

'If he wants to leave, Ellie, he'll leave.'

'Why are you doing this?'

He grabs my hand and pulls me up out of my seat, giving me just enough time to grab my bag before he almost drags me out of the hotel, away from where Michael could see us. Back towards the car park.

'What the hell are you doing?'

'You need to leave this alone. Seriously. You need to walk away before you do something really stupid.'

I pull my arm back and then I stand still. He has no choice but to face me, to listen to me.

'You saw that, right? You saw him, with that girl. And you remember what happened, the last time a student got close to Michael?'

'This isn't *that*, Ellie! *Jesus!*'

'No, you're right, this *isn't* that. This is worse. Because he's *letting* this happen, he could stop it, this time, but instead he's encouraging it. And I'm not going through that again, I can't go through that again ...'

He takes my hand and pulls me into his arms. He holds me, and he's just trying to calm me down, I know that. But I *am* calm. I'm completely in control here, I know exactly what I'm doing.

'You know, maybe it really is time to let him go, Ellie. Maybe the only way you can let all of this go is to let *Michael* go.'

I pull back. I look at him.

'It's hurting you too much, baby. It's slowly killing you, and I've had enough of watching you go through this.'

The Wife

'You think I should leave him?'

He reaches out, gently trails his fingertips over my cheek, down over my neck, my collarbone, and I feel a shiver race up my spine. 'Before he leaves *you*,' he whispers as he leans right into me, his mouth so·close to my ear it almost touches it.

I grab hold of his wrist, pull his hand away from my face. 'He isn't going to leave me, Liam.'

He isn't going to get the chance ...

Chapter 34

'Come back to bed', he murmurs into my hair, his body pressed up against mine as I stand at the window, looking out over the garden.

I fall back against him, let his arm circle my waist. 'I need to get ready. I have to go to work, and so do you.'

I glance over at the clock on the wall as Liam kisses my neck, drops his hand to my hip. It's almost seven-thirty. Monday morning. Michael's in Cardiff now. Alone? I have no idea. Liam made me leave the hotel yesterday before I had a chance to see what happened between my husband and Ava. He may be alone, she may be with him, I don't know.

I lay my head against Liam's shoulder and stare back out at the garden. 'I should call him. I should call Michael.'

Liam's fingers sink into my flesh, and I feel his body stiffen behind mine. 'Why?'

'I want to know if he's okay. He didn't leave on the best of terms, but we've both calmed down now. I need to know if he's coming home.'

'Give him some space, Ellie.'

'He's in Cardiff. How much more space does he want?'

He slides a hand underneath my short nightdress, trails his fingers along my inner thigh. My widening my stance is nothing more than a reflex action.

'I need to talk to him, Liam.'

'No, you don't. Calling him is a mistake, Ellie. It makes you look needy. Let him come to *you*.'

'And what if he doesn't?'

He's touching me now, and I like it. He's calming me, and I reach behind me for his hand, feel his fingers slide between mine.

A beautiful inner peace floods me, and I squeeze his hand tight as my knees give way slightly. But I know he'd catch me if I fell.

'Let him come to *you*, Ellie,' he whispers, and I turn around in his arms, lean back against the glass door behind me. Maybe he's right. If I give Michael the space he needs, he'll come back to me. Maybe. I'm still not sure.

'I thought you wanted me to leave him? I thought you wanted *us* to leave here, together?'

'I do. I've wanted that for a long time.'

'You're his best friend, Liam.'

'And I'm fucking his wife ... Can you not see what's happening here, Ellie?'

I start to walk away, I'm not in the mood for a long conversation. I need to get to work. But he grabs my wrist, pulls me back around to face him.

'Can you not see the huge mess we're all in?'

He has no idea, of the mess we're in. He has no fucking idea.

'You're all kinds of messed-up, because you think your husband is sleeping with one of his students, yet you're sleeping with *me*.'

'And you know why I'm doing that.'

'So, it's okay for *you* to cheat on *him*, but if he does it to you that's wrong?'

'Why are you doing this? I don't understand ...'

He slips an arm around my waist, drops his hand to my bottom as he pushes me against him; as he kisses me, deep and dirty, I feel my stomach do a million tiny somersaults. I'm breathless, slowly being dragged under by this man, but I need to pull myself back. He's my distraction, nothing more. He's my best friend with a thousand benefits, but he can never be anything more than that. I love my husband.

'I love you, Ellie. *I* love you.'

'Michael loves me,' I whisper, and Liam kisses me again, he pushes me deeper under, and I may flail for a second or two but I'm not drowning.

'How can he love you? When he treats you the way he does? How can *you* really love *him* when you're here, with me?'

I shake my head, but he rests his palm against my cheek, he makes me look at him. Makes me look into his eyes. I feel like I'm drowning now. And then he comes even closer, his breath warm on my neck, his lips vibrating against my skin as he speaks.

'Maybe it's time to let go.'

He steps back from me, his eyes remaining fixed on mine for a couple more beats before he grabs his suit jacket from the back of a chair and shrugs it on. He drags a hand through his hair, grabs his car keys from the dresser and he turns to look at me. Dr Liam Kennedy. Tall. Handsome. So different to Michael. And I don't want to need him, but I do.

'Don't call him, Ellie. That really would be a mistake.'

Chapter 35

It's been good to have to place so much focus on work. I need to have something other than Liam to take my mind off Michael. Off *her*. The spa is busy so much of the time, and it's only going to get busier as we start to take on weddings. And the salons are all thriving. I have so many distractions ... Is that all Liam is? Just a distraction?

I'm behind reception in the Durham salon when I hear the door open, and I glance up, smiling, ready to greet another client. But it isn't a client. It's Michael.

'Hi.' He smiles a small smile, his hands in his pockets, a look on his face I can't read.

'Hi ... When did you get back?'

'A couple of hours ago. I dropped my stuff back at home, popped into work ... I rang the spa, to see if you were there, but Carmen said you were working from here today.'

'I am.' He's been home. Had he realized Liam stayed the weekend? With me? Had we left any trace of him there? No. We were careful. We're always careful. 'Did everything go okay? In Cardiff?'

Were you alone, Michael? Did you go there, alone?

'It was fine.' He shrugs. 'It was a guest lecture. I do that stuff day in, day out.'

Was she there, with you? Did she make the monotony seem that little bit easier to deal with? Your distraction?

'We need to talk, Ellie.'

My stomach sinks, my breath catching in my throat. Is this it? Is he going to tell me he's leaving me? Or is he coming back to me? Has time away really healed some of those wounds? Has it started to fix something?

'Okay.'

'Somewhere more private. How about we go to lunch? We could go to our restaurant. We haven't been there for a long time, have we?'

My stomach dips again. I know he's been there without me. I've been there without him, but I was alone. He wasn't.

'I'm not really hungry.'

'Liam says you haven't been eating ...'

'You've spoken to Liam?'

'I asked him to keep an eye on you, while I was away. I'm worried about you, Ellie.'

Liam never told me, that Michael had asked him to keep an eye on me. He never told me he'd even spoken to Michael before he went to Cardiff. Is *he* lying to me too?

'You shouldn't be. I'm fine. And I'm eating plenty, Liam shouldn't be telling you anything otherwise.'

'He's our friend. He cares about you.'

In ways you'll never know, Michael.

'Did he tell you anything else?'

'No. Just that ... that you're keeping yourself busy.'

I start to gather my things together, leave instructions with the salon manager about a delivery that's coming this afternoon, and then I leave. With Michael. We walk side by side, not touching each other, through the streets of Durham city, heading towards our restaurant. But it doesn't feel like our place anymore. It stopped being that the second I found out he'd taken someone else there.

'It's been a while, hasn't it? Since we came here.'

I look at Michael as he quickly scans the menu outside. But I don't say anything.

'Shall we go in?'

I nod and follow him into the restaurant. We're seated at a table by the window, which is nice, I like to people-watch sometimes. I like to imagine what's going on in the lives of others, it's another way of escaping my own.

We order drinks, tapas, bread and olives, and I look at my husband across the table as a hundred memories of previous visits here flood my brain. Happy memories. They're all tainted now.

'I'm not having an affair, Ellie.'

Liar.

'I didn't say you were.'

'You implied it.'

'Then I'm sorry.' I'm not.

He narrows his eyes as he looks at me. And I suddenly realize I haven't checked the tracker all morning. I knew he was flying home today, and yet, I didn't check to see where he really went after he landed at Newcastle airport. *Did* he go home? *Did* he go to the university? Call the spa? I need to check now. Before he starts talking.

'I won't be a minute,' I say, pushing my chair back and making my way to the toilets.

Once inside I lock myself in a cubicle and pull out my phone. I log onto the app, check his movements from the second he arrived back at the airport. He did go home. He did go to the university. He called the spa. Everything he told me he did, that was true. Has he seen *her*? If she wasn't with him, in Cardiff, has he seen her since he got back? She's one of his students, he could have seen her at work. He certainly hasn't called her today. She hasn't called him. Yet. I really need to be more vigilant. I've been spending too much time with Liam lately, I'm forgetting to check things as often as I should.

I go back into the restaurant, but I wait a second before I head back to our table. I'm watching Michael as he chats to one of the waitresses, a pretty red-head who can't be much older than eighteen or nineteen. She could be another one of his students, a lot of them work jobs like this. He could know her, or he could just be using his charm to flirt, he can't seem to stop himself from doing that. He certainly has her transfixed as he speaks, as he smiles at her. She laughs at something he says, and I feel sick, my stomach once more twisting itself up into a tight and painful knot.

Do you not see what you do, Michael? How you encourage them to come to you? Can you not see how dangerous that is?

I wait until she's finished placing our food and drinks down on the table and finally leaves before I make my way back to Michael.

He looks up as I sit down, and I reach for my glass of wine, taking a long sip.

'Is everything okay, Ellie?'

I look at him. And I feel sad and confused. I feel angry, that we've let ourselves become these people. 'Everything's fine. What did you want to talk about?'

He averts his gaze, starts fiddling with the napkin next to his plate. 'I think I should move out. Just for a while. I really think it's for the best.'

I don't know what to say. How to feel. Give him space, Liam said, and he'll come to me. But he isn't, is he? He isn't coming to me, he's leaving me.

'*Do* you? Think it's for the best? You think that's going to solve all our problems, you, walking away from them?'

'I'm not walking away from anything, Ellie ...'

'You are.'

'I'm not walking away. I'm giving us some space.'

'You've just *had* space, Michael.'

'I've had a couple of days. It isn't enough.'

His words floor me. They're like a knife to my heart, the hardest punch to my stomach. They hurt.

I keep my eyes on him, he isn't going to think I'm weak, I'm not letting that happen. I'm not weak, and I'm not losing this fight. I know he's still lying to me; telling me to my face that he isn't having an affair, that's just a smokescreen. He thinks by telling me that I'll believe him, I'll take his word. No. I'm not doing that. I can't stop him from leaving, if that's what he wants to do, but I *will* make sure I know where he is at all times. He isn't going to get away with this dangerous game he's playing. And *she* isn't going to win.

'Then go. If that's what you want.'

He frowns. What did he expect here? Did he think I'd break down in a wailing heap and beg him to stay? I *want* him to stay. I'm not begging him. But I *am* going to confront him, with the truth. When I finally get it. I'll make him realize the mistake he made; the mistake *she's* making. And mistakes have to be paid for.

'I really do think it's for the best, Ellie. I don't think either of us has really had time to deal with what happened, not properly. I'm not sure we've let the enormity of it all sink in, not yet, and I don't want it to pull us apart, I really don't – but I feel like that's what it's doing.'

'What *I'm* doing?'

'I didn't say that. Don't put words in my mouth. What we went through, it was incredibly difficult, we faced something no couple should ever have to face, but instead of time healing, I think it's only made things worse.'

No, Michael, you've done that. You've made things worse, by your reckless actions. Your betrayal. Your inability to see that you're encouraging history to repeat itself.

'Where will you go?'

'A friend is going to let me stay with them.'

'A friend? Who?'

'You don't know them. Just someone I used to go to college with.'

I feel my stomach twist up again, his words – his lies, stabbing at my heart. A friend I don't know? I know all of his friends. He knows all of mine.

You're staying with her, aren't you, Michael? Your distraction. Ava. You're going to her.

'This isn't forever, Ellie.'

I look at him. And I want to believe him, I want to believe everything he tells me but I can't. I once trusted this man with every fibre of my being, but now I trust nobody. There are times I don't even trust myself.

'We *will* get through this.' He reaches across the table for my hand and I let him take it; let him squeeze it tight. 'I promise you, Ellie, we'll get through this.'

Will we?

He smiles. A smile that always used to make everything better. A smile that's now just masking the lies, hiding the truth ...

For better, for worse ...

Does he remember those wedding vows?

Do *I* ...?

Chapter 36

He wasn't angry with me. He was calm. Had he used that trip to Cardiff to think about things? Or had he let *her* persuade him that leaving me was the best thing to do? Is this the beginning of her end game? Is she building up to the point where she finally makes him leave, for good? That chance will never come. She can try, but I'll make sure it never happens. I need Michael. He needs me. End of story.

He's been gone for a couple of days now. Staying in a hotel in Durham, not with a friend like he told me he was.

More lies.

I've been keeping track, I'm still listening to his calls, and so far he hasn't spoken to *her*. Not over the phone, anyway. And he hasn't been to that house in Chester-le-Street. He's gone to work. The gym. Back to the hotel. But I keep watch, because I'll know if he goes to her. I'll know.

I feel fingers tighten around my wrist, feel Liam pull my arm back behind me, gently prising the phone from my hand, his other hand on my hip as he puts my phone down on the countertop.

'Enough, Ellie.'

I turn around, remove his hand from my hip and I look at him. Right into his eyes. I can't even remember asking him to come round, but I must've done. I must've needed him, for him to be here.

'I'll decide when it's enough, Liam. Not you.'

He edges past me, picks up my phone and slides it into his pocket. 'It's not healthy, what you're doing.'

He always did have an air of arrogance about him, something Michael never had. Arrogance. But with Liam, it was always there, in the background. I can see it now, more clearly than I ever could.

I reach for his pocket, for my phone, he doesn't get to take shit away from me, what am I? Some errant teenager he feels the need to punish? But he grabs my wrist, grasps it tight. He stops me from retrieving what's mine.

'Let go of me.'

He shakes his head, his eyes burning into mine. 'You know where he is. You're just torturing yourself now.'

I laugh, and I try to wrench my arm free of his grip but he's holding onto me too tightly. 'Who do you think you are? You have no right to take my things ...'

'He's asked me to make sure you're okay, did you know that?'

'Like he did when he was in Cardiff? Why didn't you tell me, huh? That you'd spoken to him?'

'There was no need to tell you. I didn't have to tell you anything just now, but sometimes I think you need to see the messed-up irony of this entire situation. Maybe then you'll think about ending it. All of it. Maybe then you'll think about moving on because it's time, Ellie. To move on.'

'With you?'

The corner of his mouth curls up into a smirk, and I narrow my eyes as I stare at him.

'I love you, Ellie, and I don't know how many more times I can tell you that before you finally start to believe it. I love you, I've loved you for so fucking long, I've wanted you, for so fucking long ...'

'Give me my phone,' I hiss, and I reach out with my other hand, which he knocks away, and I'm starting to feel anger rise up inside me now. It isn't his place to police me. He doesn't get to say what I can and can't do.

'Give me my fucking phone, Liam.'

'He's gone for a reason, Ellie. Do you get that yet?'

I slap him so hard I feel the vibrations race up my arm, it tingles with the force. And his grip on my wrist tightens as he turns his head back to me. I feel my throat tighten, I can't get any breath out, and then he pushes me back against the counter, his mouth crashing down onto mine in a kiss that does nothing to help loosen that breath. Until he breathes into me. Until his breath is my breath and I've got my fingers wound in his hair, my legs wrapped around his waist. He's inside me. He's fucking me, because this isn't making love, this isn't even sex, it's fucking. Hard. Frantic. Fucking. He's taking his shit out on me, I'm taking mine out on him, we're hurting each other, but that's fine. We both need this. And as he thrusts into me I slide my phone from his pocket, slip it into the drawer beside me, and then I pull my legs tighter around him, I make him come, and when he does he cries out, his loud, guttural groans merging with mine as we both climax in a flurry of pent up frustration, confusion, anger. I dig the heels of my stilettos into the small of his back. I want to cause him pain, because I'm angry with him. Because I need him. I scratch at his neck, nip his lip with my teeth as he kisses me, and in turn his fingers dig into my thighs, pressing so hard it hurts. And then, it's like the storm cloud has passed and a moment of calm descends. Only the sound of our breathing pierces the silence as he slides a hand around the back of my neck, pushing my head down so my forehead touches his. I feel his fingers in my hair, his other hand lightly stroking my thigh. It's over. Whatever that was, it's done.

'I'm sorry,' he whispers, and I take his face in my hands and I kiss him. 'I just hate seeing what this is doing to you, and I can stop it, Ellie. I can make it all stop.'

I look at him. I tilt my head to one side and I stare so deep into his eyes it makes me shiver. 'How?'

He cups my cheek in the palm of his hand, and he smiles slightly. He kisses me gently. 'You just need to trust me. Okay? You need to trust me.'

He reaches behind him, unhooks my ankles from around his waist and he lifts me down. Even though I'm wearing heels – high heels – I still have to look up at him, this tall and beautiful man. My best friend.

'I don't trust anyone, Liam.'

He tugs loosely at the neck of my shirt, his fingertips grazing the curve of my cleavage, his eyes never leaving mine. 'You should trust *me*.'

'Why?'

He smiles, and it's one that reaches his eyes but that means nothing. 'You ask too many questions, Ellie.'

And I get no answers. There are too many secrets still hiding in the shadows, too much I'm still not comfortable with. Too many things I'm still not willing to accept.

'I have to get to work,' he says, putting an end to that conversation, and I watch as he moves around the kitchen – the kitchen of a house that isn't his. It belongs to his best friend. To me. He's here because I want him here. But maybe he shouldn't be. What if Michael comes home? Finding Liam here wouldn't seem out of the ordinary, but if he caught us like this, together ...

'Liam?'

He turns around and smiles at me. 'Yeah?'

'What did you mean? You can make it all stop?'

He comes back over to me, slides a hand onto my hip and leans in to me, his mouth brushing that space just below my ear. 'I can make it all better, Ellie. I promise. All you have to do is trust me.'

I breathe in deeply as he pulls back from me; as he walks away, out of the kitchen into the hall and I exhale slowly as I hear the front door close behind him.

I don't trust anyone.

But I do want it to stop.

I want someone to make it all better.

But I think that someone has to be me.

Chapter 37

Today was a good day at work. The wedding venue project is moving along, and although we may not be ready to make the most of this summer's wedding season, we hope to be up and running in time for the winter, for those magical Christmas weddings. I want to help create a fairytale for others, even if my own marriage feels like it's crumbling around me.

I'm exhausted. It's been a long day and I'm ready for a bath, a take-away and a night in front of the TV. I don't want Liam here tonight. I've told him I need some time alone, and he wasn't happy. But he doesn't get to decide when we spend time together. I do. And tonight, I don't need him. Tonight, I'm okay with being alone.

I check the locks on the front door are all secure, and then I go around every window, every door in the rest of the house and I make sure they're all secure too. It's something I need to do before I can settle. Before I can feel safe.

I've just finished checking the house and poured myself a glass of wine when the doorbell rings. I told Liam I didn't want him here tonight, and I sigh heavily as I head out into the hall. But as I glance at the security monitor, I feel my heart skip a beat. It isn't Liam. It's Michael.

I quickly unlock the door, and as soon as it's open he pushes past me into the hall, he doesn't even look at me.

'Michael ...?'

I close the door, hurriedly redo all the locks and then I follow him into the kitchen.

'A fucking tracker, Ellie?'

It's like my blood's suddenly turned cold, freezing my veins. I feel sick, dizzy. How did he know? How did he find out?

'I mean, I knew there were things going on in your head, I knew you were acting irrationally ...'

'You wouldn't talk to me, Michael. You wouldn't tell me anything, wouldn't ...'

'So you fucking *tracked* me? You listened to my calls? *Jesus* ...!'

He drags a hand through his hair, turns his back to me and I have to hold onto the counter behind me to steady myself. Fear swamps me, I can't control this now, I don't know what to do.

'You're fucking ill, Ellie. You need help. And I can't give you that help, not anymore. I can't do *this*, anymore. I'm done.'

He turns away from me, starts to walk towards the door.

'I just needed to know that nothing was going on ...'

He swings back around, his eyes blazing. I've never seen him so angry. 'And my word should have been good enough. You can't just go around tracking people, invading their privacy ...'

'If you have nothing to hide ...'

'You really don't get this, do you? Are so you fucking deluded that you think there's anything out there that can make this scenario *right*?'

'How did you find out?'

'Your recent behaviour; the way you've been acting, the questions – that gave me every reason to think something was wrong.'

He still shouldn't have been able to find out so easily. I'm confused ...

'Did someone look at your phone?'

'It doesn't matter how I found out, Ellie. What matters is that my own *wife* put an app on my fucking phone, without my knowledge, to keep track of me. To record my calls. My own wife *spied* on me.'

'Who is she, Michael? Is that Ava? The girl in the lecture theatre. The same girl you met at the airport hotel ...'

'Jesus Christ ... You really have been following me, haven't you?'

'Who is she, Michael?'

He comes closer, so close he's up in my face, his voice nothing more than a hiss but I'm staying calm. I have to. I have no other choice.

'She's none of your fucking business.'

And then he steps back from me, backs off towards the door, he's leaving. I can't let him go, not like this.

'Michael ...'

'You need help, Ellie. Seriously. And until you get that help, I don't even want to talk to you. Just ... just get some help. Please.'

I can't move, my feet are stuck to the floor. I can't stop him from leaving. All I can do is listen helplessly as he unlocks the door. As his car drives off. Only then do my feet finally move and I run to the door, swinging it open, I need to stop him. But I'm too late, he's already out of the driveway. He's gone.

I slump back against the wall, take a second to let what's happened sink in before I go back inside. Relock the door. Before I call Liam. I need him now. I need him, to help make this better ...

*

'How did he find out?'

I'm sitting by the edge of the pool, looking down into the water, watching as the moonlight hits the surface, casting strange patterns up at the ceiling. I'm remembering that night. Remembering how it changed everything. I'm remembering what happened, in this room.

'I don't think that matters now, Ellie. Do you?'

'He was so angry.'

'He'd just found out his wife's been spying on him, how else did you think he'd react?'

I turn my head to face Liam. He's sitting with his back against the wall, his knees drawn up, drinking from a bottle of beer, his shirtsleeves rolled up to his elbows.

'I can't lose him, Liam.'

He throws back his head, closes his eyes and he sighs, a heavy, frustrated sigh. 'It might already be too late, Ellie. You've killed any trust he might have had left in you. You were listening in to his calls, for Christ's sake. Tracking his every fucking move, to him you're this crazy person he doesn't understand anymore.'

'I'm not crazy.'

I turn away from him, look back into the water. I reach down and I trail my fingers through it, disturbing the patterns the moonlight's still casting.

Another sigh from behind me, but I ignore it. I'm not crazy. I know something's going on, I know my husband has a secret he isn't willing to share. I know *she's* still around, I just can't prove it now. And that lack of control is unsettling me. I don't like it.

Pulling my hand out of the water I realize I haven't swam in this pool since that night. Before, we used to swim all the time. Me and Michael. It was a way of relaxing, for us. We loved having our own pool. Loved having sex in our own pool. But she destroyed all that. Our dream. Our fucking lives. She destroyed everything. That night destroyed everything.

I start to undress. I'm going to swim in my pool again. I'm going to do something I haven't done since before that night, I think getting back in the water is something I need to do.

'Ellie ...?'

I turn to look at Liam, and I smile. 'Are you going to join me?'

He hauls himself to his feet and comes over to me, pulling my naked body against his still-clothed one. 'I might.' He smiles back, and I laugh quietly. I let go of him and I back off towards the steps of the pool, lowering myself slowly down into the water. It's a little colder than I first anticipated, and I shiver slightly as my skin breaks out in goosebumps, but the second I start swimming the only feeling I have is one of freedom. As I glide through the water it feels like everything I don't want to think about is drifting away. I'm leaving it all behind, even if it's only a temporary feeling.

I stop at the far end of the pool and I watch as Liam swims towards me, his strong, toned body cutting through the water far faster than mine. Dr Liam Kennedy. My drug of choice. A bad addiction I should never have gone back to.

You made me do it, Michael. You made me run to him. You, my father, and all men like you. You all did this …

'I need to know, Liam.'

He stops in front of me, pushes his wet hair back off his face, his grey eyes staring deep into mine. 'Don't you know enough, Ellie?'

I shake my head and he drops a hand beneath the water, parting my legs, his thumb running gently over my inner thigh.

'Then do what I told you to do in the first place. Hire a private detective.'

I frown slightly. 'Won't he be more aware than ever now? Of being watched?'

He leans in closer to me, and I gasp as his fingers start playing with me, his mouth dropping warm, damp kisses all over my shoulder. 'So, hire a good one.'

'Because I have so many in my address book.'

He pushes his fingers inside me, and I bite down on my lip as his eyes lock on mine. 'I'll help you. Find a good one.'

I think this may be my only choice now. Hiring someone else to watch my husband. Someone who can get me evidence. Proof. Photographs. Someone who'll be able to follow him everywhere. Yes. I think I need to do this, Liam's right.

'Okay ...'

His face breaks into a grin, and he thrusts his fingers deeper into me before he yanks them out, swings me around. He pulls me back against him before entering me from behind, his hands on my hips keeping me where he needs me to be.

With him.

For now.

But everything has to come to an end, sometime ...

Chapter 38

'Here.' Liam slides a slip of paper towards me and I pick it up. I read the name and the number he's written down. 'Give him a call. Go talk to him.'

'How did you find one so quickly?'

'I'm good at seeking out the best. Of everything.' I let a small shiver run down my spine as I remember last night. Sex in the pool. Once. Twice. Wrong but incredible sex. 'If you're going to do this, you need to hire someone with a good track record. This guy has one of the best.'

'And you know that, how?'

'I told you to trust me, Ellie. So, just do that. Okay?'

I look down at the piece of paper in my hand. 'Do *you* think I should do this?' I look back up at him, and he shrugs.

'I'm not going to make that decision for you.' He stands at the side of the table I'm sitting at outside on the spa's Garden Room terrace, his hands in his pockets, his hair pushed back off his face. 'But, if you're hell bent on finding out the truth ...'

'All right. Maybe I will get in touch with him. See what he can do.'

It feels odd, that's all. Handing the control over to someone else. But I have no other option now.

'But, you know, if it was up to me ...'

I look at him. 'It's *not* up to you, though. Is it?'

'Just do whatever you have to do, Ellie. I need to get back to work.'

He starts to walk away. I'm not going after him. Instead, I look back down at the piece of paper in my hand. And then I feel him behind me, leaning over me; he hasn't gone anywhere.

'I forgot to say,' he murmurs, his hands on my shoulders, his mouth so close to my ear I can feel his breath on my neck. 'You look beautiful today.'

His fingers lightly brush the back of my neck as he pulls away from me and I turn my head to watch him walk away. He's leaving now. My escape. And I look down at the piece of paper again. I pull out my phone and I tap in the number Liam wrote down for me.

This is what it's come to, Michael.

I need to know, once and for all.

I can't do this alone now.

Not anymore.

*

It's hard, losing the control I once had. I want to call him – Michael. I want to speak to him, but Liam thinks that's a bad idea. He thinks I should leave him alone, for a while. He thinks that's best. But I'm struggling. I feel like I'm stumbling through every day, wondering what my husband's doing. Who he's with. That's why I had to get in touch with Karl. The private investigator. I met with him this afternoon, gave him all the information he needed to keep track of Michael. And I'm not proud, that I'm stooping to levels I never thought I was capable of, but I've been pushed too far. I need to finish this now.

Liam sits down on the chair by the fire. He's making himself at home, and I haven't stopped him. I don't want to be here alone, and Liam, he makes me feel safe.

'What if I'm wrong?'

Liam looks up and he frowns. 'Wrong? About what?'

'About Michael.'

He drops his gaze. 'You're not wrong.'

It's my turn to frown. 'How do you know? Liam? How do you *know*?'

He doesn't know. I can tell, the way he nervously drags his hand along the back of his neck, the way he doesn't look at me. He knows as much as I do.

'Don't do that.'

This time he does look up, his eyes hard. Cold. 'Do what?'

'Lie to me. I'm surrounded by enough lies, I don't need any more. Not from you.'

'You're not wrong, Ellie. About Michael.'

I shake my head, get up from the couch; I walk over to the window, folding my arms as I look outside, although there isn't a lot to see. It's dark. The only light out there is coming from the solar lights we have lining the driveway, and even they're a little dimmer tonight.

I feel him come up behind me, feel his arms wrap around my waist, pulling me back against him but I keep my eyes fixed on the darkness outside.

'It all adds up. What you've seen. The way he's been acting ...'

'Don't, Liam.'

He kisses the side of my neck and I shiver. I'm not in the mood for this, yet I don't push him away.

'He never deserved you, Ellie.'

I swing around, my eyes locking on his. 'And you do?'

'I won't hurt you.'

'Yeah, well, he made that promise too.'

I lower my eyes, but he tucks a finger under my chin, tilting my head back up. 'I won't break it.'

I shake my head again, knocking his hand away from my face. 'Promises always get broken, Liam. Vows always get broken.'

'Remember what I said, Ellie. We could leave all this behind. What I said before, I meant it. I can make this all go away, we can start again. You and me ...'

'Please, don't do this. Don't make this something it's not.'

'What happened, that almost killed you. Remember? *She* almost killed you, and Michael, he brought her to your door ...'

'It wasn't his fault ...'

'She came to you because of *him*, Ellie. And he must've encouraged her, somehow, he must have given her some kind of sign ...'

I push past him, walk away from him. I don't want to listen to this.

'How can you be so sure he *wasn't* sleeping with her? That something *hadn't* been going on?'

He wasn't saying these things before, why is he saying them now?

I stop. I turn around and face him. 'Michael told me nothing had gone on. He gave her no signs, he didn't encourage her.'

'And you believed him?'

I pause. Because I don't know if I believe what Michael told me. I don't know ...

'Do you believe him now?'

I back up against the wall, I'm too tired for this fight. 'This is different.'

'Is it? How? *How* is this different, Ellie? You have *no* idea what went on with this student and Michael before she showed up in your house acting all crazy. You know nothing, except what he told you.'

'She wasn't well, Liam.'

'What if he'd just driven her to that point, huh? Do you ever think about that?'

'He – he wouldn't do that ...'

'Because you know him so well, right?'

'Why are you doing this?'

'Because I care about you. I *love* you, Ellie. Does *he*?'

'He loves me.'

'Are you sure about that?'

'I'm not doing this ...'

I start to walk away but he grabs my arm, pushes me back against the wall. 'You know what he's like, what he's always been like. The way he piles on the charm, isn't afraid to be tactile, the flirting ...'

'It's all harmless, Liam. That's just who he is.'

'When that crazy bitch was kicking your baby out of you, was *that* harmless?'

'That wasn't his fault ...'

'She wouldn't have been there if it wasn't for him. She wouldn't have been here, in your home.'

I feel tears start to stream down my face. He's supposed to be the one keeping me safe, making me feel better, why is he doing this? Why is he hurting me?

'Don't, Liam, please ...'

'Let's go, Ellie. Let's get out of here, leave all this shit behind, what's left for you here now, huh?'

I feel something shift inside me, a kind of reset, kicking me into action and I push him away. I walk out of the room and into the hall, I don't need this crap.

'My businesses are here, Liam. My life is here, I'm not walking away. I'm not doing what Michael chose to do, I'm not turning my back on everything ...'

'Michael isn't here, Ellie. I am.'

I swing around to face him. I'm angry now, he isn't being fair. 'I don't love you, Liam.'

'Don't you?'

I narrow my eyes, I stare at him as he comes closer. 'No. I don't.'

He leans in to me and kisses my open mouth before stepping back. 'You need to face up to things, Ellie. You need to face up to the truth.'

The Wife

I watch as he picks up his jacket from the rack by the door and strides out without looking back.

I need to face up to the truth.

If I knew what that was ...

Chapter 39

'You've seen him, haven't you?'

I wait for Liam to answer me. I wait for him to lie to me, but I hope he won't.

'No, Ellie, I haven't. But I have spoken to him.'

I turn away from him and look out of the window. It's a grey day outside, weather to match my mood. 'What did he say?'

'We talked about football, a squash match we've got coming up ...'

'So, you *will* be seeing him, then?' I turn around, my eyes locking on his. 'At some point?'

'Ellie, I don't know. Okay? All of this, it feels like I'm losing him, too ...'

I laugh, I can't help it. 'This was never about *you*, Liam. What the hell do *you* care if you never see him again, huh? You told me you resented him, that you've resented him for years, because he had me ... You're not his friend. You never were, not really, or you wouldn't feel those things. You wouldn't *say* those things. You wouldn't want to take me from him ...'

'He doesn't deserve you, Ellie.'

'Did you tell him that? Did you tell him he didn't deserve me? Did you tell him how you really feel, about me?'

'Of course I fucking didn't. Jesus, what the hell is wrong with you?'

I laugh again. He really has to ask that? 'Did he say anything, about me?'

Liam looks away. I don't often come here, to his laboratories, but I was travelling through Newcastle, and I guess I needed to see him, even if all I've done since I got here is be defensive. Angry. I need someone to take my frustration out on, and Liam's my go-to person for that.

'He asked how you were. Asked me to make sure you're all right.'

I turn my head to look back out of the window. Out at the rain starting to fall from that gunmetal-grey sky. I don't know what to say. I'm not sleeping all that well, I'd rather lie awake and imagine what my husband's doing. Where he is. Who he's with. I'd rather torture myself than get the rest I need.

'Why don't I move in, Ellie. You shouldn't be on your own ...'

'I'm not ill, Liam.'

I don't like being alone in that house for too long, but I'm not sure I want Liam there permanently. It doesn't feel right, it feels like I'm giving up. Like I'm accepting that Michael's never coming back, and I can't do that. I'll never accept that. I can't give up.

'I don't want you to move in. I'm fine.'

'You hate being alone in that house.'

'I'm not there that often.'

That's true. I've started working later, avoiding going home until I have to. I even went out with Carmen and some of the girls from the spa a couple of nights ago, anything to keep me from going home too early.

'Ellie? Look at me.'

He's right beside me now. He's almost touching me, and I hate that I feel a weakness hit me whenever he's this near; the power he has over me – how did I let that happen? How did I let him be this person, the one thing I need to keep me from completely falling apart?

'Ellie?'

I slowly turn my head towards him, and I'm fighting it now. That power, that hold he has over me. I'm fighting it.

'I should go. I've got a meeting in Durham in an hour.'

He grabs hold of my wrist, forcing me to stay where I am. 'I used to watch him all the time, the way he'd act around other women, not caring that you were in the same room. That you could see what he was doing.'

'He wasn't doing anything, Liam. That's just who Michael is, you know that ...'

He bends down, lowers his mouth so it almost touches mine. 'Open your eyes, Ellie. See what's right in front of you.'

I shake my head. I try to tug my wrist free of his grip, but do I really want to leave?

My phone ringing suddenly distracts me, and I reach into my pocket, pull out my phone, and I look at the screen.

'It's Karl. I'm taking this.'

Liam lets go of me and I step away, holding my phone to my ear as I listen to what Karl has to tell me. And as he speaks I feel my heart start to race, my gut twist up into a knot.

I end the call and look over at Liam. He's leaning back against his desk, his arms folded, his expression impassive.

'He's got something. He wants to meet me ...'

Liam comes over, takes my hand, makes me look at him. 'What does he have?'

'He didn't say. Just that – that it might be important.'

'Are you meeting him now?'

I nod. And then I realize I need to call Carmen, tell her to take over the meeting we had planned for this afternoon. I won't be able to make it. I need to meet Karl, I need to know what he's got. What he's found out.

'Do you want me to come with you?'

Liam's right there in front of me but it sounds like he's miles away.

'Ellie?'

My mind snaps back into focus, and I look at him. 'Yes, I – I want you to come with me.' I need him there. I don't know what Karl's going to show me, I just know that I want Liam there.

'Okay. Come on, let's go.'

This time it's me who stops him from leaving. I grab his hand, make him stay where he is. 'Liam, I ... thank you. For being here. For listening to me.'

He takes my face in his hand and kisses me, his mouth warm against mine, and I fall against him. I let his arms hold me, his body shield me, he keeps me safe.

But I don't love him.

I don't ...

*

The rain's eased off as we head towards the coffee shop in the centre of Durham Karl asked us to meet him in. I don't even know how I managed to get here; my head was all over the place, imagining every scenario, anything that Karl could have found. Something I missed? Or something new? Why is this meeting so important? I've had updates from him before over the past few days, but so far he hasn't come up with anything concrete, nothing to prove that Michael is doing anything wrong. He's visited the pub with some of his university colleagues for lunch or after-work drinks and then he goes back to the hotel he's staying at. That's all that's happened, so far. He goes to work. He goes back to the hotel. And I don't know whether I'm frustrated, that he's doing nothing out of the ordinary, that he isn't seeing *her*, or whether I'm angry at myself for thinking he was capable of that. Of cheating. Have I really been making something out of nothing? *Could* I have been wrong?

That knot in my stomach twists tighter as we reach the coffee shop, and Liam reaches for my hand before we go in, squeezing it tight. I give him a small smile and I let him kiss me, a quick kiss. We shouldn't even be risking that, not here. But I need him to make me feel safe, because right now I feel anything but.

'It's going to be okay, Ellie.'

He can't know that. How can anything ever be okay again? After everything we've done. Everything we've said. Every secret we've kept. Every lie we've told ...

I turn away and walk inside, scanning the room until I find Karl over in the corner of the coffee shop, his laptop open in front of him.

My heart's beating wild and fast as we make our way over to him, and while the bigger part of me desperately needs to see what he's got that he thinks is so important, there's another, smaller part of me that doesn't want to see anything that could suddenly make it all real.

I sit down and Liam slides into the booth beside me, his thigh resting against mine and I need him that close to me. I need to know he's there.

Karl smiles at us both, and I reach under the table for Liam's hand. I don't let out a breath until his fingers curl around mine. I'm not letting go of him.

'You said you wanted me to see this as soon as possible.'

Karl nods, and presses a few keys on his laptop, before he slowly turns the computer around to face me and Liam.

'I took these this morning,' Karl begins, and I look at the screen. At an image of Michael, getting out of his car. Going into a health centre that I know isn't ours. 'He left the university at about ten-thirty and drove into Chester-le-Street, to this doctors' surgery.'

I'm aware of my fingers tightening around Liam's, of my heart beating faster, I'm confused. Is he ill? Is that what he's hiding? Is something wrong with him? Oh, Jesus, what if he's only been trying to protect me all this time?

I look at Liam, but he's as confused as I am.

'Do you recognize that surgery, Ellie?'

I shake my head, glance back down at the laptop screen.

'He was inside for about fifteen minutes. And when he left ...' Karl presses another key, and another image pops up on the screen, one that makes that knot in my gut tighten even more, nausea rising up in my throat. 'He wasn't alone.'

Liam's hand squeezes mine even tighter as I stare at the screen. At my husband.

With *her*.

Ava.

I watch as more images appear, of my husband and his distraction. I stare at her leaning into him as he talks to her. Comforts her.

His pregnant whore ...

Chapter 40

'Can you see it now, Ellie?'

He's talking, but I'm not listening. I'm tuning him out, letting his voice fade into the background.

'Can you see what's happening?'

Why is he here? I'm almost sure I told him I wanted to be alone, so why is he in my kitchen?

'You need to go, Liam.'

'I'm not going anywhere. I'm not leaving you alone, not now.'

I raise my head slowly to look at him. 'Why? What are you scared of? Do you think I'm going to do something stupid? Is that it?'

'No ...'

'Then you can go, can't you?'

'Come home with me, Ellie. Please.'

I shake my head. I want to be on my own. For the first time in a long time I actually want to be alone, in this house.

He comes over to me, takes hold of my wrists and unfolds my arms. He takes my hands in his, his grip tight around my fingers.

'I don't think you should stay here. This house, it isn't good for you.'

'It's my home.'

'Pack a few things and come back to mine. Please, Ellie.'

I tug my hands free of his and walk over to the counter. I pour myself a large measure of whisky, but before I can drink it he's taken the glass from me. Poured the whisky down the sink.

'What the hell are you doing?'

'Pack a bag and come home with me.'

'Just go, Liam. Please.'

'She's pregnant, Ellie. You saw that, right? You saw Michael, with her ...'

I swing around and stare at him. I'm tired of him now, I don't want him here. I need to think. 'We don't know the baby is his.'

'Jesus, Ellie, come on ...!'

He rakes a hand through his hair, throws his head back and sighs heavily.

'You *want* it to be true, don't you? You want to believe that my husband is sleeping with her, that he got her pregnant, you want that to be true. Why, Liam? Because you think that'll make me stop loving him? Make me run to you ...?'

'You've already run to me, Ellie.' He moves a little closer, reaches out to touch my cheek. 'And you didn't do that for the hell of it. You did it for a reason, you're just too scared to admit it.'

'You need to go. Please.'

He pulls his hand back, steps away from me, but his eyes

remain fixed on mine. 'I love you, have you got that yet? I love you so much, and I won't let him do this to you. I won't let him hurt you like this.'

I say nothing. I just keep staring at him, hoping he'll get the message. That he'll leave, I really do need to be alone now.

'This is killing you, *he* is killing you, and I can't stand by and watch him do that.'

Still, I remain silent. I want him to go, I can't think with him here, he's too much of a distraction.

'Ellie?'

I shake my head. He needs to go. And he does, eventually. But I wait until I hear his car leave the driveway before I move, before I head into the hall, pull the bolts across the door. Make myself safe. And as soon as that's done I lean back against the wall, close my eyes, and take a second to breathe. A second to let what I saw today sink in.

Her.

Ava.

Pregnant.

My husband, holding her in his arms, her fingers clinging onto his jacket. She'd looked upset. Scared. She should be.

My eyes spring open and I stare at the door. I glance at the security monitor. I look down at my left hand, at the wedding band there on my third finger. A symbol of those vows Michael and I made to each other.

To have and to hold.
For better, for worse.
In sickness and in health.
Till death do us part …

They mean something, those vows. We said them, and we meant them. All of them.

Didn't we, Michael …?

Chapter 41

I can't get those images out of my head. His concerned expression. His finger tucked under her chin as she looked up into his eyes. I couldn't sleep, I spent the night lying awake staring at the ceiling, thinking about everything I'm losing. My husband. My life. My mind ...

I need to see him. Michael. I need to see him. I need to confront him once and for all; I need to do that, even though Karl – the private investigator – told me to do nothing until he's got more information. It's what I'm paying him for after all, isn't it? To gather more information. To watch my husband, track his movements, because I can't do that anymore. He told me to wait, until he has more proof. Do I need more proof? Weren't those pictures enough?

I push open the revolving doors of the hotel I know Michael's staying in and stride into the lobby. Why did he never go to that friend he claimed he was going to stay with? Was there ever a friend? Or was that just another lie? After all, it's easier to bring *her* here, isn't it? Easier to carry out that deception and betrayal in a place full of people who don't know you. Who won't judge you. How many times has he lied to my face?

How many times have I lied to his?

Despite the fact it's only just gone 8 a.m., the reception area is busy. There seems to be a large group of people trying to check out so I hang back a little, sit down in the foyer, my gaze shifting between the front desk and the door. I have no idea if they'll tell me Michael's room number, but I'm his wife. I'll make up some kind of emergency, I can lie just as well as he can. Probably even better.

My phone vibrating momentarily distracts me, and I pull it from my pocket. It's Liam.

I glance quickly outside, and then I realize Karl is probably parked up somewhere, watching the hotel. Has he noticed me come in here? He should have done, if he's doing his job properly. And he won't be happy that I've done this, that I've come here, but rather than confront me himself, has he called Liam? Is he too scared to tackle the woman he can see I've become? Would he rather Liam come and handle this? Handle *me*? Is that who I am now? Something to be 'handled'?

I ignore the call and slide the phone back into my pocket, but within seconds it vibrates again, so this time I turn it off and throw it into my bag. I don't need the distraction. And then I hear it – his voice. Michael's voice. Deep. Bold. Perfect diction. It carries well, my husband's voice.

He's at the front desk, talking to the receptionist, smiling at her the way he smiles at every woman he comes into contact with. And she's just like all the others, sucked in by his handsome face and easy charm. And I'm tired of it, the way he flirts with them, attracting these women like some modern-day pied piper.

I get up, make my way over to him, and as he turns his head his smile evaporates.

'What are you doing here, Ellie?'

He speaks to me like I mean nothing to him. It stings, further ripping that hole in my heart that he's already put there.

'I need to talk to you.'

He turns away, signs something the receptionist slides over to him, and he looks at her as he hands it back. He throws her that smile, again, but this time she doesn't return it. She quickly glances in my direction. I'm making her uncomfortable.

'There's nothing to talk about,' he says, slipping his newspaper into his bag before sliding it up onto his shoulder. 'I think you should go.'

'I'm not going anywhere, Michael. I'm quite happy to say all I have to say right here, if that's what you'd prefer.'

The way he looks at me, it makes me feel sad and angry. Tired. Defeated. But I can't let those feelings win out. I need the truth. I need to know how to end this.

He sighs heavily. A frustrated sigh. 'Come to my room.'

He turns and heads towards the lifts, and I follow him, neither of us saying anything. The silence between us is almost foreboding, and I feel my heart start to pick up a faster rhythm as we approach his room. She's obviously not with him. But that doesn't mean she hasn't been here.

He closes the door behind him, throws his bag down on the bed. He stares at me, and again I feel sadness and anger merge, I still love him so much. That's why I've been driven to this, because I love him. He's my husband ... *my* husband.

'What do you want, Ellie?'

I tilt my head to one side, and look at him. Right at him. I hold his gaze and he narrows his eyes, he's confused. Good. I'm the one in control now, and I need to make sure it stays that way.

'I want *you*, Michael.'

He narrows his eyes a little more, and then he breaks the stare; he laughs, turns his head away from me, runs a hand along the back of his neck. 'Jesus Christ ...'

I walk over to him, pull his hand away from his neck and I force his head around to look at me. 'There's nothing funny about this. I'm your wife, and that's something you seem to be forgetting ...'

His fingers grasp my wrist, so tight they dig into my skin, but I don't even flinch.

'You haven't been my wife for a long time now, Ellie.'

'And whose fault is that?'

'I didn't drive you to this ...'

'You helped.'

His eyes lock on mine, it's like he's staring into my very soul. Trying to find the woman he married. The woman he loved – no. He still loves me. Whatever he's done, we can fix it. We can move on. We can get past this, I know we can. I wasn't sure before, but being this close to him ... I'm not willing to let him go.

I reach out with my free hand, lightly touch his mouth with my fingertips and he doesn't stop me. He keeps his eyes on mine, and I know he feels it too. That connection, that bond between us that can't be broken.

'Do you still love me, Michael?'

'Ellie, please ...'

'Do you still love me?'

'Of course I still love you, but ...'

'Ssh.' I shake my head, press my fingers against his mouth to silence him. 'You still love me. I still love you. We can save this, Michael. We can save *us* ...'

He grasps my wrist a little tighter, but still the pain means nothing. I *feel* nothing. 'Ellie, you're not well ...'

'I'm fine.'

'You need to talk to someone. You need to go back to the counsellor ...'

I wrench my arm free and step back from him. 'All I ever wanted was to talk to *you*. My husband. What happened that night ... we vowed we'd stick together, remember? You promised me that, you said ...'

'And I'll never break that promise, but right now – right now, I can't do *this*. You need help, Ellie.'

I walk back over to him, run my fingertips lightly over his jacket collar. 'I don't need help.' I pull him gently towards me, and he doesn't protest, doesn't make any attempt to stop me. Because he's weak? I think we might all be a little guilty of that. I rest my mouth against his, smiling slightly as I feel his erection nudge my thigh. 'I just need my husband back.'

He slides a hand around on to the small of my back, lowers it to my bottom, cupping it gently as he kisses me; as he pushes me back against the wall.

Weak.

Weak.

Weak …

'You want me because I'm *not* the woman you married,' I breathe as his hand presses against my breast. 'That's what's making you hard, right?'

He looks at me for a second, his eyes burning into mine, and then he steps back. It's like he's suddenly been yanked from a trance; like he can't quite believe what he's doing, and it breaks my heart. It fills me with anger. Two very different emotions clashing, fighting against each other.

'You need to go, Ellie. Now.'

The anger's winning. Sadness is just a waste of time, it's sucking up the energy I need to fight this battle.

'Because I'm not Ava?'

He takes another step back, rakes a hand through his hair as he stares at me again. 'I'm not doing this, okay? I want you to go.'

I walk towards him. I hold his gaze, I need to stay strong. Focused. He needs to know I'm not just going to roll over and give up without fighting this.

'What does she do to you, Michael, to make you keep running to her?'

'You need to go.'

'Is it the prospect of a younger body, hmm? A body that isn't damaged, like mine? A body that isn't scarred? Does she fuck you in ways you never dreamt of …?'

He grabs hold of my wrist again, his eyes blazing with an anger I haven't seen in him before, but he doesn't scare me. I don't think anything scares me anymore. I think I passed that point a long time ago.

'You need to leave, right now.'

What nerve have I touched? What button did I press?

He opens the door and lets go of me. He's giving me the chance to leave without a scene – which I have every intention of doing, but this isn't over. This is so far from over.

I reach out, cup his cheek, move my mouth so very close to his. 'You caused this, Michael. You did this, with your reckless behaviour.'

'I did a lot of things I'm not proud of, Ellie. Remember?'

We stare at each other for a few loaded beats, and then I step back from him. I turn and walk away. As I head towards the lift I feel that anger rising, bubbling away inside of me, threatening to explode. I need to get out of here now, I need to go to work, do something normal. If I knew what normal was anymore.

'Ellie?'

I stop walking, and look up to see Liam standing there in reception, his hands in his pockets, his face serious. Concerned? He might be. I'm not sure, I can't really read his expression.

'I need to get to work ...'

He grabs my hand as I pass him, swinging me around to face him. 'What've you done?'

I don't know, what I've done. But that anger's filling me now, flooding my veins. I'm angry with myself, with Michael. Liam. I'm so fucking angry ...

I look up into his eyes, and he gets it, he feels that anger coursing through me, burning my gut, it's relentless. I need to channel it, rid myself of it before I go anywhere or do anything, and he knows that. Liam won't turn me down. Liam is the weakest of them all, I know that now.

I kiss him, and he responds in a heartbeat, he always does. His fingers wind in my hair, his body hard against mine, but we can't stay here. People are watching, we're in too public a place ...

He takes my hand and we walk briskly towards the toilets, we can't wait. I don't want to wait, I need him now. He's my medicine, my fix – and this is urgent. Michael may have rejected me, but Liam would never do that.

Michael. My husband. Rejected me ...

I lean back against the wall as Liam quickly checks inside, then he takes my hand again, drags me into a cubicle, kicking the door shut as he throws me back against the side of the stall. And for a beat or two we just look at each other. He smiles at me and my heart starts racing; he's a beautiful man, Dr Liam Kennedy. But that momentary second of calm quickly dissipates. I'm here for a reason. I need to vent, I need to release that anger, let it seem like I'm making Michael pay for his deceit. His betrayal. By fucking his best friend? By taking part in my *own* deceit? My *own* betrayal? It's so messed up, so confusing. So wrong. But we're all in so deep now, I can't see a way out.

I reach down to unzip him, I take him in my hand, feel his hardness grow and I ache for this release now, I need him. This man. *This*.

He rests a hand on my hip, swings me around, then yanks my jeans down. He nudges my legs apart with his knee, and he's inside me before I have a chance to draw breath, his fingers sliding between mine up against the wall. He thrusts into me with an almost violent force, and I buck back just as hard, I grip him tight, I want to hurt him. That's why he's here, a vehicle for me to take my anger out on in the only twisted way I know how.

He lets go of my hand, reaches down, and he touches me. It's all I can do to stop myself from crying out. And he senses that, pushes my head around slightly so my mouth catches his; so my cries seep into him.

'Harder,' I whisper. I need him to go deeper, it makes me feel safe. Protected. But I also need to feel pain. To know that I'm still alive and not just sleepwalking my way through the nightmare that my life has become.

He takes hold of my hand again, grips my fingers tight as he pulls out of me. Then he slams back into me with a force that pushes the breath from my body, but the pain it causes is beautiful.

Your best friend wants me, Michael.

He *wants me …*

It's crazy, brutal sex. Hard and fast. Wrong. Sordid. Dirty. Sex.

He makes me come with his fingers, his body buried deep within mine as I tense up. And as my release ends, his begins. I feel him explode inside me, feel him flood me with his toxic power, and I fall back against him, his arm circling my waist, holding me. For a second we stay there, in silence, my head resting against his shoulder, his breath hot on my neck as his breathing slows down.

His fingers remain curled around mine. He's still inside me, and for a second or two I allow calm to spread through me. I breathe in deeply and squeeze his hand before I ready myself to let go of this, to head back to reality. I have a job to do.

I needed him. He temporarily fixed me, but I'll break again. I always do. But I know he'll be there. To fix me ...

Chapter 42

I don't want Michael to know that I called Ernie. And I asked Ernie not to tell Michael I'd been in touch; asked if we could meet away from the university. I don't want my husband to know I've talked to him. And Ernie's going to ask why, of course he is. As far as I'm aware Michael hasn't told any of his colleagues that we're not even living in the same house anymore, that we're barely talking. Or maybe he has, I don't know. I'm about to find out.

I park the car and head inside the pub – one I chose because it's a little way out of Durham. A country pub, in the true sense of the word. Cosy seating, a real fire, beams on the ceiling; it's quaint. I've been here before, once, with Liam, so I'm vaguely familiar with its layout, and I scan the room as I look for Ernie. Professor Ernie Waterford, a man who isn't just Michael's work colleague, he's also his friend. *Our* friend. He was Michael's lecturer before he became his mentor, and he's always been there, on the periphery of our lives. I just have no idea how much Michael's confided in him over the past year or so, if at all. Maybe he hasn't needed to. He's had *her*, hasn't he?

He's sitting at a table in the corner, by the fire, which isn't lit today because we're heading into summer. I make my way over to him and as I approach, he stands up, holds out his arms and hugs me. The usual, familiar bear hug I always receive from Ernie.

'Ellie, my darling, how are you?'

He waits for me to sit down before he takes his seat. A gentleman to the end. 'I'm fine.'

I'm not. I'm so far from fine.

He looks at me, sits back down in his chair, crosses his legs and clasps his hands together in his lap. He knows something's wrong. It's obvious something's wrong, otherwise why would I insist that he keeps this meeting secret from Michael?

'Why did you want to speak to me?' he asks. 'Don't get me wrong, it's always a pleasure to spend time with you, it's just a little unusual for you to request something so ... clandestine?'

I pause, and for a second I wonder if I've done the right thing, coming here. I'm still not sure who I can trust, but that brief moment of clarity soon disappears. I've been left with so few choices now. This is what I've been driven to. 'You ... you know that Michael and I – we've been through a lot. Things have been tough – really tough, and I don't know how much Michael's told you ...'

'He hasn't spoken to me in any great detail about anything personal, Ellie.'

I briefly look down, aware that I'm fiddling with my wedding ring, twisting it round and round my finger. And then I raise my gaze, look Ernie in the eye.

'Have you noticed anything ... odd about Michael's behaviour over the past few months?'

He frowns slightly. 'Odd? No, not really, but to be honest, Ellie, I'm not around as much as I used to be. I don't see Michael all that often ... is something wrong?'

I shake my head, even though it's obvious I'm lying. I just don't want to tell him too much. But there are things I need to know, so I'm pushing this.

'That student – the one who invaded our home, the one who ...' I look down again, closing my eyes for a second or two while I try to compose myself. And then I feel his hand on my shoulder, squeezing it gently, his voice quiet as he leans in to me.

'I'll go and get us some drinks. The usual?'

His tone is kind and I nod without looking up. I'm scared that if I look at him right now I might cry. There've been times over the years when Ernie has felt more like a father to me than my own ever was. He's always cared, even from a distance. That's why I'm here now, because he cares about me and Michael, and whatever I need to know, he'll tell me if he can. I'm sure of that.

My phone ringing out distracts me and I reach for it on the table, turning the volume down as I glance at the screen. It's Liam. It's nearly always Liam. I answer it, sitting back in my chair as I look around the pub. It's fairly busy for a weekday afternoon, and I wonder if Michael brings *her* to places like this. Out of the way places. Secluded, secret places where he has little chance of his infidelity being discovered. The kind of places I come to with Liam, but that's different. Our situation is different. I need Liam. He doesn't need Ava.

'You're not at work, Ellie. Where are you?'

Sometimes he treats me like a child. He has no right to know my every move.

And I have every right to know my husband's?

'I'm in a meeting, Liam.'

That's not entirely a lie. This is a meeting, of sorts.

'Come to mine tonight. Please. I don't like the idea of you being in that house alone.'

'Then you come to me.'

Strange though it may seem, whilst I once hated being alone there, I don't want to leave my home, even though it doesn't feel much like one right now. There are times when it feels more like a prison. But I don't want to walk away, I'm not giving up. It's going to feel like a home again, one day. When Michael's back and all that's broken is fixed.

'Is that what you want?'

'Yes.'

'Okay ... are you all right?'

'You keep asking me that, Liam.'

'Because I care about you. I love you ...'

'Stop saying that. Please.'

I glance over at the bar. Ernie's coming back with our drinks.

'I have to go. I'll call you later.'

I hang up and toss my phone into my bag.

'Here we go. Gin and tonic, ice and lemon. Just how you like it.'

'Thank you.' I smile and take a sip of the gin, enjoying the feeling of the cold liquid hitting my throat.

'Is there something you need to talk about, Ellie?'

I look up, his eyes meeting mine, and I'm back in control now. I'm good. 'Before it happened – that night ... Ernie, you know the kind of man Michael is.'

He raises an eyebrow, steeples his fingers together under his chin. 'The kind of man ...?'

'Tactile. Flirtatious. Charming.'

'There's nothing wrong in being that kind of man, Ellie.'

'There is if that kind of man takes advantage of his position.'

He frowns again, his eyes still fixed on mine, but he remains silent. He waits for me to expand on that.

'Has he ever – have *you* ever seen him act in an inappropriate way with any of his students?'

Ernie leans forward and drops his hands, his eyes staring deep into mine. 'What are you trying to say, Ellie?'

'You know why she did what she did. Why she came to our home, why she attacked me, you know why she did that. She did it because she had some ridiculous notion that Michael had promised her some warped kind of happy-ever-after, and I just need to know ...' I take a second to breathe. 'I need to know if it really *was* a ridiculous notion.' I raise my head, and look back at Ernie. 'I need to know if his behaviour is something I should've been worried about a lot sooner.'

Ernie's frown deepens. 'You think Michael may have had inappropriate relationships with students?'

'The way he is – the way he behaves ...'

'He's an excellent lecturer, Ellie. The kind of person who draws people in, holds their attention. It's a very special quality, not one many possess. And it isn't unusual for students to sometimes develop crushes on their professors ...'

'What she felt was more than a crush, Ernie.'

He throws me an apologetic look. 'I'm sorry. I didn't mean that to sound as flippant as it may have come across.'

I sit back, and try to ignore the anger that's starting to kick up inside of me. All around me life continues, and I'm envious of all those people who don't have a darkness surrounding them. They're lucky.

'There's another student ... Ava. I can't remember her surname ... I think he might be ...' I can't bring myself to say it. I've already said too much. 'I think he might be sleeping with her.'

I turn back to face Ernie. His expression is one of confusion, surprise; concern. For what I've just told him? Or for me? Has Michael told him how unstable he thinks I've become? No. Ernie said he hasn't spoken to him in any detail about anything personal, but then, I'm surrounded by liars, aren't I? Ernie could be lying too. I really don't know who I can trust anymore.

'What makes you think something's going on between Michael and this student?'

I drop my gaze, look back down at that gold band on my finger. 'I've seen them together. Outside of the university ...' I stop talking. I can't let him know I've had Michael followed. I can't let him know I listened in to his calls, read his texts. If I tell him that then he's just going to think that I'm crazy. Unhinged. Paranoid. Everything my husband thinks I am, but I'm none of those things. He's just driven me to this with his lack of concern. Lack of comfort.

'Have you seen anything that makes you think he's sleeping with her?' Ernie asks, and the tone of his voice now is akin to that of someone speaking to a child. It irritates me, makes my skin prickle. I can feel that anger edging back now.

It was a mistake, coming here. I shouldn't have done it. I stupidly thought Ernie might have been able to help me, when all this has done is make him pity me.

'He's changed, Ernie. He isn't the man I used to know.'

I'm not the woman I once was either, and all I wanted to do was bring us back to those people. *Be* those people, again. I thought we could do that. Now I'm not so sure.

Ernie leans forward, and when he looks at me this time the pity is so clear in his eyes it makes me flinch.

'I thought you'd both come through the other side, Ellie. Every time I saw you, either of you, together or alone, you always seemed like you'd fought what happened and won.'

'Sometimes everything you see isn't the truth.'

I pick up my bag and reach into it for my car keys. This *was* a mistake.

'I should go now. I have a meeting in Newcastle later, I don't want to be late.'

A lie. I have no meetings. Carmen's looking after everything today.

'Ellie, are you sure you're okay?'

I try to summon up a smile, but I'm not convinced the one I give him reaches my eyes.

'I'm fine. I'm sorry, I shouldn't have come here, and I shouldn't have said what I did, I'm just being stupid. Me and Michael are going through a bit of a rough patch, that's all.

It happens. Especially when you've been through everything we have. We'll be fine. We'll work it out.'

'I'm sure that whatever it was you thought you saw, between Michael and this student – it's just his way, Ellie.'

Just his way ... Something I'm expected to accept, right?

'Forget I said anything, Ernie, I really am sorry. You're right. I'm probably just reading something into a situation that doesn't exist.'

Am I? Really?

He stands up, comes over to me, takes both my hands in his and smiles. He seems almost relieved. 'You have nothing to apologize for, my darling. I had no idea things were still affecting you so badly.'

Nobody has any idea how badly everything is still affecting me. Nobody.

'I'll be fine, *we'll* be fine. We just need a bit more time, that's all.'

I lean in to kiss his cheek, but I do need to go now.

'You take care, Ellie.'

I throw him what I hope is a more convincing smile and start to walk away, but then I stop. I turn back around.

'You won't tell Michael we met today, will you? Only, I don't want to worry him. He still worries, you know?'

Ernie nods, just the slightest dip of his head, and I can only hope that he'll respect my wishes. I just have to trust him.

As I walk out of the pub into the afternoon sunshine, I feel everything from anger and frustration at my own naivety to an overwhelming sadness at what I've become. What my life has become. I feel alone. Isolated, confused and scared, and I can't have that. Those feelings can't take over, I haven't stopped fighting yet. I'm tired, and there's a tiny part of me that wants to give up but I refuse to do that.

Michael loved me once.

He'll love me again.

He'll love me. Again …

Chapter 43

'Hey, you,' Liam murmurs into my neck as he slides his arms around me from behind, his hands edging up under my T-shirt. *His* T-shirt. It's all I'm wearing. We've just had sex in the shower, my skin's still damp, my body tingling with the memory of him pounding into me against the tiled wall as the water cascaded down over us. I shiver, and he laughs, a sound which vibrates into my shoulder and I shiver again.

I turn around and look at him, all tall and handsome in nothing but his jeans, his dark-blonde hair pushed back off his face, those steel-grey eyes of his shining. He's been a part of my life for so long, will I ever be able to let him go? That thought scares me, because this was never meant to be anything more than sex. Fun. An escape. I'm fighting for my husband, for that life I want back – I don't want this. Not forever.

I reach out, grab hold of the waistband of his jeans and I pull him towards me. I kiss him, and he smiles, and for one wonderful, fleeting moment everything feels okay. The darkness lifts and I see light, but it doesn't last. The darkness always returns.

He tucks a finger under my chin, and tilts up my face, his eyes locking on mine. 'I hate seeing you so sad, Ellie. What I said before, about us leaving here, leaving all this shit behind, I still mean that. We can still *do* that.'

'I can't, Liam ...'

I pull away from him, walk out of the kitchen, into the living room. I don't want to talk about leaving. I'm not leaving.

'You and Michael – it's over, Ellie.'

I swing around to face him, shaking my head, I refuse to believe him.

'And I'm not doing this to hurt you ...'

'Then stop saying it.'

He comes over to me, and rests his palm against my cheek, forcing me to look at him. 'He's sleeping with a student. A student who's pregnant ...'

'We don't know it's his.'

'Jesus, Ellie, wake up! If it isn't his then why the hell is he with her? All those meetings, those pictures Karl showed you ... Baby, you need to stop fighting this. You've put your life on hold for far too long while he's been out there living his. Without you.'

I shake my head again, he's wrong. He's wrong.

'He doesn't love you anymore, how can he? But *I* do.' He leans in to me, his thumb stroking my cheek, his mouth almost touching mine as he speaks. '*I* love you.'

He kisses me, and I press my hand against his chest, feel his heart beating hard. Fast. I don't want him to love me, so I should push him away and end this. I should. But I can't.

Without him I'm weak. Alone. I need him to lean on. Or do I really just need to feel loved ...?

He reaches down, takes hold of the T-shirt and pulls it off over my head. I gasp as the cool breeze blowing in through the slightly open window hits my naked skin.

'I love you, Ellie,' he whispers, his eyes staring deep into mine, and I'm confused and tired; I don't love *him*. I don't, love him ...

I back up against the wall, close my eyes as he touches me, slides a hand between my legs, forcing them apart. But I'm not fighting this. This is another welcome moment of relief.

He rests his hand lightly on the curve of my waist, dipping his head to kiss my shoulder, moving down until he reaches my breasts. His touch is so different to Michael's. Had he been this way back then? Had we fucked the way we fuck now, back then? I can't remember.

I wind my fingers in his hair, bite down on my lip as his beard scratches my skin. It tickles slightly but that only seems to heighten everything. And when he raises his head and his eyes meet mine, the corner of his mouth curls up into a smirk and I laugh. He makes the shit go away, he makes it all go away, he chases it down. He gives me a few moments of peace. Calm. Escape ...

I pull gently on his hair as he pushes inside me, his thrusts slow at first but picking up speed. I trail my fingers up and down his spine, dig them into his flesh, scratch at his skin, because that makes him fuck me harder. It makes him hurt me like I'm hurting him; the pain is all part of what we do, I crave it.

'What the hell ...?'

Michael.

I slowly open my eyes. I look at Liam, but he doesn't move. He makes no attempt to pull out of me and for a second it's like my world's stopped turning. Maybe this is just a dream ...

'Does somebody want to tell me what the fuck is going on?'

I hadn't pulled the bolts over the door, because Liam's here. I hadn't done that, but I hadn't thought for one second that Michael would come home, not yet. After what happened at the hotel? No ... Why is he here? Why?

My breath catches in my throat. I'm aware of my heart hammering away, so fast it's not making my attempts at breathing any easier, and the silence that fills the room now is dark and heavy, punctuated only by the ticking of the clock on the wall above the fireplace.

Liam takes my face in his hands, and whispers something to me I don't catch, because I'm not hearing anything other than the wild beating of my heart. Then he finally pulls out of me, and turns slowly around to face Michael. I crouch down, reach for the discarded T-shirt, slipping it on as I back up against the wall, my eyes fixed on Liam and Michael. Best friends. Brothers, almost. And I watch as that friendship crumbles around them. It's over. Now.

The silence is still there, still hanging heavy in the air, and I don't know what to do. I don't even know if I'm scared, I don't know what I'm feeling. But I know there's a tiny part of me that's glad Michael's found us. I'm glad, because seeing Liam touch me like that, it'll shake him up, won't it? Make him see what the consequences of his actions have been. He drove me to this, his indifference to my feelings pushed me into Liam's arms, he'll see that now. He did this. He caused this ...

'How long?' Michael's the first one to break the silence, and his eyes, they don't move from Liam. He hasn't looked at me, maybe he can't. 'How long have you been fucking my wife?'

Liam takes a few steps forward, and it's then that I realize how much taller than Michael he is. How much stronger he seems.

'Do you care?'

Michael laughs ... no. He sneers, but Liam doesn't react. He doesn't do anything, he just stands there, a face-off that is more terrifying than any fight. I expected a fight, I didn't expect this. My stomach's pulled into a knot so tight I'm still finding it hard to breathe. So when Michael finally looks at me, when he walks past Liam as though he doesn't exist, it feels like someone's grabbed hold of my throat, like they're squeezing it; I really can't breathe.

'You accuse *me* of sleeping with my student and all the time you've been fucking *him*?'

'All you had to do was talk to me ...'

'Oh no ... no, Ellie, don't you dare use me as an excuse for *this*. I have done *nothing* wrong, it's *you* ...' He stops talking, but he's looking right at me and he doesn't break that stare. I've never seen his eyes so cold. Never seen him look so angry. So disappointed. So distant. 'You really are a fucking mess, aren't you?'

'How can I be anything else, Michael?'

He cocks his head slightly, as though he's trying to read my mind; see deeper into my fucked-up soul.

'I did something really bad, we both know that. But this – *this* isn't it. *This* was how I got through it, this was what I needed, to help me forget, to help me deal with everything – because I wasn't dealing with it. And you refused to see that ...'

'You refused to let it go, Ellie. You refused to accept what happened despite everyone telling you it was what you needed to do, what you *had* to do. You didn't need to do *this*.'

'I'm sorry,' I whisper, and I feel stupid tears start to burn the back of my eyes. I think he's right. I am a fucking mess. But I'm still in control. Still hanging on. 'I'm so sorry. For everything.'

'You should've listened to me, Ellie. I told you, to let it go, to leave it alone. What I did for you ...' He trails off, but his eyes remain locked on mine as he backs away from me. I feel numb, detached from the situation, almost. I watch as he faces Liam one more time; hold my breath as I wait for something to happen, but once more they just stare each other down. 'You're not fucking worth it.' Michael almost spits the words out, but Liam doesn't flinch. Only his eyes move, following Michael as he walks away. As the door slams shut out in the hall. Still he keeps his back to me, his gaze focused on the open living room door. And then he holds out his hand – he just reaches behind him, and I take his hand. I let him pull me against him because I don't know what else to do.

'What did he do for you, Ellie?' he murmurs into my forehead, his fingers winding in my hair. I slide my hand down over his hard body, rest it on his hip, dig my fingers gently into his skin as memories of that night come flooding forward again.

What did he do ...?

Chapter 44

Fourteen Months Ago ...

A sharp kick to the lower back jolts me awake and I wonder how long I was out. Seconds? Minutes? Have I been lying here for hours? All I know is my body hurts, wave after wave of pain washes over me.

'I need to think ... I need to think ...'

She repeats those words over and over like a mantra as she paces backwards and forwards along the edge of the pool, her hand in her hair, she's pulling at it, her behaviour's terrifying to watch.

I drop my hand to my stomach and flinch as another wave of pain hits me, before I carefully lift my top up, wincing at the bruises already forming on my skin.

'Hey!'

My head jolts up and I see her, standing over me, her eyes glaring down at me. Cold, lifeless eyes.

'Get up,' she instructs, and I try to pull myself to my feet but my ankle gives way beneath me. It's too painful to put any weight on. 'Jesus ...'

She reaches down, grabs hold of my arm and yanks me to my feet, forcing me to put weight on my injured ankle. I don't know if it's broken but the pain is harsh, and standing up is difficult. Then she pushes me back against the wall, and I'm actually relieved that I have something to lean on, something to support me.

'Okay ... okay, I know what I have to do ...'

She's talking to herself, she isn't directing that at me, and I watch as she wanders over to the pool edge, crouches down, dips her hand in the water. She stays there for a good few seconds, staring down at her hand as she moves it around, and I know I have a chance now, to get out of here, to run, and no matter how painful that's going to be it's what I need to do. I need to run. Find a phone. I need to call for help because I have no idea what this woman is going to do.

I take a deep breath and make for the door, but the second I turn my back she's there, the swift kick she delivers to the back of my knees sending me crashing to the floor, hitting the tiles with a heavy thud. I land on my stomach, and I close my eyes and try to breathe, try to believe that my baby is okay, that he or she can survive this but the fear that's inside me now is too much. I'm scared, I'm tired, and once again I think about just giving in. I don't know if I can fight this anymore.

I keep my eyes squeezed shut, my body tensing up as I wait for her to do whatever it is she's going to do next, and I cry out in pain as she kicks me over onto my back. Tears start to stream down my face as my hand drops to my stomach, but she yanks it away and I open my eyes. I stare at her as she crouches down beside me, grasps my wrist, and places her own hand on my stomach, tilting her head as she rubs it slowly.

'Michael's baby is in there, huh?'

'What do you want?' I hiss, my voice can barely rise above a whisper. It hurts to speak.

She twists her head around to look at me. 'I thought I'd made that clear. I want Michael. He wants me. I don't even know what you're doing here.'

She stands up, pulls me up with her and pain floods my body again as she forces me back to my feet.

'You need to go now.' She lets go of my wrist and wanders over to the floor-to-ceiling windows that overlook the front lawn and the driveway, but it's dark outside. There really isn't anything to see. 'Michael will be home soon. You can't be here.'

She turns around to face me, and her expression is something that fills me with a new kind of fear. She believes what she's saying, that she's the one Michael comes home to, not me.

'You had no business touching him.' Her voice has an edge to it now, and I back away as she walks towards me. Maybe I can make it to the door again, before she reaches me, but I don't think my legs are strong enough. I try to quicken my pace, but the pain is too much. I start to feel my legs give way again and she grabs me before I fall, just to slam me back against the wall. 'You had no business, touching him,' she repeats, and she's so close to me now. Her face is right up in mine, and my heart is beating so fast, so hard I feel like I'm about to pass out. 'He's mine, not yours, you crossed a line ...'

349

From somewhere, I don't know where, a rush of something comes flooding forward, a strength I didn't think I had left in me suddenly takes over, and I grab hold of her hair, yank her head back, and twist her around so *she's* the one with her back to the wall. She has no right – no fucking right to invade my home, to inflict her sick shit on me. To hurt my baby.

'Get out of my house, you fucked-up bitch.'

I twist her hair around my fingers, pulling it harder; I'm fucking angry now. But something outside momentarily distracts me. Headlights. Their bright beams briefly flooding the room and I turn my head to look outside ... a mistake. She pushes me forward and I crash back to the floor, back onto my stomach, and I cry out as a fresh wave of pain swamps me. It's incessant, and I try to crawl away but she grabs hold of my ankle and drags me back, kicking me over. I cry out again as she brings her boot down onto my stomach, not just once, but again and again. She rains those kicks down on me like she's stamping on some random insect, and I can't do anything to stop her. But then I remember the headlights ... someone's outside ... the car ... someone's here, they can help me. They can help ...

I try to scream but she pulls me to my feet and presses her hand over my mouth, her eyes blazing as they burn into mine. She shakes her head, and I feel her other hand touch my neck, she starts to squeeze it, pressing her fingers into it and I don't know if I have any fight left in me now, I just know I have to try. Or she's going to kill me. She might have already killed my baby, and that thought is what fires me up, what gives me the strength to push her away. The pain wracking my body is brutal and raw as she rushes back towards me, grabs my arm, and twists it up and around; I scream out loud, the sound of bones breaking making me sick to my stomach. The pain is so intense now I almost pass out, but I can't do that. I can't stop fighting, I can't give up, and despite the pain I fight with everything I have left inside of me.

I somehow wrench my injured arm free and I punch her in the stomach with my other balled-up fist, but she staggers back just a couple of steps before she comes for me again, and I can already feel what little strength I had left ebbing away. The room's starting to spin, and I know I have only one option left to me now, if I want to survive this. One chance. And I take it. I push the pain aside and I kick out, one hard kick that floors her. That brings *her* crashing down, the sound of her head hitting the edge of the pool echoing off the walls. And for a second I think that's it. Is she unconscious? But she slowly lifts her head, puts her hand down, tries to raise herself up but I can't have that, I haven't got the strength to let this carry on and I stamp down on her hand, as hard as she was stamping on my baby. I crush her fingers, I don't care that bones are breaking beneath me, she's broken mine. And despite the pain that's taken over every inch of my body I sink to my knees, press my hand against her neck ...

'Ellie!'

His voice momentarily distracts me, and I look up. Michael ... Michael's here. But he's too late. This has to stop, now, he's too late.

'Ellie, *Jesus* ...! Ellie, *stop!*'

I feel her move beneath me, feel her start to struggle and I look down into her eyes. And I feel nothing.

'Ellie, please ...'

I tune him out, I'm not listening. I'm finishing this, now. I'm ending it. He's too fucking late.

I grab hold of her hair and slam her head back against the edge of the pool, watching as blood floods out into the water, turning the surface a deep red. I'm not here anymore, in this room, in this place. It's like I'm watching this play out from the sidelines, like someone else has taken over my body and I press my hand against her neck one more time. Just to make sure. But her eyes, they really are dead now. *She's* dead, and I watch as the puddle of blood around her head grows bigger, trickling down over the tiles, more of it spilling out into the water.

I pull my hand from her neck, try to raise myself to my feet, ignoring the pain because I need to step back from this now.

What have I done?

What the fuck have I done?

I can't move, I can't go anywhere, I just keep staring as that pool of blood around her spreads wider, it's almost reached my feet now.

'Jesus Christ, Ellie ...'

His voice snaps me out of that trance and I turn my head to face him. 'You weren't here, Michael.'

The panic on his face is clear as he rushes towards me, pulling me into his arms, and I cling onto him. I hold him so tight, I'm scared to let go. I close my eyes, I don't want to look anymore. I don't want to see what I've done. I know what I've done. I killed her. I killed her ... did she deserve that?

'I know, sweetheart, I know ...' He strokes my hair, kisses the top of my head. 'I'm so sorry, darling ...'

His voice is fading and the pain's taking over – it's too strong now. I feel myself start to fall, feel him catch me and lower me down, before he sinks down with me. He sits next to me, keeping an arm around me as he pulls out his phone. He's calling the police. Paramedics. Soon this place will be flooded with people, all asking questions, and I've never been so scared.

I killed her.

I took someone's life ...

'I'll take care of this, Ellie. Okay?'

I look at him. My handsome husband. Is it his fault she was here? Is what happened here, tonight, Michael's fault? I'm so confused ...

I look down, and I don't know whether the blood pooling around me is from her or whether it's mine. Is something happening to my baby? Am I losing my child?

A numbness starts to spread through me. I feel cold and clammy, the pain, it's fading now as that numbness takes over.

'I'll take care of this,' Michael repeats. 'I promise you, Ellie, I won't let anything happen to you.'

And I have no choice but to believe him.

Chapter 45

'I killed her, Liam.'

He hands me a tumbler of whisky and sits down on the stair beside me.

I look at him. 'I killed her.'

'It was self-defence, Ellie. You had no choice.'

I stare down into the tumbler and shake my head. 'No. She was still alive, she wasn't trying to hurt me, not at that point ... if I'd left her ... if I hadn't slammed her head back a second time ...' I take another sip of whisky. 'Michael was there, he told me to stop, and I just carried on ... I didn't give him a chance to help, I just ... I killed her. Because I was so fucking angry.'

'The police didn't see it that way.'

'The police believed the story Michael told them. The story he told me to stick to. He saw her slip as she lunged towards me, saw her fall and hit her head. She tried to get back up, slipped again, hit her head a second time. The fatal blow.' I shrug. 'They believed it.'

Liam stays silent, staring out ahead of him at the now locked and bolted front door.

I down the last of the whisky and stand up, head into the kitchen.

'None of this is your fault, Ellie.'

I turn around and lean back against the counter. I fold my arms and look at Liam. 'He saw me kill her. I murdered her, Liam, she was still alive ...' I drag a hand back through my hair and turn my head away. 'And he covered for me. He lied, for me. And all I had to do was leave it alone ...'

He comes over to me, gently turns my head back to face him. 'None of this is your fault, do you hear me? All you wanted to do was talk, and he refused to listen ...'

'He told me not to drag it up, he told me to just let it go, and I didn't. I couldn't. I took someone's life, and I still can't deal with that, but I should have tried to.'

'She killed your baby, Ellie. She kicked your child out of you ...'

'That doesn't mean she deserved to die too.'

He takes my face in his hands, he forces me to look at him. 'You did what you had to do, but it's over now. Okay? It's over.'

I shake my head, pull his hands away from my face. 'No, Liam, it'll never be over.'

'Jesus Christ ... It's over! What else has to happen before you finally start to believe that?'

'Michael said he's done nothing wrong, but he's lying. I know he is. He's still lying to me.'

He takes my hand and clutches it tight. 'It's time to walk away now, Ellie.'

I look down at his hand holding mine, just for a second or two before I raise my eyes to meet his. 'What if he goes to the police? What if he tells them the truth, about that night? We've given him every reason to be angry, every reason to want to hurt us.'

'He won't do that.'

'How can you be sure? We've both betrayed him. We've both hurt him ...'

'If he goes to the police he'd be in just as much trouble as you, and he knows that. Withholding evidence. Lying. Covering up a crime. He isn't going to risk that happening.'

I don't know ... I want to believe him, I want to believe he's right but the look in Michael's eyes ...

'You should have talked to me, Ellie. You should have told me about this ...'

A hammering on the front door disturbs us both and I almost jump back from Liam in shock. Whoever it is, they're not letting up. The banging is incessant.

Liam heads out into the hall and I follow a little way behind, glancing down at the security monitor by the door.

It's Michael. He's back. Why?

'Let him in.'

Liam frowns. 'No. I'll go out there, try to calm him down.'

'Let him in,' I repeat.

Liam sighs, starts pulling back the bolts, and I watch on the monitor as Michael steps back from the door. He waits for it to open. And the second it does he steps inside, stops in front of Liam, and I feel my stomach twist up into another tight and painful knot.

But he does nothing. He comes over to me, and I feel my heart start to pump the blood around my body so fast I have to lean back against the wall to steady myself.

'I came here tonight because Ernie called me.'

I close my eyes for a second, and it feels like my entire world is crashing down around me, crumbling quicker than I ever thought it could.

'You went to him, Ellie. Behind my back. You went to him, and you accused me of sleeping with my students ...'

'I didn't accuse you ...'

'You fucking did!' He raises his voice, takes a step towards me, until Liam pulls him back.

'That's enough.'

Michael swings around to face Liam, his mouth twisting up into a sneer. 'Enough? I'm not even close to starting.' He looks back at me. 'How long, huh? How long have you two been sleeping together?'

I don't answer him. I can't.

'How fucking long, Ellie?'

He raises his voice again, and as Liam's fist connects with Michael's jaw I flinch. All I can do is watch as Michael staggers back, his hand clutching the side of his face.

I wait for him to retaliate, but at the same time I don't think he will. He isn't that kind of man; then again, none of us are the same people we were a few months ago. Was that really all my fault? Did I drive him to this? Drive *us*, to this?

'How long have *you* been sleeping with *her*?' The words fall from my mouth before I even have time to realize I'm saying them. I was thinking them, and I'm not sure I meant to say them out loud.

Michael narrows his eyes, steadies himself, and I quickly glance over at Liam. He's sitting down on the stairs, his head in his hands.

'With who, Ellie?'

'Ava.'

He comes over to me, puts himself back in my space, and I look over his shoulder to see Liam stand up but I shake my head. I don't want him to do anything, I'll be fine. Michael won't hurt me, not like that.

'I told you, Ellie, she is none of your business ...'

'Why? *Why* is she none of my business, Michael? Why is *your* betrayal acceptable but mine isn't?'

'Have you heard yourself? Justifying something so wrong? There *is* no betrayal on my part, that's all on you.'

'You're lying.'

'I'm lying, huh?'

'I've seen you both, together, there's something there ...'

'I'm done with this shit, Ellie. I'm done, with you.' He steps back, shakes his head. He looks from me to Liam. 'You deserve each other.'

'You're lying, Michael.'

His eyes darken as he steps forward, and this time Liam's there, I can't stop him. He pulls Michael away from me again, yanking him back hard but Michael wrenches his arm free, turning his anger on his one-time best friend ... were they ever really friends? How could they have been? Knowing what I know now – Liam told me he's resented

358

Michael, all that time. And friends, they don't resent each other.

'Touch me again and I will fucking kill you.'

I watch in horror as they face off once more, the air heavy with an atmosphere so thick it's cloying. Suffocating.

'You never deserved her, Michael.'

'And you do?'

'She was mine before you even knew her, did you know that? I loved her before you'd even had a chance to ...'

'What the hell are you talking about?'

'Liam, please ...'

He holds up a hand to silence me and I sink to my haunches, drop my head, if I don't look at what's going on in front of me, maybe it won't seem so real.

'No, Ellie, let him talk. I want to know how deep this betrayal actually goes. Were you two fucking the whole time we were married? Hmm? Have I been a complete idiot the entire time?'

I stand up, I'm not taking this. He isn't making out like he's the innocent one here, we're all to blame. All of us. The secrets we kept, they're coming back to haunt us now. And we should've seen that coming.

'Me and Liam, we had a brief relationship, before I met you, Michael. I had no idea you two were friends ...'

'Hang on. You two knew each other before we got together, and neither of you said anything?'

'Because there was no need. It was nothing serious, just sex, that's all it was ...'

'Are you sure about that? Because he just said he loved you, he said you were his ...'

'It was sex. Nothing more.'

He looks at Liam, then back at me, and he laughs. 'Yeah. And you stand there and tell me *I'm* the one who's lying.'

'You have secrets too, Michael.'

He shakes his head, backing away towards the door. 'This is too much. It's too fucking much. I did everything I could for you, Ellie. I did everything I could ...'

I go after him but Liam pulls me back. He stops me, and I look at him as I try to break free of his grip but he's holding my arm too tight. All I can do is watch as Michael drives away.

'What have we done?' I whisper.

What have we done ...?

Chapter 46

He's still lying. I don't care what he said, what he thinks, he's lying. He keeps telling me Ava is none of my business, and the more I replay those moments – those two, brief moments when he told me that, when he told me she was none of my business – the more I know for sure that he's hiding something.

I tap my pen on the desk in front of me as I stare out of the window, at the rain falling lightly on the terrace outside. The spa's garden room is busy, due to the rain, but the atmosphere is peaceful. Calm. Just the low hum of chatter in the background.

I turn my attention back to the envelope lying on the table in front of me. Karl gave it to me this morning, dropped it by on his way to keep tabs on my husband. I'm beginning to wonder if having Karl following him is such a good idea now. I never could get used to the lack of control, I feel helpless. Useless. And I don't like that. I think I need to start taking matters back into my own hands. The game's changed. The rules are different. I can play this on my own. It's for the best.

I open the envelope and slide the pictures out. They were

taken the day after Michael found Liam and I together, apparently. The day after it all came out. I look down at the first photograph on the top of the pile. One of Michael outside his university building, talking into his phone, his eyes down on the ground.

I move that one to the back of the pile and look at the next one. Michael's still outside his building, but she's with him now. Ava. Looking up at him like he's everything to her. I feel surprisingly empty as I look at those photographs. I can't feel anger, I don't even feel sad, and that scares me. Have I become that numb? That cold?

I look back out of the window, rest my chin in my hand and raise my eyes to the sky. There's no break in those clouds; it's growing darker, if anything.

I reach down and pick up another photograph. And this one causes a tiny flicker of something to kick up inside me. I don't know what, exactly, but the way she's leaning in to him – her face is almost touching his as she speaks, and she's smiling, his hand is on the small of her back ...

He's still lying to me.

And I've never lied to him?

I slide the photographs inside the envelope and head back out to reception.

'Everything okay?' Carmen asks.

I smile and nod. 'Everything's fine. I can take over here if you want to go grab a coffee.'

'You sure?'

'Go on. Take a break.'

She returns my smile and makes her way out to the staff

room at the back of the spa while I take over reception. I'm working on autopilot most of the time but these brief moments of normality help me cope. I need them.

I check the bookings we have coming in today, take a couple more over the phone for the upcoming weekend, and for a while everything feels okay. It's just another ordinary day; life goes on, doesn't it?

I look up as I hear people approach the desk, and I smile as a group of young women give me their details; they're booked in for lunch and an afternoon of pampering.

As they head off towards the changing rooms I glance back outside. It's still raining, the kind of rain that's more of a mist. I always found that kind of rain irritating. And then I see it, his car, pulling up into one of the few free spaces left out front. Michael's car. I watch as he gets out, walks briskly towards the entrance and I take a deep breath. I wasn't expecting to see him here. I haven't seen him since that night, haven't heard from him. I thought it best to leave things for a day or two.

His eyes meet mine the second he walks through the door, but his expression is too hard to read.

He strides over to the desk, and throws a white A4 envelope down in front of me, his eyes never once leaving mine.

'Get a lawyer, Ellie.'

I feel like I've been punched in the gut. I reach down, pick up the envelope and I open it, even though I already know what's inside.

'And let's do this the easy way, okay?'

He's divorcing me.

He's leaving me.

I look up, that now-familiar numbness sweeping over me again, and the man standing in front of me feels like a stranger. 'What've you done to your wrist?'

His left hand and wrist are strapped up. I couldn't help but notice that; it was his left hand he'd used to throw the envelope at me. But he doesn't answer me. He doesn't want a conversation, whereas me, I'm going through the motions, asking ordinary, everyday questions while I try to pretend everything's all right – try to block out what's really happening.

'Just sign the papers, Ellie.'

He's already out of the door before I can say anything else. He's walking away, and I can't stop him.

I look down, at my fingers scrunching up the corner of the envelope. I feel sick. Yeah, *now* I'm feeling everything, it's all flooding back at once, engulfing me. Anger and pain, a breath-taking sadness.

I reach into my pocket for my phone, I need to speak to Liam, but the call goes straight to voicemail. I leave a message asking him to call me back, and I scroll down my list of contacts for another number.

It's time.

Chapter 47

It was easier to get the train from Durham into Newcastle than take the car, a quick ten-minute journey preferable to what could be hours stuck in afternoon rush-hour traffic. As I head out of Central Station I notice the rain's eased off now, although the sky is still dark, making it seem later than it really is.

I slide my bag up onto my shoulder and make my way across the road to the hotel opposite the station. Liam's offices and laboratories aren't far from here, we use this hotel regularly, Liam and I. But as I make my way into the lobby I can't see him, so I reach for my phone to text him just as I spot him at reception. I discard the message and go over to him, gently tugging on his belt to get his attention, and he turns his head and smiles at me.

'You just get here?' he asks, finishing whatever he was doing there before he gives me his full attention.

I nod, and he smiles again as he takes my hand, leading me away from reception towards the lifts.

'Where are we going?'

'I've booked a room.'

I stop, and let go of his hand; he swings around to face me. 'I didn't come here to sleep with you, Liam. I need to talk to you.'

He comes closer, holding his hand against my cheek and I hate myself for that growing weakness he elicits from me when he touches me.

'I know. And we can talk, of course we can …'

I pull his hand away from my face. 'Michael's divorcing me.' I look at him, right into his eyes. 'You don't even look surprised.'

'That's because I'm not. I mean, come on! It's only you who's been convinced that this was all going to go away, that you could make it all better … you can't. You never could.'

I shake my head, and step back from him. 'You're supposed to be my friend.'

'I am. Baby, I am, but I can't stand by and let you believe that this was going to end any other way.'

'I love him,' I whisper, leaning back against the wall. I take a second to breathe, to think. 'I thought he loved me too.' I look back at Liam. 'I was wrong.'

He rests his forehead against mine, his fingers lightly stroking my cheek. 'It's time to let go now, Ellie. Of Michael, of any guilt you might still feel; it's time to let go of the past.'

'I can't.'

'You have to try. Or this is going to destroy you, and is that what you want him to see? What you want him to think he's done to you? Show him you can move on, Ellie. Show him he doesn't matter anymore.'

Does he matter anymore? Is Liam right? Am I really fighting a losing battle now?

'What if he goes to the police, Liam?'

'Ellie, we've been over this, I told you, he won't go to the police.'

I take his hand, push him gently away. 'Let's go somewhere more private. I don't want to talk about this out here.'

'Do you want to go to the room?'

It sounds so sordid – booking a room, one we're only going to use for an hour or so. But it's not like we haven't done this before. Except, this time, sex isn't something I want. I just want his company.

I nod, take his hand again and we head up to the double room he's booked. A clean, modern room that we're not entirely unfamiliar with.

He closes the door and takes off his jacket. I take off mine, throwing it down on a nearby chair before I go over to the window. I watch people streaming out of the station opposite, onto the streets of Newcastle, everyone from students to shoppers to businesspeople. It's a busy area of town. Bustling. Vibrant. A mix of bars, restaurants and grand hotels.

I feel Liam's hand on my waist and I lean back against him, closing my eyes briefly as he kisses my neck. I need that second of calm, that moment of peace.

'Did you see him?' Liam asks, his mouth still resting against the side of my neck. 'Did he tell you, in person, that he wanted a divorce?'

I turn around and he steps back from me as I go over to my bag, reaching inside for the envelope Michael threw at me this morning.

'He doesn't *want* a divorce, Liam. He's demanding one.'

He takes the envelope, slides the papers out and looks at them. 'Adultery, huh?'

I sit down on the edge of the bed, and I'm trying to make sense of all these feelings – all the emotions whirring around inside of me because they're changing. They're not the same as they were before, I'm not feeling the way I did before. I've lost the hope. And that doesn't even scare me, I don't think I care that he wants to leave me ... no. That's a lie. I care. I want to know *why* it's come to this, because him finding out about me and Liam, that isn't the only reason. If anything, I think he was just waiting for an excuse to do this, to walk away from me without making it look like *he* was to blame. Now he can blame me. Now he can tell everyone how I was too broken to fix, how I never got over what happened; how *we* could never go back to what we were. I slept with his best friend. We've given him the perfect excuse. Okay, now I'm angry. Now I'm fucking angry.

'No.' I stand up, start pacing the floor, shaking my head. 'No, he isn't doing this to me. He isn't *blaming* me, for this ...'

Liam catches my hand and I stop pacing. I turn to look at him, and the second I do I know I was right, to let Karl go. I couldn't settle, having someone else in control, because to some extent I don't think I fully trusted him. I don't fully trust anyone, so I called him before I came here. I told him I didn't need him anymore, because I don't. I can do this myself, it's better that way. I was right, to take back control. I was right.

'What I did was wrong, Liam. And that's something I have to live with, but I don't have to live with his lies. He thinks I'm damaged ...' I shake my head again, feel Liam squeeze my hand a little tighter. 'I don't have to live with his lies.'

Chapter 48

Something changed, the second Michael tossed those divorce papers at me. Something shifted inside me, unravelling all those emotions, all those messed-up feelings. Things became clearer. He doesn't want me anymore, okay, I get that. But he doesn't just get to walk away, that's not how this works.

He lied to me.

I lied to him.

Together we killed our marriage.

Even our darkest secret couldn't keep us together. That night was too much. We really couldn't come back from it. We couldn't deal with it.

But he knows what my distraction was. Is. Now it's time to expose his.

Sue looks up as I walk in, and the smile she gives me tells me Michael still hasn't made our separation public knowledge yet.

'Ellie, hello.'

'Hi, Sue, is Michael in his office?'

I know he's in his office. I may not be able to track him anymore, not the way I used to do, but I can still get hold of his timetable. His schedule. So I know he's here, somewhere.

'Yes, he's just preparing for this morning's lectures. Do you need a word?'

'Just a quick one, if that's okay?'

She smiles again and nods. 'Go on in.'

'Thanks.' I tap gently on his office door but don't wait for a response before I push it open, immediately closing it behind me.

He looks up from his work, takes off his glasses and lays them down on the desk as he stands up. 'What are you doing here, Ellie?'

I take an envelope out of my bag and throw it down in front of him. And I don't need to tell him what's in there, he knows. I'll give him his divorce, but that isn't the end of it.

His eyes stay fixed on mine for a second or two before he drops his gaze. Looks down at the envelope. 'Do you think this is what I wanted, Ellie?'

'I don't know, Michael. Is it?'

He raises his head and his eyes lock back on mine. 'I didn't want this.'

'You should've thought about that before you slept with *her* ...'

He slams his fist down on the desk, his eyes blazing, and I quickly glance outside. Sue's looking in our direction and Michael goes over to the window; he closes the blinds. Then he turns back to face me.

'*I* haven't slept with anyone.'

He's lying.

'I'm not the one who's cheated. I'm not the one who's lied.'

I saw it, just there, that small but still visible twitch of his eye; that's how I know he's lying. He's still fucking lying.

'You and Liam ...' He drags a hand back through his hair. 'I can't forgive that kind of betrayal, Ellie.' His expression is one of sadness. 'What you two did, that fucking hurt. And if you can't understand that ...' He briefly turns away again, and for a couple of seconds he stays there, silent, with his back to me. And when he turns to face me the anger's returned, his eyes are cold and hard. 'You followed me. You recorded my phone calls, read my texts, you thought *I* was cheating on *you*, and all the time you were sleeping with my best friend. And the fact you can't see how wrong that is ...' He shakes his head, goes back behind his desk. 'I didn't want this. I didn't want to lose you, I didn't want to lose *us* ...'

'Who is she, Michael?'

'You need to stop this ridiculous obsession, Ellie, because I ...'

'Who is she?'

He comes back out from behind his desk, walks right up to me, and he looks so deep into my eyes I flinch slightly.

'She is nothing to you, do you understand? You leave her alone, you leave *me* alone, because if you don't ...' He stops talking. He takes a couple of steps back from me and I wait for him to finish that sentence.

'If I don't, you'll what, Michael? What will you do?'

He stares at me, and for a second or two I think we both remember just what it was we used to share. The people we used to be, how we lost it all, and it makes my heart break all over again. But then his expression hardens, and I take a deep breath. *This* is what we are now. This is *who* we are.

'I know what really happened that night, Ellie. I tried to stop you, but you wouldn't listen, you wouldn't ...'

'You won't go to the police. Why would you? You'd be in trouble too, you covered for me ... What's going to happen to *her* if she loses you, huh?'

He steps forward, he's back in my space but I stand my ground. He isn't threatening me with that, I'm not taking it.

'I said, leave her alone. She is a student, that's all she is, she has nothing to do with any of this. Whatever warped scenario you've created in your head, she doesn't deserve to be a part of it. She has nothing to do with *us*.'

'Protecting her ... how noble of you, professor.'

'I'm done with protecting *you*. Now go. Please. And thank you, for signing the papers. At least you've made one thing easy.'

I hold his gaze for a few more beats, but I'm not looking at the man I loved. The man I married. The man I *loved*? When did the past tense become the preferred one?

I reach behind me for the door handle, turn my back to him, but he suddenly takes hold of my other hand and swings me around to face him. And when he speaks his voice is softer. Kinder.

'I really am sorry, Ellie.'

'So am I, Michael. So am I.'

I'm sorry, for what happened to us.

I'm sorry, for killing the woman who tried to kill me.

I'm not sorry for the things I still have left to do.

Chapter 49

'You're quiet.'

Liam slowly glances up at me, he can barely manage a smile. 'Sorry. I was just thinking.'

'About anything in particular?'

We're in a bar across the street from Central Station. Another of our regular places, we come here a lot. This area of Newcastle is our secret haven – this bar, the hotel over the road. The coffee shop I sometimes hang out in while I wait for Liam to finish work.

He shakes his head, but I know he's got things on his mind. We all have.

'Okay ...'

'I've been offered a job, Ellie.'

'A job?' I narrow my eyes. 'What kind of job? I thought you were happy where you were?'

'I was – I am, it's just that ...' He leans forward, looks right at me. 'It's an assistant professor position, at a university in northern California.'

California? No ... why is he suddenly talking about new

jobs and a move to America? He's changing everything and that unsettles me. I still need him, here.

'They've heard about the research I've been doing, the projects I've been working on, and they want me to come over there, on a twelve-month contract initially, to work with them in their research facilities.'

I'm a little stunned. This has come from out of nowhere; something I can't control. Can I?

'Are you taking the job?'

He says nothing for a second or two, he just continues to stare into my eyes. 'Yes. I'm taking it. It's a great opportunity, Ellie, to take my work over to America ...'

'When are you leaving?'

'Soon. Within the next couple of weeks.'

I turn my head away. I'm losing him too, and that scares me more than anything.

'I want you to come with me, Ellie.'

I keep my eyes on the street outside, watching people walk by the window, getting on with their lives. Ordinary, everyday people. I envy them, I want to *be* them.

I slowly turn back to face him. 'I can't, Liam.'

I'm not ready. I may never be ready. I didn't sign up for this. When we started this affair it was never meant to be anything but sex. An escape. I'm not comfortable with what it's become – what he *assumes* it's become. Even if it means losing him ...?

I sigh quietly.

'You knew what this was, Liam. I never promised you forever.'

His head snaps up, his eyes staring right into mine. 'Things have changed, Ellie. Circumstances, people – everything's changed. Your marriage is over ...'

'That doesn't mean I'm ready to jump straight into another relationship. I don't *want* another relationship, you really think I'm ready for that? You think I'm ready to follow you to America? Leave everything I know behind?'

'I think you need me.'

'I think you're wrong. I don't need anybody, not anymore.'

That's a lie. I do need him, I just don't want him to know that. It puts me at a disadvantage.

'So, that's it? We're done?'

'That isn't what I said ...'

'I'm leaving the country, but I don't want to lose you.' He leans in closer to me, lowers his voice. 'I was there for you, Ellie.'

'And for that I am truly grateful, but it doesn't give you the right to suddenly claim me as yours. You knew from the outset that this was nothing more than sex, *you* changed the rules. Not me. And if you can't live with that then maybe it's best we *do* call it a day.'

I don't mean that. I really don't mean that.

He stares at me for what feels like an eternity, and then he sits back in his chair, turning his head away slightly.

'Liam?'

He leaves a few beats before he looks back at me.

'I'm sorry, okay? But everything that's happened ... I told you I killed someone, I actually said it out loud, admitted it to myself because – because up until that point I think I've been kidding myself that it didn't really happen. If I never spoke about it, never said the words out loud then it never happened, I never did what I did ...'

'I don't care, that you did that.'

I frown. 'I took a life, Liam.'

'And she took your baby's. She stamped on your stomach so many times that child never stood a chance. You were bleeding out before the paramedics got there, according to Michael. So whatever guilt you might still feel over what you did, forget it, Ellie. Don't even go there.'

I've tried to forget it. Every day since it happened, I've tried to forget what I did. But I can't. It's why we're here, why we're all in this mess, because I couldn't forget what I did. I couldn't forget what *she* did, who she was ... *had* Michael encouraged her? Were the lies happening even back then?

'It all leads back to him, Ellie.'

Liam's voice drags me from those thoughts, and I look at him. 'Sorry?'

'Everything that happened – it's all his fault.'

Is it? Or is he just telling me this in the hope that I'll finally start to believe him?

'But we can leave all this behind. We've got the perfect opportunity now, to get away from everything, to start again. You and me, we can make a new life for ourselves in California ...'

'You make it sound so easy.'

'There's nothing hard about it. We pack a few bags, and we go to America. It really is that simple. And I promise you, it *will* get better. I'll *make* it better.'

I look at him again, right into those deep grey eyes. 'What about *my* work, Liam? What about the salons, the spa ...?'

'You've got people you trust who can run your businesses, you don't need to be here.'

I do. For now. I need to be here, I just can't tell him why. Because he'll stop me. He'll tell me to walk away, and I will, when I've done what I need to do. When I've finished the job.

'I can make this better.'

I don't know. Am I willing to hurt him, to be with him in the way he wants me to be with him when I'm just not ready? I care about him, I really do, I just don't know if I love him. And maybe, just maybe, it's getting to a point where I'm tired of the lies. I just want them to end.

I look down at the wedding band still there on my finger.

'Give me your hand, Ellie.'

I look up. I hold out my left hand, I watch as he slides the wedding band off my finger and slips it into his pocket.

'It's over. He doesn't want you anymore, and you don't need him. Okay? It's over.'

It will be.

Soon.

It'll all be over ...

Chapter 50

He told me to leave her alone.

I can't do that.

I won't do that.

Our marriage might be over but I still need to expose the lies I'm convinced he's been telling. The lie he's been living. I still need to know why he's so defensive of this woman. This girl. I need to see his betrayal once and for all, and I won't settle until that happens.

He knows everything now. He knows of my betrayal, I still know so little of his. But that's going to change.

I watch as she leaves the house, pulling her jacket around herself, but I can still make out her baby bump, as small as it still is. She's made no attempt to hide it today.

What happened to those baggy jumpers I saw you wearing before, Ava? Now it's all out in the open – now you have my husband, did he tell you it's okay to flaunt that bump? Tell the world what you're doing?

I watch as she climbs into her car, takes out her phone and makes a call. Is she calling Michael? Are they arranging to meet? If they are, I'll find out. I'm not leaving anyone alone.

She puts her phone away, starts the car and drives off, and I wait just a second or two before I start to follow her. I don't want to lose sight of her, but I need to remain discreet.

She heads towards Durham, and I manage to stay just a car or so behind her. I'm keeping her well within my sights. And when I realize where it is she's actually heading my stomach tightens, but I can't let it get to me. I have to stay focused, remember why I'm doing this.

She pulls into the hospital car park, and I park up a little way away from her, keeping that distance. But just being here again ... I haven't been here since that night. The night I lost my baby. Now she's here to check up on hers.

I watch her walk towards the Obstetrics and Gynaecology department, and I hang back a little before I start to follow her. I don't want to be seen, even though she has no idea who I am. It's obvious where she's going, but I need to see if she's come here alone, that's why I need to hang back, why I need to keep out of sight. When she reaches the entrance and stops to look at her watch, I know for sure that she isn't going in there on her own.

My heart starts beating hard and fast, a sickening anticipation flooding my gut as she leans back against the wall, and the way she's looking around – she's waiting for someone. For Michael?

I've been keeping close tabs on Ava Douglas – I remember her surname now – for a few days. I can't follow Michael anymore, he's too aware, too suspicious, so I'm following *her* instead. And it's harder than following Michael. I have to second guess a lot of things. I check Michael's schedule as much as I can, for lectures. Tutorials. I assume she's going to be places, and sometimes I'm right. I get lucky. Other times she isn't where I think she might be. But she almost always goes home at some point, and that's where I watch her most. At home. I'm there most evenings, every morning. I'll be there, until I see what I need to see. Until I've exposed my husband's secret, because he doesn't get to play the innocent victim here. We're all to blame. All of us. Nobody gets to be the good guy.

She checks her watch again, looks around her, again, and then she steps away from the wall. I shift my gaze to follow hers, because she's obviously caught sight of whoever it is she's meeting.

I take a step back, just to make sure I can't be seen, but I don't move my eyes. I keep staring at her, until I see him approach. Michael. Of course she's meeting Michael.

She smiles when she sees him, and as he envelopes her in a hug that sick feeling in my stomach intensifies. I raise my phone and click away, take as many photographs as I can of the two of them together before they disappear inside. Do the staff in there remember him? From that night? The night we lost our baby ... but he has another chance, to be a parent. I don't have that, I never will, and I have to swallow down that realization before the grief engulfs me again. That can't happen here, not here. Not now. But it's hard, keeping it at bay.

I lower my phone, and I frown, because they don't seem to be heading inside just yet. Michael's checking his watch now, both of them looking over towards the car park, and then Ava leans in to him. She takes his hand and she squeezes it, and he smiles at her, and I'm struggling to know what I'm really feeling here.

And then she stands up on tip toes and waves at someone, I can't see who yet. Who else could they be waiting for? I crane my neck to see if anyone else is coming, and I'm surprised and slightly confused to see another couple approach them. A dark-haired woman and a man of around Michael's age. They reach Michael and Ava, and I watch as he shakes the man's hand, leans in to the woman to kiss her cheek. I watch as they both hug Ava, and then I quickly remember why I'm here, and I raise my phone again, capture a few more images before they all finally head inside.

For a few seconds I just stand there, watching the doors they've disappeared through. I can only assume that other couple were Ava's parents. They seemed to be the right age – Michael's age? Are they really that accepting of their daughter's relationship with a man almost twice her age? A man who got her pregnant? Her fucking English professor?

I know exactly what I'm feeling now. I hate him. All the love I thought I still felt for him, that's been sucked out of me. His lies. His deceit. His willingness to break his promise to protect me, in order to protect *her* ... I hate him.

I turn to go, making my way back to my car.

I've accepted the inevitable, but this ends only one way.

My way.

Chapter 51

He slams me back against the wall, grasps my wrists tight so I can't struggle free. Because I'm fighting him. I want this, I do, but not with him. Yes, with him. I don't know. What I saw this morning messed with my already fucked up head, all I could think of as I drove away from the hospital was seeing this man. Doing this.

'Pretend I'm him, if that's what you need to do,' Liam murmurs into my neck, his beard rough against my skin. 'Hurt me, the way you want to hurt him.'

I wrench one hand free of his grip and I push his head up, so he looks at me. I make him look at me, and then I push him away. I pull my dress off over my head. He smiles, and takes a step towards me; he's ready. He's always ready.

He reaches out to touch my hip, lowers his head to kiss my neck, my breasts. I breathe in as he pushes me back onto the bed. But this is happening my way today, and I nudge him over onto his back. I straddle him, scrape my nails down his chest as I lower myself down onto him. And he knows how to fight back. He's over me in a heartbeat, still inside me as his body bears down on mine, as he thrusts and pounds into me despite

382

the fact I'm clawing at his shoulders, his neck. I'm closing my eyes and pretending he's my lying, cheating husband. A man I never thought I'd stop loving ... maybe I haven't stopped loving him. Maybe wanting to hurt him – maybe it's because I know I've lost him, and I still can't deal with that. Is it myself I'm really angry with? That thought only serves to intensify my growing anger and I push Liam away with an almost violent force. But he's right back at me, grabbing me by the hips, digging his fingers into my flesh so hard I can already feel the bruises appearing. He pulls me back down onto him, sitting up as I wrap my legs around him. I pull at his hair, kiss him so hard I feel his blood on my lips, the bitter metallic taste filling my mouth, but I don't stop. He doesn't want me to stop, this is what we do. Fucked up sex. We're fucked up people. Now.

It's brutal, harsh, violent sex. Hate sex, but I don't hate *him*. I'm just transferring the hate and the anger I'm feeling towards Michael – towards myself? – onto him, because I know he'll take it. And as he comes, as I feel that rush explode inside me, he pushes me onto my back, presses the weight of his body against mine until he's done. Until he's finished. Then he flips me over onto my stomach, thrusts a hand between my legs, and he's back inside me, his hand on the side of my throat as he fucks me, forcing my head up, his other hand touching me, helping me reach my own climax. And when it comes it hits me with a force I wasn't ready for. My body collapses beneath him as I cry out, biting down on his fingers as they catch my mouth.

We're done.

It's over, whatever that was.

I close my eyes, feel his fingers slide between mine, his breath warm and heavy on the back of my neck. We take a minute, to slow down, to recover. And I like that he's still lying over me, that his body still covers mine. I like him here. Like this.

'I told you I can make it all better, Ellie,' he murmurs as his fingers squeeze mine a little tighter.

I say nothing. I believe him.

'But you need to trust me.'

I let go of his hand, turn over and sit up, pulling the sheet between my legs up over my chest. He reaches out, pulls the sheet away from me and I try to grab it back but he tosses it to the floor. His eyes burn into mine, and I feel a cold shiver tear up my spine but I'm not fighting anymore.

'Is it him you really want to hurt, Ellie? Or are you trying to hurt yourself?'

I attempt to get up off the bed but he pulls me back, grasping my wrist tight as he moves up behind me. He pulls me back against him, his fingers still gripping my wrist while his other hand rests gently on the curve of my waist.

'I want to hurt all men like him.'

He lets go of my wrist and I reach behind me, touch his face, feel his fingers slide back between mine.

'All men like my father.'

Men who cheat.

Men who lie.

Men who deserve everything that's coming to them.

'You need to stop following him.'

I gasp as his warm breath dances over my skin. 'I'm not following him, I'm following *her*.'

'Don't.'

His hand moves down, gently nudging my legs apart and I gasp quietly as he touches me.

'I need to know who they are, Liam. Those people. At the hospital. I need to know who they are.'

'No, Ellie, you don't. Whoever they are, they're nothing to you. Michael wants you out of his life, it's time to let him have what he wants. You don't need to know anything else. You know enough.'

I take his hand and pull it from between my legs; I get up, walk over to the window, and I look outside at the street below. I've become obsessed with watching people, imagining what their lives might be like behind closed doors, because I'm almost certain that too many of us become very different people the minute we enter our own homes. Our own private space.

'I want to go with you. To California.'

I feel him come up behind me; I feel his hands on my hips, his mouth brush the back of my neck.

'You were always coming with me, Ellie.'

Was I? Maybe he's right ...

'But I need to finish what I started first.'

Before I go anywhere.

I feel him touch me, he's back inside me, and I continue staring out of the window as he fucks me, again.

Staring down at people I don't know.

Do we ever really know ourselves?

Know what we're capable of?

When pushed ...?

Chapter 52

I'm putting Carmen in charge of all my businesses. She's the only one I trust, the only one I feel comfortable with to keep everything running smoothly while I'm not here.

She was slightly shocked, when I explained that Michael and I are divorcing, that I'm leaving for America with Liam, and her reaction was understandable. The situation is complicated. The truth is still something so few people know, and it has to stay that way. People know what they need to know. Nothing else is their business.

The past few days have been filled with meetings; business meetings and visits to my lawyer. To sort out the divorce. Michael isn't fighting, he doesn't want this to be something that has to end badly, he just wants rid of me. He'll get his wish. Soon. And then he'll be free to start a new life with his very own Lolita, bring up their child knowing I'm safely out of the picture. Only, I'll never be out of the picture, not until I've exposed him for what he really is. People need to see that he lied, too. That he took advantage of his position. That this, maybe, isn't the first time he's done that. What *she* told me, the night she invaded my home, I'm starting to think she may not have been the one who was lying. She was young. She was pretty. She was everything Ava is, had she just been pushed too far by my preening husband? Had he realized his mistake, with her? Is that why he's so protective of Ava? He doesn't want his lies to be exposed, he doesn't want the truth to come out ...

Too bad, Michael. Too fucking bad ...

I drop my head, take a deep breath, and when I look back up I paint a smile on my face. I'm ready to greet customers, play the hostess I need to be when I'm here, at work. We have a group of students coming into the spa this afternoon, a birthday party, apparently. I know they're students because they're paying the discounted rate, and they're good customers, students. They spend money in the café, buy drinks, splash out on a lot of the creams and lotions on sale in the small store here in reception.

I check the bookings in front of me and see that they're expected any time now, so I remain behind the desk, checking my phone while I wait. I haven't heard from Liam all day, but he's busy sorting out the move. He spends a lot of time in Skype meetings with the university over in Stanford, so it isn't unusual for me not to hear from him. He'll call me, when he's free.

The sound of loud chatter causes me to look up and I plaster that smile back on my face as a group of young women make their way over to me. Happy, carefree young women, all ready for an afternoon of pampering. The expected group of students, I'm assuming.

There are seven of them, all of them pretty in their own

unique ways. I notice that as I explain the treatments they're booked in for, and let them know about the café and the bar and the shop here in reception. As I point out the small, glass-fronted store in the corner of the lobby, I see her, making her way over to the group here in front of my desk. Ava. Beautiful, pregnant Ava.

She's the last one to arrive. She's late, as she hurriedly explains to her friends, apologizing breathlessly as she hugs them all, one by one, and I glance down at the booking again. It was made for eight. Eight are here now.

I look back up, look right at her, I catch her eye and she smiles at me. She has no idea who I am, but that doesn't surprise me. Michael won't have had any photographs of me around, he won't have given her any chance to see me, to know who I am. Has he even told her he's married?

'Excuse me ... can I just ask about the massage I've got booked?'

Her voice – I recognize it from the phone calls I listened to – interrupts my thoughts and I smile at her. 'We have a specially trained pre-natal massage therapist here at the spa, she's going to look after you this afternoon.'

'Thank you.' She returns my smile, and I can't help but notice how much prettier she is close-up. Her hair's shining, and so are her eyes; she really is an extremely beautiful young woman. Pregnancy suits her. 'And the pedicure? Is that safe?'

'Perfectly safe. Don't worry, you'll be well looked after. All of you. And if you want to make your way to the changing room through there we'll get you all started on your individual treatments.'

I wait until they've disappeared from view, their happy chatter still filtering through to reception, before I breathe out properly. Before I take a second to think …

'Libby! Can you come and take over on reception, please? I've got a few things I need to sort out before I leave this afternoon.'

I grab my phone and head towards the massage rooms. If I'd looked at the booking more closely I would have seen that Jo, our pre-natal massage therapist, is working today. But why would I have questioned that? She's here most days, Ava isn't the first pregnant woman we've had visit the spa so, no. I wouldn't have questioned anything. But now I know.

I push open the door of Jo's room, and she's busy setting up for her next client. Ava.

'I'll finish this, Jo, if you want to grab a quick coffee before your next client comes in. She's just getting ready now, so you've got a few minutes.'

'Are you sure? There isn't much left to do.'

'I'm sure. Go on, grab a quick break while you can.'

'Okay, thanks. I won't be long.'

'Take your time.'

She closes the door behind her and I finish getting the room ready. For Ava. I line up the lotions and the wipes, fetch a pile of freshly laundered towels from the cupboard, and clean down the massage table, the smell of antiseptic filling the room.

I light scented candles to mask the antiseptic smell, dim the lighting, make sure the air conditioning is set to the right level. The room is calm. Serene. So am I.

It's ready for you. Ava.

I'm *ready for you* …

There's a light tap on the door and I swing around as it opens. I paint that smile on my face once more as she walks inside, wrapped in a thick white robe, her dark hair piled up on top of her head, her pretty face devoid of all make-up now. She looks so much younger, without the make-up.

'Oh, I'm sorry, should I wait outside?'

'No, no, come in. I was just getting everything ready for Jo – she's going to look after you this afternoon. She won't be a minute. Sit down.'

I indicate a brown leather couch by the door, watch as she takes a seat, as the robe rides up her leg slightly, giving me a glimpse of her toned thigh.

Does she wrap those legs around you, Michael, when you fuck her?

I busy myself sorting out the pile of towels, making sure all the right sizes are there.

'I hope you don't mind me asking, but how far along are you?'

She looks at me, and she smiles slightly, she seems a little shy. 'Almost six months.' She rests a hand on her bump, a reflex action, and I have to stop myself from letting the memories swamp me. I never really had a bump. It was too soon. Too early. I never even got the chance to feel my baby move inside me. 'Do you have any kids?'

An innocent question, of course, but one that cuts through me like a knife, slicing my heart in two. I shake my head. 'No. I don't.'

'Would you like any? Kids, I mean.'

I want her to stop, to not ask me these questions, but she doesn't know, does she? She doesn't know, what I went through. How someone just like her took away any chance I had of being a mother in the cruelest, most terrifying of ways.

I look at her, and her expression suddenly changes, she looks slightly horrified. Embarrassed, that she's asked me something so personal.

'Oh, I am so sorry. I didn't mean to pry ...'

I smile at her, I don't want her to feel uncomfortable. I want her to feel relaxed. I want her to talk. And if that means I have to deal with painful memories in order for her to do that, I can take it. I'm fine with that.

'You're not prying. Besides, I asked you a personal question first.'

She smiles back. She seems okay now. Good. Because I haven't finished yet.

'Are you – sorry, I'm the one who should be apologizing for prying now.'

'No, it's okay. I don't mind. I like talking about the baby.'

I lean back against the massage table, slide my hands into my pockets. 'Is the father involved?'

She looks away, and I frown. But then she turns back and she's still smiling. It's just a weaker smile, that's all.

'It's complicated. The relationship we have ...' She trails off. 'He's a bit older than me.'

I feel my stomach tighten, but I can deal with this. After all, this is what I want, isn't it? This is what I need, I need her to talk, that's why I made sure my phone is recording this conversation.

'Is that a problem?' I ask, keeping my eyes on her, I'm waiting for her to meet my eyes again. I want to look at her, when she talks to me. When she tells me what I need to hear.

She shakes her head. 'No. It's just ...' She shrugs. 'It's complicated.'

'Any particular reason why?'

She leaves a brief pause before she answers me. 'He's a lecturer. At the university.'

'The father of your baby? He's one of *your* lecturers?'

That knot in my stomach tightens even more as she nods. And there's almost a sense of relief emanating out of her as she speaks. Just how secret *is* my husband's relationship with this girl? How hard is she finding it, keeping that secret?

'Do people know, that your lecturer got you pregnant?'

'He said we shouldn't tell anyone, not yet.'

'But, you're quite obviously pregnant. You can't hide it forever.'

Are you making her lie, too, Michael?

'No, he ... he hasn't made me keep the pregnancy secret, just that he's the father. He doesn't think it's a good idea, for that to be common knowledge yet.'

Because that could ruin you, couldn't it, professor?

There's a part of me that feels sorry for this girl, that she's letting him manipulate her like this, but then I remember what she's done. She's carrying my husband's child, and that isn't right. She doesn't deserve my sympathy.

'Is he married?'

That question just fell from my mouth, and it shocks her, I can see it on her face. There's a panic there, like she's just been caught out.

You have, Ava. I caught you.

'I ... yes.' She drops her head, lowers her voice as she answers, her tone almost apologetic as she admits what she is – a teenage whore who took a man she had no right to take.

'Doesn't that bother you?'

She slowly raises her gaze, and I realize I need to pull back from this now, this isn't supposed to be an interrogation. I'm not here to judge her, not outwardly, anyway.

'Yes, it bothers me.' She sounds almost defensive now. 'But I fell in love. And he loves me, too.'

How fucking perfect. How gloriously idealistic, I hope their rose-tinted utopia is all they wish it to be. But I've heard enough now, I've *said* enough. It's time for me to go. To let Jo take over, and I almost breathe a sigh of relief as she walks into the room.

'Anyway, it was lovely to meet you.' I smile at my husband's mistress. His beautiful distraction. His dirty little secret. 'You have a lovely afternoon, and I hope everything goes well for you. And the baby.'

I leave without looking back.

I walk away.

It's almost over, I've accepted that now.

It's almost over.

Almost ...

Chapter 53

The house is being put up for sale, it's what both Michael and I want. It makes sense. We're getting divorced. I'm moving away, although, I haven't told Michael that part yet. He doesn't know that I'm going to California, with Liam. I'll tell him when I'm ready. If I tell him at all.

I'm expecting a visit from the estate agent – we need a valuation, before we can put this place on the market – but when the front doorbell rings I frown, because the appointment isn't for another hour and a half. Surely they would call if they were going to be this early?

I go into the hall, check the security monitor by the door. It's Michael. I have no idea why he's here, and I wait for a second or two before I start to pull back the bolts; before I unlock the door.

'We need to talk, Ellie.'

Words I've waited a long time to hear, from him. But it's too late, for talking. It's too fucking late.

I stand aside, let him walk through into the hall, but I don't say anything.

'Look, I ... everything that's happened ... I don't want this to end badly ...'

'I think we passed that point a while ago, Michael.'

'Can we just talk, Ellie? Please?'

I fold my arms, I laugh. I can't help it. 'You *want* to talk now, huh?'

'Don't do this. Don't make this any worse than it already is ...'

'I'm going away.'

I cut him off, and he narrows his eyes as he looks at me.

'That's what you want, isn't it? For me to go away?'

'Going where, Ellie?'

'America. Stanford, to be exact. Liam's been offered an assistant professor post at the university ...'

'Hang on ... you're leaving, with Liam?'

'Why would I be going to California on my own?'

'Jesus ...' He drags a hand through his hair, turns away from me for a second. 'I don't fucking believe this ...' He swings back around to face me. 'You said it was just sex. That you and him ... you said it meant nothing, it was just sex.'

'It is just sex. For me.'

'Yet, you're willing to move to America with him? For what, exactly? A lifetime of great fucks?'

'Grow up, Michael.'

He grabs my wrist, pushes me back against the wall, but I wrench my arm free. I push him away, I'm not doing this.

'What the hell is going on between you two, huh?'

'Does it matter now? Does any of this matter, now?'

Does it? I'm beginning to wonder myself. Beginning to think that putting ourselves through all this pain ... is it really worth it?

'Jesus, Ellie, I still love you. I still fucking love you ...'

'No, you don't. You don't.'

'Don't tell me how I feel, you have no idea ... My best friend, Ellie. You slept with my fucking best friend ...'

'Because I needed someone to be there for me.'

'*I* was there for you.'

I shake my head, wrap my arms back around myself. 'No, Michael, you weren't. Not in the way I needed you to be.'

'So, what? He gives you the come-on and you open your legs without a single thought for what the consequences are going to be?'

'None of this has anything to do with what me and Liam—'

'You're kidding yourself, if you believe that.'

I walk away from him, into the kitchen, and he follows me. I need a drink, and I reach for the bottle of whisky on the counter, but his hand closes around mine the second I touch it.

'That doesn't help anything.'

I loosen my grip on the bottle, but he keeps his hand on mine. And for a second neither of us says anything. The atmosphere surrounding us is loaded and heavy and I'm filled with a mixture of anger and sadness and – hate? Do I really hate him? For what he's done? Do I hate myself? For what *I've* done?

'Don't go with him, Ellie.'

His words vibrate against the side of my neck as his mouth

touches my skin, and I shiver. I look down as his fingers tighten around mine, as his lips brush my shoulder.

It isn't right, what's happening. I don't want him to touch me now, I don't want him, anymore. I can't get past what he's done, what he's still doing, I can't forgive the lies. I just tried to ignore them by creating my own, and that was a mistake. Like I said, we're all to blame ...

I let go of his hand and turn around. I reach for my phone, my eyes locked with his as I press *play*; as the sound of her voice echoes around the kitchen. Our conversation, from earlier, he needs to hear it. He needs to know that he has no right to ask me anything anymore. No right to tell me what to do.

'She was at the spa, this afternoon. Did you know that?'

His eyes remain fixed on mine, he just narrows them slightly. He's looking at me like I'm nothing. That moment we shared just a few seconds ago, that's over. Gone. That's forgotten. His eyes have darkened, their once bright blue colour dimmed by the hatred and pity he feels for me now.

'What did you say to her?'

I hold the phone up. 'It's all here. I just asked her a few questions ...'

He takes a swipe at my wrist, knocks the phone from my hand so hard it hits the wall behind me; smashes to the floor, and I watch as it hits the tiles, shattering on impact.

'You don't know what you're dealing with, Ellie. You have no idea what's going on ...'

'Then tell me! Just tell me, Michael, let's end this right here, right now. Let's stop all the lies and just tell the fucking truth. Is she having your baby?'

He looks at me, right into my eyes, and I swallow hard. I feel my heart start to race. My skin feels cold, like there's no blood rushing through my veins. I feel empty. I'm not even sure I care whether he tells me the truth or not now. I'm tired of it all. But then, do I really want all this mess, all this fucking heartache – do I want that all to have been for nothing?

'Ellie, I ...'

He drops his head, rubs the back of his neck. He seems nervous. Is he finally going to admit what he's done? And then his eyes meet mine, and I take a deep breath, grip the counter behind me to steady myself.

'I can't do this ...' He steps back, shakes his head, and I watch as he turns and leaves. Walks away. Like he always does. He walks away.

I grab the whisky; I sink to the floor and look over at my shattered phone as I take a swig straight from the bottle. One mouthful. Two. Three. I'm not satisfied until I feel the hit, feel the edges of my world begin to blur again.

'Ellie?'

I slowly look up, shift my gaze to the door as Liam runs through it. He takes the bottle from my hand and yanks me to my feet, he holds onto me because I'm swaying slightly. Too much alcohol, not enough food. That's how I live now.

'Did you know your front door was open?'

'Michael was here,' I say quietly, clutching his T-shirt, I'm still a little unsteady on my feet.

'Here? Why?'

'He wanted to talk. Wanted to clear the air ...' I look up

into his eyes, and I smile slightly. 'The irony, huh? Now he wants to talk ...'

I let go of Liam, start to make my way out of the kitchen, into the living room. I turn around to face him as he leans against the doorpost.

'It didn't really go all that well.'

'What happened to your phone?'

I tell him, about Ava, about her visit to the spa; about Michael's reaction to the recording.

'He told me not to go with you. To America.'

'Are you taking any notice?'

I don't answer that.

'Did something happen, Ellie?'

'Like what?' I go over to the window, look outside at the late evening sunshine beating down on the gravel driveway.

'If he's telling you not to go with me ...'

I spin around, my eyes locking with his. 'We had a moment.'

He frowns. 'A moment?'

I don't respond, he knows what that means.

He comes over to me and he kisses me. 'Do you trust me, Ellie?' His mouth still touches mine as he speaks, and I nod, grasping his T-shirt tighter between my fingers. 'Then know that this *will* get better, okay? And once we're out of here ...' He smiles and slides a hand around the back of my neck; he strokes my skin ever-so-lightly with his fingertips. 'All of this will be forgotten. I'll make this better, I promise you.'

But promises, they get broken, don't they?

'All you have to do is trust me.'

Chapter 54

The phone ringing jolts me from my sleep and I glance over at the clock on the wall. It's just gone 10 p.m.; I must've dozed off in front of the TV.

The phone continues to ring and I reach over to the table next to the couch to retrieve it. I don't recognize the number but I answer it anyway.

'Hello?'

'I need to speak to Ellie Travers.'

'Speaking.'

'It's about your husband ...'

'Michael?'

'Mrs Travers, your husband was brought into hospital a couple of hours ago ...'

I sit bolt upright, switch the TV off.

'He collapsed ...'

I get up off the couch, start pacing the floor, I'm confused. Am I actually awake? I'm not dreaming this, am I?

'Collapsed ...? Is he – is he okay?'

Was he with *her*? Is *she* there, with him, by his side?

'Mrs Travers, if you'd just ...'

'Which hospital is he in?'

'North Durham ...'

I cut her off. I'll find out the facts when I get there, I can't do anything here.

I grab my jacket and head straight out, I don't even double check I've locked the door, I don't care about that right now. I just need to get to Michael. I can't think about anything else, and I'm thankful the drive to the hospital is a short one.

Pulling the car into the car park I hurriedly try to find some change, pay for the parking and run into the building. I'm assuming he's in A&E, so that's where I head first. But he's been moved now, and a kind-faced nurse directs me to the ward they've taken him to. And when I get there, the first person I see is Liam, leaning back against the wall closest to the nurses' station. Why's *he* here? I don't understand ...

'Hello? Can I help you?'

I turn around as one of the nurses approaches me.

'Are you Mrs Travers? We spoke on the phone earlier ...'

'Sorry, yes, I'm Ellie Travers.'

'Okay, Mrs Travers ...'

'Ellie, please.'

'Ellie ... if you'd just like to wait here someone will be out to speak to you in a little while.'

I want to ask a million more questions but I know she won't be able to answer all that many. I need to wait for the doctor. I still don't understand why Liam's here ...

I walk over to him, ignoring the hand he holds out for me. 'What are you doing here?'

'I was there. When it happened.'

Now I'm really confused. 'Where? Where *were* you, when it happened?'

'We were at the squash club ...'

'Why the hell were you with Michael, Liam?'

'I still go to the club, Ellie. Just because me and Michael aren't ...' He stops talking, looks around the ward; does he know where Michael is?

'Have you seen him? Since he was brought in?'

He looks back at me. He nods, and I feel sick, I don't think this has sunk in yet.

'I tried to bring him round, when he collapsed. I wasn't there at the time, he was in the changing rooms ... I heard people shouting for me, they knew I was around, knew I could help, so ...'

'So ... what? Liam, what happened to my husband?'

'They don't know for sure, they're doing tests ... Ellie, it's going to be ...'

'No. No, don't you stand there and tell me it's going to be okay, don't do that.'

'Ellie ...'

He reaches for my hand but I pull it away, I don't want to be touched. I want to know what happened to my husband.

'Ellie, please, look at me. Look at me.'

I do as he says, I look at him. I hold his gaze and I wait for him to say something.

'I told you to trust me. I still need you to do that.'

I'm only half-listening now, because something else is distracting me. Some*one* else, her voice ... she *is* here. Why the hell is *she* here?

I slowly turn my head, look back over at the nurses' station, and I see her. Her hair's pulled back into a ponytail, her neat little baby bump prominent beneath the sweatshirt she's wearing. She looks dishevelled. Upset. So am I, I have every right to be. She has none.

'Ellie, stop!' Liam grabs hold of my hand, to stop me from going over there, from confronting her, but I'm tired of this now. Here is where this shit ends, I don't care about the circumstances, she needs to know that she's not welcome here. 'Don't.'

I glare at him, what fucking right does he have to stop me from doing anything?

'Leave it.'

'Leave it? His fucking teenage whore has no right to be ...'

'This isn't the place ...'

'You know, I am tired of you telling me what I should and shouldn't do, this fucking ends. Right now.'

I glance back over to where Ava was, she's seen me. And the expression on her face tells me she knows exactly who I am now. She fucking knows.

I walk over to her, and she doesn't move, she doesn't back away, she doesn't make any attempt to go anywhere. Which is wise.

'I don't know what the hell you're doing here,' I hiss. 'But I'd like you to leave.'

'I need to be here,' she whispers, and I applaud her audacity, I really do, but she's pushing me now.

'Get the hell out of this hospital, you have no right to be here ...'

'I have every right.'

I raise my eyebrows; her front shows no bounds. 'You do? I wasn't aware mistresses had rights over wives now ...'

'I'm not his mistress.'

I narrow my eyes. I stare at her. She's lying, surely ...

'I'm his daughter.'

Chapter 55

I heard the words, I heard them come out of her mouth, I saw her say them. They're just not registering. They're not making any sense.

I feel Liam behind me, feel him take my hand and I don't fight it this time.

'His – his daughter?'

She's about to say something else when I hear the doctor call my name. He beckons me over to a side room – Michael's room, I'm assuming – and she makes to come with me but I stop her. I don't want her anywhere near me, this is too much for me to take in, too much for me to handle right now.

'You can see your husband now, Mrs Travers.'

I let go of Liam's hand as the doctor stands aside to let me through. Michael's sitting up, he looks pale. He doesn't look right, he looks in pain, and I stop for a second before I go any closer.

He has a daughter.

For a split second I try to forget that she told me that. I try to forget everything, but I can't, can I? So much – too much has happened.

'Ellie.'

He holds out a hand and I move closer, I take his hand in mine. His skin is cold. Clammy. And I really don't know what I'm feeling now. I'm angry, confused; I wanted his secret exposed, but this ...? I wasn't ready, for this.

'Don't trust him, Ellie.'

I frown. What does he mean, who's he talking about?

'Liam ... don't – don't trust him.'

I don't want to talk about Liam. Liam doesn't matter right now.

'She's outside, Michael. Your daughter.'

His expression changes, and despite the fact a few minutes ago all I cared about was that he was okay, I hate that he kept such a massive secret from me. I hate that his lies were so much worse than I could have imagined, that he listened to me accuse him of sleeping with her when all the time he knew ...

'You should have told me,' I whisper.

'I couldn't ...'

'You should have told me.'

I drop his hand and I walk away. I can't do this, I don't know if I even want to anymore.

'Ellie!'

I stop, but I don't turn around.

'I mean it. You can't trust him.'

I leave the room, stand back and watch as Ava takes my place.

'Do you know what caused him to collapse?' I direct that at the consultant in front of me.

'Initial tests have revealed an abnormally high level of meperidine in his blood ...'

'I'm sorry ... what?'

'It's used to treat mild to moderate pain. Your husband was taking it for an injury he acquired to his wrist a little while back.'

I look over at Liam. I'm confused. I was aware of Michael's injury, but I had no idea it was something so bad that he had to take painkillers. Why would I have cared? He'd just thrown divorce papers at me, we weren't all that close at the time.

'I don't understand ... he's injured his wrist, so, why was he at the squash club tonight?'

The consultant looks to Liam for help with that one, and Liam takes a step towards us. Slides his hands into his pockets.

'He was there for the tournament. As a spectator. He went back into the changing rooms after the final match, to see everyone, and that's when he collapsed. I was called in, to try and help.'

None of this is making sense. But what it *is* doing is making me realize, once and for all, how far Michael and I have drifted apart. How distanced our lives really had become.

'We're still trying to work out how that much meperidine ended up in his system, but what we *do* know is that it can be incredibly addictive in a very short space of time.'

'Are you telling me he's addicted to a prescription drug?'

'He assures us that isn't the case, but we have to ask, we have to make sure we cover every possibility.'

I fall back against the wall, close my eyes for a second or two. 'Is he going to be okay?'

'He's going to be fine. We'll keep him here on the ward for a little while. There are a few more tests I'd still like to carry out, just to rule out any other underlying problems that might have caused him to collapse, but all being well he should be able to go home in a couple of days. If you have any more questions, please, feel free to come and talk to me.'

'Thank you ...' The doctor walks away and I look at Liam. 'He told me not to trust you.'

He frowns. 'Michael?'

'Yes, Michael.'

'He's confused, Ellie. It's a side effect of the meperidine, confusion. Drowsiness. Fainting. He won't be thinking straight right now.'

I look into the side room, see Ava sitting on the edge of the bed, holding Michael's hand. She looks scared.

'Did you know? About *her*? Who she is?'

'No, Ellie ...'

'I need some air.'

I make my way back outside, I can't stay in there, it's suffocating. I need to breathe, need some time to think.

The cool night air hits me the second I step outside, exhaustion swamps me, and I sink to the floor, drawing my knees to my chest. I don't want company, but it seems he doesn't care about that.

'I want to be alone, Liam.'

He lowers himself down beside me, and I don't stop him. I don't have the energy.

'Why didn't he just tell me the truth?'

He doesn't reply. What can he say? He doesn't know the

answer to that one, only Michael does. And I don't know why I'm not back in there, making him tell me. Maybe I don't want to hear it. The truth.

'An affair would have been easier to deal with.'

Liam pulls out a packet of cigarettes and offers me one. I decline. He lights up, takes a drag, and I watch as he blows smoke up into the dark night sky.

'I accused him of so much shit. And all the time he knew the truth, why didn't he just tell me?'

'He must have had his reasons.'

I look at my now naked left hand, only the indent of where my wedding ring once was is there now. Where did I put it? My wedding ring? And then I remember, Liam took it from me.

'Do you have my wedding ring?'

He turns his head to look at me. 'Why do you want that back?'

'Because it's mine.'

'So, this sudden revelation means things have changed, huh?'

'Jesus, Liam, of course things have changed!'

I push myself to my feet, start to go back inside.

'Ellie, wait!'

I turn back around.

'I love you, Ellie. We've made plans, remember? Me and you, we're leaving here, we're starting that new life ...'

'I can't do that now. I can't go anywhere, not now.'

His expression darkens slightly, but what did he expect? That I'd just check on Michael, make sure he was okay, then skip happily off into the sunset with him for a new life in California?

'I've just found out he has a daughter. For all we know he could be addicted to prescription painkillers, things have fucking changed, Liam.'

'I've accepted the job now.'

'And nobody's making *you* stay. But *I'm* not going anywhere. Not anymore.'

I make my way back inside. Ava's in the relatives' room now, and she isn't alone. The woman I saw her with at the hospital a little while ago, she's with her now.

They both look up as I close the door behind me, and I'm sure I see a flicker of pity cross their faces. I don't want or need their fucking pity, I need to know what the hell is going on.

They both stand up as I approach, and I watch as the older woman slides an arm around Ava's waist. They look alike, these two women. But Ava, she bears no resemblance to Michael at all.

'Is Michael all right?' I ask, wrapping my arms around myself, it's almost a defensive action. I don't want anyone near me, I don't trust anyone, I haven't done for a long time now.

'He's sleeping,' the older woman replies. 'Look, Ellie, we need to talk ...'

'You're right. We do.'

'If you'd rather wait for Michael to explain ...'

'No. I'm sure you're quite capable of telling me everything I need to know.'

'You deserved to know sooner. He just – he didn't think you were up to it ...'

410

She trails off, and I can see she feels like she may have overstepped the mark with that comment. She has. But it isn't entirely her fault. And then it suddenly dawns on me. If she's Ava's mum, which I'm assuming she is, then she must've slept with Michael at some point. When? Was he sleeping with her when he was with me? *Is* he the kind of man who cheats and lies, is Ava just a consequence of his actions? Is she the only consequence?

I feel dizzy, this is all too much, all in one go, but I need to know everything now, I just need a second ...

I feel a hand on my hip steady me; lower me down onto a chair and I look up to see Liam beside me. I don't know whether I want him here or not, but he isn't something I'm concerned with right now. Ava and her mother are.

'My name's Sara. Sara Douglas. Michael and I, we went to university together. We were friends, stayed friends once we'd left, only, one night that friendship ...' She doesn't need to finish that sentence, we all know what she means. We all know what happened. 'It was a one-time thing ...'

'When did this happen? When, exactly, did you sleep with him?'

'I had no idea he was in a relationship, Ellie, believe me. He didn't say anything, didn't tell me he was with someone. If I'd known I would never have gone there ...'

'Jesus ...' I whisper, throwing my head back, am I right? Is my husband no better than my father? Was his perfect image nothing more than a front? Something I fell for? Was sucked in by? Believed?

'I didn't tell him I was pregnant. When I found out he'd

411

lied to me, that he was with someone when he'd slept with me, I didn't want to complicate things so I kept quiet. I moved away, brought Ava up on my own, until I met Larry ... It was only when Ava started university here, when she found out Michael was a lecturer, here ...'

'I wanted to meet my birth father,' Ava interrupts.

I turn to look at her. I've been so unfair to her, even though she has no idea how badly I've thought of her. Because my husband lied to me.

'He had no idea that I even existed, not until I contacted him a few months ago. And I wanted him to tell you, Ellie, but he was nervous ...'

'Do you – do you *know* what happened to us?'

She looks briefly at her mother before she turns back to face me, and she nods. Of course she knows. 'He said you weren't coping, weren't ...'

'He thought I was too unstable, right?'

'That isn't what he said ...'

'He should have told me.' I reach for Liam's hand. Everything's changing again, everything's shifting, again, and I feel like I'm spinning out of control. 'At the spa ... when we were talking, you told me your lecturer – you said he got you pregnant? I don't understand ...'

'I had a very brief affair with another lecturer, not long after I started uni. I'm not proud of it, and I know it was wrong, but I loved – I *love* him. And when I fell pregnant ...' She looks at her mother again, and she squeezes her hand, gives her a reassuring smile and I feel all kinds of guilt swamp me. I hated this woman, and she did nothing wrong. She didn't lie. She didn't cheat. Nothing was her fault. Everything was Michael's.

'Michael has been really good to me, Ellie. He's looked after me, supported me, I just wanted to know who my father was. And what you went through ... I can't even begin to imagine what that felt like. I'm so sorry.'

She has nothing to be sorry for.

I shake my head, keep hold of Liam's hand. 'It's okay. It's fine, I just ... we moved on. That's all we could do.'

She throws me a weak smile, drops her head, and starts picking at the hem of her sweatshirt. She seems nervous.

'Ava?'

She slowly raises her gaze, looks at me briefly then glances at her mum before turning her attention back to me. 'He's my dad and – and he's been good to me, but ... that doesn't mean I ...'

She stops talking. I'm confused.

'Doesn't mean you're what, Ava?'

She looks up at her mum, and Sara gives her daughter's hand another squeeze before she takes over.

'Ellie, it – it might not be my place to tell you this ...'

'Tell me what?'

'I don't know how honest Michael has been with you, but, from what I know – and I have no idea how much of it is true and how much of it is just hearsay ...' She holds my gaze, and I feel my fingers tighten around Liam's. 'I heard things. After I moved away I kept in touch with a few of our mutual friends ... there were rumours ...'

She leaves that sentence hanging, she doesn't really need to finish it. And I can see she wishes she hadn't said anything, but I'm glad she did. I'm glad I know who my husband really is – *what* my husband really is.

'Maybe you should talk to Michael.'

Sara's voice is fading into the background now. I don't need to talk to Michael. I don't *want* to talk to Michael, even though there's a small part of me that wants to confront him, to make him tell me I'm wrong, that what Sara's just told me is wrong; that he didn't cheat. Didn't lie. That he wasn't a coward for keeping the truth about Ava from me when he should have been man enough to tell me. What did he think I was going to do? Dissolve into an emotional heap on the floor because he was now a parent? Something I can never be. But there's also a part of me that doesn't want to know any more. I really do think it's over now.

Liam slides an arm around my waist and I lean into him. It's time to go.

I look at Ava and Sara. And I smile, because I'm genuinely grateful that this happened. That I found out what I needed to know; that my husband's secret was exposed. That my entire marriage was probably nothing more than a lie?

'Good luck, with the baby. I'm glad I met you, Ava.'

She smiles, but she's as worn out as I am. As we all are. I just want to go home now. I want to sleep. Forget, for a little while, that any of this happened.

And maybe I will, in time.

Maybe I will …

Chapter 56

I'm woken by bright sunlight streaming in through the bedroom window, and I turn over, but Liam isn't there. I reach out, splay my palm out over the space next to me. It's cold. How long has he been up?

I get out of bed, pull on my robe and head downstairs. Liam's in the kitchen, making toast, and I watch him from the doorway for a second or two. Is he the only man who hasn't lied to me? Is he the only one I can *really* trust? Michael told me not to, but Michael was a man I never really knew. A man I should *never* have trusted.

Liam turns around and sees me standing there. He looks concerned, but he shouldn't be. I'm fine. 'Hey. You okay?'

I nod and walk over to him. I step into his arms and I let him hold me. He smells of lime and coconut, and when I kiss him he tastes of toothpaste and coffee.

'How long have you been up?' I murmur as his fingers run lightly up and down my spine.

'A while. I couldn't sleep. I went out for a run, came back, grabbed a shower. You hungry?'

I shake my head and step out of his arms. Last night, what

happened, what I heard, it's all rushing back, flooding my brain, but I know one thing for sure – it really is all over now.

'You should eat, Ellie. We've got a busy few days ahead.'

'I'm fine, Liam.'

We fly in three days' time. We start a new life, in less than a week. Me, and this man here. The man I should have always been with? Who knows. Maybe I did just take a wrong turn, made a bad decision. But we're both still here. We survived.

He touches my hip and I flinch slightly, but then I relax and lean back against him. I let his arms fall back around me, close my eyes as he lightly kisses my neck.

'It really is going to be okay, Ellie.'

I reach behind me, and touch his cheek with the palm of my hand, sliding my fingers between his as his hand presses against my stomach. Maybe he's right. Maybe everything *is* going to be okay. I think I have to believe him when he tells me that now.

The phone ringing cuts through the sound of the kettle boiling, the noise of the TV playing away in the background. I answer it – I have to. It might be something to do with the salons or the spa. There's a lot still to be sorted out before we leave for California.

'Hello?'

As I talk I watch Liam make tea, butter toast, and I wonder how our life would have turned out if we'd stayed together from the start.

'Am I speaking to Ellie Travers?'

'Yes?'

'Ellie, it's the hospital. It's Michael ... Ellie, I'm so sorry, but your husband passed away a short time ago ...'

416

I drop the phone, step back against the counter and Liam rushes over to me. He picks up the phone and I raise my gaze to look at him as he speaks into it. And then I close my eyes. I squeeze them shut, I might still be dreaming. This might not be real …

'Ellie?'

I keep my eyes closed, no, I'm not awake. I'm not.

'Ellie, come on. Look at me.'

His fingers close around mine and I slowly open my eyes, I look into his, and I shake my head.

'No,' I whisper. 'No …'

'I'm sorry, baby.'

I don't know why I'm not crying. Why I don't even want to cry. Why? Because I still don't believe it's real?

'How?'

'We need to go to the hospital …'

'How did he die, Liam?'

He looks right into my eyes, and gently strokes my hair, but I feel strangely okay now. It's a shock, of course it is, but it's odd, how okay I actually am.

'He suffered a cardiac arrest, that's all they'd tell me, which is why we need to go to the hospital.'

He pulls me against him, and I hold onto him.

Michael's dead.

My husband, is dead.

My husband died a long time ago …

They'd tried their hardest, to bring him back. But it was too late. And looking at him now, lying there, at peace …

I never found peace, after that night. But if that night hadn't happened, would I ever have found out the truth?

I can't touch him, they need to do a post-mortem. But I'm okay with that. I don't want to touch him.

I feel strangely detached as I scan his face. His handsome face. I'd thought he was different, but I was wrong, and now there's a part of me that blames Liam, for letting me go so easily back then. If he'd fought for me harder, could all of this have been avoided?

I take one more look at my cold, dead husband and I wonder if he'd ever really loved me. I'd loved him, but that hadn't been enough. And that's what makes me sad – not that he's dead. That me loving him wasn't enough.

I leave the room without looking back. I've said my good-byes. And as I head out into the corridor I see Ernie Waterford on his way over to me. Come to pay his condolences, tell me how sorry he is ... I'm going to have to listen to so much of that, and I don't want to.

'Ellie, my darling ...' He envelops me in a hug, and I let him. I hold him, I'll give all these people everything they expect from me. But I'm just going through the motions, nothing else. Painting on the widow's smile, grieving like I'm supposed to while they all choose to ignore the fact that Liam and I aren't even hiding our relationship now. I'm not doing secrets and lies, not anymore. And then Ernie pulls back, looks at me, and I frown slightly. 'Listen, I ... can we go somewhere more private?'

I nod, and we walk in silence as we head outside. The relatives' room wasn't empty when I arrived, there were other families in there; grieving families. Grief isn't private here, it has to be shared.

418

'Ellie, I'm so sorry ... we're all in shock ...'

I can't say anything. I don't *want* to say anything. I don't even want to be here, I want to go back home. I want to leave all of this behind now.

'But I ... I need to clear the air. And I should have told you this before, but Michael he – he confided in me. He made me promise ... Ellie, I'm not proud, of what I did ...'

I look at him. What the hell is he talking about? 'What did you do?' I whisper.

'I knew, about Ava. I knew who she was, and I helped him – I helped Michael keep his secret.'

I fall back against the wall. So, Ernie *was* just another liar. There really was nobody I could trust.

'When I asked you, if he'd had relationships with his students ...'

'To my knowledge she was the only one ...'

'She ...?'

He's not talking about Ava now, and I feel my blood start to freeze in my veins.

Ernie briefly bows his head, and I watch as he wrings his hands. Knowing about Ava was one thing, but even he knows this was one secret he should never have kept.

'Emma Ford was a very damaged young woman, Ellie. She formed a fixation with Michael that spiralled way out of control ...'

'Did he sleep with her?'

I'm asking a question I already know the answer to, I just need to hear the words.

Ernie coughs, keeps his head bowed for a few more beats

before he finally looks at me. 'I spoke to him, I told him he needed to end the relationship, it wasn't ethical. It was wrong, especially given her fragile state of mind ...'

'Oh, Jesus ...'

I turn away, I can't take this in.

'And he obviously tried to end it, Ellie. He tried ...'

I hold up a hand to silence him, I don't want to hear any more, I feel sick.

'And you're certain, she was the only student he slept with?'

'After what happened to you, after that night ...'

I look at him, and his eyes are so full of regret but it's too late.

'There were no other students, Ellie, I'm almost certain of that ...'

He leaves that sentence hanging and I look at him. 'But?'

Ernie sighs, and I know now that everything I thought I knew was nothing more than a cruel charade.

'But I think he may have ...' He looks at me, and I feel my blood run even colder. I don't want to hear what he has to say next yet I know I have to listen. Because every word he utters is making me realize I was right. I wasn't crazy, I wasn't imagining everything. Yes, I got some things wrong, but my husband *was* lying to me. He was lying ...

'Did he have affairs, Ernie?'

The answer he gives me is only going to back up what Sara told me last night. The rumours she heard, Ernie's going to confirm them.

He sighs again, but he looks right into my eyes when he replies. 'Yes, Ellie. He did.'

I turn my head away, and I want to feel angry, I want to feel sad, I want to feel *something*, but once again all I feel is numb.

'Ellie, I'm sorry. I'm so sorry ...'

I shake my head. I'm tired now. All the betrayal; the people I thought I could trust, they turned out to be nothing more than covers for my husband's lies, and I'm tired. Of everything. 'It's fine. No, really, it is. His lies are finally exposed now, so, I should at least be grateful for that.'

'I thought I was protecting you, Ellie. I never meant to hurt you, and Michael, he never wanted to hurt you either, that was the furthest thing from his mind ...'

'The furthest thing from Michael's mind was me.'

I turn to leave.

'Ellie?'

I don't stop, I don't turn back around. I don't want to hear any more. I know enough. He sat there, just a few days ago, and he lied to my face. A man I thought cared about me. A man I'd trusted; often thought of as a father figure. But fathers have lied to me. Husbands have lied to me.

I don't want to hear any more apologies. I don't want to hear how sorry people are, I don't want their sympathy, their false promises of help. I don't want to watch as they try to pretend my life wasn't a mess. They knew. They all knew, I'm sure of that now. They all knew who my husband was.

Was I the only one who didn't?

Chapter 57

It rained, the day of Michael's funeral. The church was full, so many people wanted to say their goodbyes. How many of those people had he slept with? How many of those people had been privy to his lies? Promised to help hide his deceit? How many of those people had really been my friends?

People talked, at the funeral. People judged, because Liam was by my side throughout. Liam held my hand, stood by me when everybody else thought it best to stand back. Was their guilt too much? So, they talked and they judged and they thought what they wanted to think. I didn't care.

Ava was there. And Sara. Ava cried, Sara held her, I kept my distance. They're nothing to me, they never were, Michael saw to that. But what he'll never see now is his grandchild.

It was a long day. A tiring day. But it was a day that needed to happen, for me to be able to draw a line under everything. To end it once and for all. And when it was over, only then could I walk away and know that it was the only thing I could do.

I have Liam now. And I still don't know if I love him. I don't know if I'm capable of that emotion anymore, I feel so empty so much of the time. Even here, living our new life, in our new home, a large sprawling house on a leafy street in Palo Alto, northern California, I still feel empty.

Liam loves me, he tells me he loves me all the time, but I still feel empty. We're so far away from everything we knew before yet I still can't shake the past. I killed a woman. A fragile, damaged woman who'd been pushed to the edge because my husband had seen fit to take advantage of his position. She'd been vulnerable, and he'd played on that. What he did, it sickens me. What happened, because of him, that will stay with me forever. The only thing I take any comfort from is that I know now that I wasn't crazy; I wasn't imagining everything. I was being fed lies while Michael tried to cover his tracks. Gloss over his guilt. Keep his secrets.

I took a life, I killed someone, and that's something I will never forget, something I will have to live with for the rest of my life, but there are still days when I find it hard. Nights when I can't sleep. Moments when I wonder if dying is the only escape I have left.

I draw the curtains and look outside; it's another beautiful, bright day. There hasn't been a dull day since we arrived here. No dark clouds, no rain, just blue sky and sunshine. So that should tell me something, right? I should see that as a sign. A new beginning. I should read something into that, and push the darkness away.

Liam comes up behind me and his mouth brushes the side of my neck. I lean back against him, close my eyes as his kisses cover my skin.

He loves me.

He didn't lie.

He didn't cheat.

He was different.

And I trust him.

He promised me a happy-ever-after, do I believe that'll happen?

No. Promises always get broken.

But I trust him.

I trust him ...

Epilogue

I loved her too much to sit back and let fate take charge. I wanted her, too much, I wasn't taking that risk.

I'd made the decision a long time ago, to take her from him. To claim her back. I should never have let her go, but I was weak, back then. Too scared to admit that she'd got to me, that I'd fallen in love when it was something I'd vowed I'd never do. And then *he* got in the way. He took her from me before I had a chance to fight for her, and from that day onwards I resented him.

I knew nothing of his affairs. I'd spent all that time playing the best friend yet I never really knew him. Just as Ellie never really knew him and in the end, he hurt her. And she never got the chance for payback.

I did.

And I took it.

The night he fell and broke his wrist, that was the night it started. That was the night I knew exactly how I was going to take Ellie back, take her from him the way he took her from me. They'd already separated, by that time, so maybe it would have all played out the way I'd wanted it to without my intervention, but I couldn't take that risk. Despite everything Michael was, everything Ellie ultimately found out about him, there was always a risk that he would somehow find a way to convince her to come back to him. That she would begin to believe him, whatever he told her, because she'd loved him ... once. I didn't want her to love him again.

It was me; I caused his accident. I couldn't guarantee how awkwardly he'd fall, or how severe his injury would be, I just got lucky that it was bad. That his pain was unbearable. It was me, who advised him to take meperidine, advised him to ask his doctor for that specific drug. Then when his doctor stopped prescribing it, told him there was no need for him to take such a strong, potentially addictive painkiller any longer, I told him his doctor was wrong. Told him I could get him more, if he felt he still needed it. I fed him the drug that eventually killed him. And even after he found out about me and Ellie, he still came to me, begging me to get him more meperidine. He needed me. And I helped him. Why wouldn't I? I knew what the side effects were. I knew the risks, knew that his addiction could, one day, prove fatal. I just had to keep on top of things. Keep watching him.

The morning after he'd been brought into hospital, I did go for a run, just like I told Ellie. I didn't lie to her. But after that run I didn't go straight home, I drove to the hospital. I went to see Michael. I told the nurses looking after him that Ellie had wanted me to check in on him early because she couldn't make it until later. I lied to them, and they believed me, because I can turn on the charm just as well as he could. I can use my smile, I can flirt. I can get anything I want.

The Wife

I wanted Ellie.

They let me into your room, Michael, believing I was the concerned friend I pretended to be. After all, I was the one who'd saved your life the night before, right? And then I became the one who ended it. I administered that last, lethal dose of the drug you were slowly becoming addicted to. Your veins were already scattered with pin pricks from the tests you'd had, the blood they'd taken, they weren't going to notice another one. I killed you, Michael. I induced the cardiac arrest that eventually took your life, and I feel no guilt.

You lied to her. You hurt her. You made sure she almost lost everything, but she was never going to lose me.

You got what you deserved.

We all got what we deserved. In the end …